Trem

By Alex Baxter Scott

Conditions of Sale:

This book is sold subject to the condition that it shall not, by way of trade or otherwise, be lent, re-sold, hired out, or otherwise circulated
without the publisher's prior consent, in any form of binding or cover
other than that in which it is published.

All rights reserved. No part of this publication may be reproduced, stored in a retrieval system, or transmitted, in any form or by any means, electronic, mechanical, photocopying, recording or otherwise,
without the prior permission of the publishers and copyright holder.

Dedications:

With thanks to:
My Mum for the proof reading, making sure everything makes sense and for her constant support and love!

Amber and Cindy for the support and encouragement to get me this far, and all family and friends!

Dedicated to:
My Nan Elizabeth and Grandpa Maurice, forever in my heart and memories.

And in memory of:
My Dad Jerry, may the tides always be in your favour captain, wherever you are.

Cover art by:
sssssick.tumblr.com

Prologue: "That Place Sucks"

"It's the family you're representing, Tremera. Remember to make a good first impression. You're here to secure our legacy."

"Yes Father."

Six years ago, during a long summer, a girl was to make a decision that would change her life. The days were bright, warm and fun, mucking about like all children do. When you're in the back and beyond, all you could really do was spend time in the play areas, doss about in the woods and work on the non-existent tan by the village's castle ruins. Mortsbury was hardly excitement capital of the world.

But on one particular long, uneventful day of nothing, Gabriella "Gabby" Morgan was feeling rebellious, if her parents were to be believed, nothing new there. Her friend, Manisha was no different. Regarded by their peers as "a bit weird", they could safely say they were never really bullied. They were just left to their own devices. They were content with that, it meant they didn't need to worry about those pesky social interactions. It left them alone to do more things together, like dares. Any child will tell you that there is nothing in this world more unbreakable then a dare.

"Oh come on Manisha, be reasonable!" The twelve year old Gabby called in the middle of a laugh.

Manisha pouted as she tugged her headscarf forwards slightly. "I am being reasonable Gabby! Look, you'll be doing the village a service." Manisha raised her eyebrows and gave a little nod. "Think about it."

Gabby felt herself deflate like a balloon, she did have a point. The dare was simple, yet it made Gabby feel nervous. Go over the moss covered gates of the creepy manor in the edge of Mortsbury and see if it actually is haunted.

"It's trespassing anyway, I'm not doing anything really illegal. I'm too young for prison anyway." Gabby responded, looking at the floor.

Manisha lent down and looked at Gabby, bending over in a funny angle to catch Gabby's gaze.

"You do know you're too young for prison right? If you got caught, the cops will probably give you a slap on the wrist and send you on your way." She reached over and tapped Gabby on the back. "I'll be your backup, you can trust a friend."

Gabby straightened her back. "I'm starting to think you planned this all the time, was this why we were doing dares?"

Manisha put her hands up and grinned. "Guilty! You found out my cunning scheme."

Gabby returned a grin. "You sneaky bugger!" The two shared a chuckle.

After a deep breath, Gabby started to make her way to the edge of the village with Manisha in tow. Mortsbury is hardly a large village, from end to end it's only a few miles long, with not that many houses. It's mostly farm land backing onto the woods, which were mostly uninteresting save for an old, derelict farmhouse and some rusty, abandoned farm stuff.

The manor house hardly seemed in keeping with the village. Three levels of windows, all with shutters obscuring the view inside. Walls of discolored sandstone clad in ivy that could dwarf an average sized person twice over. Everything looked untouched, nature was left to its own devices. So much so that it was hard to determine the actual size of the manor. The gate that surrounded it was half rusted and seemed pretty useless in it's role of keeping things out, it was already open a crack. The walls around the gate were equally ivy covered too. It must have been untouched for years, decades even, maybe longer.

Gabby hoped that meant it was abandoned, any owner who was still living inside it would surely keep it maintained.

The sun was already starting to set, the dusk light bathed everything in a rich, orange glow. The two would be ghost hunters had their backs to the wall of the gate.

"So you're staying here?" Gabby asked, keeping her eyes on the manor.

"Yep." Came the reply. There was a moment's silence.

"Out of harm's way?"

Gabby jumped when she felt something hit her arm, she was so relieved to see it was Manisha, if it were anything else, she'd have had a heart attack. Safe to say she was a nervous person to begin with, so her nerves presently were pretty high.

"What good backup follows the first in line? I wouldn't be backup then!" She joked as she peered over Gabby's shoulder.

The still summer's evening was halted by a gust of wind which filled the air with the sound of rustling trees. Rather unsettling for the two. Gabby felt her hands start to feel clammy, an obvious sign to her she was getting tetchy. She swallowed hard and started to walk towards the manor.

"Wish me luck." She muttered as she began the journey to the house.

She pushed open the gate, which screeched so loud it might as well have been nails on a blackboard. Scrunching her face up, she held her breath as she pushed through the gate as quickly as she could. Gabby felt such a sense of elation when she was through.This was such a stupid idea, why did she agree to this? She wished she could go through walls, or better yet turn invisible. Just anything she could do to not get noticed. She could turn back, that would be such a clever thing for her to do. But she didn't.

Instead, she kept going, her brain screaming at her to stop. There was a crunching sound with every step she made, sure it was the gravel on the path but it sounded so meaty to her. She knew Manisha was watching but she couldn't bare to turn around because no doubt the second she'd avert her eyes, there would be some jumpscare like in a bad horror movie.

She reached the door. There was hardly anything special about it, the handle looked rather dusty, but no carved faces with contort expressions like she'd expected. The images of creepy manor house usually conjure up something more dramatic. But this house was just... Unsuspecting. Nothing about it seemed any more or less weird than any boring manor house. She'd seen more threatening mansions on those TV relocation programs her Mother likes. She took hold of the door handle, really hoping it was locked so they could call the whole thing off. There was a low clunk as Gabby pushed open the door. No such luck.

As the interior revealed itself, Gabby shivered. It felt like a sharp gust of freezing air hit her like a brick to the face. It was so dark, she couldn't focus on anything. The front of house comprised of the big, heavy wooden doors, a flight of steps almost immediately to the right and a long stretch of corridor in front of her. With her heart racing, a hundred thoughts flooded her brain. Okay, you're in now, no ghosts, you can go. That should have been what she did but, like an idiot, she let the questions continue coming. Well maybe there's something else going on? Why is it abandoned? Why is the door unlocked? Are there any people living here, and if so, why is it so decrepit?

Stairs or corridor? Corridor any day. She was only wearing flat shoes but she was getting really annoyed at how much noise they were making, every step seemed to echo. If she knew she was going to be breaking and entering, she'd have brought a torch. The manor was covered in dust which did wonders for her sinuses. An irritating tingle set in her nose and her nerves were hardly quelled. As she felt the tingling build up even more, she felt panic sink in again. She tried rubbing her nose, not breath through it, anything. It was futile.

"Aaatsssschh!" Oh that sounded loud. Gabby was convinced she could hear something, she wasn't sure what but she decided she should make her exit as quickly as possible.

A pair of black eyes peered out of the darkness, from behind the bannister of the landing on the manor's first floor. They narrowed in on the young intruder, and they were not pleased. With the onlookers eyes still trained on Gabby, their head turned to the side.

"Jenny, get her out of here. I don't care how." To anyone else, it would look as if the black eyed figure was talking to thin air. In reality, the "Jenny" she was talking to was following her instructions, fading through the wooden floors like they were made of nothing.

At the end of the long corridor was a room, which Gabby continued towards. There was a faint light coming from it, evidently the shutters didn't remove all the light from the manor. The room looked huge too, even if the details were still hard to focus on, given the dingy darkness. Gabby looked around as she approached the entrance. She could see what looked like the back of someone's head. The owner maybe? It was probably not a great idea to do so, but she was on a ball with bad ideas so she called out.

"Ummm, hello?" Gabby called out. At least she could explain things. It was a stupid dare, she didn't mean to intrude and she didn't steal anything, so there's no need to call the police. The figure didn't answer, or even seem to notice her. She took a few steps forward, entering the room.

The figure's head slowly began turning and Gabby halted when she saw the figures eyes. They were blue, bright and almost glowing in the darkness. She looked to be in her late 20s, in a plain white dress. Her short, bright blonde hair waved about as if it were underwater. Gabby immediately took a huge stride backwards, her mouth was agape and she was shaking rather violently now. The pale woman was some kind of bloody ghost! Her theory was only confirmed further when the woman walked through the sofa she was sitting on and approached Gabby, very slowly.

Okay nope, nope, she was not dying today. She took a deep breath and held it tight inside her lungs.

"Hello." Came the voice from the spirit. Gabby could have sworn she detected a broad Brooklyn accent.

But that was totally irrelevant as she was about to be violently haunted. She proceeded to run at full speed in the opposite direction, wavered only by her shoulder colliding with a suit of armor she didn't even notice was there. She ran as fast as she could, she was not going to hang around for anyone or anything. She'd clearly flown too close to the sun and was now paying for it. She teared past the staircase and bashed through the doors. The rush of warm air came as a relief, but she was still not out of danger yet. Gabby slammed open the gate and ran straight past Manisha. Her friend looked bewildered as she semi-noticed her friend shooting past at a seeming twelve miles per hour.

"Hey! Gabby wait!" She called as she followed, trying to keep up with her friend. She turned the corner and looked around. She heard a sniff and turned to the left, looking down. Gabby was sitting against a bush and was hugging her legs.

"Gabby?" Manisha asked. She sank down to her friend's level and put an arm around her shoulder. "What's happened?"

Gabby wiped her eyes. "I'm going mad, I've legitimately lost my bloody mind." She muttered as she took a deep breath.

"What the hell happened in there?" She pulled her head scarf out of the way. "I'm sorry, I shouldn't have baited you, that was really cruel of me."

Gabby just shook her head. "It was my fault for doing it."

Manisha rested her forehead on Gabby's, her voice almost a whisper. "What did you see?"

Gabby looked up and stared into her friends eyes. "I don't know. It could have been anything, I mean it was kind of dark." Gabby ran her hands through her hair. "It was nothing... I just got spooked by something I guess..."

Manisha took her hand. "Will you be okay?"

Gabby sniffed and cracked a half smile. "Manisha, when have I ever been anything but okay?"

"When Avin Shrain died in Lemuria Rising?"

This caused Gabby to blush and lightly smack Manisha's shoulder. "Shut up! That left me emotionally vulnerable!" Using her favorite show against her, how sneaky of Manisha.

Manisha chuckled and kept smiling as she patted her friend on the back. "You sure you'll be okay?"

"Yeah." Came the muted response. Manisha helped Gabby up and brushed the dust off her friend.

"Let's put this whole thing behind us, yeah? No hard feelings?" After a few seconds of silence, Manisha added, "Back round mine for movies?"

Gabby sighed. "Go on. You're forgiven, for now. Like you said, let's just....Pretend this didn't happen okay?"

Manisha nodded and lead Gabby down the gravel covered street and back to her home. The rest of the day was spent in front of the TV, watching horror movies, chugging popcorn and snacks by the bucket load.

Gabby was still plagued by what she saw. It must have been a hallucination, a trick of the light, something. Maybe the house was owned by someone with really, really bad cataract. Some freaky projection, a joke played on her by the owners of the house. There was no such thing as ghosts. There can't be, not outside of her collection of horror movies, comics and novels. Gabby would go to sleep that night still thinking on what she saw. To her, she could rationalize all she wanted, but nothing could provide a satisfactory answer in her mind.

No, what she saw was a pale woman who looked like a Hollywood movie star walking through a solid object and come to haunt her till she was a shaking mess. After a few weeks, it was a distant memory. If she lingered on it, told people about it, ranted and raved about what she saw, she'd just be another mad nut job. The months passed by and Gabby and Manisha continued their lives as if that strange day never happened. Six years later, the two former girls had turned into young women, both eighteen. Between them, nothing had changed, their friendship only grew strengthened.

Now, they were on the verge of their college A Level results, an already stressful day. Two years of hard work hang in the balance of what was written on a piece of paper. But for Gabby, the hot, summers day would prove to be even more important for her. The life of Gabby Morgan, was to never be the same.

Chapter One: "Results Day"

"Tremera, allow me to introduce Lord Tremadore, heir to the title of the Asud Manzazuu."
"Hello. It is a pleasure to meet you, my lord."
"Tremadore please my dear, formalities are such a waste of time."

The alarm clock rang out a shrill beep into Gabby's head. It drew the eighteen year old into the land of the living, slowly but surely. Half awake, her hand fumbled around her bedside desk, knocking over a pot of pencils, for the umpteenth time. Her fingers fiddled around for the buttons. Irate she couldn't find it, she proceeded to hit the clock. That did it, silence at last.

She'd been counting down the days of the last few months. This was the last day she had to use that clock for a long time. College was over, the last exams had been sat and the inhuman levels of stress were practically over. Just this one last hurdle. Results day, stress built up to the extreme. She didn't want to do it. She turned around, squinting in the sunlight.

"Bugger off....." She grunted at the bright orb shining through her curtains. She rolled onto her side and let out a strange groan as she stretched her limbs.

She lent up and rubbed the sleep out of her eyes, it felt like someone had been eating crisps over her while she was sleeping and they'd all collected in her eyes. If she was more "with it", she'd make a reference to The Night The Sandman Came, a particularly cheesy creature feature from 1970. But she was too zoned out to even think which of her catalogue of cheese best suited this situation.

Instead, she kicked off the bed sheets and, while doing her best impression of a lumbering primate, shuffled to the center of her bedroom. Some clothes had been left on the floor from last night, which she just kicked off and slept in her underwear, it was summer, she had her reasons. She slipped on her usual pair of black skinny jeans, plain gray t-shirt and red checkered shirt, she practically lived and died in this outfit. Her room was what she described as an organized mess, the dull white walls were covered in posters, some framed, others hastily stuck on with tape.

The posters were almost exclusively horror based, and all the films were of a quality less than stellar. For instance, The Zombie Dead Of Alabama from 1984. Now that was a proper stinker, and Gabby loved it, especially with the cool looking poster of a rotting hand emerging from a grave holding a tattered Bible. Her supernatural experience all those years ago would make some people mad, knowing that ghosts and spirits exist and they reside in your village could lead to many a sleepless night. However, for some reason, that never really happened. Gabby had chosen to keep the experience so buried in her mind she barely even remembered it in great detail.

What did happen though was it triggered a passionate love for the horror genre, in film, television and comic book form. Manisha was dragged along for the ride and many a late evening was spent with a bowl of crisps and dip watching the B Movie glory unfold before them. She had turned what should have been a deeply troubling experience into something good. Plus Manisha was the only one who knew about the events at the manor house, she didn't tell her parents or grandmother at all, it'd only lead to awkward dinner conversations or she'd get sectioned under the mental health act.

Gabby lightly smacked her cheeks to wake herself up before heading down the stairs to the dining room. What immediately hit her was the smell of breakfast, which was great because the kitchen stank of wood polish for the last week, having an oak kitchen had its drawbacks. It was an old fashioned looking place, the Morgan family residence. Leaded glass windows, a lot of wood, certainly no modern construction.

In fact, the television and computers were the only things in the house that really seemed to place it in the 21st century. The kitchen lead to the living room, with no doors separating the two, being an open plan design. The old wood burning fire, unused for months because it was well into the twenty degrees Celsius outside. There were old sculptures made of wood by each side of the fire place, impulse purchases holidaying abroad somewhere, before Gabby's time.

She entered the kitchen and looked to the wooden table, a plate of toast was sat in the middle. Banana on toast with a little jam, her favourite. Her Mother had her back turned to her, she was at the coffee machine brewing up something strong, the way she liked it.

Mavis Morgan's sensible bob cut reflected her overall appearance, she was practical in all aspects. Around the house, she wore a simple button up shirt and black leggings. Her blue and green eyes were kept locked on the drink she was preparing.

"Ahh the Kraken awakes." Mavis joked.

"Oh ha ha." Came the response. She smiled as she took some toast and sat down.

Sat at the table was her Grandma, a kindly woman, in her mid 80s. Her white, curly hair sat atop the head of the thin faced, bespeckled lady. Gabby always loved hearing her tales, her stories, both during the war and since. She had been as much of a constant source of support to Gabby as her Mother and Father. She greeted Gabby and returned to the newspaper's crossword puzzle. Gabby peered over as she took a large bite out of her toast.

"Stuck on something?" Came the barely comprehensible question, nearly lost amongst the sound of crunching.

Gabby's Gran stared through her glasses at the question. "Yes. This is before your time I think...." She called over to Gabby's Mum who was still making the drinks. "Mavis, do you remember what that film with Ernest Carmichael and Jenny Abernathy was called? The one where he was that lovable conman."

Gabby's Mother stopped making the drinks and stared off into space, trying to recall. There was a deafening silence of around five seconds, which honestly felt to Gabby like an eternity. Eventually, the silence was broken.

"...It was Bait & Switch wasn't it?"

The elderly woman let out a loud "Hah!" As she scribbled the answer out. Gabby laughed as she put a hand over her Nan's shoulder. The two smiled warmly at each other.

Nan had been living with them for five years now, nearly coming up on six that July. Her Grandad had passed away peacefully in his sleep, so of course they would take her in, they had enough room. Her Nan was hardly a hoarder, unlike her Mother, if all the nicknacks around the house was anything to go by, so she only had a few things to bring with her.

She always wore a simple silver bracelet that her husband had given her, nothing ornate, he wasn't made of money, but something simple and undeniable. He would joke that summed him up perfectly, that always got her Nan laughing. Gabby often wondered on the thought of an afterlife. If ghosts really did exist, if what she saw all those years ago was true, then maybe there was some way.

Nan was a bit of a spiritualist, she'd always pour a glass for Grandad, then drink it in his name, so she says. Of course they mourned, who wouldn't? But Gabby, the lover of horror, was convinced she cracked the best way of coping. Just live, that's what she always thought, live for the lost ones, because they would want you to carry on as best you could, and not get bogged down in the sadness. Have a good cry, let it all out, then don't stop for anyone.

Gabby and her Nan's tender moment was broken by the sound of footsteps from above them, followed by the sound of running water. Her Father of course, it was his wash day. Of course she joked when she called it that, it made him sound like someone's car. Yeah, give him a good wash, wax and shampoo for £10 at the garage in town. That summed up the family dynamic really, they were funny!
A little mad too, Gabby and her Nan had played pranks on her Father for years, and it ranged from mixing orange juice into his coffee, the odd jump scare of course, and none of it was mean spirited. Sometimes her Mother and Father would get their own back, as Gabby once woke up to find a (remote control) spider crawling on her face.

She was hardly an Arachnophobic, Florida's Spider Women (1978) was one of her favourite awful films. But her Mother described the shriek she made as a rendition of a Puccini opera from a distressed puppy. There was a slight madness in the family, that's what Gabby needed, especially when the stress hits.

"So, how well do you think you did?" Nan inquired as she closed the newspaper.

Gabby spoke through her mouthful of toast. "I don't want to jinx myself, but I'm pretty sure I didn't fail at any rate."

Right on cue, Gabby's Mother placed a large mug of coffee in front of her. She quickly picked it up and pointed with her little finger. "You're a saint, I swear! I don't know why you're spoiling me when I don't even know my results yet."

Mavis sat down at the table and crossed her arms. "You did your best, I know you did. Really, that's all that matters. I know you're indecisive about university, but if you don't get the points to go in, it's not the end of the world."

"Exactly. I'll walk away with three A Levels, that's more then the lot that left high school."

As she finished her breakfast, washing down the toast with a large gulp of coffee, she checked the time. 8:10, that gave her five minutes to walk down the street and to the bus stop. Plenty of time, since the road they were on was rather small. She stood up and reached over to her Mum, giving her a small kiss before doing the same to her Grandma.

"Right, better get going! It'll be weird going back for like ten minutes. I'll ring you up and let you know the results. I'll probably find Manisha and hang out with her for a bit, so I'll be back in an hour or so. I'll keep you guys posted!"

After waving her family off, she left through the wooden door and ventured out onto the street. It was the height of summer, Mortsbury looked great this time of year. For a little place, it had a certain beauty to it, a picturesque postcard village look to it. Only a few shops were in the village, a butchers, a small corner store and a post office. It was the kind of area where everyone knew each other.

The Morgan family were one of the two youngest households in the village, along with Manisha's family, the Sharma's. The rest of the village was mostly made up of older folk, Gabby had once called it the Retirement Village, which was a little unfair really. Their house was the seventh house along the great stretch up the village, with Manisha's being off a turning.

Each house had their own outside garden which meant the summer air was full of the smells of many assorted flowers, plus someone had evidently cut their grass recently. Gabby took in a deep breath, calming the nerves that were slowly building in her chest. She began the short walk down the street to the bus stop, conveniently placed at the bottom of the road, leading onto the main road which connected them to the school and the towns. As superstitious as she was, Gabby hoped that the cloudless sky, pleasant temperature and all round stunning looking day would be a good omen for her results. She'd be more concerned if it was raining sideways, thunder and lightning.

It wasn't long before she reached the bus stop, and she was greeted by Manisha when she arrived. Now there was a woman who aged well, Gabby was always envious. Gabby had gone from a spotty little greasy haired, socially awkward girl to a clear skinned, curly haired socially awkward woman.

Manisha however, always looked stunning to Gabby. She dressed modestly, a headscarf, a black zip up jacket with a white stripe going across from the arms, which was very telling about her tolerance to heat, simple black leggings and similar canvas shoes to Gabby's own. She joked how they were "right fashion icons". She silently crept up to her friend and flung herself onto Manisha, putting her arms around her shoulders.

"Glob!" She grunted as she put her weight against her friend who felt herself slowly sink to the ground.

"Gah! Gabby get off me!" She cried out in the middle of laughing. She shrugged her shoulders hard and Gabby let go, the two laughing as they composed themselves.

Manisha straightened out her top. "Well Gabs, day of reckoning eh?"

Gabby grinned. "Yeah, my favorite creature feature. I'm joking, I'm joking." She took another deep breath of the fragrant air. "You decided what your gonna do after this?"

Manisha paused for a second. "I dunno, I like where I'm at at the moment, but I guess I can always get some more qualifications. You?"

Gabby just shrugged. "No idea. I only really stayed on because of you, and the clan."

On that cue, Manisha dug into her pocket and got out her phone. "Oh on that note, did you get that text from Julia?"

Gabby pulled her own phone out of her pocket. "I don't think so, why?"

She pulled up her messages, barely anyone texted her anyway. Her last message was from her Mum, asking her if she could pick up something from that nice little deli store that was close to the school.

"Boris proposed to Julia about an hour ago." Manisha showed Gabby the message.

"No!" Gabby gasped.

"Yep." Manisha replied.

".......No!"

"Yep."

Gabby took the phone and read the message. "Oh that sly romantic!"

"Right? Took him long enough. They're keeping their grades secret till they hear ours."

The two both looked to the right as the distinctive hiss of the air brakes of the school bus interrupted their flow. Well, it was a public bus, but there weren't that many students that needed picking up around their neck of the woods. The both took their bus cards from their pockets, flashed it against the drivers machine then went to get their seats.

"Mind if I plug myself in? I don't want to use up all my conversation topics just yet." Gabby joked as she pulled out her MP3 player, an older model but one she's had for years.

"Sure, I'll do the same." Replied her friend.

Gabby scrolled through her playlists till she found what she thought best suited her mood. She lent against the glass of the window as she watched the countryside roll past her. In that little instance of time, her favourite tunes playing in her ear, next to her best friend, watching the world rush by them, the stresses and pressures of the world seemed to slip away. She drummed her fingers on her thigh in time with the piano playing in her ears.

Today was going to prove interesting, even though she had no real idea the extent of how her life would change in the next few hours. Two years of her life had gone into this, to say it was daunting was an understatement. Her mind crawled back to the good times she had her friends had shared. Her, Manisha, Bobbi, Julia and Boris, the five of them shared thick and thin, and it was fun, like, really fun.

On one of their free periods in the closing days of college, before the exam, Bobbi smuggled in a football and they played a game of two a side with Bobbi on the sidelines. It was only then that the football hit the window of the German language classroom, the relief when they saw it didn't break was unbelievable. In High School, Boris came up with the idea of using balled up tin foil to bat around the group and see how many times they could keep it circulating before someone dropped it. On a fluke of a day, the highest score was, and remains, 107.

On an open mic, Julia who actually could sing rather well took the mic with Boris as backing vocals. Boris sounded semi tone deaf, but no one complained because they were too cute together. Of course Boris and Julia both had gotten their results before Manisha and Gabby, they lived close to the college, so they were one of the first in. It must have been pretty impressive if they decided to propose after it.

The half an hour it took to get from the bottom of Mortsbury to the college felt like it took no time at all before the two hopped off the bus. The rabble of high school students got off before them, they were in no rush to get into the building. The school was both a high school and a 6th Form college, so Gabby and her peers shared the building with the high school, though they were separated for the most part. The school itself was pretty old fashioned, a high budget for renovating the place and bringing the entirety of the school into the 21st century would be very sought after.

The computer rooms, science labs and sports hall were the only things that really screamed modern. But honestly, Gabby really rather liked the rest of it. Her movie interests never really escape 1989 that much, with a rare exception, so being in such a retro environment was kinda cool to her. To see the old messages people would write in the desk, to smell the old wooden walls (which now stank of fresh paint), to marvel at the fact they still had blackboards, with chalk! Yeah they had interactive whiteboards but she remembered a brilliant case where one in her Maths class didn't work, so the teacher had to use badly drawn doodles and stick men to explain Probability Theory. The poor guy had to stop every five minutes to explain the doodles!

The results were being given out in the main hall, which was pretty much the first thing you see when you enter the school. It was fairly large, with a big stage at the front. There, a line of five teachers sat behind their desks, handing out student's futures like high street magazine sellers, but with more warmth thankfully.

Gabby and Manisha joined the queues, Manisha choosing the line leading to the head of year, and Gabby chose the line leading to her now former drama teacher. Now, there was a real cool guy. Early 30s, perpetual stubble, a cracking sense of humor and an honest and fair approach to feedback, meaning if you were total rubbish, he'd tell you! Mr Choksi was his name, but everyone called him Chris. That's what was great about 6th Form, there was a brilliant sense of camaraderie, even with the teachers. You earn their respect in high school and it paid off in college.

The wait in the line was getting unbearable. She felt her hands get clammy as they began to shake a little. This was just as bad as her high school grades, maybe even worse. She at least knew her grades were in a good place even before the exams. She knew nothing about how well she fared. She couldn't remember the last time she was this on edge. To pass the time in the queue, she spent a bit of time trying to place the last time. Seeing Bobbi for the first time after their operation was a good start. Gabby was struggling real hard to place the last time she'd be so wracked with nerves.

Then it hit her, and it hit her hard. It struck her so hard she actually had to be pushed along, she'd been stuck in place. It was that creepy manor, where she saw that... Whatever it was! She had let the whole event get forgotten about, it was like a distant dream to her. Had it really been years? Was the house even still there? She hadn't seen or heard about it since the event. But she remembered the details, they were crystal clear in her mind. The smell of the dust, the silence.... The figure. The figure who kind of reminded Gabby of that silent movie star her Nan had talked about, that Jenny woman.

That thing, whatever it was, was see through, its feet weren't visible, only the thighs up could have been clear, anything below it kind of just faded away. Gabby wondered how she could have dealt with that image in her head for all these years. She has forgotten. She'd filled her head with tacky horror movies as if it was some kind of coping mechanism, and it had worked. It worked so well that she felt the realization hit her like a brick wall.

Gabby realized she had been standing in the line for a good twenty seconds longer then she needed to. Chris' snapping fingers snapped her out of her trance like daze. Oh yeah, her future. Bugger, she forgot. She sat down on the hard, plastic chair and clasped her sweaty hands together, they left ugly hand prints whenever she put them on any surface when they leaked like this.

"So Gab, it's the day of reckoning for you eh?" Chris joked as he kept his head down, searching for Gabby's paperwork.

"Yeah, judgment day, the promised time, whatever other biblical nightmare we want to call this." She joked through an uneasy, nervous smile. Nervous was an understatement, she was pretty terrified honestly. She watched her bearded teacher flick through the papers, there can't be that many students whose surname begins with M. If he was being needlessly dramatic to give her a heart attack, she'd haunt him. Of course, given what she unearthed, that was kind of in poor taste.

"Mason, Malone.... Morgan. Your papers are in order." He then handed over the two or three sheets stapled to each other.

There was a slight, involuntary murmur from Gabby. It sounded kind of like someone kicked a bear in the bottom, but quieter. She couldn't look, but at the same time, the suspense was unbearable. She took a deep breath, placed the paper on the desk and looked down at it.

"Say what?" She blinked a few times. She picked up the paper and moved it close to her face. "Is that right?"

The paper read thus. English Language: A, Drama & Theater Studies: A, Media Production, B. After a moment's silence, she let out a shrill screech of happiness. Chris rubbed his ear.

"The audience is now deaf." He chuckled. He felt himself drawn to a hug from across the table. "Congratulations!" He patted Gabby on the back. "You really worked hard, you deserve this."

Gabby put her hands together and had the biggest grin on her face. "Thank you so much! I did have an amazing teacher."

Chris laughed to himself as he offered his hand. Gabby gave it a good, firm shake. "Too kind Gabby. You'll be at the leavers party in a fortnight, won't you?"

"Yep!" Gabby replied as she kept the papers close to her chest. "I'll see you there?"

Chris nodded in response. "I look forward to it, so long as you don't get too drunk."

"I promise... Tentatively!"

After a brief exchange, Gabby practically ran out of the hall, where she saw Manisha waiting for her. She fully charged at her friend and practically shrieked.

"I'll show you mine if you show me yours!"

Manisha snickered. "I never would have expected someone of your romantic persuasion ever say that!" She held up her paper, and of course, straight As. Gabby held her papers to her friend. They both gave each other a high five.

"Two years of our lives not entirely wasted eh?" Manisha returned Gabby's dork grin.

Gabby took out her wallet from her pocket. "Shall we treat ourselves?"

"You know it!" Came the response.

The two now former students left the hallowed halls of their place of learning one last time and ventured out to the summer sun once again. The school was at the top of a road that lead to a T junction, if one turned right, walked for about ten minutes then took a sharp right by the fish and chip shop, then they'd reach the little market town that they would always spend their lunch breaks at. Lines of old fashioned looking shops lined both sides of the cobbled street, which comprised of Ye Olde craft shops, an agriculture suppliers, more tea rooms per block then Gabby had ever seen and a bank or two.

The bakeries were where they usually got their lunches, a diet of pasties and sausage rolls for years. But this time, the rather nice looking deli restaurant was to be Gabby and Manisha's destination. They had enough to treat themselves, and they had every reason to as well. They spent an hour there, Manisha taking nibbles out of her vegetarian option while Gabby attacked her meat sub with extra meat. Sure her parents would treat her when they got home, but by her own admission, she was a human rubbish bin when it came to food. Her Mother was determined that her metabolism was mutated, she must have got that from her Father. Between mouthfuls, she rang her parents and gave them the news.

Manisha couldn't stop laughing hearing her friends hyperactive screeching over the phone as she chugged cola and downed huge chunks of meat and bread in tandem. The looks they got from the deli's other customers caused the nerd to sink in her chair a bit, but it wasn't going to deter her excitement. Truth be told, the sugary drink was doing no favours, especially when she ordered another to go.

The two spent the next hour walking around the town, visiting a few shops, including a sweet shop which had the unbearably sour Gobstoppers Gabby loved doing wagers with Manisha over. Of course, she'd bought them to relive some of that childish but nonetheless fun jeopardy. It was more tame than the wagers used to be, but given they'd left the school, they couldn't do the usual "Get the biology teacher to say banana" wager.

A simple rock, paper scissors had to do for now. Of course, like in most things, Manisha beat her. Manisha was kind enough to record Gabby's muffled cries of desperation as the customary stream of drool left her mouth and she started to resemble a soft tomato. Once the intensity subsided and Gabby was sure the tooth rot had kicked in, they figured the should head back. It was getting on for 2pm, and they wanted to catch the 2.30 bus, if they missed it, they'd get caught up in the school leaving time, and the less time swimming through an onslaught of high schoolers the better from now on. It was like the human equivalent of hiking through treacle. Spotty, trend obsessed treacle.

Thankfully they nabbed the bus bang on 2.30. It was quiet, barely anyone on it, aside from the old dear with the facial hair who would boot anyone out if they were in her seat. She caused a great deal of amusement. Of course, it was a bizarre feeling, this would be the last time they would do this.

Manisha had rung up the gang, they'd all arrange to meet up over the summer to celebrate Boris and Julia's engagement at Bobbi's place. Specific dates would be discussed later in their chat group. Gabby and Manisha spent the trip back recounting memories and having a good old laugh. Manisha was going to spend the summer at her job in the chemists before going off to university in September. As for Gabby, she had no idea really, she'd see what she thought over the summer. Of course her mind was set on only one thing.

As the bus stopped, the two disembarked for the last time. As they walked up the road to their respective houses, Gabby looked down a turning, the turning to the old manor house. Her hands began to feel clammy.

"Hey Manisha, I'm just gonna go check something out. We'll be in touch, yeah?"

Her friend turned and glanced down the turning Gabby had fixed her eyes on. "Okay, I'll text you tomorrow. See you soon."

Gabby didn't look to Manisha to respond, instead giving a small nod. Today had already been a day of change for her, but ever since she thought about what she saw in that dusty, dark house all those years ago, it felt like she had awoken something inside her. It was something that wouldn't be going anywhere if she didn't satisfy the.... No, curiosity wasn't the word. Curiosity is when you want to look into something. This felt like she was being forced towards it. That's why she wasn't expecting herself to go willingly, but she had already began her way down the path to that old, haunted house.

This was such a mistake. She had thought that before, and she still went into the bloody house. It was like something was drawing itself to her, her feet would act independently of her brain and like a commuter train, make her stop wherever they wanted to for however long it wanted to even if she didn't want them to. Why had it taken this long anyway? Well, Gabby wondered, maybe when you put something off for so long, you forget about things.

But she saw a ghost, why would she take it so well? She was so taken aback by this thought, she wasn't an idiot, she knew what this meant. Maybe it was for her own good she try and forget it? The fact she did forget was very telling. Her love for horror, her desire to find something to give her that rush of excitement to match that fear, it all made sense. But this was reality.

The path she walked down had been left to nature since the last time Gabby ventured down it. The bushes and trees that lined the cobbled path had grown thick and wild. In a few cases, Gabby had to trailblaze her way through. What she wouldn't do for a machete. A particularly thick branch left a scratch on her hand, which she reacted by kicking the tree that the branch belonged to. A few feet into the bramble resulted in a cut across her cheek, thanks to another scratchy branch.

Eventually, after what felt like ages, and after numerous scratches, she bested the overgrown mess. When she emerged, she was greeted with that familiar sight. The mansion house, from all those years ago. Well, this was it then. Time to face her fear and see what all the fuss was about.

"Oh bugger...."

Chapter Two: "A Rush of Cold Air"

"What about Tremarda? He's been staring at you all evening."
"Well... Father wouldn't approve."
"Father's not here is he?"

Gabby approached the door, once again. She took a moment before she reached for the doorknob, mostly because she'd noticed it was hanging loosely from the door. Blimey, whoever was inside didn't care much for security. Mind you, if the owners of the house had that little spook show for everyone who happened upon the house, they'd be pretty safe from theft. No one ever really talked about the house in the village, it seemed like it was just forgotten about, rather conveniently. She grasped the doorknob and gently put some weight on it. She jumped as there was a bit of a clunk, she moved her arm back and the knob remained in her hand.

"Bugger it...." She muttered. Great, now she broke the house.

There was a slight chill in the air, a slight breeze had picked up, and it carried along with it a faint noise from the house. Gabby moved closer to the door and put her ear to it. There was someone singing, though it was barely audible, she could work out it was a female's voice. Well, maybe it could hide the noise of her entrance. A shaky hand pressed against the door, with it's peeling paint and recently de-knobed handle. With very little effort, the house opened itself to her.

Immediately, she was hit by a wall of darkness. The light from outdoors poured in like a torrent, illuminating the landing and the small corridor that lead to the main, well, living room. Gabby didn't know what else one would call it. She hastily closed the door behind her, as much as she could since she broke it. She placed the broken knob on the floor and slowly began to walk towards the room. The singing was clearer now, which acted as a guiding force for Gabby to follow in the musky darkness.

Whoever this house belonged to, they weren't friends with the sun. Of course, maybe the ghost she saw was the owner. She'd find out soon enough. The voice filled the room around Gabby, it was a soft, gentle voice. The melody itself sounded old, like the kind of sweeping romantic number from those 50s movies her Grandmother liked, in fact, this one sounded oddly familiar. Gabby kept her steps as light as possible, using her heels as much as possible so she could make her footfall as gentle as possible. She kept her eyes fixed on the origins of the singing. Her mind was so awash with worries, concerns and paranoia that she was just not listening to it, she'd progress unabashed.

The singer was starting to come into view. She sat on the seat of an old piano, one arm leaning against the keys. She was ever so slightly translucent, her arms resting on the keys didn't affect them, they should be sunken in under the weight of her arm, but they remained unaffected. Evidently she had no mass to her body. Gabby was able to see her side profile, she looked no older than thirty, with short, blonde hair and a simple white dress. Her eyes were positively glowing in the darkness, a beautiful, radiant blue. Her round, soft face rested on her shoulder as she continued to sing. Gabby's mouth opened slightly. It was the same one as before, the same ghost.

For some reason, fear hadn't kicked in. Gabby was in awe of her pretty looks. Pretty was an understatement, Gabby thought she looked adorable, and kind of gorgeous too. She had halted in her tracks, and only realised this when those same deep blue eyes were looking right at her. Her heart immediately skipped a beat.

"Hi." The word escaped out of her lips and her voice broke.

The blonde figure sat upright and proceeded to look Gabby up and down from head to toe. Gabby attempted to swallow, but her throat was so dry and her sweat glands were working overtime. She had her trembling hands clenched into fists and took one step back. The ghost began to approach her, though she didn't as much walk as glide. The bottom of her feet kind of faded into nothingness and the further up the legs she went, the more of her there was.

She passed through one of the chairs in between her and Gabby and hovered close to the frightened teen's face. They must have locked eyes for only a few seconds but it felt like hours. Gabby could see those eyes were so full of life, they still looked hopeful, curious, happy even. The ghost floated around her, like it was inspecting her, and all the while Gabby could feel the air become thin and silent. The ghost stopped when she met Gabby's eyes again. She leant forward, her lips curved into a warm smile.

"Well hello, sugar!"

Gabby blinked, her face twisted into a confused, open mouthed gawp. She wasn't expecting that. Whoever she was, she actually seemed really pleasant. She was emitting a calming aura that gave Gabby two thoughts. Either she was totally benign and really friendly, in which case everything she'd feared about, wasn't the case and there was truly nothing creepy or threatening about this whole thing. Or she was trying to lul her into a false sense of security, gain her trust then eat her face off when she let her guard down. But that was the plot to The Chalk Friendship Circle from 1987, so chances are that may not be the case.

Gabby realised she hadn't said anything in ages and was still staring at her with her mouth open. She promptly closed it and returned the greeting by way of a little wave. Clearly words weren't going to come.

"You know your not supposed to be here. It's against the law to walk into someone's house without their permission."

Gabby had almost forgotten the accent, which made things all the more bizarre. But something about her was really nagging at the back of Gabby's memories, and it was starting to slowly creep into her mind. It was a movie she did recognise her from...

"You don't say much, do you?" The ghost joked through a little chuckle. She waved her pale hand a little. "The names Jenny! What's yours?"

Jenny... Jenny... Gabby's eyes immediately widened. "Jenny Abernathy?!" She yelped out. The ghost winked. She was the star from that movie her Gran mentioned that morning. That was causing her head to spin.

Gabby tried to form coherent words, as difficult as it was for her to do so. "How....?"

"How did I get here?" Jenny asked, pointing to herself. "Well, I guess it's a little complicated, but I guess you could say I was... Well, summoned, I suppose." She looked at the still confused mortal staring back at her blankly. "That didn't explain anything did it?"

Gabby didn't know why she started laughing, but she supposed it was the idea that she was actually talking to the ghost of Jenny Abernathy, star of the silver screen from the 1950s, the kind of woman she'd heard about for years, that she'd see listing of her movies on classic film nights and how they looked into one of her films for one of her classes. She was there, having not aged a day since she was singing and dancing with Ernest Carmichael in Bait & Switch.

So all those years ago, it really was real. She didn't know whether to walk or more advisably, run away and tell everyone about this. But then, no one would believe her. Why was she taking this all so well? Maybe because, when she saw Jenny for the first time all those years ago, she had always had this thing in the back of her head, that she knew it was real. She never told anyone about it and kept it hidden, to the point of practically forgetting about it, but the thought was always there.

Now, there was no doubt in her mind. Ghosts, or whatever they were, do exist. This was so strange... All she wanted to do is ask more questions.

"Why were you... Summoned? How does that even work anyway?" Q&A with the ghost of Jenny Abernathy, not how Gabby thought today was going to go down.

Jenny's head tilted slightly as she looked off into the distance, wondering how to put it all into words. Gabby used the quick pause to look around the room they were in. The walls were stone for the top half of the room and dark brown wood covered the lower half. In the living room, there were two world globes. Gabby wondered why they'd need two.

She squinted slightly, she couldn't see the exact details, but one globe had the sea green and the landmass brown, another had a much different looking series of landmasses in grey while what she assumed was the sea in a faded white. Two long, leather sofas faced each other in the centre of the room, with a table between them. Several books and strange, metallic looking cylinders were placed in random order on the table, with small blades layed out near the cylinder. A few strange looking, small sculptures were sat atop plinths and were darted around the room.

Details were of course rather blurry as the wall facing them was clearly an entire, giant window, the curtains of which had been drawn. Enough light was seeping through to bathe the room in a dark orange light. But what grabbed Gabby's attention the most was above the dusty old fireplace.

A large, no, enormous tapestry hung across the entire wall, which was a good thirty foot long. On it were various figures, and Gabby wished she could see it better, because it looked resplendent. She could see the faint impression of the first figure, who was brandishing a sword which they held outwards, as if leading a charge. Gabby quickly counted the figures, over fifteen at any rate.

Her eyes moved down as she saw what was between the tapestry and the fireplace. A portrait of three figures, she could see them easier then the figures on the tapestry, a woman, a man and a child. The woman, Gabby was so taken aback by her. She looked like she hadn't reached her forties, her hair was snowy white, which looked strangely modern in style for what was clearly an old painting. Her hair was all what her Gran would call "sticky uppy", the fringe was swept off her forehead and curved to the right, hanging over cheek. Her eyes may have been jet black, but Gabby couldn't believe how warm her smile was. It was a smile that showed no trace of anything else but love, compassion and caring. She wore a high collared white tunic of some description with grey piping kissing the top of the collar and running down the front of the top, with a black robe over it.

The male had his arm over her back, and his smile was just as warm and innocent as the womans. He was a little less pale as the woman, with strange, metallic looking green eyes. His hair was a soft brown and long enough to brush his shoulders. His tunic was similar to his wives, but was a dark red, almost maroon, and the same black robe was worn over it.

As for the child, the white haired Mother held her in her arms. A small mess of black hair was almost perched on the little ones head, and the eyes were just as dark as the hair, and it was laughing. Enjoying the sensation of being cradled by its Mother. It was still an infant, it's eyes so full of hope.

Gabby felt her eyes misting up. This house, something about it was getting to her... Not in a bad way either. There was something about it, calming the anxiety she felt upon entering the house. It made her come to terms with the ghost of a dead movie star very quickly, which was helpful because she worried she'd never get over it. Gabby always liked abandoned and spooky settings, but this wasn't abandoned or spooky. It was relaxing, like if she entered into a state of meditation. She wiped her eyes.

"Awww, bless you heart, sugar. I guess you're not used to this are you? I wouldn't be if I were in your shoes." The late actress wanted so hard to give the poor girl a hug, if she were corporeal maybe she could have, but alas, it was not meant to be. The two of their heads turned to the picture Gabby had been staring at, of the parents and their child.

"So pretty, isn't it? That little one, she was the one who asked me to cross over."

Gabby turned to Jenny. "What for?"

After a moments silence, Jenny inhaled. "Because she needed us I guess."

"...Us?"

The living and the dead both locked eyes for a second before Gabby felt a rush of cold air. Gabby pivoted on the spot so she could face what she felt was behind her. Jenny kind of levitated into place. A figure was standing in the doorway, leading from the living room into the landing where Gabby had entered from.

The light from the open door cast a shadow across her which made her details seem fuzzy and hard to focus on. The figure remained silent and still. Gabby was about to open her mouth when she heard something to her right which, upon seeing it, made her yelp like a little girl.

Like a bad jumpscare, she saw something come hurtling towards her at an alarming rate. Rather sickeningly, it phaised past her and latched itself onto Jenny. Gabby stumbled backwards, feeling rather disorientated by the whopping great thing that went past her.
It was like a freezing cold blast shot through her chest, knocking the air out of her. She looked up at the thing that went through her and panted.

"...Bloody hell..." She muttered.

The thing that had gone through her was another ghost. Like Jenny, it was semi translucent and seemed to hover above the ground, to make up for the lack of feet. The ghost was holding onto Jenny's shoulders, it looked like she was trying to protect her. If Jenny was adorable, then this ghost was....Wow.

Even though the feet were blending into the darkness, the ghosts long boots that reached up to their thighs were clear enough, as were the simple black trousers. They wore a long, flowing, red coat with black embroidery that reached so far down it had started to disappear, with a large belt across their waist and black gloves. First glance at the face revealed the ghost was another female, with sun kissed skin and a mess of deep, dark red hair tucked under her tricorn hat. She was a pirate, there was no other way to describe it.

The pirate ghost moved her hand down Jenny's cheek gently, resting her forehead on the actresses. She spoke in a delicate and caring tone. "Are you alright?"

Jenny took the gloved hand gently and looked into her eyes. "Skye, I'm okay..."

Skye immediately shot Gabby a deathly look, a flash of white shined from her gritted teeth. "Just what the hell do you think your doing here!?"

And then the tension kicked in. Whatever calming aura the house was exuding was well and truly shattered. Her brain quickly tried to scan for an answer, or even a response, while she tried to process the fact a dead movie star from the 1950s and a female pirate were staring at her, looking for answers. Unfortunately, she could only muster a stupid response, as she came to regret saying it the moment it left her mouth.

"Well, what are you doing here?! How and why are you ghosts here?"

Jenny's face resembled that of a hurt puppy, while Skye had the look of someone who'd deck Gabby if she had a physical presence.

"Don't say that word! That's not what we are!" Skye exclaimed as she struck her own chest. "We're Etemmu, there's a difference."

Gabby looked confused, a what now? She'd never heard of that before. They looked like ghosts, they were kind of see through, floated, were dead, what else could they be? Before she could ask, she heard the voice of the woman standing in the doorway, who she'd almost forgotten.

"That's enough Skye." Another female by the sound of it. Blimey, Gabby wondered what kind of place this was, full of dark, mysterious women and the ghosts, or Etemmu or whatever they were called.

Gabby was able to get a good look at the woman in the doorway, as she started approaching her, the silence of the room was broken by the clomping sound of her laced up boots. It was clear to Gabby that this person was alive, the figure was as solid and as tactile as she was. Around her, the same black and white robes as the family in the painting, which was wrapped around a slim, pale figure, in an oddly clasing combination of clothing. Sure the robes were present, but the black tights and black shorts felt so... Out of place.

Even her hair looked punkish, one side of her head was closely cut as her fringe hung over the side of her face in a shaved undercut style. Much like the woman in the portrait, there was such a strange mix. Several piercings were in her ears, all of them studs. Of course Gabby couldn't help but notice her eyes, black as pitch.

She glanced at the portrait, at the small child and back to the woman standing before her. My, how they grow up so fast. Her expression gave Gabby a chill, it was a probing gaze. She was methodically analysing Gabby, she could tell. The black eyes scanned over her and the woman's head tilted to the side, a small "Hmm..." escaping from her mouth.

"This is private property, and your breaking and entering." The woman's words were like a cold winter's breeze to Gabby, biting and chilling to the bone.

Gabby felt a thin layer of sweat developing on her forehead. "Well, I know the doorknob was a little loose but I'd hardly call something already broken, breaking per say..."

Okay, maybe joking wasn't such a good idea, the mood in the room was awful as it was, no need to add cringe worthy awkwardness to the mix.

"If I'm being honest, this is all kind of stupid... A couple of years ago, I made a bet. I know it was stupid but I bet my friend I wouldn't go into this house and well...I did."

She paused for a second. She looked across at the three women around her, all had patient looks on their faces. Gabby continued.

"That's when I saw Jenny. I ran straight out, screaming and half in tears yeah, but that was years ago."

The black eyed woman spoke next. "So why did you come back? Why didn't you run and tell everyone you could about us?"

Gabby responded with a scoff. "Oh come on, be fair, they'd think I've gone mad! Sane people don't see ghosts." She glanced at Jenny. "Sorry, Emu or whatever the word was."

"Etemmu!" Barked Skye.

The woman looked over. "Skye, calm down."

Jenny wrapped her arms around the pirate's arm. "Trem's right, she didn't mean any harm by it..."

That was her name? Trem? Gabby was really rather taken aback... Given her friends came from all around, unusual names weren't unheard of. But still, it wasn't like anything she'd heard of. Trem took a step or two towards Gabby, who found herself taking several steps back before realising what she was doing.

"You seem pretty smart, and harmless enough. I can respect your reasonings, but I think it's best for you to forget what you've seen today. You did it once before and for all our benefits, you should again."

Gabby let out a brief, muted chuckle. "Not meaning to sound rude or anything, but ummm, no can do. I'm sorry, I really am, but you can't expect me to just let this go! I mean, this is all mental, I'm sort of wondering why I haven't gone full on whacked in the head. Or if I have then it might give me a rational explanation for all this."

There was a low level growl coming from Skye as Jenny had to hold her back. "Skye, no!" She pleaded as she was dragged along.

"You'd better learn some respect! If you had any idea what you're dealing with then you'd watch your mouth!" The pirate snapped.

Trem turned to the spirit. "Skye, control yourself."

Skye sighed and took a deep breath before backing away. Trem moved closer to Gabby, ending up only a foot or two away from the intruder's face.

"There are things here that shouldn't be dabbled with by mortal hands. They'd prove a danger to you, and I can't afford to have anyone hurt or even killed because of ignorance."

Gabby replied so quickly she didn't even stop to think about what she'd say. "What dangers though? Look, I live in the village, if I have to just walk away from this again, knowing it's all right on my doorstep again I think I will go mad."

Jenny raised a translucent hand. "If you lived not far from here, why didn't you come earlier?"

The young woman ran her hands through her hair, this time she actually tried to think of a response. Honestly, she didn't really know why, but she couldn't say that. "I guess, at first you put things off, you know, days turn to weeks, then months and then years. Plus I had high school, then college. I guess I just wanted to forget it..."

Trem lowered her head, Gabby could clearly see she was thinking hard on something. The pale gothic woman looked back up after a few seconds. "What is your name?"

Well that she could answer confidently enough, makes a change. "Gabby Morgan."

"Gabby Morgan, I know I can't make you unsee what you've seen here, but there are rules we have to follow. No humans can learn of our existence. This has already gone out of hand, I can't risk you seeing anymore. If word of this got out, then it could put the lives of so many at risk."

Gabby was already starting to get desperate, she didn't want this to just slip away, not after all that had happened, and in such a short space of time. "You're worried I'd tell people what happened here right? Like I said, no on would believe me, and that's if I lied and told them against what you told me. I don't break promises like that, I hate it when people do. It just hurts people."

She noticed a change in Trem's expression, her eyebrows raised slightly and her lips parted a fraction. That wasn't the look of someone who wasn't believing her. Gabby decided to continue her justification.

"I know you've only got my word, but look, what harm can I really do? Do I look like some kind of necromancer or black magic user? I can barely get my head around what Wiccans do. I'm good at talking, acting and studying. This otherworldly stuff is way beyond me. I doubt any passerby can summon a pirate or a pop culture icon."

Jenny blushed, as much as she could give her pale, half see through form. "You really think I'm that big?"

Trem looked to the second level of the house, her face turning to a slight frown before turning back to Gabby. "You speak truthfully, Gabby Morgan. I can't fault your logic. I'll need some time to think on it. Till then, you're free to stay in the living room."

She turned on the spot and began heading to the landing, where a flight of wooden stairs lead to the next level of the house. Gabby quickly followed, stopping after she reached the first few steps.

"One second, there's one thing I want to know!" She called out, her voice echoing around the house.

Trem stopped halfway up the flight of steps. "What is it?"

Gabby opened her mouth to speak, but she wasn't able to think of how to phrase it, it's not something that one just asks bluntly. Since being subtle was out a bit beyond her at the moment, she let out a small "Well..." She turned to the picture of the child Trem with her parents.

The most subtle of twitches triggered in Trem's eyes. It was the look of someone who was trying to hide their feelings. It said a lot for why Trem's personality was the way it is. Gabby couldn't believe she thought that. She'd only known her for a matter of minutes and she was already making personality calls? Realising her mistakes, Gabby quickly redacted her comment.

"I'm sorry, I won't ask about it again..." Wow, she was convinced she came across as a massive bum.

"It's okay. You're curious." Came the rather muted reply. She began climbing the steps up to the first floor.

"Stupid, stupid idiot..." Gabby muttered, slapping her head with the lower part of her palm. The slapping sound reverberated around the house.

Not long after Trem had disappeared, Gabby had returned to the living room, where Jenny and Skye were waiting.

"Were you clicking your fingers just then?" Skye asked, her tone a lot less demanding and aggressive then before.

"No...Why?" Came the reply. Almost as quickly as she finished her sentence, she felt something zoom across the top of her head, an inch or two shy of clipping her curly hair. She ducked immediately and looked around aimlessly, feeling the wind it whisked up flick her hair.

"What was that!?" She yelped.

The two spirits chuckled, Jenny trying to hide her mouth behind her hand. "I'm sorry Gabby, it's kind of funny !" Jenny whistled as the thing that was flying around the dark room came to perch on the table.

Gabby slowly moved closer, trying to get a better look. "Oh my god....." She muttered.

It was a little bird, like a robin, but made of wood. It's body was carved from a light birchwood, the details were crisp and sharp. The craftsmanship looked very lifelike, very detailed. But the way it moved, it was like a proper bird. It's head darted about analytically and it made a quiet cooing sound. The noises coming out of it sounded a little clunky, like it was not quite right. Gabby slowly held her hand out, holding her breath.

The bird jumped onto her hand, Gabby couldn't help but laugh as she gently stroked the top of the little ones head.

"It's adorable..." Gabby made a ticking noise with her tongue as she continued to play with it. This was getting stranger by the minute. Ghosts, well, fair play, but living inanimate sculptures? It'd be freaky if it wasn't so cute. "Does it have a name?"

Jenny and Skye exchanged glances, the pirate shrugged her shoulders. "I don't think so...?" Jenny responded.

Gabby let the wooden robin climb up her arm as it perched onto her shoulder. She made a little friend, today wouldn't go entirely to waste. "I think I'll call him Woody. Do you like that?" The robin cooed, which came out as a wood like rattle. Gabby petted him on the head before moving over to the other side of the room.

She reached the large curtains and looked to the ghosts. "You two aren't like, allergic to sunlight are you?"

Jenny looked a bit lost and confused, Skye just had a scowling look on her face.

"Okay, I'll take that as a no." She muttered.

She yanked on the curtains and pulled them back, letting in the brilliant light. The dust from the curtains filled the air, causing Gabby to cough. The whole room was now bathed in the brilliant afternoon light. Things were so much clearer now, the once blurry details lost in the dark were now much clearer. Gabby gestured to the middle of the living room.

"Mind if I look around?"

Jenny peered at Skye, as if asking silently for permission. "Guess there's no harm in it."

Gabby took a seat on the leather sofa, and it was really comfortable. She felt like she could sink into it and never leave. She leant forward to examine the table. Woody hopped off her arm and sat on the table, cleaning the wooden wing with his beak. Gabby took one of the books, a black, leather bound volume with faded, sepia pages.

She opened the first few pages and squinted at the words. Her face twisted into a look of confusion. The writing was... Strange, like a gone wrong Arabic mixed with Japanese. She flicked through the pages, with a few diagrams drawn out. One included odd shaped diagrams, such as a circle with three orbs forming a triangle pattern inside it. Some kind of bizarre spells or incantations maybe? One thing that caught her eye was the cylinder, which caught the sun and caused it to shine rather brilliantly. She reached over and picked it up, gently as she could.

At first glance it looked like metal, but on closer inspection, it looked to be made out of a rock of some description. The Hematite cylinder had a figure depicted on it. It had one hand reached out, with some of the strange, not quite Arabic writing along the bottom.

"Trem's been working on that every day, has been for a few weeks now." Jenny explained as she moved through the sofa and hovered next to Gabby.

Gabby glanced over to Jenny for a moment before she turned her attention back to the cylinder. "Is it some kind of artwork thing? Or is it tradition?"

Skye phased through the sofa and put her arm around Jenny, pulling herself closer to her partner. "We don't know really. We don't ask that many questions. She usually asks us things, and writes down what we say."

Gabby gently placed the Hematite tube back onto the table. "Do you know why?"

Skye sighed as she rubbed her forehead, pushing her tricorn up with her thumb. "We don't really know that much about where Trem came from or what her people are. We know they summon Etemmu like us. She asked us all personally to come back to this world..."

Gabby's eyes widened. This was already starting to get a bit too much to contemplate. "Hold on, how do you mean she asked you?"

Skye bit her lip and glanced to the landing, half expecting Trem to appear at any moment. In a hushed tone, she replied. "Well, she's not exactly human...."

Gabby's eyes shot open, her eyebrows raised high. What was that supposed to mean, not exactly human? She looked human, she sounded human... If it was true, then what the hell was Trem?

Before she could ask anything else, she heard the sound of boots clomping down the steps. She turned around to see Trem entering the living room. Gabby quickly shot to her feet. Woody got to his feet as well and flew over to Trem, resting on her shoulder.

"We can't keep you here of course, so you don't need to worry about being a prisoner. We can't make you do anything, so we're relying on that trust you promised." Trem approached Gabby and stopped a few inches short of her face. "Just know, if you jeopardize what we have here..."

Gabby cut off Trem's flow, she knew where this was going to go. "You don't need to make any threats. I know it won't be easy to trust me, but I hope that you'll see you can rely on me to keep my mouth shut."

They were rather close to each other, Gabby could see into Trem's jet black eyes, there was such a sadness to them, though Trem maintained an icy disposition towards her.

Gabby started fidgeting again, rubbing her thumbs up and down her fingers. "I don't pretend to know anything about all this. Honestly, it kind of scares me. No, actually it's bloody terrifying, and it's kind of brilliant. I know I'm not making sense, it's just kind of hard to process right now." She let herself take a second to take a deep breath and calm herself down. "I want to prove myself to you, that you can trust me. Can I..."

She wasn't really sure how to phrase it, so she decided to say it out right.

"Can I come back tomorrow?"

She could hear the faint muttering from Jenny and Skye, who were whispering a conversation and looking a little concerned in the process. Trem sighed as she tilted her head. "Sure. So long as it's just you, by yourself. Understand?"

Gabby responded with a silent nod. "Guess I'll see you tomorrow then?"

Before Trem could answer, Gabby felt her pocket vibrate. She began to fumble around her pockets, trying to find it. When she did, she sighed as she saw who was calling her. With confused and bewildered looks from the other three, she put the phone to her ear.

"Hi Mum...Yeah nothing's wrong, just fancied a bit of a walk...Yes I know it's been over an hour. I should have rung, I know, sorry. Yeah, I'm on my way back now. Okay, see you soon." She turned her phone off and returned it to her jeans pocket.

She gave a final goodbye and headed out of the room. She saw the broken door knob and tried to reach down to pick it up.

"Leave it." Trem ordered. Gabby obeyed and left it on the floor as she gently pushed the door open and closed it.

After a few seconds, and with her gaze still fixed on the door, Trem gave out another command. "Have Abhay follow her."

Skye glanced over, at first she looked a little concerned, but her expression rested on that of contentment. "Will do."

Jenny kept her arm wrapped around Skye's, keeping close to her friend at all times. "What happened up there Trem? Your not usually like this..."

Trem sighed. She sat on the sofa and rubbed her eyes. Woody nuzzled her neck gently with his beak and cooed. Trem let the tips of her fingers stroke against his birchwood body. She felt exhausted, glancing up at her ghostly friends. "Treman happened."

Chapter Three: "What Have You Done?"

"I forbid you from fraternizing with the likes of him!"
"You're in no position to order me around, I'm the one who will inherit the titles after you."
"I will not have this family's name dragged through the mud!"

While Gabby was exploring the living room, Trem made her way up the stairs to the first floor. At the top of the stairs was the galleried landing, leading to some of the house's rooms. She stopped by the closest door to the steps and pushed it open.

Inside was her bedroom, complete with four poster bed. The walls depicted a desert landscape, which she had painted in her youth. The colours were looking a tad faded after all these years, but the picture itself was still pretty much clear. The two bedside cabinets had candlesticks with the candles themselves melted down to the extent that the hardened wax was running off them. A Hematite cylinder was atop one of the cabinets, as was a few stone figurines. In the centre of the room was a small, round table that had a book and some scrolls placed on it's top.

A full body mirror was covered, as were some paintings on the walls. There was a desk in the corner, by the closed windows, which had a block of clay in the process of being sculpted. Also on the desk was a large glass tank, with bronze around the top and bottom of it. A thick layer of sand coated the bottom of the tank and a variety of half logs and a little area to hide in were also placed in the tank. There was a light constantly shining on it, which was supplied by a rather old fashioned, steampunk looking device, a bronze, metal arm that connected to the wall like a dentists light. Trem always found ways to... "Acquire" the UV light bulbs.

As she walked into her room, she gently closed her door. As if on cue, a Bearded Dragon's head poked out of it's hideaway. It looked left and right, then up to Trem. It slowly came out of it's cool spot and into the centre of the tank. Smiling, Trem walked up to the container, slid open the top and reached in, gently taking her pet and friend out.

"Hey there buddy." She whispered as she walked over to her bed. Sitting on the front of it, she let the reptile climb up onto her shoulder, which still had a little bit of sand and wood dust lightly coating it.

Samiel was given to Trem for her sixteenth birthday, as is customary with her culture. At sixteen, Manzazzu are expected to learn the responsibilities of life, as well as death. What better way to teach the younglings life then by gifting them with pets? The only thing Trem objected to was the name. Sammy was much nicer than Samiel. She stroked his scaly body and sighed.

"I don't know what to do." She muttered to Sammy, not expecting an answer of course. She felt like a little vent might do her some good. "I never expected this to happen. It's not like there's a rule book for this sort of thing."

Trem gazed at her companion with sad eyes, lost in the dilemma that kept her confused and concerned.

"What have you done?" Came a voice from behind Trem. It was an old, bitter sounding voice, low and with a certain aloof smugness that made Trem's skin crawl.

Trem turned around to face the owner of the voice. Her grandfather, Treman, aka the massive pain in her backside for years now. Like Skye and Jenny, he was an Etemmu, fading from the waist down. Unlike the others, he seemed more faded, with his eyes milky and hard to see in the light. The once craggy face, which had looked like it was a caricature modeled in clay was now softened by his ghostly aspect. His thin, wispy white hair hung around his shoulders and he wore robes like Trem's.

Trem returned his question with a stern gaze, both of them locked in scowls. "It's none of your business, old man." She retorted.

Treman turned his nose up at his grandaughter, a flash of yellowing teeth could be seen from his wrinkling, cracked lips. "Watch your tongue, insolent child. Remember whose house this is..."

Before he could finish, Trem spoke over him. "Remember who summoned you in the first place. I know you're fading out of existence, but I thought that was your current state and not your mind."

Treman floated closer, his craggy face mere inches from Trem's, his ghostly aspect chilling the air around her, making Sammy shiver. "Remember why you summoned me in the first place, you brat! You were desperate, crying out for Mummy and Daddy like a wounded animal!"

Trem's teeth pressed so hard against themselves it felt like they'd crack under the pressure. Her scowl widened into a look of near rage. A deep intake of breath prevented herself from getting pushed over the edge. She held up her left hand, which had a ring on each finger. The biggest, brightest and by far the most impressive was a sapphire ring on her thumb. Around it, a ruby, emerald, amethyst and a citrine, all set in silver.

"I could always drag you back into the Styx, if that's what you want. Kicking and screaming too by the look of it." She looked at her Grandfather's fading form and scoffed. "Your always so proud aren't you? You've nearly overstayed your welcome here. How many years now? You're not gone yet. If you wanted to end it even in the afterlife, you can do it on the other side and just leave me alone."

Trem felt such a sense of satisfaction. Getting it all out was what she needed to relieve the stress of the situation. Though she had doubts it would yield anything successful.

"Are you finished?" Treman asked, in his monotonous, yet still condescending tone. Trem didn't dignify it with a response. Treman continued probing. "I heard you talking to someone. She didn't sound like those irritating women you keep company with."

Trem turned away, not wanting to continue this conversation. She knew exactly where it was going, and the last thing she wanted was to justify herself to the likes of him. Honestly, she didn't really know why Gabby was still downstairs, no doubt probing into her life, finding all she could about her, her family and the Manzazzu.

"You let a human into the house didn't you?" What was particularly chilling about it was how Treman asked it in a hushed whisper, not his usual barking tone. Trem closed her eyes and nodded slowly.

"You idiot." Treman responded, maintaining the same subdued volume. "You know how many rules you're breaking?"

Trem's eyes shot open and she turned her head to face her grandfather again. "Do you think I don't know that?"

Despite his glass like eyes being so pale and hard to see, the anger in them was clear to Trem. "Clearly you do." He jeered. "Clearly you don't recall what humans used to do to us Manzazzu. They hunted us, they rejected us...."

Trem let out a loud groan. Truth be told, she was getting sick of this. "That's ancient history. If you saw her, you'd know she doesn't have enough bravery or strength to pick a fight. This isn't even the first time she showed up. If she didn't pick a fight or go screaming to her human hordes to come with their pitchforks and flaming torches to burn us to the ground then, I doubt she'd do it now."

Treman's hand rubbed against his pale head. "You don't understand humans. They're treacherous beings. They wage wars with each other over their depiction of heaven, they slaughter waves of their own for not conforming..."

Trem stood up, one hand holding onto Sammy so he wouldn't fall off. "No, it's you who doesn't understand. You'd rather go back to the ways of old, when we summoned Etemmu to fight. Well, there's a reason why that kind of stuff has been outlawed. It's because if it wasn't, bitter old men like you would want to go on some crusade against the human race. All because of what happened in the past."

Treman scoffed. "I cannot believe I'm being lectured about being trapped in the past by you. You who are so convinced you can find Mummy and Daddy. How many years has it been now? Five? Ten? So what if they haven't appeared on the tapestry like the rest of them? Face it, you are never going to see them again, and it's time you moved on."

Trem's face slowly transitioned from a deep rage filled grown to an almost mocking smile as she chuckled. Treman looked so befuddled with her.

"Wh....What's so funny?" He demanded, clearly being laughed at was really getting on his nerves.

Trem tried to stop laughing, but she decided to keep it going for a bit, just to taunt Treman. "I just realised something...!" She said in between laughs.

"What!?" Treman barked, his fists clenching.

"You can rant and rave all you want, but there's not a damn thing you can do to stop me! You lose in every situation, so all your doing is just blowing hot air!" She looked down and continued laughing as she and Sammy locked eyes. "He's such a time waster isn't he?"

Treman got so worked up that he practically shrieked his response. "I will not be made to be a fool of!"

Trem's laughter faded, replaced instead with a malicious smirk. "You need me."

Trem watched as the rage washed over Treman and for the first time in a long time, she caught him looking concerned. He remained silent while Trem took a few steps towards him and held up both of her hands, with rings on all the fingers. She wiggled her fingers for a few seconds.

"You need me to open up the Styx again, to make sure you get returned to the afterlife before you lose every fibre of your being. Because that's what scares you, isn't it, Grandfather?"

The way she said Grandfather was unnerving for the old man. He hated not being in control after all. Trem had successfully knocked him off his high perch. Now he was desperately trying to climb back on it.

"Mark my words child, this girl will bring nothing but trouble."

Trem had a look on her face which screamed unimpressed. Was that the best he could come up with. "Yeah well, consider them marked and ignored. Now prattle off to your room like a good spoiled brat. Before I change my mind." Her sapphire ring began to glow as she held it up for Treman to see.

"If the family is ruined because of your actions, I will hound you to the end of time!" He threatened, well, it was an empty threat but a threat nonetheless. He began to slide back towards the wall. Trem walked towards him to try and hasten his exit.

"You are already hounding me, now be a good boy and shove." Her head tilted towards the direction of the wall.

Treman muttered something offensive under his breath and slid backwards through the wall. A lengthy exhale passed Trem's lips as she rubbed her eyes, walking back over to the tank. "I do not need his incessant poking his nose into my business all the time..."

She gently lowered Sammy back into the cage. After checking to make sure he was alright for food and water, she closed the tank. Sammy had been a little shaken by Treman, he always was, so Trem thought it best he should get some rest. She watched him crawl into his log and rest.

She put her hand against the glass. "I'm envious of you Sammy. You get the best kind of lifestyle. I wish it were that easy for me sometimes. But it was never going to be was it?" She pulled up the chair and sat down, holding her head on her hands. "I got to make the decision...."

She started weighing up her options, and there weren't that many. Realistically, only two logical options presented themselves. Let her go and risk exposure or...Keep her prisoner here, indefinitely too. The second option is pretty much the worst case scenario. Neither Trem, the Etemmu or the Manzazzu as a race were in the business of kidnapping young women and holding them in their manor houses against their wills. That was the kind of anti human sentiment Treman would approve of. The thought that her putrid grandfather would approve of that option, meant it was off the table very quickly.

So that left the option of let her go and hope she wouldn't scream their existence to the heavens. Jenny seemed to get along with her, that was something at least. If worse came to worst then she knew Jenny was loyal to her above all else. Well, that wasn't strictly true, she was closer to Skye. Gabby spoke a lot of sense when she was explaining herself, she clearly knew what was good for her. But what nagged at Trem was all the variables in this plan. What if she did tell someone else and they don't think she's mad? Long shot of course, but still. She couldn't keep Gabby waiting outside, she needed to come up with a solution.

She opened her desk and took out a few items. A roll of parchment, a black feather and an ink pot plus a simple wooden box with a bronze lock. It had an ornate seal on the lid, written in the same dialect as the cylinders. She began to write out the situation down to the receiver and asked for advice on how to proceed.

Trem muttered the sentences she wrote down back to herself as she proof read her letter, making sure that for a brief summary, he was in possession of all the facts. When she was convinced she had written the letter to the best of her ability, she rolled up the parchment as tightly as she could and delved back into the draw, taking out some string and tying it around the letter. She then opened the box and placed the letter into the velvet lined container. She shut the lid and locked the bolt, then waited for her citrine ring to glow a deep orange. She waited for a few seconds before opening the box again. When she looked inside, the letter had disappeared.

"Good." Trem muttered to herself. "Tremadore should get that within the hour then."

Her Etemmu followers were brilliant, they were funny and supportive and essential support for her. But, as much as she loved the four of them, Skye, Jenny, Abhay and Hogarth, they weren't Manzazzu. Sure, they learned a lot from their time with her, and she had come to learn quite a bit of human culture, even if it didn't exceed the 1950s.

But they were all human, once upon a time. In an act of lonely desperation, Trem reached through into the other world and called for Treman. She was frightened and alone without her parents. Her grandfather had been dead for years, he was the only one she knew, being only sixteen when he died. She stupidly expected him to help her, to help find her parents. But the old fool proved to be a curse in disguise. Evidently she wasn't aware just how bad he could be.

Years later, Trem received a letter from one of her Father's friends, a Manzazzu called Tremadore, who he has spoken of many times before. After explaining what had happened, Trem now finally had her Manzazzuan aid. They kept in regular contact via letters. Though she had never met him, he seemed a darn sight more friendly, agreeable and all round better in every way then Treman could ever be. She was glad to have Tremadore, even if it was just in the form of correspondence. Of course he'd not be able to help her right now, she had to make her own call.

Returning the ink bottle and the wooden box back to her desk, Trem got up from her seat and after a little goodbye to Sammy, she started to make her way to the door. She'd put her faith in a stranger's promise.

Chapter Four: "Don't Question It"

"By the end of tonight, I may have ruined Father's expectations..."
"Good."
"Yes. Because I'll have gained something far more important.

Gabby checked the time on her phone, she had only been at Trem's house just over an hour. Fortunately she was able to write that off as "just a walk". It was getting on for around 4pm, and no doubt her parents would have an early dinner for her as part of the celebrations. Of course, with the recent revelations, Gabby had forgotten all about the results. They seemed so small to her, the little problems of a mortal world. That was when her mind started racing again. All those possibilities, life beyond death, the after life... Should a nobody teenager from a nowhere backwater in England really be privy to this information? Gabby knew she wasn't worthy, it was a childish dare that put her in Trem's path years ago anyway, something so inconsequential and pointless.

Would this change her life forever now? Should she let it? And what would she tell her parents? If she was going to go back to the manor the next day, she'd need to tell them something. "Hey guys, I'm just popping off to the non human necromancer who lives in the abandoned house in the village, have dinner ready." She'd promised she wouldn't make an exhibition of herself. Well, as much as she hated lying, it wouldn't be wrong to say she's going to see a new friend. While the two were hardly on friendship terms, at least there was no hostility between them.

After a brief scrabble through the bushes, resulting in another small cut on her face, Gabby returned to the main street that lead up the village. Once there, she made the walk up the path to her house. She reached into her back pocket and took out the folded paper with her results on it. For what good they made now, she could at least talk about them, a distraction from the days events in that old house. She opened the gate which let out it's usual droning squeak. Oil the gate, another thing for her to remember.

She walked up to the wooden door and paused. Standing on the step, she dried her lips with the back side of her hand and left it hovering there while she remained in thought. She got a good grade pretending to be someone else, but she'd never expect to have to put those college drama skills to good use with her family. This wasn't right, but what else could she do? She made a promise, one she had to keep, especially if she was going to keep on Trem's good side. Calling the whole thing with her off would be too much to bear, how could anyone just walk away from this? She did when she was a child, out of fear. She was fast becoming an adult, and adults face their fears... Right?

Her stomach growled at her, sounding like an angry Rottweiler. Contemplating the true existence of existential concepts was hungry work. She'd had her sub at the deli a few hours ago but that was it. She was still a growing lady after all. As soon as she entered the house, she was hit with the unmistakable smell of pizza.

"The nomad returns." Came her Mother's voice from the other room. Gabby walked into the kitchen to find her Mum over a platter on the table with various boxes and bottles of fizzy pop around the place. Gabby took the paper out of her pocket and held it out ot her mum.

She scanned the paper and put it down on the table, pulling Gabby in for a hug. "Well done love."

Gabby returned a smile to her mum but kept rather silent, which wasn't like her. She felt her mum's hands around her head as she gently lifted her head. "What's up?" She asked.

Of course Gabby couldn't tell the truth. Time to put that Drama grade to good use. "Nothing, it's just been a funny day is all."

Gabby's mum let out a small "Awww" as she ruffled her daughters hair. "Bless you." She proceeded to the counter where she took a plate and a glass and handed it over. "Well it's all done now, so you can relax now."

Pulling up a chair, Gabby sat herself down and started loading her plate with pizza slices. In her mind, she was planning ahead for tomorrow. To avoid suspicions from her parents, she'd say she was going to Manisha's for a while, or at any rate, another friend from college. They didn't need to know the specifics. The idea of lying to them really wasn't sitting well with her, but she really couldn't do anything else. Maybe sometime in the future, if Trem would let her stay, maybe they could be slowly drip fed information, but until then, Gabby had to lie.

She looked around the room, she was so lost in her own world that she failed to notice it was only her mum in the room, they were short two family members. "Where's Dad and Gran?" She asked, taking a bite of a pepperoni slice.

"They went to get her prescription. The current lot aren't doing much for her." Her mum replied as she took a seat opposite her daughter.

Outside the house, the bushes that surrounded the house and the ivey that had crawled it's way up the walls were brushed by a cool breeze. A ghostly presence emerged from the ground. It was one of Trem's Etemmu, Abhay Singh, who was under orders to follow Gabby home. He hovered near the wall which separated him from the dining room. He moved his translucent ear to the wall, he could hear what was being discussed rather clearly, one of the advantages of his state, not that there were many mind you. As he stay floating, he overheard the two women's talk of "college" and "what the gang were up to" …. Whatever that meant. Honestly, it didn't make a lot of sense to him. This modern talk vexed the three hundred year old Indian figure of history.

"These modern people could learn a thing or two from the old days...." He thought to himself.

His concentration was shattered when he heard an annoyingly persistent yapping. He turned his head and saw, standing on its hind legs, propped up against the fence, was the neighbours small dog barking at him. Abhay tried to ignore it, but as soon as he turned, the dog's barking grew louder.

Abhay sighed as he rubbed his hand against his beard. "If I was three hundred years... If I was still alive..." He muttered. His head quickly shot to the right, he could hear someone inside approaching his location. He slid into the ground as fast as he could.

Gabby's mum opened the lead lined window and looked around. "Next door's dog's gone off on one. He's usually so well behaved." She shrugged as she closed the window.

Abhay rose out of the ground and straightened his uniform. "Follow her she said..." He moved his head back to its original position as he listened in on the conversations inside.

As Gabby and her mum continued eating, Gabby was trying to think of topics to say to break up the silences. "So, anything exciting happen in my absence?" She asked, before flicking the last bite of a crust into her mouth.

"Hmm, yeah actually." Her Mother replied, in the middle of a mouthful. After swallowing, she took a sip of water to help it go down. "You know that guy on the news, the one who's wanted by the police?"

Gabby leaned forward and put her crossed arms on the table. Honestly, she was just really glad to have something to talk about to distract her from the whole manor house thing. "Yeah, the guy who killed those three people in the coffee shop in Old Town." Mavis had a little smile on her face, clearly happy with the upcoming news, Gabby thought.

"They found him. Guess where?"

Gabby shrugged. "I don't know...."

Mavis leaned back in her seat and pointed. "They found him in the Mudd family's farm, hiding out in one of the barns."

Gabby now looked legitimately invested, in that her eyes were wide. "That's really close to us! What was he doing there?"

"He was on the run. He'd made it down here, then Old Man Mudd found him. Gave him the two barrels in the chest. When the police arrived, they found Mister Murderer Dean Jackson slouched against a hay bail in a pool of his own blood."

Gabby scoffed. "Meaty. Remind me next time I see him at the village show to buy his marrows, I don't want to end up like him." That got Gabby thinking, would the murderer be in some form of afterlife now? If there was a heaven and a hell, hopefully he'll have found himself a nice, flaming hot corner in the latter. She took another slice of pizza from the box.

"I'll call it after this, leave the rest for Dad and Gran." She downed the last dregs of pop in her glass. She let out a deep sigh as she began to fiddle with her fingers. "Mum, can I ask a weird question?"

"Of course you can." Came the response, as she finished her slice.

Gabby took a few seconds to figure out how to phrase this. "Do you know anything about that manor house in the village?"

Abhay's ears pricked up when he heard this. He continued to listen, making sure he heard every little detail.

There was a moments silence, it felt like hours for Gabby though. She'd so wished she didn't say that, the last thing she wanted to do was to blurt it out now. Her mind raced, trying to think of ways to spin this. She really was such a naff liar. She felt relaxed with her Mum, talking about college and news and stuff over pizza, very civilised. She put her hands on her lap, they were so sweaty now. She was rubbing them together in an attempt to fidget without being noticed.

"Well, your Father and I moved into Mortsbury in I think the summer of 1980. We had a walk down there and noticed it, as you do. But I've not seen anyone in it. Looked a little ratty then. Why do you ask?"

Gabby had to be so careful right now, so she tried her best to calm down and try and weave a believable tale. "Well, Manisha told me that one of our friends, well, they're kind of a friend of a friend's really... Their parents have bought the place."

Her Mum nodded slightly. "Huh, funny. I didn't see it on any of the housing sites. I'd have thought they'd want to advertise something like that. Must have done it privately."

"Yeah, that'll be it." Gabby breathed a small, muted sigh of relief. Hopefully she managed to spin that one rather well.

Outside, Abhay let out a much louder sigh of relief. Trem never gave him any other instructions, it's not like he could haunt the living daylights out of Gabby's Mother or anything.

Gabby found her throat was drying out, must be the anxiety she had to endure. This whole endeavour was not going to do her mental health any good. She drank deeply from the glass. Once she was finished, she dried her mouth with her tissue. "I only bring it up because, you know, it's not like I have many people around here to spend time with, barring Manisha and Bobbi. Julia and Boris are all further afield as you know."

Her mum drummed her fingers casually on the wooden table. "Yeah that's true. You've only been practising driving for... What, a week?"

"If that." Came the reply.

"If the new people in that house are friends then I don't mind you popping down there every now and then. It's not like your bound by a curfew or grounded or anything. I'm not that kind of Mother."

Gabby smiled and leaned forward. "Nah, your above that." She teased. The two shared a chuckle for a few seconds.

The laughter was silenced when they heard the sound of a car pulling into the driveway. Abhay immedialty ducked into the ground to avoid being seen. Gabby rose from her seat, followed by her Mother as they crossed over to the window. They watched as Gabby's Father got out of the car, bag of prescription medication in one hand, as he opened the passenger door to gently help his Mother in law out of the vehicle. She'd never been an energetic woman, even when she was younger, well, she was always older to Gabby, she was in her sixties when Gabby was born. Any woman of 87 would be showing the signs of the years, so to speak.

But today, she seemed a little off when she exited the car. Nothing glaringly alarming, a little paler in the face, eyes a little more droopy, little things. All of which pointed to the implication she wasn't altogether well. If the medication she was on wasn't working, that'd be the reason, surely. Gabby took reassurance in one thing though, she'd tell them if something was wrong.

The doors to the house gently opened as the other half of the family entered the house, welcomed by Gabby and her Mum with warming hugs.

Craig Morgan's tie was hung loose around his neck, his suit jacket was thrown over his shoulder. A middle aged man, a few years older than his wife, his blonde hair had receded to the back of his head. He always came across to his co workers as a man you could trust, a trait he took great pride in upholding. As a Father, he continued that example, encouraging openness and was always willing to listen to any problem.

"Are you alright?" Gabby asked her Gran, who was clearly looking a little shaky.

"Oh don't you worry about me, just a little flutter that's all." She reassured, giving Gabby a little pat on the back. "I just need a bit of a rest. Besides, I heard all about the excitement today."

Gabby's face turned pale and her expression turned blank. "Wh... What do you mean?"

Her Dad held up his phone, a message from her Mum informing them of the results. Gabby let out a huge sigh of relief she really wished she could stifle, given the strange looks it got. She scratched the back of her head in an awkward fidget. "Stressful day, you know?" She went to pull out two chairs but before she could, her Nan spoke up.

"Actually dear, I don't have much of an appetite, I think I might just head to bed for now." Gabby had noticed she looked a bit tired, this was true. Hospitals could be an exhausting place, waiting rooms and getting from points A to B and all that.

"Okay, we understand. You just get the rest you need okay?" Mavis responded as they watched Gran being taken to her room by her husband.

Gabby felt the need to grab another piece of pizza, now they had twice as much leftovers as they expected. Plus it gave her something to do.

"This isn't the first time this has happened is it?" Granted, she could have been more serious sounding if she didn't have a mouth full. Manners? Stuff them, this was a serious conversation.

Her mum started collecting the empty boxes and used glasses. "Well, they had to increase the doses of her medication, these things happen. It's not unheard of, doesn't mean anything bad."

Gabby's eyes trailed off into the distance. "Doesn't mean anything good either."

Gabby continued silently chewing on her food and remained stood, lent against the chair while her Mum threw the empty boxes in the bin. After about half a minute, her Dad reappeared. He flung his suit jacket over his chair and took a seat.

"No need to stand on ceremony for my sake." He joked as he gestured for Gabby to sit down. As he began to tuck into his food, he glanced over at Gabby's results. "Are you proud of them?"

Gabby nodded, wiping her hands on a tissue. "Yeah, it's nice it all paid off. I got something decent to show for years of decent work. Not bad for a non academic." She felt the ever forceful pat on the back from her dad shake her slightly.

"Now, don't go under selling yourself. You did much better than I did, leaving high school with half decent letters next to subjects. We're really proud of you."

Gabby's Dad's head pats would usually seem condescending, but it really tapped into her nostalgia, so she allowed it. At this point, anything she could do to install a bit of comfort in herself, a bit of pleasant distraction, it would be for the best.

The next hour was spent in front of the television, catching up on the fictional dramas of well paid actors in small sets getting worked up about pre planned plots. The way Gabby thought of it kind of drained any life from the program. Abhay meanwhile was trying his best to keep awake. He was pretty sure he wouldn't be getting anymore today, especially as the sun had already began setting and the sky was growing darker. Easier to get back to Trem's undetected, from that blasted mut too, who had been ushered into the house.

Just to make sure, Abhay poked his head over the bushes and looked to the Morgan family's next door neighbours. He saw the dog was behind the window, and the two locked eyes. Abhay gave the classic eye to eye "I'm watching you" gesture with his eyes which set the dog barking once again. Fortunately the glazed windows absorbed any of the sound.

After their program had finished, Gabby turned to her parents. She was sunken into her arm chair, the one her late Grandfather liked and her parents were sat next to each other on the large sofa.
"I think I'm going to go upstairs for a bit. I got some things I got to look up."

"Anything questionable?" Came the response from her Dad. Gabby just shot an unimpressed look back at him and smiled.

She got up from her arm chair and as she passed her parents, she gave them both kisses on their cheeks. As she started to climb up the stairs, she heard a faint call from her Father. "Remember, clear browsing history!"

"Hah!" She yelled back playfully as she ascended the wooden steps to her room.

Throwing her chequered shirt off, she let herself drop like a stone onto her bed, letting her bear arms feel the sheets as she rubbed her eyes. Groaning softly, she stared at her ceiling. What a day. It wasn't anywhere near her usual bed time (which would change drastically now there's no college to worry about) and yet she felt shattered. Literally, shattered into a million pieces and reassembled haphazardly with a glue gun.

Straightening out her t shirt sleeves, she got up and headed over to her desk, where her laptop was sitting. As she sat down and logged on, all she could think about was the events of that day. In one day, she got her college results, confronted a childhood fear, confirmed the existence of life after death and met a gothic looking, kind of hot necromancer. It's funny how strange a day can get. She went to the search engine and searched the most well known spirit of the two, or Etemmu in this case, whatever the difference was.

"Jenny Abernathy, born 1931, died 1962, famous American film actress and singer..." She's only 31 years old... Or was anyway. Gabby kind of didn't want to scroll down to the category marked simply "Death". She spoke to this person, she actually liked her. Staring at the picture, it really didn't sink in. The black and white publicity photo that retro film buffs adored had come to life and met her, twice in fact. Morbid curiosity got her into this in the first place, why stop now?

"On January 12th 1962, Jenny Abernathy was hit by a car which had lost control on the frozen road of New York City. She was killed instantly and pronounced dead at the scene." Gabby put her hand to her mouth, she felt herself brought to tears. She knew Jenny had died, well, that was obvious, she was a ghost. But like this? She remembered that adorable, timid little face, the same one she'd seen on her Nan's films and it just made her start to cry. She wiped her eyes on her arm and continued reading.

"The driver was also killed instantly. The lack of witnesses spurred on various conspiracy theories surrounding her death, the most prevalent being that it was a Mafia..." Gabby closed the webpage, she couldn't read anymore. Reading about how someone you've only seen in movies died was a little sombre, but when you've met them, it makes it so much worse. It makes it personal, it means you have more of an understanding of what that person was like, rather then guess from interviews or their "personal life" section. Gabby tried to dry her eyes again, as much as she could anyway. The circumstances around Jenny's death really took her off guard.

She opened the browser and had to think about what to type in. She didn't know Skye's surname... Well, there couldn't be that many female pirates called Skye. So that's what she typed. *"Female Pirate Skye"*. Sure enough, making sure not to click on the rather appealing looking female pirate anime pictures that appeared, there was something that looked hopeful. A smaller page about a Lady Skye Bloodworth, that must be her.

"Lady Skye Bloodwoth (1552- unknown) was a noblewoman who was famous for running a pirating operation in Cornwall during the reign of Queen Elizabeth." Gabby's eyes widened, Skye must have been something else, to run a pirating operation while being a member of the nobility right under the Queen's nose. She knew old Queeny Liz hated pirates and loved knocking their sea savvy blocks off if given half a chance. So that must be how Skye died then, the law must have caught up with her.

"Bloodworth was the only person accused of piracy to be given a pardon by the Queen..." Okay, what? Honestly that took Gabby by surprise. As she studied the information, she found out that her estate housed an

old castle which they used to house the treasures and wealth they stole from ships that passed their part of Cornwall. There was nothing about how Skye died though, only that, obviously, she did die and there was a lot of squabbling about inheritance with her family. No changes there then.

A sudden sound made Gabby almost jump out of her skin. She spun around on her seat and saw the window had been blown open. Time had really gotten away from her, it was already night and she had only the light from her laptop illuminating the room. She walked over to the light switch, slowly as she could, and turned it on. With the room much easier to see, she approached the window. She looked down, checking the ground below her window. All clear, and yet Gabby wasn't convinced. It should have been a warm evening, so why was she shivering?

She closed the windows, making sure to lock them tight. Turning on the spot, she looked up and let out a loud yelp, which sounded like someone taking helium was punched in the stomach, not a dignified sound. In Front of her was Abhay, floating a foot above the ground.

"Are you one of Trem's?" Gabby asked through a wheeze.

"Yes, I am." Came the reply.

Gabby looked over to her door, remembering her parents were no doubt able to hear her yelp from downstairs. She spoke in a harsh, stifled whisper. "What are you doing here? Are you stalking me or something!?"

Abhay held out his hands and gestured for Gabby to calm down. "That's not what I'm doing. Trem asked me to follow you to make sure you wouldn't let slip what you saw."

She scoffed as she crossed her arms. "So she didn't even take my word for it? That's nice isn't it?"

"No, that's not it." Came the response. "She knows you were telling the truth, she'll trust you a lot more now."

Gabby observed the new ghost, or Etemmu, a phrase she'd have to get used to saying more and more now. His skin tone and accent were very clearly Indian, and his mouth was hidden behind a thick but well groomed beard. He wore a green military uniform with a sash over his chest. Several medals were pinned to said sash and around his waist was a belt with a sword hanging from it. He looked to be of a different period from the others. Victorian era maybe?

"Who are you anyway?" Gabby asked.

"Abhay Singh, at your service" The Etemmu responded with a bow.

Gabby nodded slightly, returning the bow. "Gabby Morgan." Straightening her back, she gave him one last look over. More to research later no doubt. "So, how many of you are in that house anyway?"

Abhay wasn't sure how much information he was allowed to give out, but it was common decency to answer her question at any rate. "There are four of us. Myself, Hogarth, Jenny and Skye. I believe you've met the fine ladies?"

"...We're acquainted yeah, you could say that." Kind of an understatement really, one was really friendly to her and the other one wanted to smash her face in. "Hogarth? I've not met him yet."

A devious little smile came across Abhay's face. "Thomas Hogarth, you'll see him soon, no doubt."

Before Gabby could continue, she heard footsteps approaching her room. Her stomach felt like it had just had a block of bricks thrown into it, and panic hit her. She reverted back to a strained whisper.

"Oh bugger...." She turned to Abhay. "Hide!"

Abhay stared blankly for a second. Gabby's hands flailed slightly as she gestured to the floor and walls. "Do the phaisy thing, go through the walls or something!"

"Oh!" Abhay obliged by descending into the floor and into the room below. He remained hovering about a foot off the ground as was the norm for Etemmu like himself. Thinking he was in the clear, he was about to sigh, when he heard someone else make a noise. He slowly turned around to see Gabby's Dad, his back facing away from Abhay, taking his clothes off. He'd descended into the bathroom, right as Craig was about to go into the shower.

"Wrong room, wrong room!" Abhay yellped internally as he shot out of the room at great speed, ending up in the garden. Craig shivered as he put the shower on, a few degrees warmer than he usually would.

Mavis knocked on the door as Gabby scrambled to her seat and loaded up a random page from her web browser. "Can I come in?" Came the muffled voice from behind the door.

"I'm decent!" Gabby called back, pretending to look through cosplay accessories on her usual shopping sites. Her mum entered with a steaming hot cup of coffee in one hand, which she put on her desk.

"Is everything okay? I heard you shouting." Her mum asked.

Gabby took the mug and started drinking from it. "Thanks mum." She took a few sips before responding. "Yeah I'm okay, I just stubbed my toe on the desk is all, you know what I'm like."

The two chuckled, Mavis ruffling Gabby's hair.

"Clumsy. I just wanted to check up on you really. You seemed a little befuzzled over dinner."

Gabby's eyes began to wonder, they ended up staring out the window, into the night sky. "Yeah, it's been a funny old day really. A lot's happened, and I guess I'm still processing it."

Her mum gave her a little kiss on the forehead. "Well, we've very proud of you. You should be proud of yourself too."

Gabby held her Mother's hand for a moment. "Thanks mum, I love you."

With a warm smile, her Mum walked out of the room and closed the door behind her. Gabby got up out of her seat and walked over to the window, unlocking it and peering out. She looked below her window but couldn't see any sign of the Etemmu. Abhay wouldn't have left already would he? She still had some things she needed to ask.

"Abhay?" She called in a hushed tone. After a few seconds, she repeated herself, a little louder.

"Yes?" He appeared right in front of Gabby.

The poor girl nearly jumped out of her skin. She swatted her hand at him.

"Stop doing that!" Her hand passed straight through Abhay's torso which caused it to ripple, as if it were made of water. After a few seconds, it settled and reverted back to its original shape.

Gabby clutched her hand, it was absolutely freezing. Ice crystals had formed on her skin and her fingers were stiff and really hard to move. She dashed over to her cup of coffee and warmed her hand against it. "Ahhh....." That felt much better, actual feeling was coming back to her hand.

She looked back at Abhay, looking a little guilty. "Sorry about that, it was kind of a reflex."

Abhay straightened out his sash and patted his torso.
"Not to worry, no harm done. Pros and cons of being an Etemmu, unkillable but we have to keep up a... Well, a frosty disposition and a pretty shallow form."

Gabby sank back into her seat and kept her drink close to her. "Jenny said Trem asked you all to come, something about being lonely?"

The ghostly figure floated closer to Gabby and the ground. "I know I shouldn't tell you this, so if you ask, you didn't hear this from me, okay?"

Gabby nodded as she listened intently to Abhay's explanation.
"Truth is, when I was in the afterlife, I felt something pulling me back. It was sort of like a feeling, and well... It's hard to explain."
He rested his bearded chin on his thumb. "Have you ever heard someone in distress and the only thing you want to do is help them?"

Gabby leaned forward, her cup resting on her lap. "Yeah... Yeah, I know what you mean."

"Etemmu like me can't leave the afterlife of our own choosing, we have to be called, summoned if you will. Only Manzazzu like Trem can do that. Getting out of the afterlife itself isn't really that hard. You end up in the Styx, limbo, with me so far?" Gabby confirmed, and Abhay continued.

"When your in the Styx, you'd get a chance to cross over, back into the world of the living. Manzazzu can open a doorway from the living world to the Styx."

So there is such a thing as an afterlife, and Trem certainly wasn't human. No human could ever possess these kind of powers, this is life and death stuff. Gabby's suspicions were true after all.

"So you can cross over into the living again, just like that?" She asked, taking another sip.

"If we choose to. Manzazzu can't make us if we don't want to cross over."

Gabby and Abhay locked eyes for a moment, and when Gabby asked the next question, his eyes were very telling, they spoke volumes about the kind of person he was, or still is. "What made you want to come back?"

There was a sadness in the Etemmu's eyes, he was clearly remembering the experience well, and it was having an effect on him. "Because, I know you don't know me, Gabby Morgan, but I can't abide people suffering. If I can help it, I want to be there for anyone who needs it. When I crossed over, I saw a lonely and desperate girl who was at the end of her rope. Her parents were gone and she didn't know what to do. She was clinging onto anyone she could find. She pleaded with me to stay, I couldn't refuse her. At the same time, I couldn't exactly help her. But I gave her the thing she needed."

Gabby found her voice breaking as a few tear drops fell into her coffee. "Which was?"

Abhay's shoulders and eyebrows rose up and he smiled warmly. "Company. Sometimes the thing we need most in our lives are each other. Someone to confide in, to share our woes and help us in our times of need. I'm sure you know the feeling."

Gabby couldn't form any words. She felt so sorry for Trem, she'd lost her parents, she knew that, but seeking the comfort in Jenny, Skye and Abhay... It made Gabby want to go back even more, just to give her a hug. No doubt she wasn't looking for sympathy, but she was at least going to get the offer of support.

"Abhay, I'm going back to the house tomorrow, first thing. Thanks for telling me this, it was very ...Enlightening. No, it wasn't, it was very good of you to tell me this."

Abhay rose to his usual height, suspended a foot in the air. "Your welcome. Thank you, Gabby Morgan, for being an excellent listener." The two exchanged warm smiles before Abhay floated backwards, through the wall and disappeared into the night.

As soon as Abhay left, Gabby walked over to her wardrobe. She opened the door and inspected herself in the mirror. She ran her hands through her thick, curly hair and flicked it all onto the right side of her head in an attempt to see what it would look like in Trem's style. It looked okay in her opinion, nothing great.

She opened the other door and looked into her wardrobe. She scanned through some of the items till she found an old, black trench coat she'd got from a charity shop for a college cosplay event. She also found a pair of PVC leggings which she'd bought once on a discount and never worn, some black boots with thick soles, which she usually only wore during the winter and a grey t shirt. She threw off her white shirt and jeans and slipped on the outfit.

Honestly, it didn't look half bad. Rather gothic, and it did wonders in flushing out her pale skin, but it was a decent fit. If imitation was a finer form of flattery, then this should be quite a flattering outfit for her venture back to Trem's house tomorrow. She put the jacket, shirt and leggings on a hanger and left it hanging from her wardrobe and put the boots in front of them.

That night, Gabby slept, putting the days events out of her mind for the sake of getting rested. The next day would be another long one, but she felt a lot more confident, armed with the knowledge Abhay told her.

Chapter Five: "Some Kind Of Tapestry Of Death"

"Let the families squabble amongst themselves. By the time they notice, we'll be long gone."
"You make it sound so romantic."
"How else am I going to keep you for myself?"

The events of the previous day had drained Gabby, so as soon as she put her head on her pillow, she was dead to the world. It was going on for 10am when she woke up, which made a change from her usual 7am wake up time. Her hair messy and her eyes half open, she sat up and yawned. For a few minutes, she sat bolt upright in her bed, her creased and ruffled sheets covering her torso as she ran through the events of the previous day in her mind. Maybe it was all some really freaky dream. But that would be such a cop out, of course it happened. She met three ghosts, or whatever the funny name they were called was, a rather attractive necromancer type that wasn't even human, and she got her college results.

Now she was to go back to the manor house and meet up with Trem again. Hopefully she could get more answers this time. Though, she was in no position to demand answers, if someone walked into her home demanding to know every little detail about the Morgans, Gabby wouldn't exactly be open to telling them anything. The fact Trem was being so open and honest was a saving grace in itself, but she couldn't rely solely on it.

In a trance like zombie state, Gabby dragged herself out of bed, squinting as the daylight peeped out of her closed blinds. She grabbed her towel and headed downstairs for a much needed shower. She spent so much of yesterday caked in fear sweat, she needed to cleanse herself and wash the layers of stink off her body. She reached the bottom of the stairs where her parents were sat on the sofa, cups of tea in hand, with a plate of toast on the table in front of them. Flicking a rather large bit of eye crust away, Gabby dragged herself towards them.

"Morning." Is what she tried to say, but it sounded more like a Mandrel grunting. She leant on the sofa, behind her parents.

Gabby's Father turned his head and looked up at his daughters hair, which seemed to be modeled after the "finger in electrical socket" look, all stood up and fuzzy. "Morning sleeping beauty." He chuckled, taking a sip of tea.

Her Mum was next to comment, looking up and clearly struggling not to laugh, biting her lip. "Morning love..." She too had to take a drink to hide her smile.

"Yeah okay I know I'm gross, that's why I'm going to shower." She reached down to grab some toast, this time with just jam, not that that was a problem, jam was good. As she did, her parents held their noses as her armpit got closer to them. Gabby took a big bite out of the slice. "You remember that friend I was telling you about yesterday Mum? The one who's families in the big house just down the road?"

"Oh yeah?" Came the reply.

Gabby swallowed before continuing, wiping the smudges of jam on her face away with the back of her hand. "They've got a little gathering today. I hope you don't mind if I pop down for a bit? It's a kind of breaking in the home party."

Craig clicked his fingers, trying to remember something. "Oh yeah, what do the Americans call it? Housewarming, something like that?"

"Hmm, that's the one." Gabby's mum replied. "It's summer so I think the house is pretty warm as it is. Mind you, must cost a fortune to heat that place."

Gabby was clearly still half asleep so she didn't really clock the attempt at humor her mum was trying. Instead, she replied with a simple "Sure".

Gabby was about to head for the shower, but she suddenly remembered something from yesterday, that had gotten lost under all the excitement. "How's Nan?" She asked, slowly turning back round to her parents.

"Oh, she's okay. She was just a little tired today is all. She's going to get her strength back up, but she's probably going to stay in bed for a while today." Mavis replied, keeping her mug close to her chest.

"Nothing wrong is there?" Gabby asked, clearly any kind of health issue would be something to be a little concerned about when you reach a certain age, but fearing the worst constantly was a very unhealthy mentality.

"No, not at all. She'd let us know if there was something wrong." That was a reassuring reminder from her mum. Gabby was grateful for it, one less thing to worry about.

Feeling the mood needed a little lifting, she sprinted back to the sofa and held her arms up, exposing her armpits. "Smell my cheese!" She laughed, quoting a random thing she saw on the internet as her parents retched at the smell.

"Go shower now!" Her Mum ordered, holding her nose. Gabby left laughing, her smile hiding the dozen emotions going on under the surface.

In the shower, as the piping hot water drenched her hair, her mind was scheming, trying to decide where to start with her inquiries to Trem and more importantly, how far she wanted to probe for the information. To go too far would be invading privacy after all. Once she had finished and dried herself off, she returned to her room to try on her new outfit. The boots weren't worn that much, so needed breaking in more, the trench coat was a little too long on the sleeves, so she needed to fold them up.

Aside from that, everything else was a pretty good fit. She checked herself in the mirror, sure it was a lot of black for the summer, but she'd spend most of the day in the cool house anyway. Of course she didn't know how to explain how she went from a cheque shirt and jeans to gothic zombie hunter chique. She glanced at the poster of Lauren Cross, one of her favourite character from her more modern movie tastes, she must have looked like such a fangirl, she remembered who this outfit was based on. Well, if anyone asks, it's fancy dress.

She made her way down the wooden steps that lead to the dining room, her heavy lace up boots making a loud clompy noise as she approached. In the dining room, her dad was organising his work bag. Being the manager of the local branch of a supermarket meant that he was usually busy most of the day while her mum was a "stay at home" kind of Mother, a term she hated as she liked to call herself a "home and welfare manager". Her dad was the first one to notice the outfit.

"Well Gabby, this is a new look." His wide eyed expression meant that, if he hated it, he didn't outright say it. That was a good start.

Gabby did a little twirl, the bottom of the trench coat flapping around her ankles. "What do you think? We're all doing a gothic theme for the thing at the manor. I thought I'd go for this look which I call Going To Regret Wearing All This Black In The Height Of Summer, or Regret by Gabby Morgan for short."

That got a snort of approval from her parents, which was all she needed. She took her phone from her coat pocket and wiggled it in her fingers. "I'll call you guys when I'm heading back."

"Okay love." Came the responses. Gabby gave both her parents a kiss and headed over to the door. Before she left though, she took a few steps backwards and turned to her parents.

"Oh yeah and when Nan wakes up, let her know I gave her my best." Once her parents reassured her, Gabby headed out of the door.

Like the previous day, it was sunny and warm, a few clouds were peppered about the sky, and there was a small breeze which made Gabby's trenchcoat dance slightly in the wind. She took in a big gulp of fresh air, straightened her shoulders and looked ahead, ready to return to the manor house.

It took no time at all to scramble down the overgrown path, the trenchcoat offering a bit more protection against the brambles and thorns, even if her hands got a little cut during the process. Before long though, she was there, as promised. Gabby wondered why Trem was so okay with her coming back? She'd essentially broken in, invaded her privacy then asked for seconds. Trem must have been a very understanding woman... Manzazzu. After this, she wouldn't want to pry any further, if Trem wanted her gone, she'd stay gone.

She gently pushed open the door and took her first step inside. As soon as she entered, she could hear Jenny and Skye's voices in the distance. As much as she tried to step lightly, her clompy boots made it impossible to do so, and as soon as she started walking, she grabbed the attention of the two Etemmu. They both remained quiet, and Gabby made it as far as a few feet away from the duo when she stopped.

The expressions on the two Etemmu were sombre, both looking down at the floor. This proved unsettling for Gabby, something had clearly happened in her absence. "Guys, what happened?" Gabby's question came out so quiet it might as well be a whisper. The two didn't answer, instead, they looked to the long tapestry that hung on the wall.

At the far end, the eastern looking figure was still stood atop a rock, pointing his sword valiantly to the future, to the line of various robe clad Manzazzu, whose skin tones became paler as the generations went on. Gabby glanced at Skye and Jenny, their gazes were focused on the right side of the tapestry. Gabby followed their gaze till it ended up on a figure she was convinced she didn't see before.

It was of a female Manzazzu, layed out on one of the rocks, like how the old movie stars, including Jenny coincidently, would lie atop a piano while it was being played. The Manzazzu woman looked middle aged, with long, flowing white hair. Her eyes were the same as Trem's Mother, the same dark shade. She looked so content and happy. She could be five thousand for all Gabby knew.

"Who is she?" Gabby asked. The atmosphere in the room was like if someone had died, so hushed voices seemed to be appropriate.

Skye kept her eyes on the tapestry, one arm reaching over and putting itself on Jenny's shoulder. "Trem's aunt. She passed away this morning."

Gabby went pale, someone had died. She felt awful about that, both the comment and the fact that Trem had lost a member of her family. She remembered when she lost her grandfather, she had known it was coming for a while. She knew it was inevitable and she and the family had prepared for it, so it would lessen the blow. It still hurt, but Gabby had worried for a while that there was something wrong with her.

She could cry at fictional characters, heck, the scene where Avin Shrain sacrifices himself in The Never Ending Dream still gets her to this day, but she only managed a few tears at the funeral. She'd spoken to her parents about it, and it's when she learned that people have their own defences, their own coping mechanisms. But she didn't know Trem. She'd like to, of course, but all she knew of Trem is the differences between herself and the young Manzazzu.

Gabby was trying hard to think of something to say, but as usual it seems, the words just refuse to come to her. "I'm... So sorry to hear that..." That'll do, she figured. Saying nothing would only worsen things.

"She died giving birth to a son." Skye continued. Her gaze was finally torn away from the image of Trem's aunt and to Jenny, who had taken hold of her hand and was quietly weeping.

In Between sniffs, Jenny spoke. "Her life traded in for a new one..."

Gabby held her arm, a strange little thing she does when she feels out of place. A thought entered her mind, which evolved into a question, but she was unsure if she should ask it. It took a few seconds of pondering before she decided to. "How did you guys find out?" She glanced at the tapestry. "How did she get on that?"

Jenny used the chance to explain it to dry her eyes and collect herself. "Well, we dunno how it works exactly, but when Trem's family die, they show up on the tapestry."

Skye continued from Jenny's train of thought. "That's how Trem knows her parents aren't dead. If they were, they'd have shown up."

Oh so it's some kind of Tapestry Of Death... That's lovely. Gabby felt she needed to ask the next question, just to see how she was. "Where's Trem now?"

Skye floated towards Gabby, the air around her turning chilly and bitey. She looked down at Gabby, her expression was blank. "Let me tell you something, Gabby Morgan. If it were up to me, you'd have been booted out of here the moment you stepped in the door."

All Gabby asked was where Trem was. Truth be told, Skye Bloodworth was a scary kind of woman, god save any poor souls who thought they could cross her back in the day.

Skye's cold expression melted into a considerably warmer one as she looked back to Jenny. "But Jenny trusts you. We spoke about you at length last night, with Abhay as well. You could have told anyone about us, expose us right there and then. But you didn't. You kept true to your word. I can respect that."

Wow, something nice from Skye. Rare meteorological events happen more often than that! Snarky internalized comments aside though, the sentiment was very reassuring to Gabby. "Thank you."

Skye moved closer to Gabby, who felt like she'd stuck it in a freezer due to the cold aura surrounding Skye's Etemmu state.

"But, if I find that you did betray us, I'll rain down upon you so hard that the combined forces of Her Majesty's fleets would never be able to find your remains. Got it?"

Gabby's mouth immediately dried up, so all she could manage was a frantic head nod and a tiny, minescuel and high pitched... "Yep."

"That's what I thought." Skye started to back away from Gabby, and back into the arms of Jenny, who put her head on Skye's shoulder.

"Please, don't scare her anymore Skye. I'm sure you've intimidated her enough..." Jenny asked as she felt the pirate's hand gently place itself on her head. "Trem's in her room. It's the first door you see."

Gabby silently thanked Jenny as she began to make her way up the stairs, to the next level of the house. Skye gave Jenny a small kiss on the forehead and gestured for her to stay put as she silently followed, keeping herself at a safe distance.

Skye rounded the corner and observed Gabby, who knocked on the door. After a brief period of silence, Gabby slowly opened the door. "Trem? I'm coming in, okay?"

She watched Gabby enter the room and close the door behind her. The piratical Etemmu moved to the wall and put her ear to it. Before she could overhear anything though, a voice startled her.

"So, that's the grimy little human who's been causing all the troubles." Treman had appeared, phasing through one of the closed doors on the landing. "Not much to look at, is she?"

Skye's hands clenched into fists, the anger in her eyes hidden behind her tricorn. This sad old man installed such anger and frustration into Skye, it was fortunate he seldom showed his face, otherwise Skye would have attempted to smash it. "What concern is it of yours, old man?" She kept her gaze away from Treman, the more she she looked at him, the more she wanted to do something rash.

"The integrity and security of this house and it's name, that's what concerns me." Came the stern and blunt reply from the dead Manzazzu's rhaspy mouth.

Skye glanced at him from the corner of her eyes, her mouth curled into a devious little grin. "Well, it's not your family anymore is it? As far as Trem's concerned, she's inherited everything from you, and will continue to do so when your sent back to the afterlife where you belong, instead of giving us your useless opinions."

Treman flew towards Skye and appeared right in front of her, his craggy old face, rough with wrinkles was now only a breath away from her own. Skye got a good look at his slowly glazing over, pale eyes. "Listen here, you impudent, arrogant woman! I will not be talked down to by the likes of you..."

Before he could continue, Skye grabbed him by the neck and held him above her head, squeezing as tight as she could. "And I won't stand for any of your talk. I promised to protect her..."

Treman interrupted, forcing out his taunt while being choked by the fellow ghostly figure. "Yes you did... Quite a fall from grace for Skye Bloodworth... I'll wager they wouldn't have called you a Pirate Queen after they found out how you died...!" His grin widened, showing off his rotten teeth. "Literally quite the fall from grace, wasn't it?"

Skye's eyes widened, she let her grip slack as Treman dropped from her hand. Her face was a mixture of shock, anger and concern. "How did you know that?!" She demanded.

Treman straightened out his Manzazzu robes. "I have my ways."

The pirate Etemmu's voice became a whisper. "Look, I don't care how you found out... If you dare try anything that would hurt Trem, or Gabby..."

"Oh, concerned for the human now are you?"

Skye clenched her fists again and growled, before taking in a deep breath. "I'm concerned for Trem. If she trusts Gabby Morgan, then I will too. So you'd better not try anything, or I won't be so lenient on you okay?"

Treman smirked, a disgusting smugness that repulsed Skye. "Yes ma'am."

While Treman and Skye had their confrontation, Gabby entered the room. The first thing she noticed was Trem, who had her back to Gabby, slouched over her desk, working on something. Her

Manzazzu robes were hung up on her bed post and she wore a sleeveless, black top that reached up to her neck. Gabby could see she was lost in her work, there was a faint sound of scratching and the room smelt slightly of stone.

Gabby looked around the room, glancing at the walls, the large bed and the table topped with books and rolls of parchment. What also caught her attention was the large glass tank, with a floor of sand and some other things inside that were hard to make out from her distance.

Gabby stopped her advancing when she was a few feet away from the busy Manzazzu. She peered over Trem's shoulder to see that she was in the process of carving something into another of those strange cylinders. This time, it was an image of a woman, very possibly her late aunt. Around the top was the same odd writing she'd seen before, the Arabic/Chinese looking hybrid. Unsure of if her arrival had gone unnoticed, Gabby spoke as quietly as she could.

"It looks beautiful." Gabby complimented, watching as Trem used a small, sharp utensil to engrave the words into the soft stone.

Trem kept her eyes on her work, gently and slowly making sure every detail was precise. "Thank you." She replied as she finished the last of the strange letters. Once she was finished, she placed the cylinder on its base and stared at it.

Gabby felt a little awkward, but she felt she wanted to ask anyway, what's the worst that could happen. "It's your aunt isn't it?" Gabby waited for a response, when one didn't appear after a few seconds, she continued. "Jenny and Skye told me. That big tapestry thing downstairs is like your family tree, right?"

Trem nodded. She took the cylinder and reached over to the box on her desk, opened the lid and placed the Hematite tube inside. Once the box was locked, she turned to Gabby and gestured to her bed.

She sat down on the corner and let her hands rest on her legs.

Trem rubbed her head and sighed. "Abhay told me about last night. Thank you for being true to your word." She crossed one leg over the other, the light from the tank shining off her boots. "Sure, there's every chance you could tell someone else, or at a later time. But I think you would have done that as soon as you could."

Trem leant on her hand as she glanced at the tank. "Thank you for coming back, you didn't have to."

Gabby itched the back of her head, fiddling once again.
"Your welcome. Well, now I found out what happened, I guess I couldn't not leave you hanging. Especially after what happened." She put her hands together and looked up at Trem, glad she wasn't able to catch her gaze. "If it's any consolation, I know how it feels to lose someone."

Trem's eyes slowly turned to Trem, her eyebrows rose and her hand left her chin. Gabby noticed this and continued.
"My Grandfather, Maurice. A couple of years ago, he got pneumonia and never woke up." Gabby saw that Trem was becoming engrossed in the conversation.
"We saw it coming really, he got a cold and it wasn't getting any better after two weeks."

Gabby rubbed her eyes, taking in a deep lung full of air before she continued. "He knew too. That's why he told us not to get too worked up about it. We didn't get why, it's a death, why wouldn't you? But he said..." A dry smile came across Gabby's face. "He said he wanted us to live for him. He wanted us to feel sad and then move on. We'd never forget him, he was class. Classy Grandpa.... So yeah, we attended the funeral and had a good cry. I miss him, every day. But the more I feel sad about it, the more I feel like I'm dishonouring him in some way. Instead, I want to focus on the good times. It made it a lot easier, and made me feel like I wasn't some cold hearted, emotionally dead husk."

Gabby glanced down, noticing droplets of water on her leggings, rolling off the PVC material. Her first instinct was to see if Trem's roof was leaking, but instead, she checked her face. She felt the warm sensation of tears on her cheeks. She quickly rubbed them off and dried her eyes on her coat sleeves. "Sorry about that, I was off in my own world a bit."

Trem leant forward, placing her hand on Gabby's shoulder. "Don't apologise, you have nothing to be sorry for. In fact, I think you've gained more of my respect, Gabby Morgan."

This ellicated a confused expression from Gabby, with a hint of blush in her cheeks. "How so?" She asked, drying up the remainder of her tears.

Trem smiled back at Gabby. She couldn't help but see sadness still in Trem's eyes. She was clearly moved by what Gabby had said. "You have a mature way of going about this. We Manzazzu are fed that kind of mentality at an early age, it's the only way we don't get attached to the Etemmu we summon. Especially when we summon them to gather knowledge, you end up forming quite a bond with them, even become friends sometimes."

She returned to her desk, her bare arm rested against the top as she put her head on her fist, looking away for a moment. "But they all leave in the end."

Great, Gabby had just dried her eyes, now Trem was making her look like such a sap. But what did she mean by that? She'd probed enough for one day, questions could wait quite frankly. "Is there anything I can do for you?" She asked. It's not like she could really help much, she was just a human after all.

Trem turned to the glass tank. "The strange thing is, I didn't even know her that much. She married into another family so I think I only ever saw her once." Trem remained silent for a moment, long enough for her pet to appear. "Actually Gabby, could you go into the garden and get some greens for Sammy?"

Gabby craned her neck, getting a better look at the tank. Inside, she could see a bearded dragon had crawled out of it's shadowy hideaway, the bright light revealing it's scales in front of the sandy backdrop. "Sammy? That's the name of your pet?"

Trem nodded. "My bearded dragon. His proper name is Samiel, but I call him Sammy for short."

A slight wheeze left Gabb's throat. "That's so adorable." She whispered. She stood up and straightened her shirt. "I'll go get that for him now."

Trem looked Gabby up and down, finally taking note of the outfit. She had been so distracted, she didn't even notice it. "Nice outfit."

Gabby gave a small twirl on the spot. "Thanks! Well, I liked your style so much, I thought I'd see if I could emulate it a bit. Plus I lived and died in cheque and jeans so this sort of goth look is a nice change. Maybe the short hair look might come about one day, but I wanted to take it one step at a time." She put her hands together and pointed at the door. "Food, I'll go and get that now." With that, Gabby left the bedroom.

Once Gabby was gone, Trem turned in her seat and reached over to the box. She flicked the lock open and peered inside. The Hematite cylinder was still inside, but next to it was a rolled up piece of parchment. Trem took it out and unrolled the letter, Tremadore had responded.

Trem,

It is good to hear from you again, it has been a while. I am well, thank you for asking.

In regards to the human who you have encountered, you know the rules the Royal Family have set out about interacting with them. The good thing is that we are are far from their influence. I suppose I should have expected it from you, given how much you don't like the Manzazzuan bigwigs. Don't think for a minute though that I think any less of you. I still have a great deal of respect for you and what you've done.

If you want my advice, which is probably why you wrote to me in the first place, though it means going against our Queen, I say go for it. You have nothing to lose, and if you think she could be of any help in your cause, then do it. Here's hoping she is everything we hope she is.

You must pay us a visit soon, we can catch up over a cup of something warm.

Regards
Tremadore

"I hope she is too." Trem muttered. When she summoned her Etemmu, she was fortunate to find four people who were caring and loyal in their lives. Skye had a great comradery with her crew, Abhay was practically a prince of the people, Hogarth loved to be with people and Jenny had such a love of life that everyone couldn't help but love her. Yet these four clinged to Trem, because they all had one thing in common, they couldn't stand to see a helpless one in distress.

Of course, Trem knew that these things were a weakness in the real world. That's why they all died, they were too good. No one survives in the world by being fair and just, these were truths Trem came to realise in the years of isolation. An ugly thought hit

Trem, if Gabby was going to end up joining her, she could get put in the line of fire. Could she really ask that of her?

Gabby descended the steps and returned to the landing. Skye and Jenny approached her, both with eager expressions. "How is she?" Jenny asked.

Gabby sighed, her shoulders relaxing and her nerves eased. "She's fine. She's taking it well, all things considered. She just needs time, it's all that can make these kind of things better." She found it hard to actually look at the two in the eyes. For one, they were slightly see through anyway, but the fact they were so full of life was both unnerving and tragic in a way. "Do you guys know where the garden is?" She pointed with her thumb to the stairs. "Trem wants some greens for little Sammy."

Jenny floated towards Gabby, but not before resting her hand on Skye's arm and giving a reassuring nod. "I'll show you sugar." She smiled at Gabby, and it was that smile, the one she had seen on the old black and white movies for years.

"Thanks." Gabby responded, following the Etemmu's lead. They left the living room and entered a long corridor, a window was bringing in some light at the end of it, though moss and ivey had grown over it. Gabby looked around, several suits of armor decorated the walkways, with swords and shields above them. There was something really cool about the house, Gabby couldn't lie. Some of her favourite movies involved creepy houses, like The Satanic Butlers (1981). But the house, that should have been cold and stinking of dust and rot, was warm and had that oh so wonderful smell of old books.

They turned a corner and were greeted with a wooden door. Gabby pushed it open with little force and was hit with the smell of assorted plant life. Jenny followed close behind as Gabby entered the garden. The tall walls that surrounded the plot of land, too high to climb over, climbing ivy crawling all over. Some weeds had grown to almost waist height and once again, for the second time that day, Gabby felt like she was trail blazing. She'd give anything to have a machete. In the middle of the patch of land where the food was growing, a wire sculpture of a woman was atop a plinth.

The figure had long, wavy hair made if individual strands and was devoid of any facial features, instead, being a simple circle. At the end of each hand, exploding stars of wire emerged. Each end of the explosion had little stars twisted into shape.

"It's pretty isn't it?" Jenny observed as she floated behind Gabby. Her eyes were fixed on the sculpture. "Before my time. Before any of ours. It may have been one of Trem's family who made it."

Gabby took a minute to sink it in. "How long did it take for you to get used to all this?" She asked, finally breaking free of the locked gaze she found herself in.

Jenny started laughing to herself. "Honey, I don't think I'll ever get used to it."

Gabby unearthed a lettuce plant and pulled it out of the ground. Feeling the weight of it in her hands, and rather liking the sensation of the mud on her fingers, she turned to Jenny.
"Right, all done here..."

Before she could turn to leave, something startled her. The distant and rather loud grunt of a man, followed by a figure hurtling towards her at such a great speed, she just had time to put her hands to block her face. "Take the lettuce, I want...."

Before she could finish, the figure passed through her. Gabby gasped for breath, it was an Etemmu alright, it felt like someone had emptied a bucket of freezing, ice cold water onto her head.

She shivered and felt tiny ice crystals fall off her body. Thankfully the sun was high enough to start warming her up almost immediately. She turned to see what had hit her.

"Hogarth!" Jenny called out. "Are you okay?!"

A rather stoute man, with a thick head of brown hair was laid out on the ground. He groaned as he tried to get his bearings. A large brimmed hat sat atop his head, with a feather coming out of it. His white, ruffled shirt was kept under a brown coat and along with the tell tale tights, Gabby could tell he was from the 16th century, or thereabouts. So this was the final Etemmu, Hogarth, the actor. He grabbed his translucent sword and shot up into the standard standing, or in this case, floating position.

"Hah! Thou had best quell your fears fair maiden, for I am not so easily beasted by such inglorious hind quarters such as this villain!" Almost on cue, Abhay emerged from the house, brandishing a sword. Did he just call Abhay an asshole?

Abhay twirled his scimitar in one hand and grinned. "Are you still talking? I let me sword do the talking, I hear it speaks volume!" He adopted a readying stance, but before he struck, he turned to the right. "Morning Miss Morgan." He said with a smile.

Gabby's hand rose up into a little wave as she let out a small... "Hi."

Gabby and Jenny backed away as they watched the duel unfold. Abhay made the first move, and he was fast, really fast. His charge at Hogarth looked more like a flash of green from his uniform and all Hogarth could do was block. A flash of white teeth emerged from behind Abhay's beared. He span on the spot, adding momentum and weight to the strike that hit Hogarth's sword hard, causing him to buckle slightly.

The two were locked, Abhay pushing against Hogarth's block. Using all the energy and strength he could muster, Hogarth pushed Abhay away and made a run for it, floating as quickly as he could onto the roof of the manor house.

"Get back here!" Abhay called back, pursuing as quickly as he could. Gabby watched intently. However they were able to hold see through swords was also the same reason why they could touch each other. Whatever's Etemmu is tactile with itself, that's why they can touch, hug and feel while they just freeze the skin off any humans.

The two duelists were atop the roof of the house now, Hogarth looking like he would faint if he could, and Abhay had a satisfied grin on his face. They both stood a few feet apart, both in the primed and ready position, ready to pounce. Well, in Hogarth's case, it'd be more like an ungraceful lunge. Abhay made a few fake out moves, jumping forward ever so slightly. This proved too much for Hogarth who charged at Abhay.

"Too slow!" Abhay smacked Hogarth's sword as hard as he could, then took a step to the side, effectively acting like a Matador to a bull. Hogarth's trajectory sent him past Abhay and towards the edge of the roof. Abhay gave him a helping hand by pressing his hand to the actor's collar and pushing him off the edge.

After a high pitched yelp, Hogarth was sent plummeting to the ground. Instead of hitting the ground, he went right through it and disappeared. Abhay meanwhile gracefully floated to the ground and bowed. "That is how we do that."

Hogarth emerged from the ground, groaning. "You sir, you are a blaggard." He tilted his hat and attempted to regain composure. "For it not betwixt such fair maidens thou dost find thyself in that I would cut you open as the butcher would a cow…"

Jenny sighed and shook her head. "You can drop the act now Thomas, hun. Just talk English like the rest of us."

A rather deflated Hogarth let his shoulder droop. "Oh very well, have it your own way." He floated up to Gabby and gave a theatrical little bow. "Thomas Hogarth, at your service my lady."

Gabby was trying hard not to laugh, she was biting her own lip so hard she thought she might chew through it. "My pleasure..." She responded, in a strained kind of way. Once she'd calmed down a bit, she returned the bow. "Gabby Morgan, at your service."

Abhay put his arm around Hogarth, patting him hard on the arm. "This one here thought he could best me in a duel. As you can see, he lost!" He shook Hogarth side to side for a brief moment. "But don't look so down wordsmith, I'll get you trained up."

Hogarth responded with a nervous chuckle. "I can't be any worse then I am now."

Gabby rather hesitantly put her hand up. "Ummm, nice to meet you and everything, I just needed to grab something for Trem." She held up the lettuce in her hand.

Abhay gestured to the door. "Don't let us interrupt you. Well, more than we already have anyway."

Gabby smiled as she started walking to the door. "Impressive sword play Abhay." The three Etemmu followed her, back into the armor covered hallway. Hopefully it didn't take too long to get a vegetable.

She glanced back and winked at the Etemmu. "You must teach me sometime."

Abhay chuckled and scratched his beard. "It'd be an honor Gabby, if you think you'd be up to the challenge of course."

A devious expression ran across Gabby's face, an eyebrow raised in anticipation. "I relish a challenge."

Jenny let out a cute, high pitched little giggle. "You all are so cheeky!"

Before long, they were back in the living room. As Gabby ascended to Trem's room, she paused for a second and glanced back. It was the first time she saw all four Etemmu together. The actress, the pirate, the hero and the thespian, what a curious group. These four, hailing from different parts of history were connected through Trem. They all answered the call of a helpless little girl years ago and here they remained.

They were all fair and decent human beings back in their lives, and that trend continued after death too. Okay, so Gabby could hardly claim to know them all intimately, unlike Trem, but they all gave off that impression. Sure, Skye was rough around the edges, but it was understandable given what she was when she was alive. Abhay was a bit of a show off sure, and Hogarth is kind of a bit of a dork, but those are the little traits that make people human. Even in death, if those traits could be retained, then the person lives on.

Gabby knocked on the door to Trem's room. She slowly pushed against the door and entered the room, lettuce in hand. Trem was sat at her desk, writing something down. "I got the goods." Gabby called out.

Trem turned around in her seat, her attention seemingly half directed at Gabby. "Oh, thank you. Could I have it?" Trem was handed the vegetable and she ripped a few leafs off, placing them in the tank. She watched as Sammy proceeded to take small mouthfuls. "Thank you Gabby."

Gabby took a few steps forward, leaning in closer so that she could get a better look at Trem's pet. "Your welcome." She was fascinated by the little creature, who was happily nibbling his way through his meal. "Where did you get him?"

Trem leant on her hand as she was lost in thought. "My parents. It's common for Manzazzu to give pets to the new bloods like me. Mum has a dog, I have Sammy. It's supposed to teach us about life. It's frailty, it's shortness and well, it's importance." She reached into the tank and stroked Sammy's back. "We're not supposed to make attachments to the Etemmu we summon, so I failed spectacularly at that. But these little ones stop us from becoming emotionally apathetic."

That makes perfect sense really. Gabby glanced over at Trem, into her eyes. Hesitantly, she put an arm on her shoulder. Trem's body turned stiff, prompting Gabby to move her hand back slightly. Trem's head turned towards Gabby, after a moment, their eyes met. "You haven't failed Trem, not at anything."

Trem was ready to scoff at such a remark and reply with a swift denial, but when she felt Gabby take her hand. It had been years since someone had taken her hand, the warm sensation brought on such a feeling of nostalgia for the young Manzazzu. Gabby's hands were soft, just like her Mothers. Trem closed her eyes and took Gabby's hand, opening her palm and resting her open hand on Gabby's.

The poor human meanwhile was blushing. A little confused but she could see Trem was in her own world. Trem smiled as she closed Gabby's hand and let it go. "Sorry."

Gabby ran her fingers down her palms. "No, I, I get sweaty hands a lot."

Trem shook her head. "It's not that. Your the first human I've met in years, I forgot what it felt like. Holding a human, an actual tactile one and not another Etemmu...." Before she could continue, Gabby pulled her in for a hug. Trem didn't resist, there were no objections and no debate. This felt good, better than good, because for the first time in years, she felt she wasn't alone. She put her arms around Gabby and rested her chin on the human's shoulders.

Gabby meanwhile was really hoping she didn't do anything really stupid. After a few seconds though, the regrets started to fade, and she kind of enjoyed the sensation. They stayed locked in position for a good few seconds, all the while, Trem was remembering her parents.

The stillness of the moment was shattered when Gabby felt Trem's whole body jump, followed by a shiver, as if something chilling had passed through her body. Gabby pulled away from Trem who grabbed her head and leant back in her chair. She gasped for breath as she broke out into a cold sweat. "Trem?! What's wrong?" Gabby shouted, keeping her distance.

Trem groaned, her teeth grinding against each other. "I'm fine..." She strained through her pants. She rubbed her hand down her face, wiping off the cold sweat. "Gabby, there's a lot I haven't told you, but there's something I need you to know."

The way things were moving so fast, Gabby honestly didn't know what to say. Whatever just hit Trem, it clearly worried her, maybe even frightened her. Did she want to know? It seemed with every new thing she learned about Trem, the Manzazzu or the Etemmu, everything Gabby thought she knew felt like it was getting smaller and smaller. But, she knew she'd have to do this kind of thing one day. She signed up for it, she knew the risks when she walked into the house. "What is it?" She asked defiantly.

Trem got up from her chair, picked up her robes and started taking her assortment of rings out of the pockets. As Gabby followed, Trem explained as they left the bedroom and headed down the stairs. "This may be difficult to comprehend so let me know if I lost you."

She slipped the sapphire ring on first, on her left thumb, followed by a ruby, citrine, emerald and amethyst. "We Manzazzu have the duty to monitor the Styx, the nether space between life and death."

For once, that actually kind of made sense. Gabby couldn't pretend to understand fully, she never would, but she got that much. "Right, it's kind of like Limbo then."

Stopping in her tracks, Trem turned around, a look of confusion on her face. "Is that what you call it?" Gabby confirmed. After tilted her head and looking fascinated for a moment, she continued walking, the next hand's set of rings slid onto her fingers. "Since we Manzazzu aren't human, we have a sort of sense for disturbances in the Styx. It's sort of like... We feel if there's something wrong. With me so far?"

Gabby's mouth opened, but it took a second for the words to come out. "Sort of."

They reached the bottom of the stairs and entered the living room, walking past the rather concerned quartet of Etemmu. Trem crossed the room and looked at the world globe, specifically the grey one with the inaccurate land masses. Her finger traced around one location, and when her finger rested on one spot, she sighed.

She looked up at Gabby, her voice was sombre and chilling, as it was when they first met. "Gabby, I need to go into the Styx. Something's active inside there, and if I don't get rid of it, it could find it's way out and get loose in this world. If it's what I think it is, that would be disastrous. I won't stop you if you want to come with me, but just know it's dangerous. Really dangerous."

The four spirits started murmuring between themselves. "Trem, are you sure about this?" Abhay asked.

Jenny had her hand pointed at Gabby. "She's still so young, she could die there..."

Trem held up her hand, that silenced the four. It may not have silenced their doubts, but at least she could get a word in. "You know I wouldn't ask her to do anything she wouldn't want to do…"

Gabby spoke up, cutting Trem off mid sentence. "I'm coming with you." This could go really wrong, but Gabby knew what she wanted to do, and that was stick by Trem. Yeah, they only knew each other a short time, but Gabby knew she couldn't let her go into the Styx alone. "I know the risks, but I want this Trem."

Jenny was about to say something, but Skye held her back. Trem gave a nod to Gabby. "I understand. You'd better follow me then."

Trem marched down the hallway of the manor, but before Gabby followed, she caught a glimpse of Jenny, who looked worried sick. "Promise us you'll come back alive, won't you?"

"I have a family and friends to come back to, I won't let them down. That includes you four." With that she followed Trem into the bowls of the old house.

Chapter Six: "Into The Styx"

"Let's do it Tremarda, just you and me."
"Tremera, it'd be my honor."

Along the wall of one of the mansions corridors stood a rack of swords. Gabby followed on Trem's heels as she ran her hand along the arrays of hilts. She stopped when her hand reached a silver basket hilted sword. The hilt itself was made of a sapphire blue coloured metal and the blade itself had the same deep shade snaking around it, running parallel was a brilliant gold colour. Gabby caught a glimpse of it, and she was taken aback at its beauty. Trem took the scabbard (which was connected to a simple leather belt) that rested by the rack and slid the blade into it. Tightening the belt around her, she turned to Gabby.

"Right, we're all set." She put both her hands on Gabby's shoulders, which brought out a slight blush in Gabby. "You'll be the first human to go into the Styx. Stay close to me and do everything I say."

Gabby took Trem's soft, pale hand in her own and wrapped it in her palm. "I understand. Thank you again for this."

Trem's reply was that of a smile. Her expression changed, a hint of malice could be seen in her dark eyes. "I don't very much care for what I'm supposed to do. I'm my own Manzazzu, and I put my trust in you. For better or worse, Gabby Morgan, I'm going to make sure you're safe."

Gabby responded almost instantly. "I can look after myself...."

Likewise, Trem's retort was almost as quick. "In the world of the living, maybe. In the Styx, well, I don't know what it may do to you. The moment you feel anything wrong, you tell me okay?"

"I will." With that, Gabby continued to follow Trem, through the hallway and to the door at the end of it.

Trem pushed open the door which lead to a small flight of stairs directly below. "Remember, stay close to me." She called back as Trem slowly walked down the wooden steps. The light from the open door helped them see the steps.

When Trem reached the bottom, Gabby stayed on the steps. As soon as Trem's boots touched the ground, something triggered a blue light. Now Gabby could see more clearly. At the bottom of the steps was a structure, a large rectangular...Thing. It was much taller then Trem, maybe double her size, with navy blue walls covered in depictions of animals in gold. The same strange text as on Trem's cylinders were written beneath.

Around it, a circular hole in the ground, almost like a moat. Trem stepped over the small body of water with ease. As Gabby followed, she figured it was time to play Twenty Questions again, if they had the time. "What is it?"

Trem ran her hand over the golden writing, making sure she remembered how to do this right. It had been years, she had been out of practise. "An Ishtar Gate. Every Manzazzu clan has one, they are what we use to gain access to the Styx." She took a few steps back and fiddled with her rings, taking a few off and replacing them on other fingers.

When she was done, she held out her right hand. Gabby watched intently, the rings seemed to glow. Trem drew a simple circle in the air, which caused the air around the empty space of the Ishtar Gate to warble. As her hand rotated, the circle was formed in the air from a bright light. Trem then drew a cross through the circle and drew a line straight down. As if opening another door, she pushed on the straight line. The door to the Styx opened, the warbling air revealed a new landscape beyond the gate.

"Okay, that was cool...." Gabby muttered, peering into the Gate. She could just about make out something on the other side, it looked like water. The light was reflecting off something constantly moving, but the way it shimmered looked a bit off. She turned to Trem. Already she could feel that same rush of emotions she felt when she approached Trem's manor house all those years ago. The fear of the unknown, the uncertainty of her safety...Yet, the temptation could never be swayed. She and Trem took each other's hands. Trem counted down from three, enough time for Gabby to take a deep breath and pray.

They both stepped through the Gate, which, to Gabby, felt like walking through jelly. There was some resistance to her, she required a small amount of force to get through. When she did, she got hit by something so quick, it practically winded her. A small "Hugk..." left her mouth. The atmosphere in the Styx was unbelievable, the air was so thick, damp and humid, Gabby could barely get her breath back.

It felt so muggy and sticky, Gabby had never felt the like of it before. On top of that, the disorientation of going through the Gate made her head spin. That coupled with the heavy air and the ringing in her ears, all proved too much for Gabby's body. She didn't even really know where they were, but she quickly sank to her knees and crawled on the floor, till she was peering over the edge to the waters below. There, she proceeded to throw up.

Trem knelt down next to Gabby, leaving her hand on the poor woman's shoulder. "I didn't think Humans would take to the Styx well..." As Gabby entered a second round of upchucks, Trem grimaced a bit. "Do you want to head back?"

Gabby looked down at the black, murky water below her, and the remnants of her breakfast that sank to the bottom, which was very strange. "Well, how many people can claim they blew chunks in Limbo?" She smiled as she tried to get to her feet, only succeeding in stumbling. Trem got a hold of her and helped her stand up straight.

The poor human groaned, feeling her head spinning. As she tried to steady her wobbly head, she got a good look at their surroundings. Above their heads, well over sixty feet of concrete. The very top of the structures were tilted at an angle, giving it a triangular shape. This stretched back both behind and infront of them for a good twenty feet. The ground at their feet was blackened with dirt and ancient dust.
"Is this the Styx?" She asked, her voice straining.

Trem gently shifted weight back onto Gabby, making sure she was standing before walking to the water's edge. "Technically yes. This is the entrance. The Styx officially begins once we sail out of here."

Gabby, while still trying to get her eyes to stop floating little squiggles in her vision, tried to see what Trem was doing. She had pulled out a raft from an opening in the dock. It was held together with thick coils of metal and was layered up with three lots of logs. Around the log border that surrounded the raft, a tent was held up, strapped to the border. Trem turned to Gabby and took her hand. "Are you sure you want to do this?"

Gabby blinked hard, shaking off the remaining squiggles in her eyes. "I never go back on my word. I'm stubborn like that. Word of warning, I don't really have my sailing legs yet."

Trem stepped off the dirt covered dock and onto the large raft. "Okay, just step on. I got you, you won't fall in." She reassured, keeping a tight hold of Gabby's hand.

Breathing in the hot, dank air, Gabby reached her boot out and took a step. Trem held her by the back, making sure she was upright and safely onboard. "Welcome aboard." She smiled.

The young human glanced around the raft, it was deceptively large, it certainly looked smaller from the dock. At least there was enough room to feel comfortable and there was shelter under the tent, should the Styx be too icky to manage. A pillow and sheet were in the tent too, sleeping accomodation no doubt. Two wooden boxes were also on the deck. "Fine ship you have."

Trem walked over to the side nearest the dock and extended her arms. With one strong push, the boat floated into the centre of the dock and began to slowly float away. Gabby glanced down at the water. "Don't you need to have an oar or something? What if we stop?"

Before responding, Trem put a finger into the black waters. After a second, she pulled it out and wiped it on her robe. "Oh we won't. We're in the current now, it'll take us to the main river." She looked ahead, the ending to the long concrete tunnel they were in was in sight. A bright light shone through the murky darkness. "The real Styx, that's what lies ahead."

Gabby could feel her heart racing. Sure, her head was spinning, she wasn't getting as much air as she wanted due to the stifling humidity and her lips were tingling, but all these ailments were nothing compared to the fear and excitement of the unknown. It had been something Gabby had almost gotten used to other the past few days, but she was now going to witness something no one else would ever get to see.

The raft cut through the light and emerged into the Styx. Gabby immediately started surveying her surroundings. The sky above them was grey, as if all the clouds in the world were hanging over her head, which would explain the awful humidity. Around the blackened water, the Styx was lined with dead shrubs and rotting plant life. "Someone needed a serious word with their groundskeeper." Gabby thought.

The raft turned to the left and Gabby was faced with the main passageway of the Styx. The landscape took her by surprise, she couldn't believe what she saw. She didn't know what to expect, but a rotting dockland aesthetic wasn't it. Across the docks, twisted wood stood upright from the water, the remnants of walkways leading to land. Several rusted gantries could be seen dotted about the landscape, the metal that held it together now rusted and falling apart, exposing some of the skeletal frame inside. It all looked so.... Modern. She had expected the River Styx to be this endless ocean, not a dock that was falling apart at the seams.

"What do you think?" Trem asked, her eyes on the seemingly endless stone walkway that backed onto the water.

Gabby scoffed, sitting down on one of the boxes. "What do I think?" She shook her head, putting a sweaty palm to her forehead. "I think it's bloody mad... Why does everything look like this?"

Trem glanced back at Gabby. "Well, I don't really know, I've only been in the Styx a few times and even then, I didn't take too much notice. I suppose... When you think about it, what's not alive or dead?"

Gabby sighed. "Is that some kind of zen riddle? I'm useless at those things."

"No, not at all." Trem reassured, looking back to the rather unsightly view. "I think it's decay. When something is left to just wither away, it's not dead yet, and yet, you'd never really call it fully alive, would you."

Damn, that was a good point. "Yeah, that's true I guess...." Gabby watched the view go by as they began to pass rows of buildings. Brown and fading orange structures, with windows that all had the glass smashed and broken. Dead moss and ivy had crawled up the walls and one building in particular, a wooden one, had the once white wood turned grey with age. It looked like it was ready to sink into the river.

Trem leaned over to Gabby. "In a second, you'll be able to get a good look at it."

Gabby looked at her friend with a confused look. "Good look at what?" She felt Trem put her hand on her shoulder.

She pointed to an opening in the line of buildings. "There, here it comes."

Gabby followed Trem's finger with her eyes. An old, crumbling building passed them, with a large pile of bricks by it. As that sailed on, there was a gap in the structures, and a wall of rotten vegetation paved the way to something massive.

Set behind all these structures was one massive building. Gabby had been so preoccupied with the smaller structures built around it's base, plus the advent of the dead plant life covering a lot of it up. The structure itself was so large that the clouds were obscuring a lot of it. Gabby glanced down stream, the building stretched as far as the eye could see, off into the horizon. It was made of greystone, but due to its size, that's all Gabby could really make out.

"What is it...?" She asked, in awe of the things size and simplicity. It was so featureless, so bland, yet everything was dwarfed in its wake.

"That's the Complex. Souls bound for the afterlife come down the river, disembark at one of the docks and enter the Complex. There they go onto the afterlife." Trem explained, in such a matter of fact tone that it boggled Gabby's mind.

"They just go into that place, of their own free will? What if they don't want to?" She asked, taking her eyes off the grey mass in the distance.

Trem closed her eyes, biting her lip. "They aren't given a choice. But sometimes, accidents do happen. Usually they're drawn to the otherside, it's like a pulling force. They feel like they want to go, and well, when you consider the alternatives..." Her voice trailed off.

Gabby diverted all her gaze onto her friend. "Trem? What alternatives....?" There was a brief silence, Gabby lowered her head. "You... Don't have to answer that if you don't want to...."

"They become corrupted." Trem forced the words out. "How does a soul get corrupted you ask? Well, when you die, your soul can only last so long without a body. If, for some reason, they don't reach the other side... If they lose their way, or if they resist the pull then well, they can't get into the afterlife. That's when they corrupt." Gabby could see this was a sensitive topic, the subject was clearly causing Trem great discomfort and pain.

"You don't have to tell me anymore..." Gabby stood up and took Trem's hands.

Trem squeezed her new friend's hands when she continued. "No but I do. The reason why I'm here is because it's happened again. Someone's lost their way and become corrupted. You need to know what that means, because I don't want you to be unprepared when you see it. Trust me, it's not a pretty sight."

Gabby swallowed hard, the thought filled her with dread. This was real danger now, and for the first time since entering the Styx, she had her doubts. Before then, she had been so cocky and arrogant, but this really brought her down to Earth. "Okay...What do I need to know?"

Trem walked to the boxes and sat down. Gabby followed and perched herself on the opposite facing box. "First of all, when a soul corrupts, it becomes a Faragh. That means blank, because they literally start losing their sense of individuality. You can see the early stages in the eyes, they're the first thing to go. Once the eyes have glazed over all white, then they'll start losing their facial features. That's the point of no return, and when everything is gone, what's left is a monster. All that's left is a primal instinct, to lash out and attack wildly like an animal."

Gabby rubbed her forehead, which already had a thin layer of fear sweat resting on it. "That's what we're going to be fighting?"

Trem glanced down, Gabby following her gaze. She pulled her robe back, revealing the sword in the scabbard hung from her belt. "That's what I'm going to kill with this ." She looked back up, her eyes meeting Gabby's. "It's my duty as a Manzazzu."

Gabby let go of Trem's other hand and began fidgeting again. "There's one thing I wanted to ask. Jenny, Skye and the others, why haven't they corrupted yet?"

A slight smile crept onto Trem's face. "Good question, it's times like this where I'm grateful to have someone who asks the right questions." Gabby returned the smile before Trem continued. "Well, they've all been dead for a long time now. It works differently when Manzazzu summon spirits back from the other side. The longer they've been dead, the stronger their staying power is. Keep in mind, a soul is on the clock as soon as it leaves the other side. Take Abhay for example, he died over two hundred years ago. He's had two hundred years away from the mortal world so to speak, so now he's back, he could stay for another two hundred if he wishes."

Gabby nodded, her question answered in a way she could understand. "Right, so it works both ways. However long you're dead, means you can come back for that same time. Makes sense. I take it they can go back if they want, before then?"

The smile left Trem's face, her hands crossed herself. "Yeah, if they wanted to. I'm not going to make them stay..."

There was that loneliness the Etemmu mentioned before. It was so clear to Gabby, attachment and the fear of being abandoned. Gabby always had support from her friends and family. When her parents went missing, who did Trem have? Summoning the four Etemmu made perfect sense of course. "Sorry..."

Wiping her dark eyes on the sleeve of her robe, Trem replied. "No it's okay. You know why I summoned the five I did."

That snapped Gabby to attention as her head shot up. "Five?"

Before either of them could even think anything, the air filled with a noise that chilled Gabby to the very core. It was a very loud, very shrill scream. It sounded like a tortured scream of pain, but somehow, mixed with the sound of a ravenous beast.

"What was that?!" Gabby yelped, the flight from it gave her such a jump, she felt like she'd lept out of her skin.

Something caught Trem's gaze, a flash of something blue. "Gabby, I'm about to take us ashore, I want you to keep your distance okay? Stay on the boat at all times." She stomped on the floor, which began turning to the raft, towards one of the old, worn walkways which connected the ships to the land. Once they arrived at one of the docks, Trem stepped off the raft. Gabby watched as she reached into her scabbard and pulled out the blade. The dead and dying bushes in front of her rustled and shook.

"Out you come, there's no hiding from this." Trem called out to the creature. Her hand maintained a vice like grip on the sword's handle.

Gabby looked on in horror as the creature revealed itself. It was still human shaped, but it was walking on all fours. The wrists of the creature were mangled and twisted, it was using the backs of its hands to walk. The bones in the fingers had all broken and were all bent and contorted in a variety of ways. Where there were once fingernails, now were very sharp looking claws sticking out of the ends.

The collar bone had dislodged, giving the creature a tilted and off centred look, the head was straight, but that was the only thing it retained from it's original human form. The eyes were totally white and featureless, no iris could be seen. Where there was once a full head of brown hair, now there were just whisps, and several patches of scalp had come off the skull, leaving some white skull exposed. But the worst thing about it was the mouth. The bottom row of teeth had elongated and had turned into, as Gabby thought, jumbo fangs. In fact, they were so big and sharp, they were pushing into the creature's top lip. Because of this, a thin trail of pale blood ran down into its mouth, staining it's yellow teeth red.

As much as this hideous monster was scaring the ever loving hell out of Gabby, something about it was familiar in a way. She noticed the creature was wearing the scrappy remains of a pair of blue jeans and a white and light blue rugby top. Then it hit her, and the revelation made her stomach turn. That murderer from the papers, the one killed in the barn not too far from her... Dean Jackson, that's who this creature was. Looking down, below his chest was a large patch of dried blood, exactly where he was shot.

The corrupt Faragh of Dean Jackson growled, an inhuman clicking offset the gutteral sound. It looked like it was a bull, ready to charge. Gabby glanced back at Trem. The Manzazzu closed her eyes as she held the sword straight, so the blade was parallel to the centre of her face. Her other hand moved up to the sword, her hand opened up, and wrapped around the blade. The sapphire ring on her thumb began to glow.

Her eyes shot open and she pulled her hand up the blade, it opened up and moved back to her side as the sword ignited with blue flames, much like a flint and steel. The blue pattern that ran up the sword was generating a thick and strong blaze, with the odd sapphire ember dropping to the floor.

"Oh my..." Gabby muttered, her mouth open wide. That was so cool. Especially when Trem slowly rotated the blade in her hand, put one foot behind her and gripped the flaming sword with both hands and adopted a fighting stance.

The creature roared, the fusion of a pained human scream and a snarling beast. It charged at Trem, running at full speed, while Trem stayed in her position. The corrupt soul jumped, ready to bring it's vicious form down on Trem. While it was hanging for a split second in the air, Trem slashed the air in one swift motion with her sword. A crescent of blue fire emerged and struck the beast, sending it flying back into a wall of one of the buildings. The fire set some of the dead plants ablaze as the creature began to recover, getting back to its feet.

Gabby maintained her distance, the fighting was a good few feet away from the raft. The creature shook its head and it's deformed mouth widened, letting out another disturbing roar. Trem and the Faragh ran at each other. The Dean Jackson Faragh brought it's claw like hand down onto Trem, who slashed it with her sword. It recoiled in pain, the flames leaving a deep wound in it's hand. Gabby noticed the gash, red with blood was starting to turn blue, small crystals forming inside it.

The creature used it's other hand to strike, which Trem dodged by side stepping to the right, in the nick of time too as the strike hit the mucky ground, creating a crack in the concrete. Trem ran round to the back of the Faragh and slashed it's back, cutting through the shirt and slicing open the skin along the vertical cut. She thought she was doing well, till she was met with the blank face staring back at her. This one was tougher than the last one. She twirled the flaming sword in her hand and took a step back. When the Faragh turned around to face her front on, she pointed her blade straight and charged.

Both Trem and the Faragh screamed as she drove the blade into the beast's shoulder. Trem twisted the blade, the flames catching the creatures top, setting it ablaze. The Faragh began wildly flailing, trying to put the fire out. Trem tried to pull her sword from him, but it felt lodged in tight. While it's arms waved about in desperation, Trem was flung around like a ragdoll. She forced her boot into the Faragh's chest and tried to use it to help her pull the sword out. The Faragh used the one instant that it wasn't in a blind panic to strike Trem with the back of it's hand, sending her to the ground with a painful thud.

"Trem!" Gabby called. She realised she should have kept her mouth shut, as the horrific creature turned around and stared right at her with it's soulless, blank eyes. "Oh bugger..." The Faragh began to approach her, dragging it's injured arm across the ground. Gabby felt herself hyperventilating on the thick air. She couldn't die here, what would that do to her parents? To her friends, Manisha and their college friends... To Trem.

The Faragh was bearing down on Gabby, every step bringing it closer to her. With it's one good arm, it raised the clawed hand. Gabby closed her eyes, hopefully it will be quick and painless. "Why don't you fight someone who can fight back, you coward?!" Trem yelled, struggling to get back on her feet.

The Faragh's head shot back up and growled, a fresh trickle of blood ran into its mouth. It snarled, it's hand dragged across the dirt, and then it charged. With the sword still lodged in it's shoulder, all Trem could do was put her arms up before the thing jumped on her. It's jaw opened wide, clamping down on Trem's arm. She screamed in agony as the huge teeth went right through her arm.

"Trem no!" Gabby yelled, her eyes welling up as her panic reached an all new high.

What could she do? What should she do? Trem couldn't get the sword out, and the creature had already attacked her biting her arm. Once again, much like the other day, and all those years ago, Gabby found her mind and body doing separate things. Before she realised what she was really doing, she had already stepped off the raft and was running up to the Faragh. The last thing she was going to let happen was to allow either of them to die in bloody Limbo. Trem had as much to live for as she did. Her life may have been lonely and hopeless these past few years, but how would she find her parents if she was dead?

She ran up to the Faragh, grabbed the sword and began to pull. It really was stuck tight, the area around it had formed the small blue crystals which had stuck the sword in place. Before the creature could swing round to strike her, Gabby, with all her might, which wasn't a lot, pushed the sword down. This freed the sword, but also cut through the thing's body, leaving it's arm dangling.

Gabby looked down, the sword was in her hands. The blade was still producing the brilliant blue flames, the odd ember spitting off the side. She looked back up, the freakish thing was looking down at her.

She yelped and out of a desperate reflex, she slashed at the creature. The motion opened a new wound on the things chest, right below the half dozen puncture holes from the bullets.

Realising what she did, Gabby let out a loud "Hah!" She actually did something! Keeping the momentum, before the Faragh attacked again, she hit the thing on the other arm. It recoiled and whimpered as it lost the use of both arms. Gabby didn't show any signs of slowing as she drove the blade through the things stomach, right where the bullet wound was. She drew the sword back.

The Faragh clutched at it's chest, staggering back. It was losing a lot of blood, it was as good as dead at this rate, it must have been. It let out another pathetic whimper as it turned and ran down the walkway. Gabby used this to her advantage and ran over to Trem. She was on the floor, clutching her arm. Gabby dropped the still burning sword on the ground and helped Trem sit upright. Her robe's sleeve was shredded and the puncture holes in her arm were deep and caked in blood.

Before Gabby could ask if Trem was okay, she spoke first. "Gabby... Don't worry about me. Get after the Faragh...." She winced in pain, her wound looked so painful.

"But I can't just leave you." Gabby replied.

Trem closed her eyes tight, the pain was getting really bad now. "If you don't kill that thing... It could get into the Complex...!" She opened a tearing eye. "That's disaster for everyone if that happens... So just go!" She tried to form a smile. "I'll be okay...."

Gabby was trying hard to fight back the tears. She just nodded and gently took her hands away. She got to her feet, grabbed the still blazing blade and chased after the Faragh.

She pursued the freakish creature a few yards before it turned the corner that formed between two buildings. She rounded the corner and stopped, she was running out of breath. It was too easy to get exhausted here, with the air so heavy. At least the adrenalin was keeping the sickness at bay, for now anyway. She looked up and gazed down the alleyway. At the end of it, where the shadow of the creature was cast, was the entrance to the Complex. It was a carved opening in the grey stone. Inside, somewhere, was the gateway to the afterlife. She didn't have long.

Gabby ran into the tunnel, the ground was covered in chunks of dislodged stone and pools of black water had formed. Gabby took cautious but quick paces, taking big steps over the rubble. Every second she wasted slowing down meant that thing was getting further away.

The entrance approached, a massive archway, where stone had turned into rusting sheets of metal, the metal webbing used to hold it together was exposed and twisted. Using the blue light from the sword to illuminate her path, she entered the Complex. She looked around the dark and eerie location. The rusted walls reached high above her head, seeming to go on for miles. Around her, the walls forked off, creating multiple passageways.

It was a maze, and she didn't have time to get lost. Looking down at the damp ground, she saw something that might be of help. She knelt down and hovered the blue flames closer. A few drops of pale blood, and it looked fresh. She glanced up at one of the passageways, the blood trail was clear to follow now.

Gabby had been fighting back the nausea of the place, but this Complex was making her ears ring. Blinking hard, she tried to ignore the sickening sensation. Following the trail of blood, she ran down the passageway, which was lined with faded concrete walls. Several deep scratch marks ran along the walls, and Gabby had to step over some rubble that had been broken from the walls. The blood trail became larger, drips now became a long trail. She turned a corner and was faced with a long corridor stretching far into the distance. At the end of the grimey, dust covered passageway was a light, a brilliant white light.

There, knelt in the centre of the walkway was the Faragh of Dean Jackson, on its knees, almost as if it was mesmerized by the light. Gabby tread as carefully as she could, her boots slowly touching against the ground. She stopped when she was directly behind the creature, raised her sword and brought it down on it's head.

There was no scream, no grunt, only silence as the headless Faragh dropped to the floor. Gabby sank to her knees, making sure the flaming sword was facing downwards so it's tip touched the ground. It was done, it was over. She couldn't believe she made it out alive.

While she tried to get her breath back, she felt the sickening effect of the Styx take hold once again. Her vision began to blur as her head was ringing loud and painfully. She couldn't stay any longer. She tried to get onto her feet but found herself unable to move. The Styx had always been hot, sticky and humid, so Gabby was shocked to feel a cold chill pass through her body. She looked up, right into the light at the end of the tunnel.

The light was hypnotic, dazzling, Gabby began to feel drawn towards it. She reached out a hand, her legs may have failed her but she could still try. Whether it was her mind playing tricks on her or not, she could have sworn she heard a distant, familiar voice. It was a male voice, so familiar and yet so sad. She could smell cigarette smoke. Right before she began to pull herself closer, her stomach turned. The trance was broken when Gabby let out a strained retch. She tried to throw up, but everything came out dry. Still, it prevented her from doing anything stupid. Slowly, she pulled herself up, using the sword to keep her steady.

Heading back the way she came, following the blood trail back to the stone tunnel, Gabby felt the effects of the Styx taking hold again, in a serious way. When she was halfway down the passageway, she stopped, leant against the sword and panted, her vision getting worse. "What's...What's happening to me...?" She muttered.

She heard a metallic clunk, coming from above. Gabby glanced up and saw a metal walkway that hung roughly fifty feet in the air. She'd been following the blood trail so much, she never noticed the series of gangplanks that hung above her. Despite her blurred and spinning vision, she thought she could see something, or more specifically, someone. It was hard to focus, but what she could work out was a human form, wearing black. The face was hidden behind a mask, leaving just the eyes exposed. Gabby was about to call out, but before she could open her mouth, the figure disappeared into the darkness.

"Wh...." Gabby was about to speak when her world was quite literally plunged into darkness. As if someone had flicked a switch, all she could see was black. She thought she might have closed her eyes, but her eyelids were forced wide open. "Oh please no..." Panic struck her hard, she had lost her vision. She started to blindly stumble down the corridors, trying hard not to hyperventilate. The Styx had taken its toll on her, and she was doing herself no favours panicking about the possibility that she wouldn't be able to find Trem. If she took a wrong turn somewhere, she might never find her way back.

Suddenly, she tripped up on a large piece of rubble, sending her crashing hard into the ground. The flaming sword fell from her hand and landed with a thump. Gabby's hands and knees were in agony. She felt something wet against her face, and it smelt disgusting. It must have been black water that had collected. It was probably full of diseases and really unhealthy to be near, so she stuck her face in it.

As awful as it was, it was cold, and it did the trick, as it snapped her to attention. It must have really helped, as Gabby breathed a sigh of relief, her vision was slowly coming back to her. Putting a hand on the wall, she pulled herself up. Her head was still spinning, but she felt "with it" enough to make a mad dash for the exit. She grabbed the flaming sword which had landed on one of the larger rubble boulders.

Staggering through the tunnel, she made her way out of the Complex and back onto the water's edge. She ran back the way she came, to the docks and caught a glimpse of Trem, who was sat upright, clutching her arm. Gabby ran up to the young Manzazzu, keeping the sword at a distance.

"Did you do it?" Trem asked, soldiering through the pain.

Gabby nodded. "Yeah, I killed it... Now, how do you turn this thing off?" She asked as she gestured to the still flaming sword.

Trem held out her hand, her blue signet ring glowing. Gabby passed it to her, and the flames disappeared with a hiss, into the blue pattern of the blade. "Great job, really... Even I couldn't kill that thing."

Gabby helped her friend to her feet, leading her slowly to the raft. "Well, if you cut its head off, it's as good as dead." She put Trem down on one of the boxes as the raft floated away from the dock.

Before long, they entered the current and were being taken back to the Ishtar Gate entrance. Gabby looked at Trem's wound, the bite marks were deep and nasty looking. "What should I do?"

Trem had been clutching her arm tight. "When we get back, I'll patch it up. Don't worry, we're built of strong stuff. Guess we're more resilient than humans. No offence."

"None taken, honestly." Gabby responded. She rubbed her face, still damp from the puddle. "I am not built for this place. I feel like death." She groaned. Gabby turned to Trem. "What's up?" She noticed Trem's face was blank.

She gestured to the river. Gabby turned around to see what was going on. Passing them was a boat, a simple wooden one too. Inside, four figures were sat with hoods over their heads, hiding their faces from view. They were of varying sizes and physicalities. "Trem, who are they?"

Trem got up from her seat and walked to the edge of the raft, her voice a whisper. "The departed." She bowed her head as the boat passed the raft.

Gabby watched the boat closely. Of all the things she saw, this was what she struggled with the most. These were the dead, literally being ferried to the other side. It's not like the whole venture with Trem didn't already prove that life after death was possible... But this was it, this is what happened. Already Gabby could feel tears rolling down her face, because in a way, it made her happy. She caught a glimpse of one of the hooded figures, just enough to see a hint of nose and chin. Before she could get a better look, the figure turned away. The two women watched the boat sail away.

"Off they go then, eh?" Trem remained silent, sitting back down on her box. Gabby sat facing her. "Do you mind if I ask something?"

That snapped Trem out of her reflective trance. "Yeah, sure."

"Etemmu, they can't touch us in the land of the living. So why can one bite you and I can cut it's head off?"

Trem squeezed her injury, keeping the pressure on it as much as she could. "Well, here things work a little differently. An Etemmu here is still a disembodied soul. But in the afterlife, it's like you have your body back. Here, the Styx is slap bang in the middle. I know, it's confusing. Honestly, I was never really told much about it."

Gabby smiled and shrugged. "It's okay. So what about the sword?"

Trem looked at the hilt which was sitting comfortably in the scabbard once again. "The blue flames are the only thing that is guaranteed to affect a Faragh. As you know, it's not perfect, but it does the trick." She drew her attention back to the landscape. The buildings were now fading into the distance. "We're nearly home."

Gabby breathed a sigh of relief. The less time she'd spend in this musty place the better. She was fed up with feeling sick constantly. "Great. When we get back, I'm going to see to that arm."

Trem stood up from the box. "It's okay, I can manage it myself."

"No, please, I want to do this for you." She put her hand on her wounded Manzazzu friend. "Besides you wouldn't have been injured if I wasn't in the way."

The raft floated into the concrete structure and drifted gently to the still open portal, leading into the living world. Gabby helped Trem up onto solid ground and they both forced their way through the portal, which closed behind them.

Gabby took in a huge gulp of air, which felt so light and cool. The weight on her head lifted so quickly, Gabby wondered if she was going to get some climate shock. She turned to Trem and looked at her arm. "Come on, you need to get that looked at."

She helped Trem up the steps, through the corridor and into the living room, where the four Etemmu were waiting.

"Trem! Are you okay?" Skye called out as Jenny, Abhay and Hogarth hovered around her.

Gabby sat Trem down on the seat and remained standing. "What can I get for that?"

Trem pointed her good hand towards the exit. "Under the stairs, there's a door. Look for a big glass jar, should be full of blue liquid..." Before she could continue, she grasped at her arm, holding back a grunt.

Not choosing to wait around while her friend suffers, Gabby almost ran to the door. She opened it and was greeted with the manor's potion room. Above her head, a bamboo frame, with dried plants hanging from it. Work tables were placed on each corner of the room, with various pots and equipment sat atop them. In the centre of the room was a large wooden box, with square sections all containing pots and glasses in all shapes and sizes.

Taking a moment to look around at the fascinating place, Gabby began to scan through the sections. It wasn't long till she found the right glass. She didn't waste time in getting back to Trem.

"Got it!" She knelt down in front of her friend and helped her remove the sleeve of her robe, which was almost shredded from the teeth in the fabric. She took the cork out of the top of the glass.

"Okay, what now?"

Trem winced, one eye closed itself and she grit her teeth. "Pour it into the wound, about a quarter of the glass. Then rub it into the skin, that should do it..."

Gabby obliged and gave the wound an even coating of the liquid, which was thick and pungent. It felt like custard, but it smelt like mouldy fruit. She noticed that as she started rubbing it into the deep bite wounds, Trem was biting into her clenched fist. "Do you want me to be more gentle?"

Trem shook her head. "No, more..." It was clear to Gabby that Trem didn't want her to, she could see it in her face. But she had to, so she closed her eyes and tried not to think about it. Skye had already locked Jenny in a tight embrace and kept her gaze away from Trem.

After several torturous minutes, the work was done. The holes in Trem's arms were filled with the liquid which was already setting. "It'll heal soon enough." Trem reassured, holding her upper arm with her good hand. "Gabby, that wasn't an easy thing to do, thank you."

Gabby put the cork back into the bottle and placed it on the table. "Hey, I wasn't going to sit by and watch you bleed to death."

"I meant what happened in the Styx. I really shouldn't have taken you, it's no place for a human. I think I made a monumental mistake. What would have happened if the Faragh killed you?"

Gabby stayed silent for a moment, before her shoulders shrugged.

"Tell my parents I got hit by a car?" No, that'd be awful. "In all seriousness Trem, I wanted to do it. You gave me a choice, I took it." She sat on the sofa next to Trem.

"The most important thing is you are both safe." Jenny said, hovering behind the two, her warming smile doing wonders to ease their worried feelings.

Gabby felt something vibrate in her pocket. "My phone..." She delved into her trenchcoat and pulled it out. Trem and the four Etemmu all noticed the colour drain from Gabby's face. "Today's the 13th...."

Trem turned to the others. "Yes, the 13th August. Why?" Hogarth asked.

Gabby turned her phone around. The time and date was on display, and it read 15/08. "How have I lost two days?" Panic had started to set in, and she practically started hyperventilating when she saw "12 unread messages" appear. Her hand covered her mouth as she clicked on the first message. Her eyes began to fill with tears as she looked up from the phone. "My Nan died...."

The four Etemmu all looked at each other before looking back to Gabby. Trem was about to speak when Gabby stood up. "I... I have to go." She then headed to the door as fast as her legs would reach her. She was exhausted, still disorientated from the ill effects of the Styx, but this was far worse.

"Want me to follow her again?" Abhay asked, floating towards Trem.

She looked down at her healing arm, the skin beginning to slowly form over the wounds. She sighed as she closed her eyes. "She needs space. If she wants to, she'll come find us."

Chapter Seven: "Oak Ward"

"Sister, what are you doing?"
"You can deal with Father, I'm removing myself from the family."
"Tremera, don't walk away from me!"

Gabby sprinted through the brambles and overgrown bushes, not stopping when the thorns caught her hand and cut the skin. She'd never run this fast before in her life, not even in the Styx. The blood was rushing around her body and she was struggling to catch her breath. The feeling of dread loomed over her, she had to get back but she was not looking forward to explaining herself. She couldn't say she was in a strange form of Limbo fighting the corrupt spirit of a dead murderer. There was no way she could tell them what happened, and why she was away for two days. Why did that happen? Time must have moved slower in the Styx, she thought she'd spent no longer then an hour in there. An hour in the Styx somehow equated to forty eight hours in the living world.

At last, she reached the main street. The sun was about to start setting and there was a breeze causing the trees to sway. The living world seemed that much colder and less welcoming than the Styx for Gabby. Her face was pale and dirty, her hair was a mess and the residual ill effects from her experience, mainly a low level queasiness, was amplified by her pounding heart and the misery she knew she was in for.

She approached her home, her Father's car was parked on the driveway and the lights in the living room and dining room were on, casting squares of orange lights on the path floor. Gabby took a deep breath and opened the door.

She limped into the house, panting. Her chest was raspy, each breath was hard to take. She wished she could just drop dead right now, so

she wouldn't have to deal with this. In the past few days, she'd seen ghosts, non humans and hideously corrupted souls of murderers. This trumped all of those experiences, the worst thing that could have happened in those situations was that she'd be killed. Her parents would still love her, even posthumously. Now though? Well, she was readying herself for the worst.
Gabby closed the door behind her and approached the dining room. She peered past the open door to see her Mother, her makeup smudged due to the tears. A bottle of alcohol was on the table, next to her coffee mug. Her Father meanwhile was on the phone, his work suit was now his shirt, ruffled and creased, with his tie undone and his top two buttons undone. He was on the phone, to the police. They didn't hear her come in over Craig talking.

"Well it's not like she ran away... Look I can't deal with this now, I just lost my Mother in law. Yes I know you're trying your best..."

She'd never seen them this broken before. It was her fault they were like this. If she hadn't have gone to the manor and ventured into the Styx, then she would have been there for them. Instead, she was the one to thank for her parents being in this desperate state. She stayed hidden behind the wall, listening to the conversation take place.

"Right, well thank you Constable. Yes, if we hear anything, we'll let you know.... Yes, that will be greatly appreciated. Thanks, bye."
He turned off the phone and sat down at the table, rubbing his head.

Mavis locked eyes with her husband, the look said more than words ever could. Her eyes were so full of sorrow and hopelessness that she just seemed empty. They held each other's hands and remained in silence. Gabby couldn't take it any longer. She stepped out from behind the wall, still panting slightly. Both her parent's heads turned instantly, and they both shot up from their seats.

"Where the hell have you been?!" Mavis barked at her daughter.

Her Father continued the onslaught. "We've been scared out our minds something happened to you! You picked a fine time to disappear for two days!"

Gabby's control over her emotions were beginning to break down. She couldn't bring herself to say anything, stifling sobs with every breath. She found herself backing away as her parents advanced.

"We rang you and texted you a hundred bloody times Gabby!" The rage in her Father's face was something Gabby had never seen before, she hoped she'd never have to either.

Her Mother stormed up to her, backing Gabby onto the dining room wall. "We rang Manisha, she didn't know where you were! We phoned the police who went into that house of yours and they found no one there! Where were you?"

Her Father looked her up and down, shaking his head slightly. "You look like a mess, what were you doing?" Pale face, messy clothes, out of it for two days, that could imply... "Have you been taking drugs?"

Gabby sprang to attention with that question. "No! I haven't, I swear!"

"Then where were you!?" Her Mum shouted at her, on the verge of tears herself. "I had to lie to my Mother for your sake! I didn't want her to worry so I said you were out and you'd be along any minute. She died that evening. I had to lie to my own dying Mother Gabriella!"

All Gabby could do was mutter a simple... "I'm sorry..."

Her Mother grabbed her by the arm and pulled her into the middle of the room, the light hanging from the ceiling illuminating Gabby's face. Her face was as pale as a sheet and there was a thin layer of dirt over it. She looked awful, she must have done something, either that or she was lying about the drugs. "Gabriella Diana Morgan, you'd better not be lying to me, because I'm not in the mood. Your Gran died in her sleep in the early hours of this morning. Now you can either tell us where you've been or keep it to yourself, but you made this situation ten times worse than it could have been."

Her Father stood behind his wife and crossed his arms. "No, I think she should tell us."

Gabby looked so desperate at her parents. She was so divided, she couldn't tell them, she promised Trem they would never know, but she couldn't face lying to them. Her parents stared back at her, both demanding a good explanation, which was something she could never be able to give.

"Well..." She began. Her throat dried up and her hands began to shake,it felt like her first encounter with Jenny again, only worse. "We lost track of time..." It wasn't exactly a lie, that much was true. Granted, she wasn't to know time worked differently in the Styx.

"For two days? You lost track of time for two days?!" Her Father snapped. That really sent Gabby over the edge.

She nodded, her eyes closed tight to try and hold back the tears. "I'm so sorry..."

Her mum sighed. "Sorry isn't good enough Gabby."

"I know." She muttered, wiping her eyes on her trench coat sleeve.

Glancing at her husband, Mavis continued. "We trusted you to come home on time two days ago. We're not sure if we can keep that trust. Having said that, this is the first time this has happened, and we're still worked up over Mum...Your Gran's passing."

Sobbing quietly into her sleeve, Gabby had well and truly let her defences break down. Her Mum looked at the ground. "I think you should go to your room while your Father and me discuss things."

Gabby followed her Mother's instructions by turning on her heels and made her way up the stairs to her room.

She closed the door to her room behind her and rubbed her hands down her face. She groaned loudly, throwing her trenchcoat onto the floor, walked over to her bed and threw herself onto it.

Putting her face on the pillow, she cried into it for a good five minutes. She was never going to see her Grandmother again, and her parents really weren't keen on her anymore. She hit her head on her pillow out of sheer frustration.
"I am such an idiot..."She muttered to herself. Her parents must think she and Trem were some kind of drug taking layabouts camped out in the old house. Still, at least the police didn't see any of the Etemmu, that would have been ugly. But again, that could have jeopardized matters even more. Right now, Gabby felt awful. All she could think of was how everything that went wrong in the past few days was on her.

"Maybe I should just quit..." She thought. If she left now, neither Trem nor her friends would be put at risk. It was obvious now she wasn't meant to go into the Styx, meet the Etemmu or Trem. It was all some coincidence from years ago. A bad bet with Manisha had now turned into such a freak show.

"Trem would be better off without me anyway, all I'll be is a damn burden." She sat up and pulled off her boots, throwing them on the floor. She stared at the ceiling in silence, remembering how the family dealt with her Grandfather's death. Well, they didn't need to worry about Gabby going rogue.

She turned to her bedside table, on it was a familiar silver bracelet, the one that belonged to her Gran. She lent over and saw a note underneath. She took the bracelet in one hand and the note in the other.

"To Gabby,

I know the boring details with my will may take a while to iron out, so until then I wanted to give you something sentimental. It's not all you will be getting, don't worry. But wear this and remember me Gabby.

*Lots of love
Nan"*

Gabby looked at the bracelet and smiled behind the tears. She attached it to her wrist, it was a good fit too. This whole thing was going to be extremely tricky and taxing, but this at least made Gabby feel ever so slightly better.

She rubbed her eyes once again and sat on the side of her bed. For the first time in the last hour of despair, she felt like there might be a little bit of hope in all this. Her parents wouldn't be mad at her forever, not once the funeral was over and done with. Besides, all families fall out, it's not like this is the death knell on their relationship. What it does to her relationship with Trem though? That'd have to be sorted out later.

The sun had already set, and the moon hung in the sky. Gabby had put her small television on, as a way of breaking the silence. She was still sat on her bed, staring out of her window. She was so lost in thought that she failed to notice the tell tail rush of cold air.

"Umm... Gabby?" Came a voice.

Gabby yelped and fell back onto the bed. Peering between her fake leather leggings, she saw a concerned looking Jenny who had appeared through the wall with the television, the screen had become foggy because of the coldness.

"Ah! Jenny, what are you doing here!?" She whispered, pulling herself up. "You can't let my parents see you!"

Jenny levitated towards her. "We were all so worried about you sugar...." She crossed her arms, clearly concerned about Gabby as she kept glancing at the door, readying herself to hide if she needed to. "Trem told me not to come, but I couldn't bear the idea of you being alone right now."

Gabby scooted closer, crossing her legs and sitting at the bottom of her bed. "Well, it means a lot Jenny, but you didn't have to, not if you were going to get into trouble."

Jenny also crossed her legs as she floated down to Gabby's level. "It'll be fine, they know where I am. How is everything? I imagine this is hard for you?"

Gabby sniffed, looking down at her bracelet. "Well, I've had to lie to my parents, which really sucks. I hate telling them lies, but I guess till now I was the only teenager who didn't." She put her hand on her gift. "I never got a chance to say goodbye to Gran either." She held out her bracelet to Jenny, who leant forward to get a better look. "She gave me this too, one of her keepsakes."

The Etemmu smiled at Gabby. "It sure is pretty." She tried to reach her hand out, but stopped before she attempted to hold the bracelet. Even after the few years she had spent as an Etemmu, Jenny still wasn't used to the idea of being in this disembodied form. Her arm went limp and rested by her side. "What was your Grandma like?"

Trem put her arms around her knees, thinking back to the years gone by, losing herself in the nostalgia. "Oh, she was great Jenny. She really loved your movies. Well, everyone did, that's why you're such an icon."

If Jenny had a functioning blood supply, she would have blushed. "Shucks..."

Gabby chuckled. "She just had this great way of dealing with things, she always had such a positive mindset. It was probably because of the war. Back then, people knew how to band together and make the best out of a bad situation." Her chin rested on her knees. "I wish I had that." Her head sank, her curly thick hair falling around her face.

"I just miss her. She hasn't even been gone that long, I mean I've only known for like, half an hour at most? I've just been so drained over what happened with Trem, in the Styx. I guess I had my defences lowered, and it hit me like a ton of bricks."

All Jenny wanted to do was hug Gabby, but if she tried, she'd freeze the poor woman.

"But yeah, Nan was brilliant. Eliza, that was her real name, she never like Elizabeth. She always said you shouldn't name your child after someone famous and she always thought the most famous Elizabeth was the Queen. She was strange like that, and it made me feel better about my strangeness."

Jenny tilted her head. "Why do you think your strange?"

Gabby gestured around her room. "Just look. I'm a complete geek for weird and bad movies. People call your movies cinematic class, whereas I spent my days watching Avin Shraine & The Killer Face Eaters From flipping Neptune."

Jenny tried to hold back laughter, that title was very amusing for her. "Gabby, there's nothing wrong with that." She hovered to Gabby's side, causing the air around her to grow chilly. "I was the same, an outsider. Everyone had rich Daddies, they were businessmen in suits doing boring stuff. My Daddy was a farmer, I grew up in a ranch in Iowa. I knew everyone liked me because I was pretty and cute, they all knew I wasn't the smartest tool in the box. But I could act my way into their minds, so that helped. But I was always an outsider." Her eyes met with Gabby's. "Hey, we're kinda alike, aren't we?"

Gabby returned the smile, Jenny's iconic expression that was plastered onto all her movie posters never failed to help take the edge off a bad situation. "We are, yeah." She agreed. She took the pillow from her bed and held onto it. "I guess I've just been all over the place mentally. That stuff with Trem really screwed with my head. Was it hard for you to get all this?"

Jenny opened her mouth to speak, but didn't get a chance to even form a single letter as there was a knocking on Gabby's door. "Gabby, can we come in?" Came the muffled voice of her Mother.

Gabby shot a look at Jenny and pointed down at the floor, though it was more of a panicked flail. Jenny obliged and sank quickly into the bed.

"One second!" Gabby called, scrambling for her trenchcoat, pulling out her phone. She put it to her ear and pretended to be in a conversation. "Sorry Manisha, I have to go. Yeah, speak to you later, bye." Hopefully they bought that. "You can come in..."

Her parents slowly entered her room and sat on the bed with her. Gabby, still hugging her pillow, scooted to the other end of the bed. "Hey Gabby. Look, we know we were maybe a bit harsh in our words..." Mavis began.

Well, she wasn't wrong.

"Just tell us where you were." Craig continued, not in a demanding tone, which was surprising.

Gabby wiped her face on the pillow and took a deep breath, hoping they'd buy the lie she had formulated. "Me and my friend went into the forest for a walk. We got lost..." She glanced up, trying to gauge her parent's response. So far, so good. "As you know, the Mortsbury forest is hard to get around if you lose your way and I tried to call you guys, but there wasn't any signal."

It would be worse if they thought she was outright lying to their face, but fortunately, her parents looked at her with a sympathetic gaze. "Why didn't you tell us this before?"

Bringing the pillow closer to her chest, Gabby muttered a response. "I couldn't think with all the shouting going on." She thought she sounded so pathetic and sensitive. Though, she always thought she was a pretty strong willed person. But it turned out what she thought was strength was really her just having an easy time of life. Now that all this stuff with Trem happened, it turned her whole world upside down.

Her parents pulled her in for a hug. "We're sorry we snapped at you. With your Nan's passing and all that, we just got so worked up."

Gabby just remained silent, not out of disrespect for her parents, but because she couldn't say what she wanted to, words weren't forming naturally. Her parents let go of her, looking into her red, puffy eyes. "I know you'll want to come to terms with all this, just know we're here if you need us."

"Thanks.." Came the quiet reply. After receiving a kiss from her Mum and a hug from her Dad, they left the room.

The door closed and after a beat of silence, Jenny appeared from the bed. "I'm sorry if your parents have a frozen toilet, I panicked and may have frozen the water."

Gabby was staring off into space, facing the door. When Jenny spoke, it snapped her out of her trance. "Oh, sorry Jenny, I wasn't listening. What were you saying?"

Jenny shook her head. "It's okay, it doesn't matter. Though if you guys need a plumber, I'd pay for it if I could, but..." She held her hands up and wiggled her fingers. She crossed her legs and returned to Gabby's side. "Do you think you'll come back tomorrow? I mean, we understand if you don't want to. I guess we're all just a little worried is all..."

Gabby spoke in mutters, she didn't have the energy to speak up. "I don't know. I hope so..." Her fingers clung onto the pillow tight. Something had been on her mind for the last hour or so, but she was so unsure about asking. "Jenny?"

"Yeah sugar?"

Tear soaked eyes met with translucent blue eyes. "What's the afterlife like?" Gabby asked.

Jenny immediately began to look uneasy. She began rubbing her arm and diverted her gaze. "I hate to say this Gabby but... Have you ever tried to remember a dream you had and it never really comes?"

Gabby began to deflate like a balloon. "How can you not remember?"

Jenny thought she'd give anything in the world to be a solid, living Human once again, so she could give Gabby a comforting hug. "I don't know, but none of us can really. I guess it's so we can't mouth off to whoever we talk to about how great or how awful it is. Guess some things aren't meant to be known."

Gabby buried her face in the pillow. Of course, that was bound to happen. Coming to terms with her Grandma's passing will be harder than it was with her Grandpa, at least the signs were there. She would never get that last goodbye, and it was all because she decided to go swanning off with Trem.

"Did I make the right choice in going with Trem?" She asked, wiping her eyes with her palms.

Jenny moved closer, goosebumps forming on Gabby's skin. "Trem would have died if you weren't there to help her. You did a thing no other Human has ever done."

"I wasn't supposed to though, was I?"
Jenny bit her lip. "Well, maybe. But what's done is done. There's no point worrying over it or wanting to change it. You saved Trem's life, you stopped something fierce doing something pretty bad in the Styx. Plus how many small time country girls like you can boast they have killed a murderer, especially one that was already dead! Come on Gabby, we both know that's pretty cool."

A small chuckle left Gabby's lips. "I guess so." The two sat in silence for a moment, waiting for the other person to speak. Pondering for a second, Gabby spoke up. "Jenny, tell Trem I will be there tomorrow. I don't want her worrying."

Jenny tilted her head. "What about your parents?"

Gabby glanced at the door. "I know they'll need me, but after today... I don't know. I'm not going to leave them in the lurch." She rubbed her eye. "I just need tonight to think on things."

Jenny wanted to get closer, but given her chilly disposition, she kept her distance. "It's been a mad day hasn't it?"

Gabby nodded. "Yeah, the Styx and now this. I know there's some reason why no human's seen the stuff I've seen, I just don't get why Trem thought I'd be the one to show it to."

"Maybe because she thinks your special?" Jenny asked.

Maybe, but Gabby didn't feel like it, even despite Jenny's words.

"Tell the others I'm okay. I'll see you all tomorrow. Not sure when."

Jenny smiled back at Gabby. "I'll tell them, leave it to me sugar." With a little wave, she backed to the wall of the room and disappeared from view.

Gabby lay on her bed, staring at the ceiling for a good ten minutes in silence. The news of the day had taken its toll, her parent's outbursts and the fact she had to lie to them all resulted in Gabby feeling shattered. As if fighting the corrupted soul of a murderer in another plain of existence wasn't draining enough. There was a knock at the door, she glanced down from the ceiling, her Mother had walked in with a tray.

"Hey love, I brought you dinner. You look a little pale, so I thought a burger may help." She put the tray on Gabby's desk. "I know you might need some time to yourself, so we'll give you a bit of distance if you need it. Just know that we're here if you want to talk."

Gabby sat up and moved to the edge of the bed. "Thanks Mum. After this I think I'll have a shower."

Her Mother walked to the door. "Okay love. Take as long as you need." She closed the door gently behind her.

Gabby took the tray and tucked into the food. Since her body clock was well and truly broken, to her, she'd only had breakfast maybe two hours ago at most. As she ate her way through her meal, she wondered how Trem was.

Chapter Eight: "Bitter Old Man"

"Please think about what you're doing. Don't leave us... You wouldn't leave me would you?"
"You could come with us?"
"I can't..."

Gabby had already left the mansion, and Jenny had slipped away after her not long after. Things had begun to calm down in the empty house, the other three Etemmu had fanned out and returned to their usual places. Skye usually spent time with Jenny in the garden, but this time she went out alone. Abhay would usually watch the stars when he wasn't needed, and he'd be found in the observatory, a glass dome atop the old building. As for Hogarth, the library usually, which would have been odd, given his non corporeal form, but Trem had created a "helper" to turn the pages of the books for him. That helper was, of course, Woody. He'd take a book from the shelf and drop it onto the desk for Hogarth, and would nudge the pages of the book with his beak.

As for Trem, she returned to her room. The potion was doing her arm wonders, the deep teeth marks were being filled in with new flesh, specks of sheet white flesh peppered her already pale arm. She kept her arm as inactive as she could, letting the healing do it's thing. Having fed Sammy once again, Trem began a new correspondence with Tremadore, informing him of the days events.

She must have been breaking so many rules, interacting with humans. But it became increasingly evident to her, the reason why she heard Gabby out when she entered the manor, why she showed her the greater Manzazzu culture, the Styx. Gabby had taken all these revelations so well. That means she'd be of use. If Trem had taken this long to find her parents and still come up with nothing... Tremadore was supportive yes, but not someone she could be dependant on... Then maybe Gabby could be the one. The human touch, so to speak. She'd proven useful in the Styx, even if she did throw up a few times.

She felt exhausted, just like Gabby was. The fact she was contemplating using the woman, who considered her a friend, to be "of use" was a clear sign she needed a break. Her inner Treman was coming out, and the last thing she wanted to be like was that bitter old man.

Almost on cue, Treman emerged from the wall and floated towards her. Before he could open his mouth, ready to fire vitriolic bile at her, she spoke up. "You ever heard of privacy?" She remarked, as sarcastically as possible.

"It's still my house girl, I shall do what I like!" He snapped in return.

Trem turned around, her robe draped over her shoulder, hiding the wound. "Well, you're dead, so it's technically mine. So by that logic, I can break the lock on your room and see what you've been hiding."

She knew she hit a nerve as Treman looked so flustered he changed the subject. "I saw you take that Human into the Styx."

Trem raised an eyebrow, she loved playing his own game back at him. "What business is it of yours? My own private life. That's my business. If you can lock yourself in your room for hours on end doing who knows what, then I can do what I like with the people I invite in."

Treman was clearly reaching his limit with her, ready to burst at any second. "We are Manzazzu..." He began, about to instigate another rant, before Trem cut him off.

"Former Manzazzu, in your case."

Treman's eye twitched. "We are Manzazzu.." He continued, putting particular emphasis on the first word. "We were blessed by Ishtar to do the duty of the Gods all those thousands of years ago. To protect the Styx, to help lost souls reach the other side and to preserve knowledge. Where in that does it mention fraternizing with the lower casts?"

Trem spun her chair around to face her grandfather, taking care to make sure her robe covered her arm. "Is that what humans are to you? Just some wild animal to keep at a distance? Are they only of use to us when they're dead?"

Treman moved closer to Trem, the chill began to fill the room and his fading eyes locked with Trem's. "You've not had a proper education so I don't expect you to know. As Etemmu they aren't a threat. When they live, they will kill whatever they don't understand! When they have spent years, decades or even centuries in the afterlife, they will usually get a sense of the bigger picture. Then they will be of use."

Trem only scowled further. "Then explain to me why we have our manor in the middle of a Human settlement then?"

The old man closed his eyes and sighed. "That was to do with your Mother. She was fascinated with these beings when they were alive. They were a great thing to study, that's what she said."

The chair Trem sat in slid back as she stood up, moving closer so she was practically breathing on her grandfather. "They're not like books, they're living people. I don't know what you were taught, but if they're only good to us dead then I refuse to just sit back and wait till the interesting ones die."

Treman pointed to her door. "You like to keep their company!" He barked back.

The steely expression Trem had on her face cracked, her attempts to keep an expressionless face were failing as she felt her lips quiver slightly. She sat back down in her chair, her robe starting to slide off her shoulder.

Treman floated around so he was leaning over Trem's shoulder. "The Human goes, that is the end of it." He whispered into her ear.

He phased through her, and Trem felt the thermal shock shoot through her body. She immediately began shivering as the telltale ice crystals began forming on her skin. No sooner had they formed, the warmth of the room had began melting them. Either way, it wasn't a pleasant experience. Fighting through the shivers, she called out to him. "Is it days now, or do you still have a week left?"

Treman stopped in his tracks. The eyes were always the first things to go on an Etemmu, the first sign that they were becoming a Faragh. Treman was already in the early stages. "I told you, when I have all my affairs in order, then I will return to the other world."

Trem moved her neck, a small click came from her still unthawing form. "Well, don't take your time. You know what happens if you turn Faragh on us. Bye bye cozy afterlife and hello eternal nothingness." She just managed to get to her feet. "Let's both hope I won't be the one who has to put you down if that happens."

The robe that hung on Trem's shoulder fell to the floor, revealing her arm, still in the process of healing. Treman's eyes narrowed. "I doubt you'd have the gall, little girl." With a turn of his head, he flew through her doors and disappeared.

Trem shivered, the rest of the ice crystals dropping from her body.

Treman floated through the rooms of the manor before arriving in his own. The windows and doors had all been thoroughly and securely barred with planks of hefty wood on the outside, resulting in a gloomy and dusty abode. The only thing that was uncovered was a full body mirror, a blue and gold trim formed around it.

The former Manzazzu's mind was a mess, scattered thoughts would pass through his mind and lead to aggressive mood swings as he fought back the conflict raging between his voice and mind.

He was fiercely against the idea of the Royal Family. He hated the idea of one family owning all the power in the Manzazzu kingdom, especially if that family was his own. This would make sense, were it not that he was obsessed with the family's social standing. That's why he was adamant to put anything that would jeopardize him and the honour of his family to rest. This twisted sense of right and wrong lead him to trap Trem's parents in the Styx. After all the years Trem had spent looking in vein for her parents and in such a cruel twist of fate, the culprit was in her house all along.

Treman was in all regards a twisted individual. Aside from his cruelty and limited intelligence, he followed a belief that was outlawed in Manzazzu culture, the Mutashaeib, the Divergent Manzazzu. In a bygone age, they believed that the human race was inferior, and the great powers the Manzazzu possessed should be used to "rid the vermin called Humanity from the face of the Earth."

Using the flaming swords as weapons and the Manzazzuan command of the Styx (including the corrupted souls within), they would decimate men, women and children alike, were it not for the intervention of the Second Manzazzu Queen. She and her daughter lead a bloody battle against the Mutashaeib, ending their rebellion and killing all those who would rebel. Any Manzazzu found guilty of aligning with the Mutashaeib were put to death.

Treman had been a follower since he was a young man, all five hundred years ago now. He lived his prime years in the tail end of the war between the Royal Family's supporters and the Mutashaeib. He was born into a noble family and saw the people he believed in killed. That kind of thing can take an already warped mind and mould it into something much more concerning, even to the extent of turning on their own daughter. Her probing husband had unearthed evidence that he was a secretive Mutashaeib supporter and told his wife.

Luckily, Tremera's sister was around to continue being a source of reliability for the family. As soon as Tremera and Tremarda were in the Styx, he made sure they were rendered unconscious and sent on a raft up the river. Getting lost in the Styx is every Manzazzu's worst nightmare, as Trem knew.

With his time nearing an end, Treman's plans were still incomplete. His plotting had lasted longer than his mortal life, so the extra few years he gained enabled him to continue where he left off. He headed to the mirror and pressed his hand against the glass. As if it were made of water, the glass warped, and Treman ran his fingers through it, making a circle in the liquid like glass, drew a line down the centre and a cross through it, opening the portal to the Styx.

Something he'd set up when he was alive, an unlicensed and untrackable Ishtar Gate, allowing him to enter the Styx in secret. Stepping through the portal, he emerged in one of the decaying sidings of the Styx. He stepped onto the broken up segments of railway tracks, feeling the ground on his feet again was such a comforting feeling once again. Where his Etemmu form would fade away before it reached the feet, now it felt like he had a real body once more. Around him, light spilled out of the gaps in the corrugated metal of the roof of this hidden little segment of the Styx.

Old, faded and rusted tram carriages occupied the sidings, with their windows smashed and the glass covering the floor. Treman made his way out of the sidings and onto the Styx docklands.

Chapter Nine: "Isn't death funny?"

"If Father isn't long for this world, someone's got to look after him. One of us has to be the loyal daughter."
"Are you trying to make me feel guilty?"

Gabby was surprised she had gotten as much sleep as she did, but considering she felt shattered in every way, it shouldn't have come as a shock. She couldn't remember much of her dream, only that she was with her Grandparents again, on the pier not too far from Mortsbury. By the time she awoke, it was going on 10:30. She was not a morning person, but considering what happened yesterday, she wasn't exactly a mourning person either. Not when the whole day previous was one ugly mess.

She'd slept off the last of the ill effects of the Styx though, which was one good thing. Gabby wondered if her parents would let her go back to the manor, she wanted to check on Trem. Of course, her parents weren't stupid, they wouldn't buy her story for long. It was clear to Gabby they were just being nice for the sake of it, and that she'd need to think of a much better explanation. She never dreaded breakfast before, till now.

She'd already had a shower the night before, to wash away the dirt from the Styx, so she couldn't use that as an excuse to avoid talking. With any luck, her Dad would have already gone off to work.

Gabby sat up and groaned into her hands. This sucked, the fact it all happened so fast and without her knowing... Gran passing away, spending three days without knowing it in the Styx... Today was when she was going to start making things right. Heading downstairs, her suspicions were confirmed, only her Mum was there. She sat on the sofa in the living room, the same bottle of alcohol was on the kitchen table. Thankfully the lid was on and it looked as half full as it did the night before.

"...Morning." She called from the bottom of the stairs. Her Mum was unresponsive, staring at the television, the news was playing. Gabby walked closer, like a timid animal, her steps were light and delicate. Mavis was still staring off into space. Gabby took a seat next to her, in Gran's favourite armchair no less, in hindsight, a pretty bad move.

"I want to know more about what happened." Mavis broke the silence with her chilling monotone. She still didn't look at Gabby. "Like why you were in the forest in the first place?"

Okay, time to lie. Gabby felt nervous again, her hands had began sweating. "This sounds so stupid but... We fancied a walk, my friend said she knew the way back and yeah, we just got lost. The mobile signal there is pretty rubbish as you know..."

Her Mother cut her off with another question. "You could have called 999."

Gabby didn't think of that, this was really testing her lying skills. "Well, I guess my phone is kind of old. I have had it for years now."

Gabby couldn't gauge the response from her Mother, she was still staring off into the distance. She shuffled closer and spoke in a whisper. "When did Nan....?"

"Early hours. The nurse said it was in her sleep, about 3am."

All Gabby could do to respond was to cover her eyes with her hands. "I'm so sorry... If I knew, we wouldn't have gone." She paused and sniffed. "You must really hate me..."

That broke the trance like state her Mum was in. "Don't be stupid."

"Yeah, well it's a bit too late for that." Gabby muttered. She snapped to attention when she felt Mavis' hand on her shoulder.

"Gabby, I am still your Mother. I don't hate you."

Gabby rested her hand on her Mothers. "Yeah, but I bet you think I'm a big disappointment."

The hand moved from her shoulder to her head as she felt her Mum ruffling her curly hair. "No your not. You were just careless. But I'm not going to be the one who bans you from your friend's house, just don't do that to us again."

Gabby nodded and drew herself closer to her Mum. "So no going out in the woods from now on. I want you back before 9pm too. Can you promise me that?"

Well, she couldn't if she was ever needing to go into the Styx again. Since she couldn't gauge time there, an hour or two turning into three days means that she was bound to her Mother's word. "Yeah Mum, I can promise that."

She never said anything about sneaking out in the dead of night. The garage is just under her window, she was hardly athletic but she'd often do fake fire escape drills as a little girl. It was manageable in a scrape.

Mavis kissed Gabby on the forehead. "Sorry about this, but I need to make sure you stay safe. I already lost someone I love."

Gabby remained silent, breaking eye contact mostly because of the feeling of shame washing over her. "Still, I can't apologise enough...I should have been there."

"Yeah, you should have. But I'm not the kind of Mother who's going to hold it against you nor ban you from going to your friends. I just want to keep an eye on you is all. You know you can talk to me right?"

It took Gabby a few seconds to reply with a quiet "Yes." The silence before that however was so still it was almost chilling. "I'd better go to the toilet, freshen up." She got herself up from the sofa and headed towards the bathroom.

Before she left the room, she glanced back. "So is it okay if I do go back after this? I didn't tell them what happened." Of course they knew, but she hated people worrying about her. That was why this all hurt so much really.

"So long as your back by 9." Came the reply.

Gabby knew her Mum was bottling a lot of emotions, she did last time. The funeral for her Grandfather really helped shift a lot of the repressed feelings and time healed the rest. With any luck, the same will happen again. The cycle of grief, if you start getting used to it, you worry you become apathetic, that's what Gabby believed.

She feared it happened last time, thankfully it wasn't the case. But with this new world she had discovered, with the ghosts and Trem and this whole mad world, keeping secrets and repressing feelings and desires was going to have to become second nature.

"I will." She responded, going through the wooden doors and into the bathroom. Once she had finished her business, she turned on the tap and allowed herself to have a little cry, in an attempt to try and make herself feel better.

After a few minutes, Gabby was busy washing her face when the door opened. Mavis poked her head into the room, holding her towel. Gabby had forgotten about that. She also had her outfit, the dirt scrubbed off and the trenchcoat tails given a thorough sponging down. "I figured you'd want your Regret Outfit cleaned for today."

That nickname carried new meaning now of course. Gabby had debated whether or not to scrap the silly ripoff cosplay idea, but her Mum had gone to the trouble of cleaning it, it'd seem rude not to. "Thanks so much Mum..."

Her Mother put the towel and clothes on top of the toilet seat. "I brought your towel, I know you'll be needing that." Well, she seemed to be taking things better. Of course again, it was all a farce to hide what she was really feeling.

Gabby smiled back. "Thanks. I'd lose my own head if it wasn't screwed on." She always used to hear that from her Mum in her youth. That got a smile back, which was good.

Once she had dried herself off, Gabby sprayed on some deodorant, slipped on her outfit took the trenchcoat and made her way back into the dining room. She got herself a bowl of cereal which she finished in about ten minutes. She and her Mum kept conversation to a minimum while they ate. After a quick drink, Gabby was ready to leave.

"Are you sure your okay with me going out? I know we need each other, I'm only going out to tell them what happened. I'll be back soon." She reassured, putting on her trench coat.

"After last night's little outburst from me and your Dad, you need a little away time. Remember your phone?" Gabby took it out of her pocket, held it up and returned it safely. "Good. I'll see you soon."

Gabby said her goodbyes as she put on her boots and left the house. As soon as the doors closed, she could just about make out the sound of her Mother crying. This was all shades of messed up, and she felt so bad for it. Obviously she wasn't to blame for the death, but she didn't help. All she was going to do was go to to Trem's and bring them up to speed.

The journey to the manor this time felt numb. The scratches from the overgrown brambles barely registered anymore. Gabby was too busy trying to figure out what to do. She could just walk away, as awful as that may be. What she saw was never meant to be seen, and for good reason. The confirmation of life after death? That'd change everything. She had seen the answers to questions she didn't want to ask, and she'd paid the price for it. It was almost like it was planned, that the cruel hand of fate was toying with her.

At the same time, she and Trem... For the brief time they knew each other, they'd become friends. Gabby had saved her life in the Styx afterall. Plus the thought of abandoning her while she was still looking for her parents didn't sit well with Gabby at all. The two thoughts clashed with each other and made her feel so conflicted.

Her pace slowed down, to give her enough time to think it over. The manor house was still hidden behind the wall of overgrown vegetation, she'd have enough time. It took about five minutes to get out of the mess, eventually coming face to face with the manor again. She walked over the gravel, the silence broken by the crunching noise beneath her feet. Maybe one day the place may look inviting, but now it looked as cold and unwelcoming as ever.

Inside, everyone was concerned. Jenny and Skye were in the Observatory while Abhay was in the garden. That left Trem and Hogarth in the living room. Trem was laid out on the sofa, staring up at the ceiling while Woody flew around the top of the room.

"Hogarth, can I ask a question?" Trem called to the Etemmu.

The late actor was staring out of the window, into the light of day that had been closed off for years. He turned around and hovered over. "But of course."

Trem sat up and moved back a little, so she was sat upright on the arm of the sofa. "Did you lose anyone? Before... What happened,

happened?"

Trem noticed Hogarth's gaze dart into the distance, a dry smile crept onto his face. "Both my parents. My Father was always a bull of a man, and my Mother? Oh she suffered no fools. I clearly inherited none of that." He patted his stout belly and chuckled to himself.

"More loyal than any pet or servant to his master, more giving than any person." The smile softly faded from his face. "So they would never let any such trivial issue as illness take them out." He glanced at the floor. "Carriage accident."

Trem leant closer, both intrigued and sympathetic, though trying to convey as much of the latter as possible. "How did you cope?"

Hogarth sniffed and looked up. "The show must go on. Is that not the proverbial mandate?" He held his arms out as if addressing an audience. "All the world's a stage, and all the men and women merely players."

The young Manzazzu couldn't help but smile. "Is that what passed for English in your time?" The two shared a brief chuckle between them.

"All pain is temporary my dear. Even the worst agony, the most prolonged torture has it's time. When one loses something so close, once they have grieved, what does one do?"

Trem thought for a moment. "What do they do?" She asked.

"They exchange the pain for something else. It becomes nostalgia, so many happy memories to look back on and enjoy. The childhood experiences, when the world seemed brighter and happier. The quiet, tender moments of love. The small, inconsequential things that brought us such joy."

It was Trem's turn to be lost in memory. "I know what you mean. Like when my parents gave me Sammy for the first time. They handed me this little scaley thing and told me to treat it like a sibling. That night we had a feast and slept under the stars in the garden. What about you?"

Hogarth perched himself at the other end of the sofa, just far enough to make the room feel cool. "When they found out the news that I was cast in my first big production. A poetic retelling of the Arcadia myth."

Trem's eyebrows raised in curiosity. "Interesting. I don't know that one."

Hogarth rolled his eyes. "No one does."

Their nostalgia was broken by the sound of the door opening. The two looked up and saw Gabby enter the house, her head hung.

"Let the others know." Trem commanded as she looked back at Gabby. Hogarth nodded and sank through the floor.

Gabby dragged her feet across the marble floor, over the symbol etched into the tyles. She hadn't noticed it before, a crescent moon shape with a line going through it, curving at the top and forming an upside down triangle. It didn't really have much of an effect on her though, it hardly mattered.

Trem got up from her sofa and walked up to Gabby. They both met at the entrance to the living room.

Trem stared into Gabby's eyes. They were so tired, hopeless and missing that wonderful spark of life Trem had seen before. The two stared at each other for a good few seconds before Trem embraced Gabby. All she could do was close her eyes while she felt her friend cry into her shoulder. She already felt the tears on her bare arm. She remained silent for a while, allowing Gabby to get it all out uninterrupted.

A few minutes later, the two were sat on the sofa, with the other Etemmu around them. Jenny and Skye were the closest to Gabby, floating behind her, while Abhay and Hogarth were in front of the sofa. Trem had her arm around Gabby.

"Is there anything we can do?" Trem asked. She honestly felt really guilty about the whole thing.

Of course, she didn't know much about the time lag in the Styx, it was an unpredictable thing, following no real logic. Time was something that humans create to track the hours in the day, not something Manzazzu needed to do. She could spend days in the Styx and come out hours later. Alternatively, she could be in the Styx for minutes and come out the next day, it made no sense to her. It's why she neglected to tell Gabby. Now, they had to answer to the consequences.

Gabby was staring blankly into the distance, only managing a quiet few words. "No thanks..."

Jenny floated closer, beginning to extend her hand. She drew it back when she remembered how that would be a bad idea. "Will you be leaving us?" She asked, a slight quiver detected in her voice.

"It's not like we're keeping you a hostage, we're not that kind of people." Abhay continued. "We will understand whatever decision you make. It should be what's right for you, not for us."

Gabby's tired eyes looked up, glancing around the room. "I don't want to." Came the response. "But I hate having to tell my parents lies. It's making me feel so dirty on the inside, on top of all the guilt I feel..."

Trem put a hand on Gabby's lap. "You know I wouldn't have suggested it if I'd have known." She began, turning in her seat so she was face to face with Gabby. "I just didn't know the lag in the Styx would be that bad. I thought it may be an hour or two tops. Like I said, you're the first Human that's ever been inside the Styx, it's all a big uncertainty."

Her shoulders sank as she saw Gabby's tired expression was unchanged. "But it's no excuse is it?" She took her friend's cold hand in her own. "I don't expect you to forgive me Gabby, but know I am really truly sorry...I'll do anything I can do make things right."

Gabby gently pulled her hand out of Trem's and let it hang by her side. "There's nothing you can do Trem. I've just got to deal with it myself really. Gran died and my parents had to deal with me being missing." She caught a glimpse of Trem's face, she was so full of pity and woe that it looked like she, a Manzazzu, a ghost summoning non human from a world Gabby couldn't even fathom, was ready to break down alongside her.

"Trem, I do forgive you. Like you said, you couldn't help it. How were you supposed to know anyway." She shrugged.

Then, a thought hit Trem, causing her eyes to widen. Gabby clocked this and tilted her head. "What is it?" She asked.

Trem leaned forward, her face inches away from Gabby's. "What if I was able to give you that last goodbye?"

The heads in the room all shot towards Trem. The four Etemmu looked a mix of confused and concerned. As for Gabby, that spark in her eye that had long since extinguished was finally rekindled. "How?"

Trem looked down at her hands, at the assortment of gemstone encrusted rings on her fingers. "What if I could bring her back as an Etemmu?"

Now it was Gabby's turn for her eyes to widen. She'd never considered that, but now it seemed like the obvious choice. "You can do that?"

Skye interrupted, she looked deeply concerned at this idea. "Hold on Trem. If it works, she's only been gone a day or two. We've all been gone for years, she'd be very easy to turn corrupted."

Hogarth nodded frantically. "I'd rather not have one of those things attacking the house."

Trem held her hand out to Hogarth. "Calm down." She turned to Skye, who's worried look Trem was so unused to. It usually meant something bad would happen, but given the risks she had already endured thus far, this was pretty low on the severity scale.

"Summoning Etemmu is always a risk. I took four big risks in bringing you all back. Besides, you all came of your own free will." Trem's voice grew softer and more gentle as she turned to her friend. "Besides, we're doing this for Gabby. I owe her this much."

The two shared another hug, Gabby thanking Trem quietly while the young Manzazzu had her hand on the back of Gabby's head. Pulling away from the hug, the two rested their foreheads on each others and smiled. Regardless of how this would go, for better or worse, they would do it together.

Meanwhile, Treman emerged from the mirror in his room. There was a part of him that felt his heart sink as his once solid lower half had now been replaced with faded nothingness, the Styx was so much more ideal for his plans. But he needed to complete his work in the world of the living first. He caught his reflection in the mirror, his eyes were already past the point of no return and he could feel something boiling up inside of him. Hesitantly, he opened his lips and looked at his teeth. The bottom row had become jagged, his canine had become sharp. He had days at best, before he became lost to the Faragh state.

He ran his hand through his white hair, but stopped suddenly. His hand closed into a fist as he moved it down till it was in front of his face. He opened his palm, revealing a large patch of hair shed from his head. The process was getting faster, it must have been that last journey into the Styx, sped up the process. He had planned on playing the long game till he could play no longer, but that idea had to be scrapped now.

He heard voices coming from beyond his locked door. Moving through it, he could hear the conversation much clearer.

"Right Gabby, you stay here, I'll get things ready." He could hear his Granddaughter clearly, and she was with that blasted human again. Trem disappearing wouldn't cause much suspicion, but the human? Questions could be raised.

Treman shrugged that idea off. "Humans aren't that smart." He muttered to himself as he watched Trem leave the living room and head to the entrance of the house.

Trem opened the door which lead down to the store room. Treman descended into the same room, arriving seconds before Trem reached the bottom of the stairs.

"This is not a good time. I'm busy, old man."

She walked up to one of the many work desks and took several items. A little fabric bag full of stones, a leather bound book and several candles.

Before Trem could head out of the room, Treman blocked the door, staring her down. "You're planning to summon another Etemmu, aren't you?" He sighed under his breath. "Aren't there already enough irritating Humans crowding the house as it is?"

If Treman was solid, Trem would have given the old man such a pummeling. As that was out of the question, she instead just stared daggers at him. "It's not that. Gabby lost her Grandmother..."

Treman responded with a tone that rubbed Trem up the wrong way even then usual. "Oh how sad, what a shame. Why should we care?"

Trem held up the book and grit her teeth. "I do. I'm doing this for Gabby. I'd like to see you stop us." A devious smirk crossed her face. "Oh wait, you can't. So be a dear and shut up. All you are, the sum total of your power, it's all just meaningless words."

She walked through him, as much as it caused her to shiver and cause ice to form on her skin, it was worth it to see him cringe. She closed the door behind her, leaving Treman in the room.

The former Manzazzu elder huffed as he turned on the spot. He stopped as he caught his reflection in the mirror. Staring back at him was a young Manzazzu, with a sculptured face, his jawline angular and his eyes were as black as pitch. His silvery hair was full and thick and there was a slight stubble on his chin. He hadn't looked that way in decades.

Yet, with one brief blink, the young Manzazzu in his prime disappeared and he was left looking back at this fading, withered old Etemmu. He must really be slipping away faster then he expected.

The time for action was now. Everything had been put into motion and he was the trigger. Though, to put it into action now would be risky. Best to give Trem and the human what they want. One last pleasure before they're separated. He rose up and floated through the roof, returning to his room.

Chapter Ten: "One Last Time"

"He'll find out at any moment..."
"He can't stop me."

Trem opened the door to the Ishtar Gate chamber and lead the way down the flight of steps. Gabby was so torn, was this the right thing to do? The grief of knowing she caused her Grandmother to turn corrupted and become a hideous beast would be far worse than the thought of not saying a proper goodbye.

When they reached the bottom of the steps, Trem set to work. She opened the small book to it's second page and set it out on the floor, near the Gate. On a double page spread was a circular diagram, showing the placement of the stones and the candles.

Trem muttered the instructions under her breath. "Red, blue, green, gold, brown and orange..." She began to place the stones in a circle around the deactivated Gate, a precise distance between each other. Pausing to adjust one or two by a few centimeters, she moved onto the candles. Four of them placed at the compass points around the Gate. When they were all in the right order, her sapphire thumb ring began to glow. Kneeling down by the candles, she flicked her finger at the wicks. One by one, the candles began to burn a deep royal blue flame. Soon, the room was illuminated in the same light.

Gabby just stood back and let Trem concentrate. This looked like precise work and the last thing she wanted to do was halt her flow. If this is what it took to summon the others, no wonder there were only four of them. The process still boggled her mind, the fact that Manzazzu could coerce souls from the other side, entice them into the world of the living was just mental. Not even her movies would think up something so bizarre. Until the thought of her Grandmother reappearing as an Etemmu entered her head, Gabby hadn't really gripped how surreal the whole thing was. The fact they were ghosts was hard enough to swallow to begin with.

Once Trem was finished getting everything prepared, she turned her head, staring back at her. "We're all set." Trem said, looking slightly nervous herself.

"Trem, do you really think we should do this?" Gabby asked, holding her own hand. "What if it goes wrong? Do you have a plan?"

Gabby could see Trem biting her lip. She didn't need to answer after that, the Manzazzu's expression said enough. "I'll just make sure that won't happen. I've done this half a dozen times in the past..."

Gabby took a step forward, afraid to ask the next question. "And were they all a success?"

The two remained silent for a moment. Thankfully, the sound from the top of the stairs snapped them both out of it. The four Etemmu were watching, keeping their distance. Gabby could tell they were frightened of the Ishtar Gate. Afraid another monster would emerge and cause havoc maybe? Or fear of returning to the afterlife?

They all have made the manor their home, but according to the so called laws, they would have to return in the end. That seemed tragic in a way, make new friends like that, always knowing they would leave you in the end. Maybe that's why Trem said the Manzazzu summoned them to gather knowledge and experiences, nothing in that mission statement mentions friendship.

Being a Manzazzu must really suck, it certainly seems the case for poor Trem. Gabby knew that she had it better off then Trem, which is hardly fair as Trem is a Manzazzu, clearly something much bigger and more impressive than Humans. Despite that though, Trem felt Human to her. She could feel pain, sadness... Love.

"It's time." Trem called. Gabby could feel her heart begin to race. "Good luck everyone." Trem continued as she turned on the spot to face the Ishtar Gate.

"I trust you Trem...." Gabby replied, kind of out of nowhere, but it made her feel better. She could see that got a smile out of Trem.

Holding out her hands, Trem began the ritual to open the Ishtar Gate. The rings began to glow, like they did before. Trem drew a circle in the air, followed by a cross and finally a straight line down the middle. The Ishtar Gate opened itself once again. "Gabby, your Grandmother's name...?"

Gabby found herself mesmerized by the Ishtar Gate, the moving space within the gold and blue structure was oddly hypnotic. Trem's voice brought her out of it. "Oh, Eliza Morgan, that's her name. If you need full name, Elizabeth Patricia Morgan."

"Thank you." Trem replied. She planted her feet firmly on the ground and kept her hands held out.

Taking in a deep breath, Trem's rings began to glow at once, the stones placed around her began to pulsate. The blue flames in the candles began to grow brighter and stronger. Trem closed her eyes and called into the portal. "Elizabeth Patricia Morgan, if you can hear me... Follow my voice."

Gabby felt herself shake once again, she had already broken a sweat and was feeling a hundred emotions at once. Her heart skipped a beat when she heard what happened next.

"Hello?" Came a distant, echoing voice. It was Gabby's Grandma! "Sorry dear, you'll have to speak up, I think it's a bad reception. Are you going through a tunnel? My hearing isn't what it was..."

She thinks she's on the phone? Honestly, even though she was already tearing up just hearing her voice again, she also laughed. That was so like her Gran.

"I'm here with your Granddaughter, Gabby. She wants to talk to you. Can you hear where I am?" Trem shouted into the void.

"Maybe, I'm not sure dear, could you give me a bit of a hand?" Eliza requested.

Trem obliged by pointing a finger at one of the candles. A pillar of blue flames followed Trem's finger as she sent it straight into the Ishtar Gate. "Try following this!"

There was a moments silence, it filled the room. It was an appropriately deathly silence too, but it was finally broken when Eliza called back at them. "Oh that's much better, thank you dear! You'll have to bear with me, I'm 87 you know!"

Trem turned to face Gabby and they both shared a big grin. "Get ready, she's coming through!"

Gabby's brain was racing at light speed. What would she say? She wouldn't have time to explain it all. She had to keep things precise, to the point. Make it count and not waste any time pointlessly procrastinating. When she had a pretty good idea, she nodded in response to Trem. "Okay, I'm ready!" She really wasn't, but there was no turning back now. She'd finally get some closure in all this, and Trem was helping her do so. For better or worse, this was happening.

The Ishtar Gate's portal spat out a bright light, the surface crashed like waves on a shoreline and the air suddenly became full of... Caramel sweets, the kind Eliza would always eat. The blue flames retreated back into the candles and the stones lights flickered before going out. The portal parted and a human form aimlessly staggered out of it. Once the portal closed and the light from the candles and stones had died down, the Etemmu began to form. Gabby started to walk towards the gate, stepping over the small body of water circling the structure.

There she was, her Grandmother, reconstituted as an Etemmu. Trem lowered her hands and took hold of one of Gabby's. "Remember, we don't have long."

Gabby nodded. She could see her Grandma, clear as day. From the shins down, there was nothing, she just faded out of existence, much like the others. While she was a little see through, there was no denying it was her. Gabby put her hand to her mouth, this was so wrong, and yet it still kind of felt right in a way. The closure she'd be able to get out of this would be worth it. She could already feel she was on the verge of sobbing as it was. "Gran, it's me... It's Gabby." Her voice broke slightly.

Eliza looked back at her granddaughter and smiled. "Oh hello Gabby dear! Are you alright love? You look like you've seen a ghost!"

Because she was seeing a ghost, there was no easy way around it. Gabby thought she was re-defining the term at this point. She sniffed and returned the smile. "I'm alright. How do you feel?" She asked.

Eliza patted her chest, missing the fact that she was semi translucent. "Oh a little strange dear, but I think it's just because I didn't take my pills today."

She was still exactly the same, not wanting to cause a fuss. In a way, it made things easier for Gabby. No one wants their last memory of someone to be with a grey face and a tube up the nose. At the same time, seeing the departed as a ghost? Pick and choose your poison Gabby thought. Though this may make things worse, eat into the precious seconds before her Gran would corrupt and be lost forever, Gabby asked another question.

"What do you remember happening?"

Trem glanced over, concerned but remaining silent. Given the importance of this whole thing and the risks she was taking, was this the best thing to ask?

"Well..." Eliza began. "I was in a hospital bed, the nice doctor had taken my readings, but I was a little tired so I didn't hear what he said. I heard some people clamouring over me but I'd already nodded off at that point. I did have a funny dream though..."

Gabby took another step closer. "Go on."

"Well in my dream, I was in a funny little boat on a river. It was all a little hot for my liking, especially since I was wearing this cloak over me. Then another boat passed us, and you were on it!"

That sent a jarring shock through Gabby's body. When she and Trem saw that boat on the Styx River... It was her Gran on that boat. They were just feet away and she never realised it. Unable to hold in her emotions anymore, Gabby quietly cried.

"Oh love, what's the matter?" Eliza began to float towards Gabby with the aim to give her a hug. Gabby backed away quickly, almost stepping into the water around the Gate.

"It's okay." She sniffed. She wiped her eyes on her trench coat sleeve. "Tell me more about this dream of yours."

Straightening back up, Eliza held her hands together. "Well, if you're sure? So I was on this funny boat going up a river, then we sailed up to this manky old dockyard place. I could hear your Grandfather calling my name, so I followed his voice. He lead me to this funny old place that ended in a light, so I just followed his voice." She wiped her cheek, a few tears had rolled down her non corporeal face. "Oh, what am I like? It was just a dream anyway."

No, it wasn't. Not at all, she remembered the journey. Gabby's heart began to race... Should she tell her? How much time did she have left? Well, if she didn't have long left, she deserved to know the truth. "Gran,

I have something to tell you."

"Oh? What is it Gabby?"

Gabby felt a cold shiver go up her spine, she crossed her arms and swallowed hard. "Well...It wasn't a dream..."

Trem could feel herself sweating, she knew from experience this part of the summoning was always the hardest, telling the Etemmu they were dead, and have been for a while. Hogarth was in denial, Abhay was upset, Skye was angry and Jenny was depressed.

Eliza just looked puzzled. "Wh...What do you mean?" She stuttered, the expression turning every second from slow realisation to concern.

Gabby meanwhile was fighting to get her words out in between uncontrollable sobs, she really had reached her limit of self control. "You died Gran... Your heart gave out in your sleep...." That felt more painful than knowing her Gran died when she was away. "You said you could fight the infection..."

Eliza shook her head, her mouth slightly agape. "But...How can I be? I'm talking to you, I'm still...Aren't I?" She followed Gabby's gaze to the water around the Gate. Eliza hovered over and peered down in her reflection. What was staring back at her was a ghostly, see through version of herself. "So if it wasn't a dream... Was that me going to heaven then?"

Gabby covered her eyes and face with her hand and nodded silently, it had all become too much for her. Honestly, this hurt so much more then before. Gabby had already begun to regret her actions.

"Then how did you bring me back?" Eliza asked, hovering back to her original position in front of the Ishtar Gate.

Trem couldn't remain silent any longer. She stepped out from the shadows and gave a little bow to Eliza. "That would be me ma'am. I'm Trem, a friend of Gabby's. Your Granddaughter felt really guilty because when you... Passed away, she was with me at the time."

Eliza stared at Trem for a moment. She was finding it hard to grasp. All the years she'd been on the Earth, she'd never heard of such a thing before. But the evidence was undeniable, she was there, a ghost... All because Gabby felt so bad about things.

She turned her attention to her Granddaughter. "Oh Gabby love..."

Gabby looked up from her wet palms, her skin already wrinkling because of the moisture. She and her Gran both locked eyes, Gabby's showing nothing but sadness and regret. All Gabby wanted to do was punch herself in the face for doing something so stupid enough to make the situation worse.

But that changes when she saw her Gran smile. "You're the best Granddaughter I could have asked for. You did all this because you wanted to say a proper goodbye, is that right?"

Sniffing again, Gabby tried to regain some composure, though she thought she was still a mess. "Yeah, yeah that's right..."

Eliza moved towards Gabby and put her hands close to Gabby's face, she may not be able to hold her Granddaughter, but it was enough. Sure, Gabby could feel layers of ice forming on her cheeks, no doubt causing damage to the skin and blood cells but it felt like such a minor problem. "I love you Gabby. I'm just really happy that I could be there for you when you were growing up. Now look at you, not a child anymore. You don't need me anymore."

Gabby tried to put her hand on Eliza's arm, but instead she went right through it, succeeding in coating her hand in ice. Eventually the burn became too painful to deal with and she took a step back, covering her face with her hands.

"Oh love I'm so sorry, I didn't know...!" Eliza began, shocked and horrified she was causing Gabby pain all along.

Trem moved to Gabby's side, with one hand on her friend's shoulder. "Are you okay? Let me have a look at you."

Gabby turned to Trem, her cheeks red raw, the veins bulging and it was clear to all she was in a lot of pain. But to Gabby, it was all minor or just irrelevant, it'd pass in time. What she felt she needed to do was finish her talk with her Gran. "It's fine, I'm fine." She felt the ice melt away from her face as she continued.

"Gran, I want you to know that I love you and I'm really sorry I wasn't there when you... Well, you know."

Gabby's heart sank as she saw her Gran's eyes begin to start fading, the brown hues turning a haunting white. The worst thing is, Eliza didn't seem to notice. "I love you too Gabby. You do me a favour and keep being strong. Will you do that, for me?"

"Of course I will." She replied, trying to hold back the panic she was feeling. "I don't think you can stay any longer..." Before she could continue, Eliza turned to the Ishtar Gate.

There was a small gust of wind that ran through the chamber, causing both Gabby and Trem to shudder. For Eliza meanwhile, the wind carried a voice, one that she hadn't heard in years. It sounded like her husband. But how was that possible?

"No, your right.... Your Grandfather wants to talk to me..." She turned back to Gabby and with one last smile, she began backing to the Ishtar Gate. "I love you Gabby, tell your parents I love them too."

Gabby choked out her response rather unceremoniously, not that she cared. "I will. Thanks for everything Gran, I love you too..."

With a small wave, Eliza disappeared into the Ishtar Gate. Before the water like ripples subsided, Gabby could have sworn she heard two familiar voices talking. After a few seconds, the room fell into silence, and all that was left was an empty room. Gabby was left standing there, staring at the deactivated Gate. Trem glanced over, she couldn't tell what was melted frost and what was tears. The other Etemmu who had been watching from the top of the stairs remained silent, waiting for Trem or Gabby to make the first move.

"Gabby? Are you okay?" She asked, putting her hand gently onto her friend's shoulder.

Gabby wiped her hands over her face, a mix of warm, salty tears and freezing melted ice. She looked back at Trem. "I guess I will be."

She was able to force out a half smile to reassure her friend. Though things had taken a funny turn, she'd done what she set out to do. She had said her goodbyes to her Gran, and she managed to pass without corruption. The worst of it was over, and Gabby had come out of it feeling better. Trem lead her back up the steps, to the living room.

A few minutes later, Gabby was sat on the sofa, her trench coat draped over her legs like a blanket and a hot mug of... Something in her hands. Trem said it was made from the leafs that grew on a certain Manzazzuan plant. It smelt like some kind of tea, but it's murky pink color was rather distinctive.

Blowing on it slightly, she took a sip. It was actually rather nice, a subtle taste of rose water on top of what was resembling a weak tea. She and Trem would make an absolute steal at those health shops, they could charge stupid money for it if they said it was hand picked, organic and free range. Not that plants could be free range, who knows, maybe Manzazzu ones could be.

Her random thoughts were interrupted by the arrival of Trem and the Etemmu. Trem sat next to Gabby and the others huddled around her. It made Gabby feel a little swamped. "You don't have to crowd around me guys, I'm fine.."

On her instructions, the four slid away, Hogarth and Abhay moving to one side of the sofa while Jenny and Skye moved to the other sofa, facing directly at Gabby and Trem. "Sorry sugar, we just get worried is all." Jenny apologised.

"Guys, it's okay. I've not been in a car crash or anything." Gabby tried to reassure, though given the looks on everyone's faces, she didn't do a very good job. Everyone was still looking at her with concerned looks. "Seriously, I'm fine. I wouldn't lie to you all."

"You sure?" Skye asked as Jenny whispered something Gabby couldn't quite make out. It was actually kind of nice to see Skye worry, considering when they first met, Skye would have skinned her if she was given half a chance, and if she was solid.

"Yeah, I mean it, I am fine. It's a little draining all this, but I'll survive." Before she took another sip of her drink, she muttered. "I always seem to."

Abhay floated towards the sofa. "Do you and Trem want a minute alone? We don't mind if you want a little space."

Trem looked to Gabby for an answer, but all Gabby did was drink and remain quiet. She gave Abhay a gesture with her head and the

Etemmu slowly scattered, with Skye and Jenny going off together.

Now they were alone, Trem took Gabby's hand as gently as she could and spoke softly and quietly. "Is there anything I can do for you?"

Gabby bit her lip and drummed her fingers on the mug. Part of her was wondering what she'd unearth if she asked this, especially since it was all very clear to her that this world was not one she was meant to know about, let alone see. But she was going to be in it for the long run, and if she wanted to help Trem then she'd need to know. "Yeah, there is..." She began. She put the mug on the table and turned to Trem. "Can you tell me about you and your kind, the Manzazzu, if that's okay?"

Trem got up from the sofa and walked over to the bookcase, below the long tapestry of her family tree. She pulled out a blue and gold book, showing signs of aging and was covered in a thin layer of dust. Trem blew away the dust and shook it about for a second before sitting back down. As she did, Woody flew down from the ceiling and perched on Gabby's shoulder, receiving a light pat on the head from her finger.

Trem opened the book to it's first page and held out her palm, one of her rings glowing as she looked up from the lightly browning pages. "If this sounds like a kids book, it is. Don't take it the wrong way Gabby, but I was taught by this book, it's perfect for your first history lesson. A lot of this is either guess work or romanticized anyway. Dad told me no one really knows for sure how the Manzazzu came about exactly."

Gabby crossed her legs and leant forward, resting her hand on her hand. "That makes sense. Us Humans can't decide if the universe was created by a God or came into being in a big bang. So we've got that much in common."

Trem could see Gabby's smile was real, she really was doing alright, in light of everything. She was so strong, stronger then Trem was when she lost her parents. She really was the one... Trem swiped her hand upwards, dragging the illustration off the page and into the air before Gabby, whose mouth was agape in awe. A simple human figure, blank faced and made of colored paper emerged, brandishing a sword and shield.

Trem began reading as the paper figure swung it's blade around. "In the beginning, Man was discovered. He was a violent creature, capable of much destruction..." The paper figure put his sword down, which sank back into the paper. Trem flicked up two more figures, one of which was much smaller than the others. A family, the two new figures being a wife and child.

Trem continued reading. "But Man was also capable of great compassion. Mankind fought for power, so if they were given a new power, one greater than anything any war could give them...Maybe then they will evolve."

The figures all looked up to the sky. Trem gently moved a new figure from the pages, bathed in a dawn glow and wearing a flowing blue and gold dress, their face obscured by a hood. "The Goddess Ishtar descended onto a group of Humans, gifting them for their compassion and good deeds. She declared that they were to be her trusted servants, the Manzazzu, who will watch over the River Styx for her. She left three gifts to her followers, a ring made of a precious stone...."

Trem held her other hand up, which was still clad in all manner of gem encrusted rings as she raised her eyebrows and smiled, as if to tick it off the list. "...A sword made of brilliant blue and gold metals the likes of which they had never seen..."

Trem nodded to the corridor that connected the living room to the rest of the house, and the rack of swords matching the same description, the very same Gabby had used to kill the Faragh in the Styx.

"...And a gateway, from which you will be able to access my realm." That explains the Ishtar Gate.

The paper figures of the Humans returned to the page, but Trem kept the figure of Ishtar and held her hand out to it. The four inch living illustration hovered over Trem's hand as she put the book on her lap. "So the legend says." Trem's little finger rose up as the little Ishtar placed it's hand on it. Trem chuckled to herself as she picked the book up and lowered her hand onto the page. The mini Ishtar walked back onto the page and became two dimensional once again.

Her ring stopped glowing as she gently closed the book. "So I hope that helps with where the Manzazzu came from. Honestly, that's all I know. I never went to the Academy at Euphretia, that's the Manzazzuan homeland. I only know what my parents taught me."

Gabby finally closed her mouth. "So, Ishtar gave those first Manzazzu a ring, sword and a gateway and hundreds of years later you've got rings for each finger, loads of swords and a mini gateway into Limbo?"

Trem's shoulders shrugged and her hands were held up. "Guess so." She said with a smile. "So, what do you want to know next?" She noticed Gabby's gaze had moved to something behind her. She followed her friend's eyes and looked straight at her parents portrait. "Oh, you want to know about them?"

Gabby immediately entered fast mode as she sprung into a flurry of explanations and apologies. "Well not if you don't want to! Sorry it's just they really seem to have a great impression on you..."

Trem turned slowly away from the portrait and smiled to herself. "They are magnificent. I remember them well. My Mother's family are some minor members of the Manzazzuan aristocracy, I don't pretend to know much about that, but it gave my late Grandfather something to boast about. My Dad though? Showman, and a pretty brilliant one at that. Mum carved little Woody there, she brought him to life. That's kind of our thing." Woody cooed happily as Gabby stroked him again.

Trem put the book on the table and stood up once again. "In fact, I want to show you something." She held her hand out, ready to help Gabby off her seat. Gabby took her hand and was pulled up onto her feet, pausing only to put on her trench coat.

Trem gave her a little wave as they headed to the exit of the house. Trem turned right and began to climb up the stairs, Gabby having to almost sprint to keep pace. Catching up with her on the steps, she put her hand on the banister as she looked around the first level of the house. Woody took the opportunity to take flight and ascended to the glass ceiling. Gabby watched the little guy disappear into the sky. By the time her attention snapped back to her surroundings, Trem was already by one of the many doors. "Where are we going?" She asked, following Trem through the door, where upon they faced a wooden spiral staircase.

"Somewhere special." Trem teased as she began to climb up the steps. Gabby groaned, more steps. Still, she'd be getting a lot of exercise today. The flight was mercifully short though, only a few dozen steps before they emerged at their destination.

It was the mansion's observatory, which could be seen on the outside of the house, the glass dome on the roof was a clear giveaway. Gabby didn't notice it much though, her sight was always on the door and not the mansion itself. The glass panels were held in place by strips of bronze that stretched far into the ceiling which was a good twelve feet above them.

The view was amazing, Gabby could see all of Mortsbury, the hills the little town nestled inside. It was high noon and the sun was high in the sky.

Looking around the room, the bottom of the dome was made of

bricks, with a long, curved seat covered in cushions around it. A few drawers were nestled in the chair as well. In the middle of the room was a large, ornate telescope. Attached to it was some unusual dials and switches written in that odd Manzazzuan language Gabby couldn't even begin to understand. A small table also occupied the room, with a bottle of some drink inside it.

The other four Etemmu were already there before Trem entered, and when she emerged from the stairs, they all stood to attention. "Oh Trem, I do apologise, we can make ourselves scarce if you so wish..." Hogarth began, on another long and drawn out outburst.

"It's okay Hogarth, I'd rather you all stay anyway." Trem reassured, turning to watch Gabby walk into the observatory.

Gabby was taken aback by the size of the room, it was much larger than she expected. Stepping onto the wooden floor, she looked all around with the biggest smile on her face. "You can see so much from up here." She pointed and laughed. "I can literally see my house from here!" She pointed to the tiny little building in the distance, barely identifiable. "This is so cool Trem."

Trem had a devilish little grin on her face. "Oh you haven't seen the best thing yet." She teased. She headed over to the telescope and flicked one of the leavers. On her command, there was a loud clunk which nearly made Gabby jump out of her skin.

"What was that?"

Almost as if on cue, a series of curved metal shutters appeared and began to cover the dome. Once they had slid into the bronze girders holding the glass in place, the room was left in darkness. Before Gabby could mention the dark, the room was illuminated by the telescope. On the dark surface of the dome was projected a brilliant star field. Millions of stars which lit up the room, along with a full moon that hung high on the dome.

"Okay, this is even cooler!" Gabby was spinning on the spot, laughing to herself and being just in awe of how beautiful the massive map of the stars looked.

Trem began to fiddle with the controls of the telescope. "This does more than project stars. It records them. All I need to do is put in a date and we can see any beautiful night sky we want." Trem noticed she was using the word "we" a lot. Gabby really was leaving a great impression on her. "Prepare to be even more amazed." She finished inputting the date and pulled the lever.

Gabby wondered how she could ever be more impressed. The stars changed again, and now it morphed to a meteor shower, streaking darts of light shooting across the dome. The falling stars danced a random waltz of white across the pitch black sky and curved with the shape of the dome.

"Okay Trem, that is seriously amazing... How even...?"

Before she could finish, Trem turned away from the telescope. "Sorry, one second!" She called, going to one of the drawers. "I just have to find something, it won't be special without it..."

Gabby turned around to look at Trem. Special? She wondered what Trem meant. This whole thing was pretty special as it was.

Skye kept Jenny close and put a hand around her love. "Aren't they so cute together?" Jenny asked, watching Trem and Gabby with a smile.

Kissing her lightly on the forehead, Skye whispered her response. "Yeah, but not as cute as you." They both giggled, Jenny would be blushing if she could.

Abhay crossed his arms and leaned over to Hogarth. "Young love at it's finest, there's nothing quite like it is there?" He gestured to Trem and Gabby. "Do you have any pearls of wisdom for us, wordsmith? A limerick, a poem? A raunchy little number?" He nudged and wiggled his eyebrows playfully.

Hogarth let out a little unsure chuckle. "Well good sir, it's pure. Pure, untainted and uncorrupted. These women have their lives ahead of them do they not? Unlike us, their lives are that one adventure yet to be written. While we are left yearning the joys of lives past, they can go into the world and claim it as their own. That is what real freedom is."

Abhay's eyes widened as he turned to Gabby and Trem. "Well I'll be, Hogarth... What have you been reading?"

Trem pulled out something Gabby couldn't make out from the drawer. "I found it!" Gabby was so unfamiliar with the sound of excitement in Trem's voice, but it was so nice and refreshing.

Trem walked over to the table and placed down the device. Gabby looked at the strange thing, and it wasn't until Trem rotated a large metal speaker to its upright position that Gabby recognised it as an old fashioned gramophone. A record was already loaded and as soon as the speaker was positioned, it triggered the record to start spinning.

"What's the music for?" Gabby asked, watching Trem put the needle onto the record.

After a second, the music began to play. Gabby actually recognised it, a sweeping ballad from a few decades ago. It already made her feel happy and warm on the inside, topped with the sheer spectacle of the meteor shower around them.

Trem straightened her back and offered her hand. "Miss Morgan, may I have this dance?" She asked, in a posh, well spoken voice.

Gabby knew exactly where this was going, Trem was really set on giving her a wonderful experience, to help her with what just happened maybe? All she knew was this, it would be rude to say no. "It would be my honour my lady."

Trem took Gabby's hand and with her other one, she gently took Gabby's back. The smiling and blushing Human mirrored her hand placement and they began a slow moving ballad.

Gabby could feel Trem's breath, it tickled slightly, which caused her to chuckle quietly. Trem meanwhile maintained a warm and caring smile. They danced around the room, the lights from the telescope bouncing off their faces, their shadows moving around the dome as smoothly as if they were flying. Trem slowly span Gabby around and lowered her off her feet with one hand.

Meanwhile, Jenny had dragged Skye into the middle of the room and they took to the skies, dancing their own waltz to the music. Abhay and Hogarth watched on, content to be the audience in this charming picture. Hogarth did feel Abhay's arm slip around his shoulder. Hogarth didn't mind though, this was a nice moment, deserved to be shared.

Pulling Gabby back up onto her feet, Trem's hands returned to their original position and she lead Gabby into another waltz, circling the telescope. All the time, she was lost in Gabby's brilliant eyes. Unlike her pitch black excuses for eyes, they were so bright and beautiful. After what happened that day, Gabby could still be happy. The knowledge that she gave this Human a small amount of joy on one of the most painful days of her life brought her to tears.

Before Gabby could ask why Trem started crying, she yelped as she found herself being hoisted into the air. Trem held her stomach and held her above her head, turning slowly on the spot.
"Whaa...! Trem!" Gabby called, but she felt safe in her new friend's hands. She held out her arms and let herself be spun around several times, the stars moving around her just adding to the experience.

This was brilliant.

Trem lowered Gabby gradually and gently placed her on the ground. Putting her hands on Gabby's shoulders, she was about to say something to her, but she never got a chance to get it out. Gabby leant in and kissed Trem on the lips, bringing herself in for an embrace. She pulled away and whispered into Trem's ear. "Thank you. Thank you for everything."

Trem rested her head on Gabby's and allowed herself a little cry. "Thank you for being here Gabby." They both went in for another kiss as the music reached it's grand finale. The two women sunk to their knees and embraced each other once again while the two Etemmu danced above them. For Gabby, a new and exciting chapter in her life had well and truly opened. For Trem, she had found someone after all these years of solitude. They were never going to let each other go, they both felt as if nothing in the world could drive them apart.

Chapter Eleven: "Obey The Laws"

"You foolish girl..."
"I am my own Manzazzu, Father. You can't stop me anymore."

Treman looked in the mirror once again. Since he last checked his reflection, another tooth had burst through and turned into a sharp fang. The fangs were pushing against his lip, causing him irritation at best. Another wad of white hair had fallen from his head, leaving an unsightly bald patch. A growl left his lips and he clenched his fist, driving it into the mirror out of anger. All he managed to do was fly his fist through the glass, causing it to ice over. His thoughts were a mess, unorganised and cluttered. Once he could see his reflection again, after the frost had melted, he sighed. The plan was almost in motion, he couldn't lose himself now.

He felt at this stage, he was held together by sheer willpower alone. The one thing keeping his scattered brain together was the thought of ridding the manor and the family name of the stain that was his Granddaughter. If her actions were discovered, bringing a still living human into the house, then it would ruin everything he had worked for. Worst of all, it may lead to an investigation and he would be found out. The Sisters were strong, he had taught them well these past two decades, but they still weren't ready to take on the royal family. His selfless sacrifice would be their final test, and will strengthen their bonds. It would be their role to continue the work he started, continue the campaign he had followed for the last hundred plus years. Treman felt rather smug, he'd be instrumental in a new era, even if it meant dying all over again.

Even as an Etemmu, he could still feel the effects of a disturbance in the Styx. He shivered, a coldness struck his already freezing body. His Granddaughter had activated the Gate, prompting the old man to sigh. "Not more annoying pests..." He muttered. The prospect of more Etemmu crowding the place filled him with dread.

As he left his room, he dug his nails into his palms, he could feel the bones in his shoulders beginning to strain. Prolonging this was necessary, and it seemed to lessen the more he focused on it. "It's all under control..." He tried to reassure himself, popping his shoulder back into place. As for his jagged fangs, he plunged his boney fingers into his mouth, and with all the strength his frail, ghostly body had, he yanked out one of the teeth. The bottom of it was rotten and the fang itself was yellow with some blood staining from where it punctured his lip. Wincing, he did the same with the other. Now at least the signs of corruption would seem to not be as bad as they really were.

Treman figured he'd better inspect the damage, so he left the safety of his chambers and headed into the manor. He glanced around, no sign of any signs of life on the first floor. Descending to the ground floor, choosing to ignore the irritating tweets of anger from Trem's stupid wooden bird, he headed to the Ishtar Gate chambers.

He turned the corner to the chamber but stopped in his tracks, he was staring at the back of the heads of the four other Etemmu, all huddled together, watching the events unfold in the Chamber. Treman was able to hear the conversation going on inside the Chamber from where he was. From what he heard, he'd feel like he'd throw up any minute. "Humans are so sickly..." He thought to himself, wondering if he'd gag at all this, if he had gag reflexes still.

His Grandaughter must have been incredibly idiotic, she'd summon a freshly deceased human who could have turned Faragh any minute and ruin all his plans for the sake of her human pet's gushy sentimentality. After a few more minutes of listening to stomach turning pap, he heard the two coming back up the stairs. In order to avoid detection, he sank into the wall. Once they were en route to the living room, Treman headed down the corridor leading further into the house.

He stopped when he reached one of the many suits of armour that sat dotted around the house. In its hands was a long sword and the helmet was a great helm, leaving two thin strips for eye holes.

"This should still be the one..."

He inspected the suite's hands and sure enough, one of the the fingers had a ring on it, a sapphire to be exact. Trem's Mother's abilities to bring inanimate objects to life came from his side of the family after all, and while the ability to store souls into gemstones and crystals was theoretically possible, it was outlawed by the Manzazzuan Royal Family.

Shows what they knew. With this, Treman had a weapon, and a means to fight. Trem wasn't a gifted fighter, she would be easy to deal with. As for her friend? Treman was looking forward to seeing if Humans bleed as easily as they bruise.

He could hear the two conversing from the living room. Sound had a way of traveling around the empty houses, voices carried great distance. Treman watched from a distance as the two women headed off to the observatory. He flew into the living room and inspected the table, where the book Trem had been reading from was sitting.

"Stupid nonsense." Treman grunted.

Something did catch his eye though, one of the cylinders that Trem had been working on. Upon closer inspection, he realised it was his obituary. "That good for nothing, self entitled..." He stopped himself from screaming his words, though his anger was already boiling over. An attempt to smash the table was met with even more frustration when his fist went right through it. One of the worst things about being an Etemmu, the lack of physical form.

He caught his reflection in the glass. Once again, the young man he once was stared back at him. Around him, three women. To his right, a girl, no older than fifteen. She had deep blue eyes with black hair swept off her dark skin, with two bangs hanging down. To the left, a pale girl who must have been a similar age with sandy hair hanging over a red sash tied over her eyes. The final girl had her arms over his neck, playfully hanging onto his back. The youngest of the three, her eyes were a distinctive lilac and her dirty pink hair was held in place with a red fabric headband. All three wore the standard Manzazzuan tunic usually worn under the robes.

Sleeveless, high collared and black with a coloured trim around the corners of the shoulders, up the middle of the tunic and around the top of the collar, these being red. The Sisters, his greatest achievement. This was many years ago, they had come along so quickly. He remembered that day well, he had gifted them their weapons. A spear, an axe and a razor wire Cat's Cradle. Once he passed on permanently, they would carry on his legacy.

Treman had been lost in thought for so long, he lost track of time. His head shot up as he heard the approaching footsteps of his Granddaughter and her friend. He quickly glanced back down at the glass top of the table, hoping to get one last glimpse of the image from the past. Alas, it had gone. Treman, in a huff, sank into the floor to avoid detection.

Meanwhile, Gabby and Trem had spent a good half an hour in the Observatory, and were on their way back down, followed by the Etemmu. Gabby was wiping her eyes with her sleeve, a big smile still on her face. "Thanks for that Trem, you don't know how much that helped."

Trem kept Gabby's hand held close to hers. Her pale, cold hand being warmed by Gabby's own, returning her friend's smile. "I try my best." The two returned to the living room, where the damp patch on the table hadn't gone unnoticed.

Gabby noticed Trem's smile fade, her eyes darting around the room. "Hey, what's up?" She asked, trying to mirror Trem's glances. The room was quiet and still, no sign of any movement to Gabby.

"Has your Grandfather been in here?" Abhay asked. He looked ready for a fight, fists clenched.

Trem pointed down at the wet patch on the glass, a clear sign that an Etemmu had been in the room, their freezing presence Gabby knew well. "Your....Grandfather?" Why had Gabby not heard of this? She'd heard about Trem's parents at length, but nothing about any other relatives.

The four Etemmu looked ready to pounce at the slightest noise, though Gabby knew they could do little to harm anyone still living, they could still harm each other. Well, she'd hope so if they were going to have to fight someone. Trem pointed two fingers to Skye and Jenny, gesturing to the room containing the Ishtar Gate. Once they slipped away, Trem gestured for Abhay and Hogarth to make their way downwards. Once it was just Trem and Gabby, the Manzazzu walked up to her friend, so close she just needed to whisper. "I'll explain about Treman later, right now we need to find him."

"Why?" Came the reply.

Trem took Gabby's hand and lead her to the staircase, using their footfalls to muffle their speech. "He's...Well he's a total scumbag, and he's on the way out." She glanced back at Gabby and made a scowling face, gesturing at her teeth. "You know, about to corrupt."

Gabby felt her stomach drop from her body. "You mean he could turn into one of those monsters? Why haven't you got rid of him yet?"

Once they reached the top of the stairs, Trem began looking in the various doors, opening them and peering inside before moving onto the next one. "I can't get rid of him till he either wants to move on or if he becomes a Faragh. He's an arrogant old man, he refuses to go back until he's done...Something." She glanced into another room and after a few beats of silence, closed the door. "I don't know or care if he's planning anything, I just want to make sure he's not going to put you in any danger."

Gabby stopped in her tracks while Trem investigated the third room. "I can look after myself, I took out the monster in the Styx, I think I can deal with an old man." She reassured, walking up to Trem and patting her on the shoulder. "Besides, haven't you seen TV shows? They always spread out to cover more ground." She smiled as she joined Trem in checking the rooms.

"Well, okay Gabby. Just be careful..." Any attempt to hide her concern was promptly foiled when Trem's voice broke slightly. Not wanting to meet Gabby's worried gaze, Trem stuck her head into another opened door.

The next few doors lead to rooms with no sign of Treman. Gabby peered into several more before she came across one that seemed suspicious. Suspicious was an understatement really, as the door was locked with a heavy, metal padlock and several planks of rotten, blackened wood were keeping the room from being entered.

"Hey Trem, this isn't his room is it?" She called, pointing at the door.

Trem immediately began to get fidgety, Gabby could see she was getting nervous. "Yeah well, we've not checked the other rooms have we?" She'd not seen Trem this anxious, what was in the room she was afraid of? "We'll check the other rooms and if he's not in those, he'll be in there so we don't need to check..."

She was rambling, it was so unlike her. Gabby stepped aside, letting Trem take the lead and continue inspecting the rooms. When Trem was inspecting one room, Gabby noticed she entered the room rather then peered in. Gabby made use of the time and analysed the door.

The lock itself, on closer inspection, was actually loose. With one strong pull, the door knob came off. Story of Gabby's life she thought with a huff.

She gently placed the knob down on the floor and looked at the rotten old wood keeping the door bolted. Gabby put her hands onto the wood and intended to test its strength. In reality, her small exertion of force pulled the wood clean off the door. Staggering back, she chuckled to herself. "Super strength...." She joked to herself. The other planks were just as easy to remove and after a few seconds, the door was clear for her.

Gabby gently pushed the door open, peering inside. The room was so dark, she could barely see two foot in front of her. She dug into her trench coat pocket and pulled out her phone, turning on the inbuilt flashlight. Gabby began shining the light around the room, but it resulted in very little. Taking one hesitant step into the room, Gabby suddenly felt nervous. She was so busy looking around the place, she failed to notice a thin wire that crossed the floor.

All she heard was a very thin "ping" from the floor. She glanced down but before she could even register it, the door behind her slammed shut with a loud bang, Gabby was startled to the point where she felt like she jumped out of her own skin.

The whole thing happened so fast, the floor erupted and two chains shot out, wrapping themselves tightly around her wrists and pulling her down to the floor. Gabby found herself pinned to the ground, the chains keeping her arms pulled to the side tight. Practically hyperventilating, Gabby struggled against the metal bindings, straining and grunting. The new shot of adrenaline was helping to keep her thrashing violently but it was hardly doing anything substantial. "Trem! Trem help me!" She called in desperation.

Though the room was incredibly dark, Gabby was able to see something in the shadows move. What little light that was coming from the door was bouncing off the sides of a dozen swords, all hanging in the air.

Part of Gabby was getting really sick of fearing for her life, and she wondered why this kept happening, why she kept putting herself in dangerous situations. She thought how selfish she was, her Mum already lost a Mother, if she lost a daughter too, it would wreck her. Trem though? This might rob her of the hope she'd been clinging onto these past few days. Gabby braced herself and as the swords began to fly towards her, she closed her eyes tight and waited.

The sound of the swords flying into the door snapped Gabby out of her defeatist trance. She craned her neck back, far enough to see all the swords had missed her. "Oh thank God for that..." She sighed. Though the chains were already starting to cut the blood circulation to her arms, making them go numb, she felt considerably more comfortable, now the blades weren't pointed at her.

In the darkness, a voice rang out. "What do you think your doing?" Treman appeared from the darkness. His jaw tilted off centre with more teeth having become jagged and a thin trail of blood was trickling into his mouth. Gabby still didn't know how a ghost could bleed, but it wasn't the time for that.

Gabby leaned forwards, as far as the chains holding her to the floor could reach. "What am I doing? What are you doing?!" She yelled back. "You tied me up and threw a dozen bloody swords at me, I only came here because we were worried you turned psycho, I think it's too late for that!" The more Gabby struggle, the tighter the grip on the chains were. "Is this your idea of a sick joke?" Is this why Trem was afraid of going into the room?

Treman floated closer to Gabby, leaning down and looked Gabby up and down, sneering. "Not much to look at after all, what a disappointment."

Gabby seethed with anger. "Excuse you?!" She grit her teeth and shot a look of pure rage at Treman. "Listen here you old zombie...." Before she could continue, Treman clenched his fist and drove it through her face, the Etemmu's non corportial hand phased through Gabby's head, causing the left side of her face to become coated in ice. Gabby panted, desperate for the air that had been knocked out of her. It felt so much more painful then any of the other times it happened, her skin stung and burned under the ice and she recoiled, stifling tears from the pain.

"Let that be a lesson to you. It's about time you knew your place. You are in the presence of your superiors." Treman gloated, the condescending look and tone just oozed unpleasantness, more so than usual. "Humans like you deserve to be put in their place. This is after all how you all should be. Cowering in fear at us Manzazzu."

Gabby hung her head, the ice melting and dripping from her face. Still breathing heavily, she stared up at him. "I don't know much about you lot, but I know this... It's such a good thing you're dead!"

Treman responded swiftly by giving her another swift punch to the face, increasing the hard frost on Gabby's face, bringing the poor woman to a state of near suffocation given how much breath had been knocked out of her. "You think my pathetic Granddaughter speaks for the entire Manzazzuan race?" He burst into a mocking laugh. "She's been isolated from the larger world all her life. She's been living a childish fantasy told to her by parents too lost in their own dreams and senseless optimism to tell her that the real world for us Manzazzu is far less kinder and decent."

Feeling faint, both through lack of oxygen and the pain disorientating her, Gabby struggled to continue but soldiered on as best she could. She was better than the old man, she wouldn't give up to him. "You've been dead for years, how do you know...?"

Gabby didn't even get a chance to finish before Treman was off on another tangent, this one far more closer to home for Gabby though. "Do you know why Manzazzu summon Humans as Etemmu? Why we never interact with Humans when your alive? I'll tell you why. Because they can't harm us until we give them a form."

He moved much closer to Gabby, his snidy voice ringing in her ears. "At first we'd summon other dead Manzazzu, but once Humanity started hunting us down in witch hunts and culls and burned us by the hundreds... Well, suddenly the idea of summoning them as Etemmu to fight and to kill their own kind just seemed so perfect."

That couldn't be true... He was lying, why would he tell the truth? It wasn't the only question she had, since Treman was content to start telling her everything. "Okay then...If you ghosts can't hold anything then how are you expected to fight? What are you going to do, ice people to death?"

Treman chose to ignore that stupid sentiment. "That's none of your concern."

As the effects of the ice were starting to wear off, Gabby felt her strength return slowly and surely. Taking in a massive lung full of much needed air, she continued her inquisition. "It is actually! Besides, I'm not likely to believe some old decaying dinosaur like you, I've got no reason to believe anything you say."

The old man's eyebrow raised in curiosity. He had found a new path of inquest. "So what reason do you have to believe anything my Granddaughter says? You act like you've known her all your life. How long has it been? Two days, maybe three?"

That was a good point. This new world of Manzazzu and ghosts was all so lost and new to Gabby, she'd taken every word Trem said as gospel. But why would she lie, she wasn't hiding anything from her. Well, Gabby hoped Trem wasn't lying to her, but how would she know? How would she know Treman was lying?

He continued his line of questions, circling around Gabby as he did so. "Seems to me you don't have any real reason to trust either of us. We're the only Manzazzu you've ever seen, it's not like you can walk up to the Royal Family and ask. Not that you'd be given the chance."

Gabby turned her head to face him, her eyes following him around the room. "I'm hardly going to believe some creep who's got me chained up in his room."

Crossing his arms, Treman scowled at her. "I don't care if you don't believe me, it's not my call to make, what happens to you is not my concern. But your new little girlfriend can't deny it, she knows the rules. If she doesn't obey the laws, then she'll get punished. The Royal Family are merciless, they'll make sure she feels the full sting of Manzazzuan law." That awful grin re-appeared on his face. "So it's not a matter of convincing anymore. It's more a question of if you want to jeopardise her safety. If I'm right, then your endangering her just by being with her. If I'm wrong, then I'm wrong. But do you want to take that chance?"

Gabby had to hand it to the old man, he got her second guessing. All the time she spent with Trem, no matter how short it was, it felt legitimate. It meant something to her, and she got the impression it meant something to Trem too. Bringing her Gran back for one last goodbye, it couldn't be a front for something... Gabby clenched her fists, the chains tightness was really getting hard to bear.

"So...What are you going to do now then?"

Oh the temptation to drive his fist into her face again was so hard to resist, but twice was enough for this sitting. The real pain was to come. He felt a twinge shoot up his body, a disk in his spine dislodged. Trying hard not to show any sign of agony, he too clenched his ghostly fist. After the next few disks dislodged , he couldn't take it anymore.

Before he answered, there was a loud banging on the door. Trem called out from behind the door. "Gabby?! Gabby are you in there, are you okay?!"

Gabby yelled out at the top of her lungs. "Trem help me!" She felt the awful stabbing sensation of Treman's fist through her head, this time the ice formed over her eyes. She let out a shrill scream as Treman made a dash for the mirror in the corner of the room. With any luck, Gabby wouldn't have seen him clearly and he was certain Trem didn't know about the mirror.

Stepping through the mirror and back into the Styx was a welcome comfort, his slowly deforming body became numb to the pain on the transition between worlds, it would buy him precious hours now, time he could use to find the Sisters and put the final stage of his plan into motion. In his absence, the fallout of his actions would keep Trem and her pet girlfriend busy. That would be the last time he'd step foot in that mansion before the plan, and honestly he was glad.

Any chance of being a noble Manzazzuan house shattered when his daughter ran off with some nobody instead of elevating them to greatness like her sister. But she married the family name away, leaving Tremera the family's last hope of keeping the name alive. But she squandered that, and now she and that husband were gone, lost in the Styx. He was proud of that much, and it was just Trem left before the slate could be wiped clean. Now that she brought that Human into her life, any slim chance of greatness was gone and only ruin was left. Still, better a great family legacy then a disgraced living one.

Trem meanwhile had run to grab one of her swords. Igniting the flames red, she slashed the air as a shockwave of fire shattered the wooden door. The sight that greeted her horrified her. Gabby, her arms forced out to the side by thick metal chains and her eyes frozen over with jagged, corse ice. "Gabby! Stay still, let me get you out of that..."

Trem cut the chains with her still flaming sword, going through the metal like they were butter. Dropping to her knees, she caught Gabby and set her down on her lap, using the flames to melt the ice.

"Treman....?"

Gabby nodded weakly, the experience had been a draining one. Her face was still screaming with pain and her arms ached. She wrapped her arms around Trem who, after extinguishing the flames, cradled her lover gently in her arms. "It's okay, I'm here now."

Gabby thought she must have blacked out, because when she next opened her eyes, she was in Trem's bed. Her trench coat was left on the foot of the bed and Trem was sat on one side of the bed, a bottle of some ointment was on the bedside table and Trem was dabbing some of it onto a cloth. Around her, Hogarth and Jenny. The petite film star looked on the verge of tears and even Hogarth looked like he was struggling to keep his composure. Jenny noticed Gabby's inflamed, blotchy eyelids straining to open. "Trem, she's awake..."

Trem leant over and spoke softly to Gabby, gently putting one hand on her forehead to check her temperature. "How are you feeling?" She felt a little hot but nowhere near dangerous levels. Her calm and collected exterior was masking not only fear for Gabby's safety but absolute hate and anger at her Grandfather. This was an all new low for him and there was no going back from this.

"I think I feel as bad as I look..." She wheezed with a smile before coughing. Each cough hurt her chest which was feeling heavy and raspy. "I've had better days truth be told."

Trem took the cloth she doused with the ointment. "Just close your eyes for a second, this will help the swelling go down." She gently pressed it against Gabby's eyes. "We were having a nice moment too weren't we?"

Gabby sighed. Honestly, she was thinking the same. The time in the Observatory and even before then, summoning her Gran and all the emotional support. That couldn't be a lie, it felt too real to be anything but the truth, so why was Gabby still in doubt?

"You know how dangerous things got before, but I still can't have you risking your life again. I didn't step in when I should and I put you in danger. I was too scared to go into that room because of some dumb superstition from my youth. I put you in danger, so... I can understand if you want nothing to do with me anymore."

Jenny cut in abruptly, Gabby could feel her coming towards them as the air chilled. "Hon you can't blame yourself! It wasn't your fault!"

Hogarth continued, still unable to shake his inner actor. "Precisely, it was that blaggard Treman's fault. You were not to blame for any wrongdoings my lady."

Gabby sat up, holding the cloth to her eyes. Whatever the thing Trem put on it was working, must have been some magic Aloe Vera. Her Gran would have loved this stuff, she always swore by Aloe Vera. "Trem, they're right, it wasn't your fault. I made my choice before, it's not changed at all when I say I'm staying. I said we were in this together and I meant it. Besides, all this does is make me want to help you all the more. Not just with your parents, but sending that old git to a pretty painful afterlife."

She didn't expect to get a hug from Trem, it kind of jolted her at first, since she couldn't see. But she wrapped her arms around the Manzazzu all the same.

Abhay and Skye emerged through the wall, having spent the whole time while Gabby was recovering searching the house. "No sign of him." Abhay called. "We've searched every inch of the manor and the surrounding area..." He stopped when he noticed Gabby was awake and sitting upright.

"...We'll let you have some privacy...?" Skye asked, joining Jenny's side.

Trem turned to the others and leant back. "No, you don't have to, not if you don't want to anyway." She glanced back at Gabby. "Don't move, I'm just going to take this off your face..." She gently took the cloth away from Gabby's eyes.

The light made her squint, but if there was any face Gabby was glad to see after being nearly blinded, it would be Trem's. She was handed a mirror and inspected her eyes. A little red around the eyelids, but nothing that couldn't be brushed off as signs of crying.

"You're looking better sugar." Jenny complimented, while holding Skye's hand.

Skye's smile meanwhile faded, that scowl Gabby knew from the first time they met was clear for all to see and gave her a shiver.
"I'll kill him. The second I see him, I'll kill him..." Skye threatened, it was almost scary, if Gabby didn't know Skye had a lighter side to her.

"I think we all would. I know between us we can make him suffer for what he's done. If you wouldn't mind?" Abhay asked to Trem.

Trem got up from the bed and crossed to the centre of the room. "Look, I'm not going to ask you all to fight my battles for me. I can do it alone, I can't ask you all to put your chances to return to the afterlife in jeopardy because of me and my issues. I want you all safe too, you all matter to me..."

Hogarth raised his hand, as if he was a school child asking a question to teacher. "If I may be so bold?" He glanced around the room before getting the nod of approval from Trem. "I believe I speak for everyone here when I say that we are loyal. We stand by those who we support and would gladly forfeit our chances in paradise for your cause."

"Here here!" Chanted Abhay, giving Hogarth a hard pat on the back.

Jenny floated closer to Trem, so they could look each other in the eye when she gave her answer. "All my life, people told me I wasn't going to amount to much, and even when I did, it didn't really mean anything. Here I think I can really make a difference."

Before Trem could thank Jenny, they were all alerted to a strange noise, a sort of bizarre buzzing. Gabby looked to the end of the bed.

"Oh sorry, that'll be me." She reached into her pocket and pulled out her phone. Looking at the time, she couldn't believe she'd only been away for three hours. One new text, from her Mother.

"Hi, is everything going okay?"

Gabby held her phone up to Trem and the four Etemmu. "It's just my Mum. Checking up on me is all." She quickly typed out a response and sent the message. Once she was done, she drew her attention back to the waiting Etemmu and Trem. "I better be heading back. It's hours till the curfew but I think she needs me." She took the sheets off herself as she began getting ready to head out. "Will you all be okay till tomorrow?"

Trem looked like she was really getting angry, considering who was on her mind, it wasn't surprising. "If Treman dares show his face in this house, he'll get what's coming to him. Nothing puts fear into a heart than four angry ghosts and one really tetchy Manzazzu."

Gabby couldn't help but chuckle, that did sound rather scary. The smile slipped away when she put on her coat. "Trem, I just want you to know... He might try and separate us, but I told you when we first met that I keep my word. I promised you I'd stick by you, that's not going to change."

Honestly, that was such a relief for Trem. Poor Gabby didn't have a good time of it at all. Treman, the incident in the Styx... Her Grandmother. But after coping with all that, Trem was confident there was nothing that could deter Gabby. She was there for the long haul. Trem felt hope returning more and more, which after all these years of solitude was giving her such joy. "Gabby, the same goes for me."

Jenny's hand shot up into the air as she dramatically called out. "Me too sugar!"

Her arms crossed, Skye laughed as she looked up at Gabby, a look that finally showed a confident and determined trust from the pirate captain. "My lady does decree it." A moment of realisation came over her, troubling Skye. "I'm starting to sound like Hogarth, God help me..." She muttered.

"Come now Miss Bloodworth, there are far worse beasts of burden to mimic then yours truly!" He turned to Gabby. "This is a fate so poetic if it were to come from prose then it would be the tale of two lovers who's destiny's coincide..."

Trem made a circular gesture with her wrist, a non verbal command to get to the point and stop faffing about.

"Oh umm, right..." Hogarth fumbled. "In summation, I pledge myself as ever."

All the heads in the room turned to Abhay who was scratching his beard. Noticing the deathly silence, he looked up to see all the faces staring back at him. "Oh, I thought my answer was obvious, I'm here to stay and shed blood for you. I never do things by halves after all."

Trem scoffed. "Well, we know that much." She teased. "Well, it's decided then. Treman doesn't have a chance then when it's six against one." She turned to face Gabby. "We won't keep you, you go back to your family. They need you more than we do right now."

Honestly, after the events of that day, Gabby could do with a good rest. Besides, after being beaten up by some craggy old guy's dead spirit, a cup of coffee would be right just what was needed. Trem's odd brew was nice, but she knew what she fancied. She knew she couldn't let her normal life get swept away under all this, as hard as it would be to balance them all. "I'll be back tomorrow. Try not to murder Treman without me?" She headed towards the door, stopping to look back when Skye called back.

"No promises!" Anyone else would mistake that for a joke, but there was nothing funny about how Skye said it. It was true, she was kind of scary.

Gabby gave a silent wave before leaving the room, walking down the stairs and slowly out of the room. She was still amazed it was daylight, and that it had only been a few hours. It felt like she'd been there days. How typical, a few hours in the Styx equates to days, a few hours in the manor feels the same. Manzazzu really do know how to make the most of their time.

The Etemmu slowly left Trem's room, all going off to do their usual distractions. That left Trem alone in her room once again. Taking off her robe, she inspected her arm. It had healed completely after the bite she sustained from the Faragh, with the only evidence being a few patches of pale skin, more pale than her normal skin tone at any rate. She took a box from the drawer in her desk, taking out some lettuce leaves for Sammy. Reaching into the tank, she stroked her little friend before returning the lid.

As she sat at her desk, she checked the locked box where she and Tremadore had been exchanging letters. She opened it to reveal another roll of parchment. She broke the wax seal and read his response. Good, he agreed with her call to execute Treman. As for Gabby, he advised she proceed as she thought best.

Gabby took her time walking back, the sun was still high in the sky and the warm summer air felt amazing on her skin, which was still feeling sensitive after the freezing. But she knew she'd return home a lot happier than when she left. She found herself walking home faster and faster, to the point where she felt like she was almost running.

When she did get home, she found herself almost out of breath. "I'm back." She called, unsure where her Mother was or what state she'd be in.

Glancing round the corner, she saw Mavis reading something on the sofa, the TV on in the background. She turned around and noticed Gabby standing in the doorway. "Your back early, I wasn't expecting you to come back so quickly."

Gabby unlaced her boots and slipped them off by the door, taking off her trenchcoat and slinging it over her chair in the dining room. She landed with a flop on the sofa. "I let them at the manor know what was up, we talked, we did some... Other stuff..." Well that was a massive understatement, a first kiss is not "other stuff", but now was not the time to talk about it. "How are you doing?"

Her Mum held up a photo album, on a page of old, slightly yellowing pictures. "I wanted to see how they held up. Pictures of your Nan and Grandad." She pointed at one particular picture, her Gran's dark haired was curly and thick, much like Gabby's. "See, you even take after her a little bit. Your both notoriously hard to deal with."

Gabby gently tapped her Mum's shoulder with the back of her hand.

"So rude!" She joked as she leant against her arm. "You sure your doing okay?"

Mavis took a deep breath through her nose and closed the album. "Yeah, I think so. I think we all will, we did last time."

That was a big relief to Gabby, the last thing she wanted was to have her Mother fall into some depressive slump. The two shared a kiss on the cheek and a warm hug in front of the television, where they stayed for a good hour or two. It made Gabby feel like a kid again, which was really what she needed. Feeling content, Gabby plucked up the courage to let one of her many new secrets go.

"Mum, I had my first snog today." She glanced up to see her Mum looking back at her, the expression hard to read. "It was with my friend, I met at the manor house. She was making me feel better about Gran and it kind of just...Happened."

There was a moment of silence between them, with only the TV pouring out adverts to stop the room from being devoid of sound. It made Gabby feel a little uneasy, but once her Mother patted her on the head, she knew it wasn't that bad.

"Only took you eighteen years, you old romantic. Tell her she can always come round here if she wants. Tell you what, tomorrow I'll make a lasagne for four? Would that interest her?"
Well that's something she never expected to happen. She didn't even know if Trem would want to come outside, since she'd locked herself away for god knows how many years. If she didn't, well, more lasagne for Gabby. But it was something she was willing to suggest at any rate. "I think it might, I'll talk to her tomorrow, see what she thinks." After a moment, they returned to their viewing pleasure, Gabby's head against Mavis' arm. "Oh by the way, her name's Trem."

"Oh, that's nice. Sounds foreign."

Chapter Twelve: "The River Flows"

"I think it's time we were going now."
"Yes..."

Once Treman had entered the mirror, he appeared back in the decrepit sidings of the Styx, with the broken down trams and rolling stock surrounding him. Holding himself stable on one of the trucks, he glanced down at the small pool of blood that was forming as a result of his decaying, corrupting state. He lamented that the Sisters would have to see him like this, but at the same time, it would only help strengthen them. They needed to know what corrupting looked like after all, and they needed to know to not get emotionally attached once he slipped away.

His wandering mind slipped back to the day years ago, when he first encountered them. For the Sisters, in human terms it would have felt like twelve years, given that all three of them matured from frightened little girls to fierce warriors on the cusp of adulthood. They were all so small, filthy and abandoned by their peers. Perfect for Treman's plans.

Euphratia, capital of the Manzazzu was always a thriving place if you had a chance to do well for yourself. Treman hated the idea of the whole civilisation having to live in the shadow of the Royal Family, quite literally. The Grand Fortress where the Queen lived was perched atop a great mountain with the bustling, thriving city below them. Thousands of Manzazzu would wake up in the morning and look up at the optulant Royals and grow jealous, Treman was one of them. Of course, that kind of thinking lead to the war, when the divergent Manzazzu, the Mutashaeib who declared an open rebellion against the Royal Family.

Years of fighting ensued, stretching across the world. The thing that amused Treman about it to no end is it was the greatest wars Humanity was never aware of. As Euphratia was hidden from the world by powerful Manzazzuan magic, their actions and conflicts were sheltered from their primitive view. Given Humanity and the Manzazzu were historically violent towards each other, the Witch Trials being a prevalent case, it was just as well they were able to shield their conflict away from them.

The way the Royal Family treated Humanity was another point of anger for the Mutashaeib. The Royals were against their subjects interacting with Humans till after they died. No one really knew why but Treman agreed with the general consensus, Human beings were much less dangerous dead then alive. The Mutashaeib wanted to have the Manzazzu dominate the Human race, subjugate them and enslave them. After the years they were mistreated by Humanity, it was only fair, and a complete Manzazzu take over would be simplicity itself, especially if they brought Etemmu back and used them as warriors, just how things were in the founding days in Babylon.

All this was irrelevant though, as Treman watched the Royal Family wipe out the major clans of the Mutashaeib. Treman never openly declared his clan as a member, unlike the other great clans he'd admired from a distance. If he did, it would mean if the rebels failed then he and his clan would be wiped out, condemned as criminals or forced into exile. Either way, his dreams of glory would be dashed. In his heart, Treman was riddled with self contradiction. He hated the Royal Family but he was obsessed with the standing of his clan.

True, he hated the idea of one family having all the power, but that most likely stemmed from the idea that anyone with more power then himself was the enemy that he needed to snuff out. If absolute power corrupts absolutely, then yearning for absolute power has the same effect, it made Treman an angry, bitter Manzazzu.

It was after the war, the country was still licking its wounds. Steel faced armored guards would patrol the Bazaar's, staffs drawn and their eye on any sign of trouble making. Euphretia was under lock and key, the last remaining Mutashaeib escaping on the sea to Africa or Australia, the nearest land masses to Euphratia. Treman was walking the stone streets, among the bartering Manzazzu at the city's central Bazaar.

He glanced around at his fellow kind, they may all have been like him, born into Manzazzuan blood, all wearing the same type of robe, but to him, they could never be further apart. Treman had ambitions, he wanted to be more than this, more than the leader of some middling political clan. One daughter was a love sick idealist, the other had neither the intelligence or the social grace to amount to anything. He would never become anything more, unless he did something about it.

While buying some supplies at a stall, his attention was drawn to the patter of small feet on the cobbled ground. Glancing around, he caught sight of a small girl who was pinching fruit from one of the stalls. She was so stealthy, the stall owner didn't even notice her. Treman looked her up and down, she wore tatty, stained and filthy cloths and her light brown skin was hidden behind a messy crop of pink hair and her lilac eyes were only just visible. She scooped a few fruit into her pocket and scampered away. Treman, who had yet to age into his craggy, elderly form, instead still thin faced with finely chiseled features, slowly followed the girl.

Following from a distance, he kept on the girl's tail. The boiling hot sun was obscured by a sandstone building, shielding the two from sight. Turning a corner into the dark alley, the girl came to a halt and looked behind her. Treman lept to cover behind a corner and waited for the girl to make her move. She whistled twice and on cue, she was joined by two others. One was pale as a sheet with a strip of cloth tied over her eyes, sandy blonde hair pulled back over her head and tied in a ponytail.

The other had tanned skin and black, greasy hair and brilliant blue eyes, like sapphires. The thief took the fruit from her pockets and handed them out, the three of them scoffing the food up like animals. Treman glanced around the corner, they all looked so desperate and hungry for even the tiniest morsle.

The pale one with the blindfold stopped eating, looking up at the way the girl came. The pink haired one's head tilted. "What's wrong?"

Breathing in, the girl with the blindfold let a few seconds of silence go by. "You were followed. He's hiding behind that wall." She extended a thin, boney finger up to Treman's hiding place.

The other two spun their heads around and watched as Treman stepped out from behind the wall. How could she have known that? Unless....

The blue eyed one grabbed a piece of broken glass from the side of the alley and held it out in defence. What was she going to do, papercut Treman to death? "Who are you? Just leave us alone! What did we ever do to anyone anyway?!"

Treman put his finger to his lips. "Sssshhh...." He gestured his hand downwards as he slowly approached them, one footstep at a time. "I'm not going to hurt you. What are your names?"

The girl lowered her shard, sinking her head as she muttered her response, the pain in her voice was so evident it would be heartbreaking, if Treman was into that soppy stuff. "We're... We're nobody"

The pink haired girl's stomach growled rather loudly, loud enough for Treman to hear. He delved into his satchel and took out a loaf of bread from the Bazaar he'd bought for himself. He unwrapped it from it's paper container and held it out to the blue eyed girl.
"Here, you need to eat something ."

The two girls turned to the blindfolded one, who gave them a nod as a response. The blue eyed girl slowly took the bread, separated it and handed out pieces. The three let out stifled moans of enjoyment, it was very clear to him they'd been living on the streets for years. "Where are your parents?"

The three paused eating and the two, who could see, glanced at the floor. "We have no parents. We have to make do ourselves."

How interesting. Treman could hazard a guess where the blue eyed girl came from. The lead Mutashaeib clan, the Talon were forced to evacuate Euphretia, and she resembled the leader of that clan's wife, a fierce woman with the most gorgeous blue eyes. She must have been left behind. As for the one with the blindfold, well, Treman knew where she was from. Pink hair or lilac eyes were new to Treman, must have been from some nobody clan. Still, two of the three girls had some real Manzazzu pedigree behind them.

A thought entered Treman's head. No one would be looking for these girls, if they weren't thought dead already then it would only be a matter of time. He leant down and addressed the three of them at once. "Would you three like a comfortable bed tonight, along with a hot meal?"

The three moved into a little huddle, whispering between them. Treman stood back up to give them some privacy, though he was sure he knew what the answer would be. "We don't want to cause a fuss, but..."

Treman interrupted and stood in front of her, kneeling down and offering her his hand. "Nonsense. I'm not going to let you three starve to death on the streets. Come with me and I'll make sure you get shelter, food and comfort for as long as you want it."

As the three nodded at each other and took his hand, Treman knew he was onto something here. Children, they'd believe anything you tell them, and therein lies the beauty of it. All he had to do was teach them the ways of the Mutashaeib, turn them into fighters, into figureheads, maybe then he could secure his legacy. Treman, the Manzazzu who engineered the take over that would change the history books. It all starts out with small steps and small people.

Now, decades later, the Sisters had grown up. Treman watched them go from frightened children to fully fledged Mutashaeib warriors, training them for years after taking them in, all behind Trem's back. While his own family were squandering their status, he was raising the three Sisters. They were his greatest achievements, considerably more than his actual family. But this would be their last meeting however.

He stopped when he reached a clearing, one of the many side turnings and dead ends in the maze that was The Styx. He whistled three times and waited, as planned.

From the rotted bushes and shrubs came three figures, all of varying heights. They all wore black leather outfits, with scarlet sashes across the waists and weapon holsters across their shoulders. Two of them wore masks which obscured all but the eyeline in a thin strip while the other wore a hood and a mask that covered their entire face. Visible behind the masks of two of them, one set of deep sapphire eyes and another of lilac eyes. The Sisters, now all grown up and clad in the uniform of Mutashaeib assassins. They emerged from their hiding places and all sank to one knee, bowing their heads.

"Welcome back." The first Sister said, closing her bright eyes.

Treman's hand hovered over her shoulder, he spoke in a whisper. "Tremalor..."

She glanced up at him, her eyes widening as she saw her mentor in his twisted state, a few drops of blood from his mouth collecting on the floor. Tremalor tried to mask her surprise, it was against her training to become too emotionally attached.

"You three have been preparing for today, all your training has paid off. Because today you three are officially members of the Mutashaeib. Tremalor...." He took his hand from her and gestured to the lilac eyed Sister. "Tremalee..." He moved to the hooded figure. "Tremalan."

Stepping back, he gave the command for the three to stand. "All you have to do is take your vow and commence the ritual."

The three of them reached for their weapons. The blue eyed Tremalor took out a small silver rod, which extended into a lance with a flick of her wrist. Tremalee took her axe from her back and twirled it in her hand. Tremalan took a series of razor wires from a pouch tied to her sash.

Together, the three Sisters began to recite their vows. "I pledge my blood, my breath, my very life to the cause of the Mutashaeib. I will live, fight and die by the laws dictated to us by those who came before us. Now and forever, I swear upon my own blood."

They all took their weapons in one hand and removed their leather gloves. Pricking their fingers with their weapons, they allowed the blood to trickle down before igniting the weapons with red flames. The blood turned the flame yellow before fizzing out of existence. Once their weapons flames were snubbed out, they returned them to their original holders and slipped the gloves back on.

"Good. This will have to be the last time we meet, so do me proud my pupils. Now, let's get into position." He lead the three onto the main strip of the Styx docklands.

Tremalee leant over to Tremalor and spoke in a hushed yet excited tone. "So this is it eh sis? We've finally done it!" Her smile was easy to make out under the mask. "I was starting to think this day wouldn't come, but we did it! We proved we were good enough..."

She felt Tremalan's hand on her shoulder. "Sorry, I can't help getting excited is all! I mean we're nearly there, when we start this, we're on the high road to glory!"

Tremalor kept her eyes locked on Treman's back as he continued to lead them. "Glory is something that isn't freely gifted, it is something achieved by determination, strength and persistence. Remember, little sister, this is only the first step in a larger plan."

Treman stopped in his tracks,clenching his fists as his shoulders arched, bones in his back and shoulders popping out of place. He held back as much of the pain as he could, though a grunt escaped his lips.

"Treman...?" Tremalor came to a halt and watched as her mentor strained, straightening out his back, causing the dislocated bones to pop and scrape against each other.

He attempted to regain composure, clicking his neck and shrugging his shoulders. "I am fine."

That was a lie and the Sisters knew it, no one who's becoming a Faragh is "fine". They all knew they'd be the one that would have to kill him in the end, though they were hardly going to wait in line anxiously to do it. Treman continued down the docklands before stopping by some old bushes at the side of the docks.

Treman turned to face the others, who struggled to hide their surprise. His left eye socket was starting to sag, his teeth were pushing hard into his top lip and most of his hair had fallen out. His jaw combined with his teeth were already starting to impair his speech, turning his previously well spoken voice into muttering.

"Take up positions everyone." He ordered.

Tremalee jumped across the water and landed on the other side of the docks. She hid behind a bush and readied herself by taking her axe in hand. Peering over, she watched the others at work. Tremalan took off her glove and leaned her hand into the River. She felt the currents lap against her skin and after a few seconds, she shook off the water and put her glove back on. She gave a gesture with her hand, fifteen new arrivals to the Styx arriving in one minute.

The Sisters and Treman remained hidden as they waited for the boats to pass. After a minute exactly, the Sisters caught sight of the boats. Three, full of grey cloaked figures bound for the afterlife, or so they thought. They floated across the water at a snail's pace, the people onboard oblivious to what was coming. With her spear drawn, Tremalor stood up from the hiding place and held one hand out, to help her aim.

Once the first boat was in range, she threw the spear, which pierced the boat's hull and caused it list. The cloaked souls onboard all began to scramble and panic, unable to stop themselves falling into the River once the boat capsized. Tremalee jumped out of her hiding place and landed on the second boat. Using the butt of her axe, she slammed it into one of the soul's faces, sending them falling into the River. She hit the bottom of the boat with her axe, causing water to pour in at an alarming rate.

"No one said how much fun this would be!" She chortled as she threw one soul out of the way and into the water as she jumped to the next boat and repeated the sequence.

The souls who didn't sink to the bottom of the River desperately scrambled to the sides of the walls. When they reached there, trying to grab onto the walkways, they were greeted by the other two Sisters. Tremalor held her hand out as her spear flew back into her hand. She threw the spear which hit the Etemmu in the shoulder and propelled him to the bottom of the River, pinning him to the bottom while he flailed for air.

Tremalan meanwhile pulled her razor wire tight, her glorified Cat's

Cradle and prefered weapon. She reached down and grabbed another Etemmu, wrapping her Cradle around their neck, pulling it taught and choking the non existent "life" out of it. Tremalee jumped back onto the walkway with her other sisters after dealing with another boat and pausing to pluck an Etemmu out of the water, choking them as she spoke.

"You know what? You said this would be easy, but I never figured I'd love it so much!" Her bright eyes were filled with so much joy, too much for the others.

"Keep focused Sister." Tremalor replied as she recalled her spear. "Remember, we need them all to turn Faragh, make sure there's still some left..."

Before Tremalan could finish, Tremalee heard the unmistakable sound of a neck breaking. She looked at her victim and dropped their slumped form into the River. "Ooops! My mistake!"

Tremalan flicked her wire into the water, the ends of it wrapping around an escaping Etemmu's leg. She pulled them back and knelt by the water's edge. She grabbed the figure by the head and smacked it against the walkway. The form then sank to the bottom of the dark water.

Treman observed the carnage with interest, honestly he was proud of them, but it wasn't something he was going to tell them. They were strong, more powerful than other Mutashaeib assassins. They wouldn't be so easily killed for one. Treman taught them well, and they were the best kind of students. When they knew no other life then homelessness, it teaches someone to be bitter at those who rule, who abandoned them and left them to starve on the streets.

Decades of fueling that bitterness helped no end for the Sisters. Plus they were closer than friends, though they were not biologically related, their bonds were so deep. The thought of his impending demise was considerably lessened when Treman observed how far the Sisters had come, and how far they would go.

The last of the fifteen Etemmu had been slain by the Sisters, who dredged the drowned forms from the River. They were all pulled to the walkway and assembled in a pile.

The hoods were all lowered and Treman looked over the Etemmu. All of various ages, all male. A bus full of Football fans collided with a car on a winding country road, losing control on a corner, sending the bus and car off a great height into the valley below. A perfect collection for the Faragh. Treman walked up to one of the Etemmu, a large bald headed man. He picked up the lifeless body and looked it over. The Sisters approached but halted at Treman's silent command.

The lifeless Etemmu's eyes shot open, where once were deep brown, now were blanked with no features whatsoever. Treman stepped back as the body convulsed, the Etemmu bent over as his spine burst out of his back, snapping in half, leaving the front half of his body limp and dangling. The jaw came loose at the joint and was left hanging while the sharp teeth formed and burst out of his gums.

Tremalee clapped her hands together. "This is so cool!" She chuckled out loud.

The pile of Etemmu began to burst into life once again, their bodies twisting and turning into Faragh, each becoming something monstrous and inhuman. Treman took the first one by the head and locked soulless blank eyes to soulless blank eyes. "Go home." He ordered as he turned to Tremalor. "You remember where the Ishtar Gate portal is?"

When she nodded a response, he continued. "Keep these aside for now. Tremalan, Tremalee, your sister and I will enter the manor house and make sure the Ishtar Gate is active. When I give the command, send them through. Understood?"

"Yes sir." The two responded.

Treman let the Faragh out of his sight, the others standing aimless. Faragh created in this way were generally less hostile to those who created them. Some inbuilt mechanism with the Faragh, or maybe self defence for the Manzazzu. What good is creating a vile beast that attacks you as soon as you birth it? "Tremalor, come with me."

Treman lead his protege away from the group while the others kept an eye on the Faragh. Turning a corner, he stopped and leant against a wall. Tremalor watched with a slightly concerned look to her eyes. "You can remove your mask here, we are in private."

Tremalor shook her head. "No sir, while we carry out your will, we will remain masked."

Treman knew he taught her well. "Now, to business. When I die, for the final time, I want you to take over. You're the strongest, oldest and most mature. I know you won't disappoint me, you've proved yourself time and time again." His voice lowered, taking his gnarled hand with its decaying fingernails and placing it over her shoulder. "I also want you to be the one to end me. Will you do it?"

Tremalor should have answered instantly, she wanted to... But she found the words hard to get out. It had been so long since they were saved by him, he really was like a father figure to them all, so the thought of having to be the one to kill him felt wrong. She should have been apathetic about it, but she couldn't help but feel something.

Deep down, she didn't want to do it, who would? She felt Treman's hand move from her shoulder to her masked face. "Tremalor, will you make me proud?"

Tremalor took his hand and closed her eyes. "Yes sir." She responded. She'd need to stifle these emotions if she was to follow his orders to the letter.

Treman's hands returned to his side. "Good, now let us return to the others."

When they walked back, they found Tremalee looking one of the Faragh over, poking it's disfigured form while Tremalan was in her own little world. Noticing Treman, they snapped to attention. With Tremalor by his side, it was pretty obvious what was coming for the two Sisters.

"The time is now, this is when I will leave you three " His tone was almost matter of fact were it not for a slight voice break, no doubt due to the fact he felt one of the bones in his neck give out, leaving his head on a tilted angle, held up by his shoulder. "Since this will be the last chance I will have to say it, I want you three to know how proud I am of your progress these past few decades."

He turned to Tremalee first. "Tremalee, your strength with your axe is undeniable, you will be a force to be reckoned with. But in order to achieve your peak, you must learn to focus. Hone in that energy and use it in bursts. Then you, along with your sisters will win many victories in the future."

Tremalee responded with a quiet and respectable bow of thanks. Of course what she really wanted to do was to get emotional and actually feel sad he was going, but she had to keep a straight face. One of the advantages of the masks, the enemies can't see when you're scared.

Treman moved onto Tremalan, whose face was still totally obscured by the hood and full face mask. "Tremalan, you are unfeeling in battle, it will serve you well in the conflicts to come. With time, your skills will be second to none. Remember to keep practising your vision and your close quarter combat." Tremalan returned the bow that Tremalee gave Treman.

"When you win your first victory, follow the plan as we discussed. But once you've eliminated my Granddaughter and her Human pet, you should allow yourselves a moment of rest. I want you three to lift a glass to your achievements..And to me."

Tremalor spoke up for the first time in a while. "We shall, rest assured."

He gave one last look to the two Sisters and after a moment of stillness, he turned on his heels and began his journey to the decrepit old sidings to venture back to the manor.

It wasn't enough to just have Trem and Gabby killed, in a fight, the Sisters could easily kill them. He wanted to make a statement to the Royal Family. The Mutasheib once installed fear in all Manzazzu, but that fear had gone from their race. What better way to mark their return then to show them the absolute level of control they had over Faragh, using them to decimate a Manzazzuan house?

The corruption really had twisted Treman's mind. By doing this, his desires to have his clan be remembered with greatness would be dashed, as his recent actions included trapping Trem's parents in the Styx, setting Faragh into the human world, thus sealing Trem and her pet's fate. That's a guarantee to drag his name through the mud. But he'd passed the point of reason long ago.

He and Tremalor disappeared into the distance, turning a corner and continuing their journey while the remaining Sisters watched. The calm and stillness of the moment was dashed when one of the Faragh landed a swing of it's club like hand on another's head. It made a mad dash, trying to escape from the dazed and confused pack.

Tremalan primed her razor wire Cat's Cradle, pulling the metal strands tight before flinging one end like a whip. It wrapped itself around the Faragh's leg as she pulled it back into the group.

Tremalee removed her glove, revealing the rings on her fingers. The ruby stone began to glow as she drew a circle around the fifteen Faragh, which combusted in a burst of red flames. As the Faragh cried out in alarm at the wall of flames blocking them in, Tremalee smiled.

"That'll keep them controlled."

The smile soon faded however. Tremalee pulled off her mask revealing the same messy crop of pink hair and her lilac eyes were still as bright as they were all those years ago. The only change is a maroon colored band of cloth tied in her hair. She lazily dragged herself over to the water's edge and sank to the floor. Letting her booted feet hang over the edge, she looked into the murky water, where, not long ago, she'd just drowned an Etemmu.

Tremalan watched her actions from a distance, eventually crossing over and sitting next to her "sister". She lowered her hood and removed her mask. The sandy hair was cut much shorter and her blindfold had been removed, revealing no eyes or sockets, just blank flesh. Tremalan reached out to Tremalee, taking her warm, ring clad hand in hers gently and holding her fingers out straight. Tremalee did the same, so now their open palms were touching.

Tremalee couldn't contain herself anymore and began to cry. Tremalan pulled her in for a hug, patting her back gently.

"I'm not ready for this..." Tremalee began, closing her eyes tight. "I thought I'd be ready by now, but I'm not... How can I be...?" She stopped when she opened her eyes when she felt Tremalan run her pale hands through her hair. Honestly, having her hair played with always made her feel happy.

Tremalan then produced her Cat's Cradle. She created a simple figure of eight and flicked a small blue ember which ran around the figure of eight like a tiny sparkler. That got Tremalee chuckling, it was another of her favourite things, watching her Sister's handiwork. Tremalan then rotated her wrists, working her fingers to create a more complex lattice pattern with the spark dancing around it. Even without the benefit of sight, Tremalan could feel the joy this was bringing her Sister. Her wrists and fingers sped up, with a good ten seconds of work going into her grand finale. The string like razor wire was now worked into the shape of a human weilding an axe.

"No way! Is that me!?" Tremalee was practically screaming that out she was so excited. Tremalan nodded with a big smile on her face. "Tremalan, you're the best!"

Tremalan unwound the Cradle just in time to receive a big hug from her Sister. Tremalee was a sensitive Manzazzu, still so childlike after all this time. She never had a childhood, so she was having a new lease of life. Was that new lease of life suitable for a Mutashaeib assassin though? Not likely, but it's what made Tremalee unique. It also made it harder for her to accept anything else but what she was told to be the truth.

The three Sisters had no reason to debate Treman's teachings. To them, he was this generous, kind and considerate man who took them in when they had nowhere else to go, how would they know they were nothing to him except pawns to kickstart a plan he'd come up with, but was too cowardly and conflicted to do himself? No doubt that was the reason why he waited till he was dead and returned as a Etemmu to put this plan into action.

But the Sisters didn't see it that way. As Tremalan and Tremalee shared a hug and a sisterly kiss on the banks of the River Styx, they were oblivious to the malice intentions they were being used in. But for that moment, Tremalee felt as if she might be ready to live up to Treman's expectations. A skilled and strong fighter, quick moving despite her heavy war axe, she was, to use her own words "pretty awesome". Tremalan meanwhile just wanted to make sure Tremalee was safe. Tremalor was always ever so slightly distant with those two, no doubt because she was Treman's favourite. His best student in other words.

Plus, Tremalan's ability was to be able to see the likely events in the future. In being robbed of her eyesight at birth, she gained the gift of foresight, though future vision it was not. All she could see were likely outcomes, each as unpredictable as the next. For instance, she could see the most likely outcome, to her anyway, which was they succeed in their plan. But other visions plagued her minds, all of which she hoped would never happen and she would fight hard to stop from ever happening.

One outcome where they fail in their mission and are put to death on the Queen's orders. One where Tremalee dies in a battle, and the most unlikely, that they allied themselves with Trem and her Human. As she sat there, holding onto Tremalee tight, like a newborn, she vowed to herself she would never let that happen.

Treman and Tremalor stepped through the portal and emerged in Treman's room in the manor house. The room had been turned upside down, the curtains open, letting light in for the first time in decades. Drawers and containers opened and books were strewn across the floor. Trem had clearly turned the place upside down, in vein of course. Treman wouldn't have been so stupid as to leave any incriminating evidence before he died.

The door was still broken open, hanging loose from one remaining hinge. Treman and his follower stayed with their backs to the wall to avoid detection. Treman glanced beyond the door, the house was silent, no sign of life. They both made a mad dash out of the room and stopped before they reached the stairs. Tremalor remained silent, the sound of her boots against the wooden floor were muffled and muted.

After a second listening out for any voices, they made their way down the steps and through the living room. Before long, they had reached the door leading to the Ishtar Gate. Tremalor opened the door and gently closed it behind her, while Treman floated through the wall itself. Tremalor made sure it was locked and secured so they wouldn't be disturbed. She headed down the flight of stairs to join Treman at the Ishtar Gate. After getting the nod from Treman, she removed her glove, straightening out her rings. She made the appropriate motions with her fingers and wrists to open the Gate.

"Good work. Go through and tell the others to bring the Faragh across the River. On my command, you bring them through and then close the Gate behind you. Understood?"

"Understood." Came the reply. Tremalor stayed still for a moment before removing her mask, her black bangs falling onto her face. "I will do you proud in the wars to come, sir."

Now he was no longer tactile, he couldn't touch her without giving her the certain icy chill only Etemmu can give. That annoyed him, especially given how long he'd just spent getting used to being somewhat tactile in the Styx. Undeterred, he continued his discussion. "I know you will. Your sisters still need your guidance though Tremalor. You are a natural born leader after all." That's when his eye fell out of its socket and disappeared once it dropped into the floor. "Oh you..." Treman began, stopping before he exerted himself too much.

"We shouldn't waste time sir." Tremalor was about to enter the Gate when she was halted by a click of Treman's fingers.

"Don't walk away when we are in discussion." Tremalor couldn't believe he was seemingly undeterred by his missing eye. The truth of the matter was that he was becoming so unattached to his senses due to the corruption that it felt like nothing much had happened. "Tremalee and Tremalan aren't up to the standards they should be. You need to push them harder, do you understand? Harder. They will thank you for it later."

Tremalor knew he was already starting to go. All she could do was agree with him. "I shall sir, you have my word."

Treman nodded and turned away from her. "Now go and do me proud."

Tremalor's face was a mix of confusion and concern, did he not remember what was just said? No matter, she still had a job to do. She pulled the mask over her face and entered the Gate.

Treman shuddered as he felt the last of his hair fall out. Looking down at his hands, with his nails turning into claws, his veins were bulging and turning black. Blotchy patches had bean to form on his skin and were starting to form on his head and face. He scrambled to the water surrounding the Gate and peered in at his reflection.

His heart sank when he saw his own twisted form staring back, at the very least he expected to see his younger form looking back at him like before. An awful, stabbing pain began to course through his body. He bit down so hard on his lip to hold back grunts of pain that his bottom lip was ripped straight off his chin, leaving blood gushing out of the wound. Out of anger, he let the lip fall into the floor.

"I...I will control it..." He muttered, his voice becoming almost unintelligible. This was humiliating for him, he was beyond this. But he knew this was all for a reason. The pain was worth it, it was good pain. Though, when another disc in his spine gave out, he had his doubts.

The good thing was by the time he and Tremalor came back from the Styx, day had turned to night and they were in the next day.

Trem and her Etemmu would be active in the house, especially with the imminent return of Gabby. It was up to him to decide when the best time to release the Faragh would be. All he had to do was wait.

Chapter Thirteen: "Was It Painless?"

"Even Manzazzu aren't the exception to the rule. Everyone dies eventually."

Gabby knew today was going to be a strange one, when she would invite Trem to the house. She was half hoping she'd say no honestly, especially when she considered the possibility Trem may never have left that house before. Then there's the cultural factor, Manzazzu clearly were way more advanced than humans. Of course, her parents didn't need to know about the whole summoning ghosts thing. The most realistic story would be she was home taught hence why she never went to the schools, due to... Cultural differences. Sure Trem had a generic, nondescript English accent, not well spoken, no trace of any regional dialect, but that could means she could be from anywhere, she could have picked the accent up. This would all be things they discussed on the walk to the house later.

But for now, as Gabby resurfaced from "the land of nod", she knew she wanted to spend a few hours with her parents, to make sure they were still okay before going back to the manor. After throwing on her leggings and shirt, the new outfit she seemingly lived in (and the one inspired by Trem), she made her way downstairs. Her Father was preparing himself breakfast, which he never did, throwing Gabby off entirely. She noticed her Mother, sitting on the sofa with the TV on, sipping a coffee. On her lap, atop a cushion was the last remains of a bowl of cereal.

Gabby passed her Mum with a pat on the shoulder. "Morning all." She called as she moved to the kitchen.

"Morning." Both parents said in unison. Craig, all dressed up for work sans an undone tie, handed her a cup of steaming coffee. "What do you want for breakfast kid?" He asked as he finished making his toast, which he pushed to one side.

"I'll have what Mum had please." She moved closer to her Father and whispered as quietly as she could. "How's she doing?"

Her Dad glanced to his wife, making sure she wasn't paying too much attention. "As well as can be expected. She's stopped drinking the hard alcohol, helps I've thrown it all out. I'm not having her drink herself stupid."

He took out a bowl from the cupboard and a box of Gabby's go to cereal, a bowl of granola. Making sure the bowl was suitably full before adding the milk, he continued. "Honestly, I'm going to have serious words with management, see if I can book some time off so we can get away and be a family for once. It's bad to bring this up after we lost Gran I know, but after the funeral I think we need a bit of life affirmation."

Now there Gabby could agree. The last few days felt so strange and long and well, full of so much to process that she'd still be figuring out for weeks to come. "Where did you have in mind?"

She caught the bowl as it slid down the counter towards her. "Not sure yet. The summer holidays may have started for you, but for the rest of us it's still two more weeks. I'll see what I can find before I let your Mum know."

The two of them turned to the living room as they heard Mavis call out. "My ears are burning!"

That morning was spent doing something Gabby was actually missing, they were being a happy family. In light of what happened, Gabby's "disappearance" and her Gran passing away, she was surprised how things almost felt normal. But that's what they did, it happened last time and it would happen again. Knowing that the dearly departed wouldn't want them to become so depressed that they'd struggle to get out of bed in the morning would be against their wishes. Like before, they'd grieve and then continue to live on, always remembering.

After half an hour of bonding time, it was time for her Dad to leave for work. Fixing his tie and straightening his jacket, he gave Mavis a goodbye kiss and did the same to Gabby, but not before playfully ruffling her hair. After he left, the two sat, watching the film review program they followed.

A good horror comic, Nightmare On D Wing had been adapted into a feature film, and the reviews for it was getting were strong. It was about a Nurse, Shreela Chowdhury who was murdered by a patient in a mental institute who had come back to life and was targeting the wards once again. Gabby wondered if she'd be able to watch her cheesy horror movies the same way, with the notion that they might be in poor taste given her company. Still, she'd never look at a Jenny Abernathy movie the same way, being on first name basis with her disembodied spirit.

"I might go and see Nightmare On D Wing with Manisha and Bobbi in a few days time." Gabby commented, breaking the silence between them. She had got a text that had slipped her mind, Manisha wanted to get everyone together before having a day in Mortsbury town centre. Maybe if she convinced Trem to come to their meal tonight then maybe she could come along. Introducing her to Bobbi and Manisha would be interesting.

"With your friends?" Mavis asked, taking a sip of her second coffee of the day.

Gabby leant her head against her Mum and grinned. "Yeah, I wouldn't drag you to one of my blood fests. I know you don't have the stomach for it!" She teased.

"Oh hush you!" Came the response. Sharing the laugh together really did make Gabby feel better. Any animosity Mavis may have felt towards her daughter was nowhere to be seen.

After a rather pleasant lunch, Gabby put on her boots and trench coat and was preparing to head out. "Right, I'm just going to talk with Trem and see if she's still okay for tonight. I'll say there's plenty of lasagne but we both know that's an understatement. Your meals would keep the entire Ninth Legion happy."

As she finished slipping her foot into her boot, her Mum called out from the other room. "No need to flash off your History GCSE Gabby, we all know you did well!"

Gabby snorted as she flicked her hair out from behind the coat's collar. "Right, see you in a bit!"

"Got your phone?" Came the quick fire question.

Her mobile was sat comfortably in her deep pocket. "Mobile present and correct! Won't be long!"

After saying their brief goodbyes, Gabby headed out, back to the manor. Hopefully the search for Treman would yield results and she wouldn't have to go through that ordeal again. Her skin still was delicate against the slight breeze, stinging ever so slightly. She might have permanently damaged her skin, but it gave her more reason to hate that bitter old man. What was his deal anyway?

She didn't know or care, she knew she defeated a Faragh in the Styx and she could do it again. Though, only just, which filled her with less confidence, getting lucky isn't a great show of skill. With the house looming, she took a moment to savour the warm sunlight and the sweet air. The house was always on the gloomier side, and was always colder inside than outside so in the height of summer that was a useful thing to have.

When she entered the house, she saw Jenny and Abhay in the living room, both conversing with worried looks on their faces. She overheard some of the conversation from the half opened door.

"Still no sign of him. Trem's checked the Ishtar Gate, but it's not like we can use it." Jenny said, holding her arm.

"There's nowhere else he could have gone, unless he escaped out of the manor. If he corrupts in the outside world he could do more damage..." Abhay stopped when he heard the door to the manor close.

Gabby poked her head around the corner. "Hey guys." She called.

"Gabby! Great to see you're okay sugar." Jenny flew over, inspecting Gabby's head. "Your looking right as rain all things considered."

Gabby stepped into the living room, Jenny following close to her. "Nothing a good night's sleep didn't cure. So, I'm guessing the search isn't going well?"

Abhay ran his hands through his thick black hair and sighed. "We spent all night turning the house upside down and no luck. We're just hoping he didn't slip outside."

That thought filled Gabby with dred, the last thing she'd want to see is that old fool bringing harm to anyone. "The good news is at least if he did start to cause any problems, we'd have heard about it. Our neighbors are massive gossips so they'd know if something was amiss."

A familiar sensation brushed against Gabby's shoulder. Glancing to her side, she saw Woody had perched on her, sitting down and cooing quietly. Gabby stroked the wooden bird's head gently with her finger.

"I know yesterday was hard on you, but do you remember seeing anything...?" Abhay began, trailing off at the end. He didn't want to cause any unnecessary distress by making Gabby recall the incident.

Gabby sat down on the sofa and put her head in her hands, trying to recall any details. Her vision had blurred, all she could see were fuzzy outlines. She could just about make out Treman before she blacked out, his outline turned his back to her. "He wasn't facing the window, I think there was something else..."

Jenny turned to Abhay. "There's that mirror in his room, with that gold and blue metal around it."

Abhay began to head out the room as he responded. "I'll let Trem know."

With the two alone, Jenny floated towards her friend and sat vaguely on the sofa. Gabby had been wanting to ask her something for ages, since they first started talking like friends. She was an icon, a pop culture symbol of a romantic bygone age. Her Gran was a big fan, she had grown up seeing her face for years, always eternal in youth and always with a smile on her face. She swallowed hard and addressed Jenny eye to eye. "Jenny, there's something I've been meaning to ask you."

The smile she returned was a welcome thing, it eased Gabby somewhat from her slightly tense state. "Sure, fire away sugar."

Gabby itched the back of her head out of nerves and continued hesitantly. "When you... Died..." She could already see the smile fade from Jenny's face. "...Were you aware of the rumors flying around about you?"

Then came a deathly silence, which chilled the room more then Jenny's ghostly presence did. Thankfully, Jenny began to laugh. "Rumors, really? I didn't think I was worth anything so silly! What were they saying about me?"

Gabby felt the weight lift off and began chuckling with her. "Well for one that you owed money to the Mafia and your death was an assassination. The other was that you were having an affair with Ernest Carmichael and his ex wife was the one who arranged to... You know..."

She honestly found it a relief when Jenny found this all amusing, she laughed hard for a while before she was able to form words. "Oh my, how exciting did they think my life was? I'm kind of flattered honestly!" She let her chin rest on her fist as she continued.

"Well I was never that smart enough to do any risky business with anyone, so the only way I had anything to do with the Mafia was that small role I did in Crimes By The Strike Of Midnight when I was starting out. As for Ernest, he was a sweetheart yeah but he treated me like a daughter, he really looked after me but he never did anything like that. He loved his wife too much, he was always showing me the family polaroids in between filming." She chuckled to herself. "I'm kind of surprised they figured my life was that thrilling."

That actually felt good to know, it means at least Gabby could know the truth. She really wondered about the next question, so she bit her lip and kept her voice down to a barely audible mutter. "Was it painless?"

Jenny looked away for a moment, gazing off into the distance. Part of Gabby really didn't want to know honestly. "Well, I got a bit of a startle when I saw the station wagon come up the road towards me... Then everything went black and I heard a crunch. I felt a little woozy, like I'd been spinning in circles and next thing I knew, I was on the high road to the promised land. Well, high river I guess."

Gabby moved towards Jenny, hovering by the Etemmu's hand. Gabby kept hers open and curled her fingers, putting them around Jenny's non corporeal hand. The two locked gaze's once again and smiled at each other. Their quiet moment was broken when Skye appeared at the door. "Oh, hi there love." Jenny called to Skye.

"Hello dear. Is it okay if I have a word with Gabby?" She asked, one hand resting on the hilt of her sword, which would worry Gabby were it not for her realisation it was Skye's go to pose to relax and reassure herself.

"Sure love." Jenny flew over and gave her lover a kiss. "I'll give you two some privacy. I need to tell Trem something." With that, Jenny left the room, through the wall as per usual.

Skye moved towards Gabby hesitantly, drumming her fingers on her sword's hilt. "Listen, Gabby... I know we got off on the wrong foot." That much was obvious, the former pirate nearly scared Gabby to death and certainly came across as fierce as her research suggested. "...But I want you to know I'm sorry for how I treated you."

Gabby was very quick to respond. Even though she knew Skye was more or less benign towards her, she still felt a little intimidated by her. In time though, that was likely to fade. "No need to apologise Skye. But I accept it. Honestly you were all in the right. I was the one who barged in here, twice without Trem's permission. I'd be like that to any intruder honestly."

Skye bowed her head and moved to the sofa, taking off her tricorn. Her deep red hair fell to her shoulders in a messy pile, something Gabby had never seen before. Skye never took her hat off, so this must mean something pretty important.

"You're very understanding. It's refreshing to see." She put her hat on her lap and crossed her leg, glancing at Gabby from the corner of her eyes. "If there's anything you need..." She began. A non corporeal ghost couldn't offer much to a mortal like Gabby, except what Etemmu always offer Manzazzu, knowledge, experiences and wisdom. Gabby had come to figure that out pretty clearly.

Well, she asked Jenny the same question, so it couldn't hurt to ask Skye. Though, unlike her lover, Skye was more defensive and brash, so probing into her past may not be a great thing to do. But, in for a penny and what not. "Yeah, can I ask a personal question?" All she needed was a nod from Skye and she hesitantly continued, as much as the build up did flare up her anxiety. Clenching her sweaty hands, she chose to avoid Skye's gaze.

"When I found out who you were, I did some research. I found out all about you." She started smiling, still avoiding Skye's gaze, which was just as well because the pirate Etemmu was gazing back at her. "Honestly, I thought you were pretty awesome. You went against the society you were in and lead a life of bravery. It's kind of inspiring."

Skye remained silent, her mouth was slightly agape and her eyes were misty with memories of those days. "Well, Jenny taught me this quote I've come to like. It was the best of times, it was the worst of times. We didn't just go against the law because we thought it would be fun, it's a dangerous thing. You can't take open rebellion like that lightly, not with the punishment being execution if you're caught." She shrugged her shoulders, her hand pivoting in the air.

"Plus it's the same old story about women and how we shouldn't be in charge, no one would take us seriously if a woman took command. Especially as I was a noble woman." She put her hand on her jacket's lapel and adopted a snooty, upper class accent. "The Lady Skye Bloodworth of Trent, daughter of Lord Maximilian Bloodworth." She scoffed and shook her head disapprovingly. "No, that could never be me. I always was a tomboy at heart."

Gabby glanced over while Skye was staring off into the distance. Seeing her smile certainly eased her. "So how did you get into piracy?"

As Skye began to reminisce, she acted out the story with her hands. She held her hand out to the window of the living room. "It was the winter of 1580, the worst storm on record. The fierce winds and the violent seas brought a foreign trade ship far off course and right into our family owned port. We owned land by the coast and had our own little jetty. We couldn't pass on a chance like this, so I assembled the house staff and we took the ship and it's cargo! The crew were sent on their way and we took the ship as our own. Over the next few years, the men and women under my employment became my crew. Think about it, maids and butlers casting off their serving duties to sail the seas."

Honestly? That sounded unbelievably cool to Gabby. She could just imagine it now, Skye on deck surrounded by the formerly stuffy butlers and the silent, timid maids who were all transformed into swashbuckling lords and ladies of the oceans. "Sounds amazing. So, what about those bad times you mentioned?"

The smile faded from her face rather slowly. "Well, of course it meant the rest of my family lost all their money and land. In hindsight, I should have spared at least a thought to them, but no. I was too quick and impulsive to consider anything else. I wanted adventure and to break out of society's shackles and I dragged my Father and two brothers down with me." She stood up and put her hat back onto her head, her red hair still around her shoulders.

"They turned on me in the end. We bribed and bought our way out of execution with the Queen and managed to land a pardon, after giving her all the riches we accumulated. Can you imagine how that feels? You vow to give your life to fight against your foes, but you end up so afraid of death that you give your enemy what they want. We wanted to send her a message, that we won't stand for her money grabbing and strangle hold taxations and we just gave her more money."

She put her hand back on her sword and tilted the tip of her tricorn over her eyes. "In the end, it wasn't enough. My father died in poverty and one of my brothers contracted a disease. With no money to go to a doctor, he died soon after. That just left one last brother, who wanted to get revenge on me for ruining the family."

Gabby could already hear a slight tremor in Skye's voice. She stood up and slowly and hesitantly approached Skye. The red head turned away and kept her eyes hidden under her hat. "He found the ship when we were docked. He set the whole thing on fire and came for me. The rest of the crew got out fine, I bought them time. In the end..."

She almost choked on her words, putting a hand to her eyes. She was really trying not to break up in front of Gabby. She sniffed and rubbed her hand down her face, holding her neck high and forcing the last words out. "In the end, I wasn't as good as I thought I was. He killed me in that duel, got me right in my black heart as he said."

Gabby covered her mouth in shock. She always knew Skye as this strong and iron hard pirate, but the way this revelation brought it all into perspective was hard to stomach, much less believe. "Skye, I'm so sorry..."

She caught a glimpse of the sadness in Skye's eyes, they were so unlike her. All the time she had given off this facade of confidence and strength, but in reality, she was just like the rest of the Etemmu, Trem and Gabby herself. Someone who had been hurt by the world and was just trying to make her time on it as bearable as possible. "Hey, don't apologise. Things are better now, I have Trem and Jenny. They make me feel like I can serve some higher purpose in this world anyway."

Neither Gabby nor Skye said anything for a while, either they were both unable to say anything or wanted to remain quiet out of respect. Having felt she said her bit, Skye was about to start heading for the door, before Gabby called to her. "Skye, I think your pretty awesome you know. We shouldn't linger on the past, I don't think. I think we should keep looking forward."

Skye turned to Gabby, her lips curling into a smile and her eyes closing. "That's a good idea. Thanks for hearing me out. We'll... We'll talk later?" She asked, the confidence and valour of her voice now replaced with a quiet, somber tone.

"Yeah, of course. I'll see you soon Skye." Gabby watched as Skye left the room through the wall, leaving a thin layer of frost.

Gabby stood up from her seat and sighed, walking to the window. The afternoon sun was already visible from the high wall of the garden, the wire statue reflecting the light and sending it back at Gabby. Glancing around, she noticed Hogarth entering the garden. Gabby made her way out of the living room and to the door leading to the outside. Opening the door, she took in a big gulp of the sweet air, the warm sunlight felt great on her skin. Approaching Hogarth, she kept her footsteps light on the ground. "Umm, Hogarth?" She called.

The actor span on the spot, clearly jumpy and on high alert. He looked relieved to see Gabby. "Oh thank goodness it's you. What can I do for you?"

Gabby held out her hands, as if showing she was unarmed...For some reason. "Hi. How are things going?"

The on edge actor glanced around the garden before replying. He really wasn't taking Treman's disappearance well. "I will be of ease when that scoundrel is put to rest once and for all. Though, presently... Some distraction wouldn't go amiss."

The way the day was going, it felt like Gabby was going through all the Etemmu, getting them to recount their life stories. Still, if they were to work together, the less secrets kept the better. "If you want a distraction, I do have a few questions I'd like to ask if that's okay with you?"

Hogarth's face light up like a Christmas Tree, which was nice for Gabby to see. Clapping his hands together rather playfully, it looked like the worry drained out of his body. "Oh please do Miss Morgan!"

Honestly, that was kind of adorable. It made him so excited, it really helped ease any nerves about the current situation. "Call me Gabby please. So, I was wondering what it was like, being one of Shakespeare's actors? I've done my research on you all and you sound like you had a lot of fun in those days."

Hogarth bowed in front of Gabby. "And you may address me as Thomas, if you so wish." He straightened out his back and began to tell his tale. "When we first started, I was but a mere amateur searching for my chance to eat at the top table. I had heard of the good Bard but never would have guessed I would fit his criteria." He paused to dramatically flick a lock of hair back off his face. "He saw I had a decent enough capacity to retain lines and asked me to read one of his passages. After that, he requested my presence at the Globe, that is when the great adventure began!"

Hogarth always had a way of diffusing the tension of a situation, but maybe it was because he was always played "the fool" character for his whole life. Gabby understood that, as she was much like that with her own group. If she was always the eager and energetic one then it would hopefully make everyone else feel better. Ever the clown, she thought. "Did you flub your lines at all?"

The former actor scoffed and chortled. "Every other night! We only had a few days to learn the plays, a week if we were lucky. The audience knew not what the script said, so we could get away with anything! The skill lies not in the memory, but in the recovery when you... Flub." Clearly struggling with the 21st century vocab but still, Hogarth took it in his stride.

"Nice." She replied, trailing off into the distance when she contemplated asking what was vast becoming The Question.
She was sure it was in very poor taste, but things had gone so well with Skye, why not give it a go? They didn't need to answer if they didn't want to. "I wanted to ask you something, you don't have to answer if you don't want to..."

He held out his arms and returned her concerned look with a confident and bright smile. "The forum is open, submit your questions."

Blimey, there really was no end to his expansive syntax. "Okay... Well it struck me you're kind of young. Can I ask what happened?"

She was really taken back to see the expression on his face, he was still smiling. "Oh a rather fast and graceless end actually. Fell from a horse. A swift dislodge of the neck and fare thee well mortal world. Twas as simple as that."

Simple as that? Not the words Gabby would have chosen. She of all people knew people take death in different ways, but to be so blase' about your own death? Suddenly Thomas Hogarth didn't seem like the quirky funny man, the real man began to break through the cracks.

Of course, we all wear a mask for every occasion. For Gabby, she had acquired a new mask in light of her time with Trem. Before then, she was the geeky horror movie fan who treated life like a game during her time in high school and college. In the presence of her parents, she was outspoken but respectful, having been brought up with manners and common courtesy, something her Dad says is lacking these days.

Now of course this new world that had presented itself to her was constantly tugging at her mind, she had to hide it from her parents as best she could, for as long as possible.

Drawing her attention back to Hogarth, she peered up at his still smiling face. "Right. Well, history did remember you. I did some research before I came here and you're regarded as one of the influential Shakespearean actors."

For an Etemmu to blush was something so strange to look at. They had no blood supply, but their forms certainly mimicked blood, sweat and tears in it's non corporeal form. "Gabby, you drive an old man to modest embarrassment! But thank you though." He glanced back at the house, a hint of unease disrupted his smile. "I should be joining the others."

Gabby looked at the house, Treman's windows, now uncovered, let the light flood into them. She could see the distant outline of Trem inside the room. "Yeah, I think we'd better."

The two made their way out of the garden and back into the cool, dark manor house. As they round a corner ready to climb up the stairs, Abhay emerged from a wall and intercepted the two. "Hogarth, did you find anything in the garden?"

The response was a shake of the head, prompting Abhay to mutter under his breath. He noticed they were in Gabby's company and gave Hogarth a light pat. "Hey I'll catch up in a sec." The former actor nodded and disappeared up the stairs, leaving Gabby and Abhay alone.

"I spoke with Skye and Jenny. I'm glad to see you're okay. What you had to go through was pretty hard I imagine."

Gabby shrugged casually, trying to seem offhand and indifferent, and failing. "We get through hardships in life don't we? I'm sure you know about that, being a war hero and all that."

Abhay looked impressed as he crossed his arms. "Is that right? Where did you hear this?"

How do you explain the internet to an 18th century Indian soldier? "Umm, well, research. I looked up all four of you, I wanted to know what you guys were like back in the day." Gabby responded.

Abhay let out a small chuckle from behind his beard as he closed his eyes. "Well, I'm no hero. All I did was serve my country."

Well that was total nonsense. In the most respectable tone she could, she contradicted his statement. "Oh be fair! You united your soldiers and lead them to victory, it's a pretty awesome sounding thing."

The Etemmu began to get fidgety, scratching his non corporeal beard. "Well, yes... But it was more because I wanted to see our land be free, so we all did what we had to." The modesty was a far cry from the jovial swordsman she thought she knew before. He and Skye really were just putting on fronts to hide parts of themselves they didn't want anyone to see. But they'd both opened up to Gabby, which was something she wasn't expecting.

"That's very selfless Abhay, I feel really fortunate to know you." Gabby smiled, really wanting to shake his hand or do something. Given his physical state, that wasn't such a good idea. What Treman did to her was still slightly stinging her face, so she wanted to avoid it as much as possible.

Abhay bowed his head and gave Gabby a smile. "The same for you too Gabby. Oh, I take it you know how...You know..." He held his hands up and pointed to his head.

"Yeah..." Gabby's research into Abhay had produced more results then it did for Skye and Hogarth. A brief illness claimed Abhay while he was away from India, ending his time on the Earth.

"Good, why should we focus on the depressing anyway?" He reached in to give Gabby a friendly pat on the shoulder but stopped himself, the glimmer fading from his eye as he looked at his hand for a moment. Clenching his fist, he glanced back up at Gabby. "Anyway, I better not keep you."

Gabby sprung into life, as if she received an electric shock, she jolted upright and started stammering. "No, no it's okay, really! I was just going to talk with Trem that's all."

Abhay moved to the side and held his hand out, as if presenting the way like a butler would. "Then I will let you get on. If you want to talk further Gabby, you know you can talk to me, to any of us."

Gabby slowly made her way up the steps to the next level of the house, turning to Abhay as she did. "Thank you, same to you all."

Once Abhay vanished into the lower levels, Gabby's thoughts drew to Trem. Last time she saw her, she had made a swift exit to be with her parents, Trem no doubt would still be worrying about her. She reached the top of the stairs and spied an open door, specifically the door to Treman's room. Slowly and gently, she approached the open door and peered inside.

Trem was standing in the room, her back to Gabby. In her hands was Sammy, who she was petting gently. The room had been turned upside down, the window had been smashed open and the floorboards were ripped up, both because of the chains which were still strewn on the ground, but others had been torn up in a vain attempt to search for clues.

Woody had perched himself on the shattered remains of the full body mirror in the room. Gabby couldn't help but notice Trem's hand was covered by blood stained bandages. Whatever Gabby missed, must have been pretty bad.

"Trem?" Gabby called.

Trem turned on the spot, her bandaged hand still petting Sammy. She looked exhausted, like she'd been up all night working really hard to find anything of use, and this was the case. Her eyes looked heavy and her black and white robe was creased. "Gabby. How are you feeling?"

Being careful not to step on any of the broken floorboards, Gabby took a big step into the room. Keeping her eyes on the ground, she replied. "Much better thanks. I just spent the evening with my parents." When she finished traversing the upturned room, she leaned in and kissed Trem on the cheek. After receiving the same from Trem, she gestured to her hand. "Do you mind me asking what happened?"

Trem pointed nonchalantly to the mirror, and Woody dipped his head so his beak pointed to the broken mirror. "I wanted to make sure nothing could be hidden there, and I may have taken out some anger on it." Trem flinched slightly, Gabby had taken her injured hand in her warm and soft hands, holding it gently.

"I'm so sorry for all this. If I just listened to you, then I would have been fine. But I ignored you and barged in here anyway."

Trem slowly took her hand from Gabby's grip and put her uneasy hand to her face. Feeling the heat from it brought a tingle through Trem's body. The manor was usually dark and cool, she wanted to keep it that way. The only times she'd ever venture outside was to the garden, to get the food for Sammy or herself. "Gabby…" She began, speaking in a whisper. "…You have nothing to apologise for. I should have come in here years ago, but I was afraid of this room, ever since I was a little girl. It's stupid I know but…"

Gabby interrupted Trem by giving her a kiss on the lips, causing the Manzazzu to turn a light shade of pink. "Trem, it's fine. Really, it's all fine. I'm okay, you don't need to worry." The two put their hands on the backs of each other's heads and rested their foreheads against each other, having a moment to take it all in.

Trem was the first to open her eyes, her jet black iris' staring at Gabby and misting over slightly, thinking of how long she had spent alone. The happiness Gabby was giving her... It was bliss. Which was why she decided on her next course of action. "There's something I'd like to give you."

Gabby opened her eyes and leant out of their embrace. "Oh?"

Taking her friend's hand, Trem lead her out of Treman's room and into her own, where she gently returned Sammy to the tank, pausing to give him one last stroke. She then walked to the table in the centre of the room, where a wooden box was sat. On it was Manzazzu writing embossed in gold. Trem moved her fingers over the lid. "I found these, they belonged to my Father. Until they come back, I don't think they'd mind if I borrowed them..."

Gabby watched as Trem opened the box. Peering inside, she saw that inside was a full set of ten rings, all with gemstones attached. They were the same as Trem's. She looked at Trem, as if to ask if they really were her's. She chortled as she gave Trem a big old hug. "Thank you Trem!"

Trem span Gabby on the spot for a few rotations, laughing with her. "I thought it was about time!" She slowed down, enough to reach into the box and take out the sapphire ring. "I want to teach you how to use a sword, just as I was. Manzazzu style." She slipped the ring on Gabby's right thumb. "That way we can both make Treman regret crossing us, and anyone who thinks of doing the same."

It was a good fit on Gabby, a little loose, but better than being too tight. The ring encircled the blue stone with a band of silver and it caught the light from the window. Now Gabby could use the flaming swords, just like she did in the Styx. "Heck yeah we will! It's perfect Trem, thanks so much. You're the best." She made a tight fist as she decided to herself that now would be as good a time as any to ask. "Oh, and Trem?"

Still blushing after the compliment, she replied with a small... "Yes?"

"Can I invite you to dinner at my place?"

Chapter Fourteen: "Outside"

"This world of Manzazzu and Etemmu isn't the be all and end all. There's a whole other world out there."
"Yes, a Human world."

Trem stared blankly at Gabby, this one simple question took her so off guard. She had been born in the manor and had stayed in it's confines all her life. The only times she went out into the garden, the walls were always too high to see anything over. Her Manzazzu training had always taught her to avoid the Human world, Manzazzu have no place in it. Manzazzu needed to remain unattached to the things they summon.

They always expected a certain level of distance, so they wouldn't grow attached to the Etemmu. But this wasn't the case with Trem, she'd broken all the rules as it was. She had formed a friendship with her four Etemmu and then there was Gabby. It wasn't a case of not wanting to break anymore rules, she could go for broke on that front. It was more that she was afraid. Her house offered security, protection and the comfort of familiarity.

"Gabby... I don't know what to say..." Trem began, sitting down on her bed.

Gabby hesitantly perched on the bed. "If you're not comfortable with it, I'm not going to make you come or anything, it's your decision."

Going against Treman's orders and inviting Gabby into the house felt so good, mainly due her going out her way to spite him. But that was a stranger coming into her territory, one that she knew every nook and cranny of, save for Treman's room. There was a whole world out there, totally unexplored. Gabby had more than proved capable of giving her new found confidence and support, but this was no small task.

"I've never been outside of the house before..." She began, feeling the nerves and anxiety kick in. "I barely know anything about your world, and what I do know is at least fifty years out of date."

Gabby reached out and rested her hand on top of Trem's. The two lifted their heads and Gabby leaned in closer. "Hey it's okay, I understand. I imagine it's all going to be a little disorientating anyway..."

Trem spun her wrist and and closed her fingers around Gabby's. "I mean...Can you show me? If it's with you, I think I can do it."

Gabby felt Trem's grip, it was pretty strong. She could see it in her eyes too, she was so nervous. "Of course I will, as much as you want to see."

Trem's face light up so bright, it certainly eased up Gabby's worries. "I want to see what you do. What's normal for you?"

That wasn't exactly an easy question to answer, since the last word Gabby would use to describe herself and her friends was normal. "Well, we were talking about meeting up, going into town, grabbing lunch and watching a film, I can let my friends know and we can do it today."

Trem looked like an excitable child being told a bedtime story. "Watching a film? Like one of Jenny's?" She asked.

Nightmare On D Wing was hardly the fluffiest bit of nostalgic romance Jenny starred in, more like a psychological horror. But Trem dealt with Faragh, nothing a movie could show would come close to that real horror.

"Let's just say it's closer to your experiences." Gabby explained. "Then after that maybe I could take you to see my parents, have a nice meal while we do so?"

Interacting with Humans...Humans who weren't Gabby... As a Manzazzu there were probably a hundred things wrong with that. But as far as Trem was concerned, there were no Manzazzu to tell her otherwise. As much as her nerves were really building up, she knew that if she had Gabby's guidance, she couldn't do too much wrong.

"That sounds nice. Okay Gabby, yeah I'll join you." She replied, after a moment of quiet contemplation.

They made their way out of the room and to the staircase, where they were met by Woody who perched himself on the desk as they arrived in the living room. Trem explained the situation to the four Etemmu, who were all unfamiliar with the idea of being left alone in the house. But they all were in agreement and supported Trem's decision. With Abhay being put in charge in their absence, Gabby and Trem headed to the door.

"You ready?" Gaby asked, taking Trem's hand as she placed the other on the door.

"I am." Came the confident reply.

The door slowly opened, letting the sunlight burst into the room. Gabby went first, taking a few steps to clear the door before stopping. Trem was hesitant to say the least. Her black eyes squinted at the light, causing them to leak. Gabby held out her hand, reaching out for Trem, ready to take her to this new world, just as Trem had done with her. As Trem reached out to take her friend's hand, she felt the warmth of the sun against her skin, and it felt good. Trem took the extended hand and closed the door behind her. Taking in a deep breath, she could smell the aromas of grass and feel the fresh air against her skin.

"Shall we?" Gabby asked, beckoning to the path leading onto the road, her usual journey to the manor.

They both locked hands. "Yes." Trem responded as they began their journey.

The overgrown brambles were another matter though. Gabby had forgotten they were still a bit of a chore to overcome. "Ahh, yeah this is a bit of a bugger to get through..."

While Gabby was looking at the thick obstruction, she didn't notice that Trem had unsheathed her sword from the scabbard on her belt and was walking up to the mess of plant life. "You brought the sword?"

Trem slashed at the brambles like a knife through butter, barely breaking a sweat. "Of course!" A few seconds later and she successfully trailblazed a clear path for them both.

"You can be pretty scary sometimes you know? Attractive, brilliant and a little bit scary." Gabby stated as she watched Trem returned her blade.

"Thank you." She replied as they climbed through the cleared passage.

It wasn't long before they arrived on the main street. Glancing around, Trem was taken aback by the row of houses lined up across the road. "They're all so small..." She muttered. Her big house was certainly not the norm to the Humans who lived around her. Human beings settled for so much less than the Manzazzu, in all aspects of life.

Manzazzu lived longer, were more resilient, were taught how to use magic and understood a higher plain of existence. Trem had often wondered why Manzazzu summon Humans back from the dead, if it was for accumulating knowledge then why rely on a race that should be their inferior? But it came to Trem years ago, Manzazzu must be curious by nature. If they couldn't go into the Human world and see for themselves, then they would learn vicariously through the Etemmu.

"What did you say?" Gabby asked.

Trem didn't even realise she was staring off into space. "Hmm? Oh nothing. It's just...Is this a normal Human settlement?"

Gabby scanned her eyes across the row of houses. "Yeah, I guess so. It's pretty quaint by our standards. Not the most exciting or adventurous place, but you know, it's home."

The sound of an approaching car alerted Trem, she reached for her sword and adopted a fighting stance. "What is that?"

Oh yeah, why would she know about cars? It's not like Jenny explained in great detail what they were. "Trem, relax please!" She took Trem by the hand, preventing her from drawing her blade. "It's a car, it's transportation! Don't worry, they're not dangerous."

They watched as a grey saloon car drove past them and pulled up into one of the drives. They watched as a blonde woman climbed out of the car, grabbed a bag of shopping and entered the house. Trem turned to Gabby. "I thought Jenny said one of those things killed her?"

This was going to be hard to explain, describing things that are so mundane was going to be difficult, because one generally doesn't think about them that much. "Well yeah, but on a rare occasion, they go out of control. The driver can get distracted or the weather might be bad and they could crash. It's not like they're anything evil. Well, except maybe any car made by Skorda." Trem just stared blankly at her. "It doesn't matter."

"So this is all your technology then."

Gabby lead Trem down the road as she took her phone from her trench coat pocket. "Yeah, it serves its purpose." She showed off her phone to Trem. "Useful things like communicating with each other for instance." She began texting Manisha, asking her if she and Bobbi are free.

Trem watched Gabby type. She had been communicating with Tremadore for years through handwritten scrolls sent via the little wooden box she has. It all seemed so redundant with the advent of Gabby's device. Gabby waited for a response, and when it arrived, she flashed it at Trem. "Great, they're going to meet us at the bus stop. They live in this village anyway so it's pretty quick to get us all together."

After reaching the bus stop, Gabby proceeded to answer more of Trem's questions and explained how phones work, electricity and satellites. The thought of actually being able to go into space floored Trem, she found it all rather difficult to believe. Ten minutes flew by, during which Gabby informed her Mum of the plan and gained her approval, so long as they were done by 6pm so she could get dinner on. Gabby could tell Trem was getting nervous, the new revelations must have been hard for her to take in.

Their waiting came to an end when two figures rounded the corner. Manisha, who was now in a white buttoned up shirt and Bobbi. Bobbi was around the same age as Gabby and Manisha, with dark skin and thick, black hair. Their Mother and Father came from Spain and Iran, settling down in the UK after marrying in their Mother's maiden region, Aragon. Bobbi's dream was to be a historian one day, hence taking and pretty much aceing History as a subject.

It was how Bobbi and Gabby first met. That love of history was reflected in Bobbi's outfit, pure steampunk. They wore a burgundy jacket which had gold embroidery sewn into it over a black shirt, a leather skirt with black tights and a pair of boots. The outfits never seemed to change, even in the summer, but Bobbi was much better at dealing with heat then Gabby ever could be.

Everytime Gabby saw Bobbi, it always put her in a good mood and never failed to excite her to see her friend again. Since they made the big decision, Bobbi had become such an outgoing and confident person. Now Bobbi and Manisha would meet Trem.

"Guys!" Gabby called, running up to the two who all joined together in a group hug.

Manisha and Bobbi buckled under Gabby's weight, not expecting her to do such a passionate run up. "We've not been gone that long Gabs!" Bobbi joked, patting her on the back.

Gabby stepped back from the others and gestured to Trem. "Bobbi, Manisha... I'd like to introduce you to a new friend of mine."

The rather flustered Trem gave a stiff wave of the hand. "Hello, I'm Trem." Came the blunt and graceless response. What really struck Trem was that, despite them being Human, there was a sense of familiarity with Manisha and Bobbi. Sure Manzazzu and Humans were non distinguishable on the outside, but a Manzazzu knows when they see someone of their kind.

Manisha reminded Trem of one of the pictures of the Manzazzuan Queen's aids, only younger. As for Bobbi, something about them took Trem's mind back to Priests of Ishtar, though she wasn't quite sure why.

Manisha rose her hand in a stiff manner before extending it out for a hand shake. "Hi Trem! I'm Manisha Sharma, it's great to meet you."

Trem took Manisha's hand in her own and shook it gently. "You too."

Bobbi stepped forth and presented their hand. "I'm Bobbi!" They looked Trem up and down. "I love your outfit, proper mix of styles."

Trem never really thought about it much, to her it was just her usual dress. The top and robes were all standard for Manzazzu. "Thank you. You're rather stylish yourself."

Manisha gestured to Gabby. "Speaking of which, you've made a big impression on Gabby! You did the impossible, you got her out of lumberjack shirts."

Gabby retorted with a fake laugh before clapping her hands together. "So, the battle plan, go into town for lunch and then catch Nightmare On D Wing for the 3pm showing?"

"Sounds good to me." Manisha replied.

Bobbi shuffled up next to Trem. "So, where have you been our entire lives?" They joked, nudging Trem gently when she looked confused. "I've not seen you about, you local?"

Trem scratched the back of her head. "Yes, I live in the manor house."

That got Manisha's attention as she glanced away from Gabby. "Hold on..." She turned to her friend and whispered. "As in the one where you...?"

"Yep." Came the swift reply from Gabby.

The thing that surprised Manisha the most is how matter of fact Gabby seemed about it all. "So, you know what happened all those years ago?"

Before Gabby could answer, the hiss of air brakes broke the ambiance. It certainly alerted Trem who reached for her sword. Gabby dashed over and took her hand. "Trem, seriously, it's okay. It's just the bus. Nothing's going to attack you here, don't worry."

Bobbi caught a glimpse of Trem's sheathed sword hanging from her belt as the bus pulled in. "Hey, is that real?" They asked, following Gabby onto the bus.

As Gabby took out her bus pass and ordered two returns for herself and Trem, the Manzazzu held her robe out, revealing the hilt more clearly. She pulled it out of the sheath, enough to let the sunlight bounce off the blade. Trem followed Gabby to the back of the bus and sat next to her. "This is all still so bizzare. So how far can these cars and busses take you?"

Gabby rubbed her forehead, wiping off a small layer of sweat, thinking on what was a pretty meta question. "Well, pretty far. Anywhere we want to go, if you can't drive, or walk it. Then there's flying or sailing." She became deeply concerned when Trem looked at her with a shocked look on her face.

"Humans can fly?"

Before Gabby could continue, Manisha and Bobbi joined them on the back seat as the bus began to drive off again. There was only two other people on the bus with them, they picked a good time. Bobbi sat next to Trem and Manisha next to Gabby.

Bobbi gestured to the sword. "That looks like a Talwar, from India. Where did you get it?"

Trem shuffled in her seat, the scabbard made sitting on the seats a little hard to make comfortable so she moved it about a bit. "Oh the house has a few of them around."

Bobbi shook their head in amazement. "Brilliant. You have an interest in that?"

Trem wondered why she was starting to loose her nervousness. Maybe that vague familiarity with Bobbi was settling her. Certainly,

Bobbi was someone Trem felt she could open up to, just a little bit. "My family... Originate from that area let's say. The history there is rather fascinating."

Bobbi crossed a leg and leant back on the seat. "Oh I know, I'm the same! History has always been my love, it's why I'm hoping I can get into being a historian. Ancient civilisations, that's what I love. Ancient Egypt, Babylonian, Roman Empire..."

Trem's ears pricked up, her interests peaked. "Babylonian?" So, Humans did know about the Manzazzu then?

Bobbi nodded. "Yep, I did some looking into that on my own time. I'd love to be able to go more into detail one day. Same with weapons too, anything with a blade I just find so cool. They don't make them like they used to. It's pretty cool you have one actually!"

Trem was still thinking about what Bobbi might know about her people. "Thank you..." She replied, half paying attention. "Does the word Manzazzu mean anything to you?"

There was a few brief seconds where Bobbi was scouring their memory, looking up into space while doing so. "No, I don't think so. Like I say, I'm not an expert, but if there's anything new I could learn then I'll get onto it."

Well, it's certainly not common knowledge, that was good at least. Don't want the whole world knowing they're out there. "Right, good."

Manisha leaned over to Gabby while Bobbi and Trem were talking. "So, you've been inside the house again? Did you see anything strange like last time?"

Gabby was starting to get sick of lying to her friends, but what could she really say? She promised she wouldn't let Trem's secrets slip. "Well I explained what happened all those years ago. I just saw

Trem's... Grandfather. I just thought he was a ghost, kind of disappointing really." She tried to make it look like she was joking, but in reality she was hoping Manisha would buy it, she wasn't stupid though.

"Right, that makes sense. So, what's it like in there?" She asked, ever the curious soul.

At that point Gabby didn't need to lie so strongly, more like stretching the truth. "Oh very cool. Classic gothic, massive house. I'll see if Trem will allow us to have our next get together there." Oh that was so unlikely, but it never hurt to make one empty promise. Gabby always liked to think she was an honest person, so her self esteem was really taking a battering these last few days.

"Oh can I ask, Trem, I've not heard that name before, do you know where it's from?" Bobbi asked.

Trem immediately glanced to Gabby, trying and failing to mask a worried look. When Gabby looked back at her blankly she looked back to Bobbi. "Oh it's short for... Well, it's shortened. It's a very common name in our culture."

Bobbi was full of the bright curiosity of a child, enthralled by the answers Trem was giving. "Fascinating. What culture is this, if you don't mind me asking?"

Something slipped in Trem's mind, whether she got distracted, didn't think or replied on impulse, Trem didn't know. But she didn't realise she replied with the incriminating answer before it was too late. "Oh, Babylonian."

"...What?" Came Bobbi's reply.

When the bus finally pulled up at the bus stop in Mortsbury town square, the four stepped out of the bus and made their way to the shops. The first port of call would be a return for Manisha and Gabby to the deli they visited a few days previous. Having picked their seat and discussed orders, all of which served to further confuse Trem, Manisha went to collect them.

Trem observed the brick walls, the bright lights and heat from the counter. The thing that always seemed to keep Trem anxious was the vast, open spaces the outside world always seemed to favour. Being cooped up in her house all her life really did get her used to the dark, enclosed spaces.

Gabby meanwhile was juggling three conflicting worries at the same time. The first was a worry about leaving her Mum at home. Coming to terms with her Grandma's passing was already becoming easier for her, both due to being able to say a proper goodbye and that she had this little distraction. This was something her Mum didn't have, and the thought of her turning to alcohol was a bit of a fearful one. Her Dad reassured her he wouldn't let that happen, and she was pretty sure that would put an end to that issue.

The second was whether Trem would be fine venturing out into the world. She said she'd be fine, but Gabby couldn't help but have her doubts. You can't spend your whole life inside and just be fine with the larger, wider world beyond the four walls of the manor. Especially since she wasn't Human. She still wasn't that well informed on the differences between the two races, they looked the same physically. The use of magic and living longer seemed to be the big crux of the matter. This would be a conversation for another day.

Of course the third and more pressing matter would be how Manisha and Bobbi would take to her. She'd already let slip about her family's origins, and Bobbi wasn't stupid, they could piece two and two together. They knew a lot about history, that much was obvious and of course Bobbi would know about Babylon and other ancient civilisations.

Maybe that could play into their hands, who knows? But a woman who carries around a sword, dresses one half punk and the other half robes and has jet black eyes would, even by Gabby's friendship circle's standards, look a tad strange.

Manisha arrived with the orders and sat them down on the table. They each received a sub and drink. Trem looked down at the items placed before her and poked Gabby on the shoulder. "What's this?"

Gabby took a bite out of hers and replied with her mouth full. "It's a meat sub with extra meat, you're not a vegetarian are you?" Trem tilted her head, looking rather lost. "I mean you eat meat? You don't just eat vegetables and stuff?" She continued as she swallowed her mouth full.

"No I don't think so, I just haven't had meat in years." She sniffed the sub, the aroma of piping hot bacon, sausage and other meats made her salivate. She took a mouth full and chewed gently. Her face quickly light up as she attacked the sandwich with passion while the others watched on.

Anyone would think she hadn't eaten anything like it in decades and that would be true. Since her parents vanished, Trem's few meals a month she needed, came from things grown in the garden. Manzazzuan metabolism was so slow they could function on one small meal every three weeks on average, and a pint of fluid a month.

Trem was already halfway through the food when Gabby held onto her arm. "Slow down Trem, jeez! Don't inhale the food! Take it slowly, it'll last longer."

After tearing off a piece of bread with her sharp teeth, Trem stopped, a bit of black pudding poking out of her mouth. "Okay."

Manisha couldn't help but laugh as she took slow bites out of her's. "Trem, your such a riot."

Trem blinked and slowly took another small bite. "I am?"

Gabby rubbed her lip to try and hide her mouth. "Don't worry, that's a good thing." She explained.

Bobbi used the time to pass the drinks around. A juice for themselves and Manisha and a cola for Gabby. She opened the drink with the ring pull and offered it to Trem. "Here, try this."

Trem moved the can closer to her mouth, recoiling when one of the bouncing bubbles brushed against her lip. "Is it supposed to do that?" Gabby gestured for her to take a sip, which she did with great caution. She took a small sip and quickly put the can down. Putting her hands to her lip, she started to panic, was that poison or something?

Detecting Trem's alarm, Gabby took the can from her. "Trem look, it's fine! It's just cola, it's meant to be like that." She took a sip to show her. "See? Totally safe."

Finishing a mouth full, Bobbi leaned over. "I don't want to sound rude or anything, but how long have you been in that house ?"

Trem had already begun inspecting the cola can when she gave her reply. "Oh, all my life."

Manisha coughed on her drink. "Seriously? I mean it makes sense, we've never seen you around before but... Isn't that kind of lonely?"

Trem gave the cola another go. Gently taking the drink to her lips, she flinched as the bubbles hit her. She took a sip again, followed by a larger gulp. It wasn't bad, far from it, but it was very strange for her. "I was taught everything by my parents before they went missing, but

I found out ways to stop myself feeling alone. Well, till Gabby found me anyway."

She turned to Gabby and the two exchanged warm smiles. "Yeah." Gabby patted Trem on the shoulder and allowed herself a moment to just stare at her.

"You guys are adorable." Bobbi grinned, taking another swig, with a naughty little expression on their face.

Gabby and Trem blushed, the smiles replaced by embarrassed glances, Gabby slowly taking her hand away and going back to her meal. "So, after this we'll head up to the cinema. What do you guys think, yay or nay to popcorn?"

Manisha pushed in a rogue piece of lettuce into her mouth as she replied through her mouthful. "I'm not fussed."

Bobbi also agreed. They spent a good half an hour talking, joking and discussing further plans for the future. In the middle of a conversation about Manisha going into the pharmaceutical sector, Bobbi got a message on their phone.

They shared it with the group, a picture from their absent friends, Boris and Julia who had arrived and were enjoying their time on holiday, their post results day treat. Trem looked at the image, seeing Gabby's unseen friends for the first time. Julia was holding the phone in one hand and holding the blonde, lanky Boris up with her other hand.

She was a muscular woman, with her arms very much on show. She wore a sleeveless tank top whole Boris was just in his swimming shorts. Both Julia's round, freckle covered face, and Boris' thin, pasty face both had massive grins pasted on them. Gabby explained how they met at school and how Boris got his first part time job at Julia's Father's bar. From there, their friendship blossomed into a romantic one before they knew it. Now they were engaged, they never were ones to waste time.

So this was all of Gabby's social circle. Herself, Bobbi, Manisha, Boris and Julia. So like Trem, Gabby surrounded herself with friends, people who respected her and watched out for each other. People to confide in and trust. They were similar in that regard, but there was one glaring difference, all of Gabby's friends were still alive.

The cinema was a short walk from the town centre, up a small slope and perched at the top of the road. Because of the time of day, the fact it was a horror movie and that it had been out for a few days now, Gabby was sure the cinema would be pretty quiet. Gabby stopped the group and pointed to the large poster framed on the exterior of the building. A figure in a blood stained nurse's uniform was holding a large knife, the blood dripping off into a puddle, the run off forming the words "Nightmare On D Wing."

"Well...That looks pleasant." Trem exclaimed at the poster.

Gabby brought everyone into a huddle, including the clueless Trem. "Okay, now the reviews of this are good, not amazing, but good. We've all read the comics, we all know what we should expect. Let's see how it goes."

Trem could tell this meant a lot to Gabby, this was her passion. Whatever it was. She was glad she braved the outside world, there was no way she would have been tempted without Gabby. The last few days may have been very strange for both parties, but Trem would be lying if she didn't find it all such fun. Certainly the most fun she's had in decades. This Human just appears in her life and as random as it was, Trem did feel a certain confidence with Gabby, and that was what drew the two together, the confidence and trust they shared.

They made their way into the cinema, with one bucket of popcorn to share between them, which Trem politely passed on. Gabby explained her relationship with the source material, and what comic books were too. The premise seemed gruesome and violent, and Gabby's excitement was strange.

"...So you're looking forward to seeing all these murders?" Trem knew it was fictional yes, but the only fictions she was ever exposed to were cultural tales of the Manzazzu, Ishtar and wary cautionary tales of the past.

"Yeah well, in this case they make the murderer sympathetic in a way, like you understand and feel for them because you see the origins. You know she was an innocent nurse doing her job at the ward when she was murdered, and when she came back to take revenge on her killer she couldn't help herself when she continued killing. That inability to control your actions is what makes it so engaging."

It sounded like the Faragh honestly, eerily close to them in fact. An argument could be made for how much influence Manzazzuan culture had on earlier Human culture, maybe the personification of Death as a hooded, black robed figure came from the Manzazzu. Certainly the Styx became Limbo, and Gabby saw the typical light at the end of the tunnel in the complex. As much as Manzazzu were told to keep their distance from Humans, some cracks in the woodwork would evidently slip through.

The lights dimmed and the advertisements began to play. Gabby told Trem to ignore them, though the numerous car promotions made it rather hard to do so. The fact they showed a four wheel drive off road traversing arctic landscapes was an over exaggeration and something Trem couldn't wrap her head around, why would they lie so blatantly?

Gabby quickly summed up the whole concept as it being just a ploy to make their product as appealing as possible so audiences will buy them. It was strange, and very telling of the world Humanity resides in.

Not long after, the film began. From the go, Trem was fixated on the screen. Gabby occasionally glanced over to see what Trem was thinking. She was locked on the screen, never leaving her position, leaning forwards with her mouth slightly agape.

As the movie continued, Trem didn't move an inch. During a quiet moment when the main hero looks over reports of the murders, Gabby put her hand on Trem's and leaned over, mouthing her words quietly. "You okay? Enjoying it?"

Severing her link with the screen, Trem looked around at Gabby and nodded, her open mouthed wonder never fading. Gabby felt good about that, it was always a bit of a gamble to drag her out of her house and take her to strange places, offering bizzare food and drink and then plonk her infront of an 18+ rated horror movie, where a man was hung by his small intestines not five minutes prior.

While the movie played, an odd thought entered Gabby's head. What was this all in aid of? Trem showed Gabby her world and was given the choice to stay or leave. Gabby could and would never ask Trem to abandon her world for the sake of the comparatively primitive and dull world she lived in, what would be there for her? The others in the house still needed her, she still wanted to look for her parents, the last thing she'd need is to be tempted otherwise.

Gabby did worry that she may have caused some conflict in Trem, but in reality, the truth was far less worrying. For Trem, it was all a lot to take in, and she wouldn't be able to manage it all in one sitting. She'd be reliant on the fact that she could return to the house whenever she wanted, which was reassuring.

Plus she knew Gabby was the right person to show her the world. She thought she could trust her, though there was always the one random, rogue, what if. Fortunately she managed to silence those fears every time they surfaced. While she watched the movie, taking in the loud sounds and the bright flashing lights, she wondered if her parents would approve of all this. Maybe one day she'd find out.

Chapter Fifteen: "My Turn"

"I know a place, out of the way, miles away from prying eyes."
"Go on."

Treman used the time Trem inadvertently granted him to his advantage. While she talked with the four Etemmu, Treman slid away to the corridors were the rows of armour were. The rather impressive suit with the great helm helmet and sapphire ring was still there. Treman purred with delight as he moved closer to the suit.

The ring began to glow brighter the nearer he got. Treman could feel the pull the ring was giving off, it was magnetising. He allowed himself to be sucked in, his whole spiritual form acting like water down a sinkhole, twirling and spinning until it was no more. As the glow faded on the ring, the helmet's slits lit up a dark navy blue. In the gaps of the armour was a glowing form. Treman moved his arm, the suit following is actions.

Even though his thoughts were becoming chaotic and maddening, the smug sense of satisfaction now that he had a physical form silenced them all. He reached into the rack of swords and pulled one out.

At this point, Gabby and Trem had already left, the door had closed behind them and the others had already begun to disperse. Now was Treman's time. It was exciting for him, years and decades of planning were finally happening. With the other Etemmu already going their separate ways to other parts of the house, Treman emerged from the hallway and into the living room. He stopped momentarily to look up at the picture of his daughter. His growl sounded more like a wild animal then a person's, he practically snapped at the image of his disgrace of a son in law. Tearing himself away from the image, he headed for the stairs.

The sound the armour made going up the steps was a loud, dull clunk. With every footstep he was giving himself away, but he really didn't care. There was nothing they could do, not now he had taken solid form. Once he reached the top of the stairs, he proceeded straight to his room. The door was open and the room was still a mess. Fortunately it looked like no one had found his hidden items.

In his fragmented state, Treman wasn't sure if he could remember exactly where they were either. He knew it was somewhere on the wall, he ran the hefty metal gauntlet over it. Knocking on one part, he heard the telltale hollow sound. Clenching his fist, he drove his hand into the wall. Treman didn't expect the pain, so he stifled a groan as blue blood trickled from the gauntlet. Inside the punctured wall was a mouldy wooden box, the paint had all but withered away.

He reached in and pulled the box out. Inside was his set of rings, the metal rusting and the gemstones scratched. The sapphire, ruby and emeralds were all in good condition, so he slipped them onto his gauntlet's fingers. To give them a test, he took his sword and ran his hand up the blade. The sword ignited red, unlocking the ability to kill the living, incinerating whoever the fire consumes. The fire returned to the ruby ring and Treman sheathed the blade.

Another quick blast of pain hit him once again. He hunched his back and groaned, several ribs bursting out of his back, forced out by a crushing pressure on his chest which shot them out in one agonising motion. The odd colored blood gushed from his back and his helmet. No more waiting, he had waited decades. He staggered, took out his sword and came bursting back out of the room, making an almighty racket as he did.

Hogarth was in the observatory, watching the world go by when he was startled by the loud crashing noise from below. His nerves began to flair up, something awful was happening. He floated over to the door and listened out for anything else, to his dismay, the sounds were getting closer. They sounded metallic, like someone in armour was dragging themselves through the house. Of course that was the case, someone in armour was, in fact, dragging themselves through the house, and it couldn't be any of the other three.

"Oh good lord..." He muttered, swallowing hard. Abhay's training had given him some experience, but it was hardly anything useful for the present situation.

The footfalls kept getting closer and closer. Hogarth knew he had to act. He backed away from the door, counted down to three and charged. He flew through the solid entrance, leaving a frost mark on the door behind him. He quickly glanced around, to his left, right, above and below. No sign of anyone. He breathed a sigh of relief and was about to make his way to Abhay to alert him when he froze. Issue is, he didn't want to freeze.

Hogarth felt glued to the spot, unable to move an inch. He tried to move his arm, but it felt like a great strength was pinning it to his body. Now on the verge of a panic attack, his eyes turned to the shadows behind him. He could only move his head a few inches, but it was enough to make out the form of the walking armour.

Treman let out a long, wheezing and strained laugh, holding his hand out, his emerald ring beginning to glow. With every laugh, blue blood gushed from his helmet, staining the once shining silver helmet and chest plate. Hogarth felt himself begin to drift backwards, towards the deranged Treman. He scrambled to grab hold of the guard rail, but his hand went straight through it. He must have been twelve feet away, and that distance was growing smaller and smaller. He yelped, desperate to try and get away, to no avail.

"You can't do this! You won't get away with this do you hear me?!" He screamed out, at the top of his lungs. Maybe someone would hear his cries and come to help him. "Someone help me!"

Treman extended his arm straight, his horrendous, twisted voice roared out of the helmet. "No one can help any of you now!"

All Hogarth could do is scream for help as he was pulled closer into the emerald. Before he could let out another plea, he felt his non corporeal body being lifted on its own accord. The vice like grip around his body dissipated and was replaced by a sensation that was akin to being dragged along by a fierce tide. He held his arm out, desperate to try and grab onto anything. The emerald was now glowing so bright the light was white. Hogarth began to be pulled inside, the feeling of hopelessness crushed his soul and with one final pathetic wail, he vanished into the gemstone.

The process complete, Treman held his hand up to the light. A slightly dark imperfection began to float around inside the gemstone. What a fitting description, Treman thought, an unsightly imperfection in his perfect plan. One down, three to go. Next was that simpering female.

Jenny was by one of the windows in the living room. Since Gabby had opened the light to them, she had grown fond of poking the glass with her fingers, watching frost and ice form and melt away. It was rather pretty. She wanted a little time to herself, to think about things, Gabby in particular. All those years ago, Jenny had scared her as a child. She'd felt pretty bad about that ever since she appeared and was planning on offering another apology, when they came back. As for Trem, Jenny could hardly fathom what that poor thing had gone through. Losing your family was bad enough, but the knowledge they were still alive somewhere and you're unable to find them? That was just cruel.

Jenny put her whole hand against the glass, watching the ice form around her. She was like Jack Frost now, Jackie Frost maybe? That ould have been a cute movie idea, if she was still in the industry. Come to think of it, if it were the 1950s and she were still alive. Oh well, it was a cute idea to explore in her head. She could always tell Skye about it and she and Hogarth could act it out. Sure his acting style was different to hers, but if one thing coming back into this crazy world taught her, is opposites attract.

Treman slowly made his way down the stairs, each step filling the air with a heavy, metallic thud. Jenny could hear it approaching. She drew her hand back from the glass and slowly turned around. Facing her was the walking suit of armour itself. Treman's posture had become hunched and blood continued to come from his helmet, though it was more a trickle now. Skye had always told her to be brave, to not show the enemy any sign of fear. She straightened herself out and maintained a blank expression. Of course, she was terrified, but she wasn't going to let Treman get the satisfaction of seeing her in a state.

"You came here to kill me, take me out of existence?" She asked, clenching her fists, trying her best to hold back the tears. She and Skye... They'd promised each other they were in it till the end, but if that was to be this run in with Treman then so be it. Jenny knew what her reputation was, a pretty thing to look at and sounds nice on film. Since she came back to the world of the living, she gained a new sense of perspective.

Treman shook his head and held up the emerald ring, the black impurity shooting around, desperate to get out. That did nothing to reassure Jenny, but she tried to keep as straight a face as possible. "That's Hogarth isn't it?" She knew he was in the observatory, he was never much of a fighter the poor man. "Well, if you think I'm going to come quietly, you got another think coming, sugar."

Jenny lurched out, flying towards Treman. She phased through his helmet, the blood leaking from the helmet's eyes froze, blocking his vision. Treman screamed out, clutching his head. As he staggered back, Jenny watched his pathetic attempts to claw the ice away. She hovered behind him and drove her hand through his chest. "That was for Gabby. I might be just a dead actress from decades ago, but you mess with any of us and you get what's coming to you."

Treman's hand shot up and the emerald ring began to glow. Jenny had little knowledge of Manzazzu magic but she knew to make a mad dash out of the room. She shot through the wall and into the corridor. Treman scratched away the last of the frozen blood from his helmet and caught sight of Jenny rushing down to one of the rooms deeper in the manor. He gave chase, as slow as he was in the armour.

Skye must have been around somewhere, though Jenny had no idea. She didn't tell her where she had gone. With Treman out of sight, she allowed panic to really kick in. She glanced around the room she found herself in, it was, for some reason, full of clocks. She jumped as they all struck the top of the hour, alerting Treman. She could hear the thuds from his armour approaching. Acting fast, she sank into the ground and waited.

She closed her eyes tight and held her breath, even if she was only breathing out of habit and not necessity. She could hear the thundering steps above her head, the low level growling from Treman and the odd spot of blue blood that dripped on the floor. Treman spent a few seconds looking around the room, becoming increasingly frustrated as he turned on his heels and stormed out of the room.

Jenny emerged from the ground and panted. That was too close for comfort, she needed to find Skye as quickly as possible. She rose up into the room above, which happened to be Trem's. Woody was sleeping on the table in the middle of the room and Sammy was in his little hiding place. Treman would know to check in this room, so she sped off through the wall into the next room, an unused guest bedroom.

She used the time it bought her to collect her thoughts and calm down. When Skye wanted to be on her own, she'd spend time reminiscing. Slowly emerging from the locked door, she glanced around to make sure the coast was clear. Craning her neck upwards, she could make out a figure sat on the glass dome shaped roof of the house. She shot upwards and emerged on the roof of the house. Sure enough, her suspicions were true. Skye was looking out at the view the manor had of the village.

"Skye!" Jenny almost screamed as she dashed towards her.

Skye span on the spot and without hesitation, she rushed to Jenny. The two met in the middle of the roof and embraced tightly. "Jenny, what happened? Are you okay?"

Jenny glanced down at the house below her, making sure there was no sign of the old man before she explained herself. "It's Treman. He's found a way to make himself whole again and he's got Hogarth."

Any attempt by Skye to mask the look of utter dread on her face, failed. "Please don't tell me you tried to fight him?"

Jenny just looked confused. All the times Skye had threatened Treman before, it couldn't all be for show. Skye had taught her how to be stronger, how to stand up for the people she loved. That's why she attacked Treman. "Of course I did. You told me I have to stand up to anyone who wrongs us."

Skye grabbed Jenny by the arms and brought her closer. "Yes but I don't want to see you in danger. You're not a fighter Jenny, if anything happens to you..." She couldn't finish her sentence. Swallowing hard, she spoke in a quiet hush. "Look, we can't deal with this right now. We have to get a message out to Trem."

"How are we going to do that?" They had no idea where she was. They knew how vast their worlds were, but they were all relics of the past. The 21st century would be no different than it being another planet for all of them, and finding one Manzazzu in the middle of it all would be impossible.

Snapping her fingers, Skye had an idea. "That wooden bird of Trem's, it might not find her but if it goes to Gabby's house then at least it can warn them when they get back."

Jenny took Skye's hand and kept it close to her chest. "That's a great idea. I know where it is, I'll go tell Woody. I don't know where Abhay is but hopefully we can get the message out before Treman finds us."

They sank back into the house and made their way to Trem's bedroom. Meanwhile, the armour clad old man was becoming increasingly frustrated, his search for Jenny had produced no results. In a bout of pure rage, he punched a sizable hole in the wall.

"Is that any way to respect the house?" A female voice rang through his mind. He turned around to see where the voice had come from, and what he saw chilled his corrupted soul to the very core. Standing before him, as clear as day, was his other daughter, Trem's late aunt. She wasn't half faded like the Etemmu, she was as clear and as alive as the day he saw her off to Euphretia to marry a high status Manzazzu.

Of course, in reality he was talking to thin air. Hallucinations weren't always common with corruption, but since Treman was insistent on drawing his out as long as possible and resisting it at every step, anything could happen.

He looked her up and down, she still wore the white Manzazzu robes with the black trim her sister wore in the portrait. She was also wearing Manzazzu rings, set in gold rather than silver and a sapphire pendant was around her neck. Like Treman and her sister, she possessed the clan's telltale white hair, but hers was balled up into one large hair bun with a jewel encrusted hair pin protruding from the top of it. A few strands had come loose and fell across her face, forming bangs.

"It's you..." Treman grunted, the sounds coming out of his mouth barely sounded human anymore.

The vision of his daughter raised her hand and slapped him across the face. If she was actually there, the helmet would have shielded himself from the pain he felt.

"Have all your plans paid off yet, Father? Have you finally gained the glory you wanted so badly?" She asked. For a figment of his imagination, she was being rather brutal in her honesty. "Have you preserved your precious family name enough? Have you shaken up the world and ripped down the root of power?" She took several slow steps, approaching Treman who was backing up, trying to avoid getting any closer to her.

Eventually Treman stopped, he had his back up against the wall and could go no further. "The Queen still rules, your Granddaughter is with the Humans and your mighty fighting force are three orphans you plucked from the streets. Face it Father, admit it. You don't have a chance."

Treman shook his head, his eyes leaking blood, creating tear streaks down the helmet. "You're wrong...!"

Trem's aunt smiled, the same smug, self satisfied look she wore on the tribute tapestry. "Even your attempts to get rid of my Sister have failed. You thought throwing them into the Styx would be enough? You coward, you should have killed her. But you didn't, you could never bring yourself to do it could you? Too much of her Mother in her!"

Treman roared as he brought his gauntlet down, slashing through the hallucination which shattered into tiny pieces before fading away. He breathed a rattling, horse sigh of relief. At least he wouldn't have to listen to her anymore.

After a moment of blissful silence, the voices continued. "That's your biggest fear, isn't it? Failure. You scare yourself senseless that all your efforts will come to nothing. You want to change the world so badly you can't cope with the idea that you will change nothing, and will be forgotten. Treman, lord of nothing, remembered for nothing."

The panic and rage in Treman boiled. "Shut up!" He bellowed as he turned to face the wall and drove his head into it, denting the helmet and creating a crack in his skull. His helmet fell from his head, his soul now nothing but a twisted mess of deformed bones and rage. With his ribs and spine now malformed, he had lost more of his posture and was so slouched it almost looked ape like, close to dragging his hands on the floor.

In Trem's bedroom, Jenny had finished explaining the directions to Gabby's house to Woody. "Now, you fly there as quick as you can, alright hun?"

The little bird chirped and nodded it's head. It flew out of the small opening in the window and off into the distance. Skye and Jenny watched it disappear for a moment before turning back to the door. The footsteps were getting closer now.

"What are we going to do about him?" Skye asked.

Jenny took her hand. "We fight him, that's what we do. You taught me to be brave love, I got to thank you for that."

Skye wiped a thin layer of ethereal sweat from her brow, it was more like an impression of the real thing her spirit was mimicking. "Guess I got to practise what I preach. Easy to say a lot of things when you're dead."

Jenny brought her hand to Skye's cheek and leaned in for a kiss.

"Listen here, I love you and you're the bravest person I've ever known. I'm not about to let you down now." She ran her fingers gently down Skye's face. "It's okay to be afraid. We'll get through this together."

Skye took her sword from her scabbard and held it out to Jenny. "Yeah, together."

Hesitantly, Jenny took the sword and held it tight. Taking each others hands, they descended from the roof and into the house. Treman had burst through the guest bedroom and was looking for them when he saw the duo hovering thirty feet off the ground in the open section of the first level. Jenny raised her sword and adopted a ready stance, just as Skye had taught her.

Treman moved so he faced the two straight on. He held his position, fixated to the spot. Jenny inhaled, held her breath and like a shot from a cannon, charged at Treman. The shattered Etemmu acted quickly, grabbing his right arm with his left and holding it up so that the emerald ring was held up towards Jenny.

The ring flashed with a bright light and Jenny couldn't react quickly enough. Soon, she found herself in the ring's intense pull. She yelped as she felt herself being yanked violently towards Treman. She spun around and called back to Skye, throwing the sword at her.

"Skye, help me!" She pleaded as she reached her arm out as far as it could go.

Skye caught the sword and looked on in horror, watching as Jenny struggled and strained against the invisible force pulling her backwards. She froze in her spot, her hands shaking as they gripped the sword. All she could do was watch as the woman she loved was being dragged away from her.

Jenny's cries for help were causing Skye to experience bursts of memory, from when she died. A feeling of utter hopelessness came over her, keeping her tied to her spot. Her eyes filled with tears and her grip on the sword loosened. "Not again, I can't..." She muttered.

"Please Skye! Skye!" Jenny's screams began to fade away as her body disappeared into the green gemstone.

A hideous laugh came from Treman once again, that chilled Skye to the very core. Acting on pure instinct, she dashed from her spot and charged through the manor house as fast as she could. Treman dropped his arm and followed, dragging his useless body down the steps.

Circling through the rooms, Skye stopped when she reached the store room. She hid herself behind one of the many boxes, held her sword close to her chest and quietly wept. She felt like such a miserable failure, she couldn't save Jenny like she couldn't save her crew all those years ago. Skye's tricorn fell from her head, her red hair falling about her face.

"I can't do this, I can't do this again..." She muttered to herself. All she could see is Treman's twisted face, which had slowly warped in her mind into the face of the man who killed her all those years ago. The vivid memories all came flooding back, as did a stabbing sensation in her chest.

She recalled herself on the deck of her burning ship, the masts collapsing around them. Her crew had all abandoned ship and she was buying them time to escape. As brave and fearless as she always made herself out to be for her crew, Skye was far from the hero they believed her to be. In truth, she was terrified. Like she did when faced with Treman, she froze to the spot and her hands shook.

She put up a good fight, but the fight came to an end with both combatants' swords puncturing each others chests. Skye fell from the side of the ship and hit the water, her last sight before she died was of the surface world getting further and further away, then darkness.

"I don't want to go back to the darkness..." She sobbed to herself. What was the use in all that false bravery if she couldn't save the one she loved? "I'm such a failure."

The silence was broken by a familiar voice. "Skye?"

Skye jumped and tensed up. She slowly moved around to the direction of the figure, breathing a sigh of relief when she saw it was Abhay. "Oh thank....Where have you been?"

The late soldier ducked down to Skye's level, both hidden behind one of the wooden containers full of materials for Manzazzuan sorcery. "I was out in the garden. What happened? I can't find Hogarth or Jenny anywhere..." Looking at Skye's face, the fact she was so riddled with panic and trauma answered his question well enough. "Treman?"

Skye nodded. Her words were struggling to get through her mouth. "Jenny tried to fight him, but he's got her and Hogarth trapped in that ring of his, the green one."

Abhay scratched his beard and pondered for a minute. "We need to let Trem know."

Sniffing, Skye tried to calm herself, taking a breath and slowing her breathing. "We already took care of that. Trem's bird's gone to Gabby's house to warn them." Her head shot up as she felt Abhay holding her by the arms.

"Good. Now Skye, I'm not going to ask you to stand and fight, not if you think you can't. If that's the case then stay put and I'll draw Treman off your scent. That way at least I can buy some time before Trem and Gabby can come back."

Skye's thoughts drifted to Jenny. She had so much faith in her, such confidence in her bravery. She wondered how Jenny would react if she could see her in this sorry state. The spirit of a woman who went against her country's law and took it into her own hands, who faced the British Navy and the full might of an empire, now reduced to a mess of anxiety? Jenny would have some choice words to say about that.

Abhay reached down and picked up the translucent tricorn and held it out to Skye. She looked down at it, for her it represented many things. First and foremost it was a symbol of her position, both as a pirate and as a leader amongst her flock. Second and most importantly for her, it was a sign of a promise she made. That promise was to stand up for herself and her friends and never leave them behind. To resist any odds they would face and come out victorious. She wiped her eyes, she had become such a shadow of the woman who made that vow all those years ago. Sure, the fear still remained, but it went hand in hand with a new fighting spirit, freshly ignited.

"No Abhay, let's do this together. We might lose, but we'll give that monster something to think about."

Abhay smiled and reached for his sword. "That's the spirit." He pulled his sword from its sheath and straightened out into a standing pose.

"What are our offences and defences?" Ever the strategist was Abhay.

"Two ghosts with swords. At a pinch we can make him uncomfortable, maybe inflict some lasting damage." It really didn't seem like they could do much at all, but it was better than doing nothing.

Abhay moved towards the locked storeroom door. "I like those odds. I've worked with less." His head hovered near the wall, he could hear the distinctive crunching footsteps were approaching. "He's coming. Shall we strike hard and fast?"

Skye joined him, hovering beside him. "Constantly moving so we're a harder target, sounds like a good plan, Captain Singh."

She could see a little smile on Abhay's face. "Thank you, Captain Bloodworth." He turned to the wall and kept the grip on his weapon firm. "This is for Hogarth."

Following Abhay, Skye's sword rose high. "This is for Jenny."

After a countdown from five, the two Etemmu charged from the room, where Treman was waiting for them. Abhay quickly got a look at the ring where their friends were stored, a swift attack plan formed in his head. As Treman reached for his arm, Abhay took off like a shot and slashed Treman's face through the helmet.

Both Etemmu expected that to phase him, but the frozen slash mark across the head barely registered. He had slipped past the point of feeling any pain inflicted by exterior forces. Abhay acted fast, shooting through his body and out the other side as Skye reached over, grabbing at Treman's one arm he was still able to lift. She forced her hand into the armour, the frost turning hard and eventually forming into a solid sheet of ice.

When she was sure the ice was strong enough, she dashed backwards to Abhay's side. "This isn't working. How is he still with it? He should have lost it by now."

Gritting his teeth together, Abhay grunted in frustration. "I don't know, he should have gone ages ago. We don't know what a Manzazzu Etemmu can do, we know Trem's more durable than Humans, maybe their souls are too."

Treman strained against the ice freezing his arm in place. Staggering to the wall, he began to bash it against the side of the wood. Skye responded by extending her sword out as far as she could and charged. She went right through his head and out the other side. He barely noticed the fact his helmet was completely frosted over, she hit new levels of frustration she hadn't felt in a long time.

"Well now what do we do?"

Abhay's mouth opened to say something, to offer a new strategy or issue some new commands. But nothing came out. "I don't know... I don't know!" He responded.

With one almighty bellow, Treman freed his arm and grabbed his dead, useless one. He directed the gemstone at Abhay and the glow began. "Abhay, get out of there!" Skye begged.

"Trem will finish what we started old man. You'll see, she's going to put you down like the dog you are." He jerked as he felt the pulling force begin to drag him towards the emerald. "You know something Skye?" He called to his friend, looking past Treman.

"I never thought my death was that dignified, just getting sick. Second time's the charm eh?" He smiled, a slight mist in his eye. He used all his energy to break his arm free and fly head first into the gem, at least this way he could instigate his fate by his own hand.

Skye watched Abhay disappear into the light, she was the last one left. There was no way she could win, if she hid then Treman would find her eventually. They didn't buy them any time at all. She tried her best, Jenny would have been proud of her for that.

Treman slowly turned on the spot and stared her down. As he laughed to himself, looking the sorry state before him up and down, more blue blood oozed from the helmet. This time, several of his non deformed teeth were scattered in the blood.

Skye had pretty much resigned herself to her fate, but she wasn't expecting to feel one thing. She expected she'd face it with fear, but instead she felt calmness. "I'm coming love..." She whispered as she, like Abhay, charged into the blinding white light.

Treman observed the ring. The four small trails of black smoke like imperfections were dashing about madly, desperate to get out. Those fools thought they were going to their deaths, far from it. That would be coming later.

A feeling of exhaustion flooded Treman, but he still found the whole situation with Trem's Etemmu very amusing. As he laughed to himself, he laid down on the stairs. He was still fighting to keep control of the corruption eating away at him, but he was still beating it. Certainly, putting his soul into the ring and using it to maintain his form that little bit longer did buy him some time. Maybe an extra twelve hours?

It would be enough. He thought he'd just rest his eyes for a minute. As he lay there, a disgusting, bleeding mess locked inside a suit of armour, he felt a small bit of peace. That was however promptly broken by a certain female voice.

"Father, that is no way to behave at such an event!" Scolded his daughter, the same as before.

He opened his eyes and saw her looking down at him. He caught a glimpse of something other then armour on his body. He was in his Manzazzuan robes once again. Treman's eyes widened as he looked at his hands. The same pale skin as before and now tactile. He felt his jaw, his lips and his hair. They were all intact, he was alive once again. His daughter took his hand and helped him up.

"Did you have too much to drink?" She asked rather innocently.

Treman shook her off, straightened out the robes and adjusted his collar. "Don't be so stupid, of course I haven't. I just felt tired, I needed a rest."

Looking around, it didn't take Treman long to realise where he was. The place was bathed in a golden light, with pillars sculptured out of fine, pale stone. Exotic plants were dotted about the place and the air was thick with the smell of spices and perfume. This was Euphretia, the Queen's primary function chambers. He saw the door that lead to the dance hall and staggered towards it.

"Father, are you alright?" His daughter followed closely behind, trying to find an opening to maybe help take the weight off his legs.

Treman fumbled with the door knob but eventually got the thing open, looking into the grand structure that lay before him. The ceiling seemingly stretched for miles, topped with a coloured glass canopy, bathing everyone in that same brilliant golden light. Golden laced curtains hung from the pillars and the centre of the room had a circle of glass on the floor. The glass formed an isle which lead straight to the throne of the Queen herself. The room was full of Manzazzu from all walks of life, for it was one time Treman gave a lot of attention to.

Manzazzu would often flock to Euphretia whenever an important event would occur in their calendar. This was a rare event, the time when Venus' orbit would match the sun's and become visible from Earth. Treman hardly held belief in the goddess Ishtar, but if it meant the Manzazzuan elite could all gather together under one roof, then it would do nicely.

The group of Manzazzu numbered in the hundreds, and they filled the room with space to spare. Treman looked up at the centre of the room, trying to see if she was there. Sure enough, there she was. Tremera, Trem's mother and the blight on the house's name.

Back in the day, her appearance differed from that presented on the portrait in the manor's living room. Her paper white hair was thicker, with a braid tied tightly around her head, emphasising her pale eyebrows and pitch black eyes. Her smile was as delicate as ever though.

Those assembled in the room all took their partner's hands as the inaugural dance was about to begin. Treman soon began to seethe with anger when she saw who had taken Tremera's hands. The romantic fool Tremarda, with his metallic green eyes and hazelnut hair. The one who came from no great family, was armed with nothing but sickening words and a passable smile.

He dared to even approach Tremera, let alone have the gall to ask for her hand in a dance. But to Treman's dismay, she accepted, and even liked it. The Queen gave the word and the music began to play, a grand, sweeping ballad.

Treman couldn't bear to watch it, they looked so happy with each other. They were both lost in each other's eyes as they began to dance, it was sickening. Soon they became part of the great wave of dancing Manzazzu.

At first, Treman resisted the urge to approach them, push past the others and tear her away from that nobody of a Manzazzu. However, the first time he resisted the urge to do so, she ran off and got married to that fool. He marched into the crowd.

"Father wait, what are you doing?" Called his other daughter as she tried to follow him. She stopped dead in her tracks when he span around and yelled at her.

"You stay out of this!" He barked.

He marched up to his daughter and was about to shout orders at her when one of the dancers spun his partner right through his chest. The Manzazzu went through him like he was nothing... Like he was an Etemmu. He was still dead, he was no more alive then his favourite daughter was. Maybe she could hear him? Worth a try.

"Listen to me girl!" He shouted. His fears were confirmed however, she didn't react to him at all. Treman felt so hopeless as he watched everything wrong with his family slowly get worse and worse.

Putting his head in his hands, he screamed into them as loud as he could. When he opened his eyes once again, he was looking at the ceiling of the manor house once again. Every inch of his body ached and felt like it was burning, on top of all the individual pains such as his burst ribs, lack of a top lip and eye. He sighed, even if it came out as a growl.

He looked at his hand, the emerald ring had come loose and was on the step near him. He picked it up and inspected it. The imperfections in the rock were still darting about the place, that was good at least. Everything was going to plan, not long left and then he could die once again. He couldn't wait.

Chapter Sixteen: "So Green"

"To have an Ishtar Gate in a place like this, will it be dangerous?"
"To a Human, this will all be meaningless."

"So, how was that for you?" Gabby asked as she lead Trem away from the bus stop, waving one last time to Bobbi and Manisha who had begun their journey back to their respective houses.

How was it? How would anyone describe what she felt? The Human world was loud, frightening in its size, smelt rather suspect on occasion and yet... Trem couldn't help but find the whole thing exhilarating. When the ancient Manzazzu left Babylon for a new land before the fall, was this what they felt? Trem had often wondered. She never had the bravery till today, but she had always admired those first explorers.

"Well... Exciting for one. Confusing and mad but exciting." She admitted. It wasn't easy to put into words but she tried her best.

Gabby placed her hand on Trem's arm gently and patted. "I'm proud of what you've done today. You didn't have to come along."

Trem's eyes hovered away from Gabby, she was showing signs of shame which worried Gabby. "I did cause you problems, your Grandmother's passing... I was hoping I could make it up to you in some small way."

Oh yeah, Gabby had spent the time with Bobbi and Manisha to take her mind off things but as a result of that, she had almost forgotten. That certainly made Gabby feel a little rubbish. She decided to sweep that under the rug and cross the bridge when she came to it. She put on a smile and pulled Trem in for a small embrace. "That's very sweet of you, love."

Love? Trem blushed, is that what she thought too? That certainly lifted a small weight on Trem's mind. "So..." She began, rather flustered and failing to hide it. "...Is this when I introduce myself to your parents?"

"Yep." Gabby began, looking up at her approaching house. "I'll do the explaining, they won't know you're a Manzazzu. Then we'll head to my room while we wait for Dad to get back and then we eat. Sound good?"

After the rather meaty lunch and the snacks in the cinema, Trem felt rather full. Given the slower metabolism in Manzazzu, she would be content with no food for the foreseeable future. The good thing was that to humans, it would sound like a compliment.

"It does sound good." She agreed.

They stopped outside Gabby's house, which she pointed to in a rather theatrical way. "The homestead." She announced. "What do you think?"

Trem was surprised by it, but not in the way she was expecting to be. There were parts of it that reminded her of her manor house. Sure it was smaller, but there were little details that were familiar. The wooden door, the hedge around the house, a certain archaic quality the houses in inner town Mortsbury didn't have.

"I think it looks nice." As honest as it was, it still felt like an underwhelming response, so Trem tried to develop it further. "It looks homely."

Bless her, she was trying, Gabby thought. "Shall we head in?"

With a not so confident nod, she took Gabby's hand and was lead towards the door. As Gabby pushed it open, Trem was hit with the smell of wood polish and coffee. Not knowing what either smell was, it took her off guard. Trem wondered if Gabby felt the same emotions as she was currently experiencing when she arrived at the manor, a mixture of nervousness and curiosity. Her grip on Gabby's hand tightened when she heard a voice.

"Hello." Called Mavis.

Trem peered around the corner, her first look at Gabby's mother. It had been so long since she last been with her own mother, so when Trem saw Mavis Morgan, she instantly felt envious. She was searching the cupboards for sheets of lasagne when they arrived.

"Hi Mum!" Gabby called. She felt her hand slip away from Trem's as she walked into the kitchen. She looked back and saw her friend was hanging back from the doorway.

Mavis counted the sheets, her back still to the two girls. "How was your time out, did you enjoy the film?"

Gabby turned on the spot and held out her hand, mouthing that it was okay for Trem to come in. Bless her, she was still nervous. "It was pretty good, the ending was a little weak because they wanted to leave it open for a sequel. But yeah we had fun." Trem held onto Gabby as she lead her into the kitchen. "So, Mum, introduction time!"

Mavis closed the box and faced her daughter. "Sorry about that, just making sure I don't need to ask your Dad to get more from the shop…" Her voice trailed off when she saw Trem.

She was surprised by her appearance, but it wasn't exactly a bad surprise. It was more taken aback that someone who looked around 20 went about wearing such an odd combination of clothing. The black shorts and boots were fair enough…She wasn't up on the youthful trends, but black robes and high collared tunics? Were the 1600s trendy now?

As for the haircut, nice for some she'd admit. The black eyes were what took Mavis off guard though, there was something hypnotising about them, she found herself staring at them.

"Mum, this is Trem. Trem, my Mum." Gabby introduced, gesturing to them both.

Mavis ripped herself from the black eyes and extended her hand out. "Please, call me Mavis dear."

Trem took the hand and allowed it to be shaken a few times. "Okay, Mavis Dear."

That got a laugh out of Mavis, though both Trem and Gabby knew it wasn't meant as a joke. Still, if they could get her on side and make it seem like they were all jovial and taking everything in good humour then it'd be for the best.

"Oh you're cute." Mavis managed to say through the laughs.

This caused Trem to blush. "Thank you." She replied under her breath.

"Your Dad should be home in about an hour. Think you can keep yourselves out of trouble till then?"

Out of trouble? Trem wondered what she meant by that. "No trouble." Trem replied.

Gabby cut in before things could get awkward, or more awkward anyway. "Right I'll show Trem up to my room."

"Okay. When you do, can I have a quick word Gabby?" Mavis asked.

"Sure." Came the reply as she lead Trem out of the kitchen. "Won't be a mo." She gestured for Trem to follow as they climbed up the wooden stairs to Gabby's bedroom.

Once they reached Gabby's room, she opened the door and lead Trem into what was perhaps the most bizarre room she'd been in for a long time. "Right, I'll just have a quick chat with Mum and I'll be back in a second. You'll be okay if I leave you here for a minute?" Given that Trem was too busy staring at her posters, she had the answer pretty quickly. "I'll take that as a yes." Gently pulling the door too, she made her way back down the steps.

Back in the kitchen, she addressed her Mother in a quieter voice. "So, what's new?"

Mavis leant against the cooker and took a sip out of a glass of water she had recently topped up. "Tomorrow we're going to go into town and have a meeting about Nan's funeral. I had a word with them over the phone, Ms Emeka will be ready to discuss things with us."

Feeling a need to show respect, she straightened herself and kept her responses muted. "Okay, I understand. Shall I come with? I know I won't really be able to contribute to much…"

"Just being there will be more than enough Gabby. I mean I won't force you to come if you don't want to." Mavis continued.

"Oh no, I want to come. I want to be there for you and Dad as well. I mean I do kind of need to make it up to you for going AWOL the other day." She admitted, the regret and embarrassment was palpable in her voice.

Mavis patted the top of Gabby's head playfully. "If anyone should apologise, it's me. I let the stress get to me. I promised you and your Father I wouldn't go down that path again and I let you both down there. It's not like you did it on purpose, you couldn't help getting lost."

Well, that certainly helped ease a weight of Gabby's shoulder. "Cheers Mum. I love you." The two shared a kiss and smiled at each other.

"I love you too. Now go and have fun. Your Father will be back soon and then we eat."

Gabby headed back up to her room with a smile. Well, at least she wasn't too angry at her, or angry at all, which was shocking. But still, she wasn't going to knock it. As fewer problems as she encountered that day would be ideal. Of course, the fact Trem's Etemmu friends had been sealed away by Treman would certainly shatter that cozy evening for them.

Gabby peered into her room to see Trem with one of her comics, specifically the most recent issue of Nightmare On D Wing. Trem had one hand holding the comic and the other hovered over the panel as the sketchy illustration of the titular nurse, complete with Indian complexion, bloody uniform and bone saw in hand was brought to life. The two dimensional image had gained another dimension and was hovering above the page, bone saw at the ready. Once it noticed Gabby, it retreated into the pages from whence it came.

"That is still so cool Trem. Can all Manzazzu do that?" Gabby asked, pushing her door open.

Trem put the comic back on it's shelf gently, being careful not to crease the thin paper. Books in this world were nowhere near as sturdy as she was used to. "I know my Father couldn't do it, but my Mother could. I'm not sure, but she told me once that each Manzazzu clan has their own unique ability. This is ours."

Her face lighting up like a bulb, Gabby dashed for one of the shelves of comics on the other side of her room and pulled out a hardback collection. She flicked through the pages till she found a double spread and presented it to Trem. She pointed to a figure in the comics, a finely dressed noble lady with red eyes, blue hair and a long braid. "Can youdo that thing on her? I always had a crush on the Grand Duchess when I was younger!"

Gabby passed the book, allowing a few seconds for Trem to study the figure. She held one hand over the page, one of her rings glowing along with the page itself. With a smooth gesture, Trem pulled the image from the comic, resulting in a perfect three dimensional rendering of Gabby's favourite character. Trem lowered her hand slightly, resulting in a bow from the figure, as if she was controlling a puppet on strings.

"Trem, you are just the most awesome person, I swear." She confessed as she watched the Grand Duchess pirouette on the spot.

Trem couldn't help but blush. She reached into the page and pulled out another three dimensional rendering, this time of the character's tomboyish female assistant. She maneuvered them into a romantic slow dance, with the pages of the book as their dance floor. Gabby watched as the two moved in closer and kissed, a rather accurate recreation of the other day. Gabby had always hoped her first real kiss would be special, if she knew how special it would end up being, she'd never believe it.

Gabby put her hands together and stifled a giggle. "Seriously, you're just the best."

Gently biting her lip, Trem replied with a smile as she let the two figures rest back onto the page as she pressed the covers of the book together and handed it back. "As are you, Gabby."

Rather suddenly, Gabby threw the book on the bed and drew Trem in for a hug. She loved being able to show her affection now, without any fears or concerns of rejection. At this point, they were both strapped in for the long ride. Gabby pulled away and the two shared loving smiles at each other.

Gabby lead Trem to her bedside, taking off her trenchcoat and leaving it on the front of her bed. Trem perched on the side as Gabby sat cross legged on the bed, taking off her boots and getting comfortable. "You can make yourself at home if you want to. I don't mind, you can leave stuff about the place, it's not going to get anymore messy!" She left her boots on the floor by the bottom of her bed.

Trem hesitantly complied by slipping her robes off and undoing her footwear, leaving them neatly by Gabby's.

"So, what do you think of the humble abode?" She asked, gesturing around the room, the collection of posters certainly leaving a striking impression on Trem.

"Well…" Trem began. The posters all looked rather disconcerting, a hand emerging from a grave for instance seemed like a not too kind nod to the Etemmu. It's not like Gabby would have known though. "….It looks nice."

That lead to a scoff and chortle from Gabby. "Oh come on, we both know it's tacky! Truth be told, when I stupidly broke into your house all those years ago, I guess it kind of woke something up in me. It shaped my interest in the supernatural which lead me to tacky, sub par horror movies. I guess that was my way of coping." She put her hand on Trem's. "So I have to thank you for that."

"You're welcome…"

Gabby shuffled over and put her arms around Trem's stomach, resting her head on her friend's bare shoulder. "I only ever told Manisha. Bobbi, Boris and Julia never knew. It's been hard keeping it all a secret for years, really hard. I don't blame you in any way, you know that. It was just hard, so to see you out there with me, Bobbi and Manisha… I can understand if you say no, but would you do all that again if you were asked?"

Trem was wondering that very same question herself earlier. Her time in the Human world felt new, the first time she'd ever had any new experience was so many years ago. With Gabby guiding her, the stories she heard about how the Manzazzu should keep themselves away from Humans for fear of their own safety, didn't seem to apply here. Instead, the most she got was spooked by some of the content in the film she saw.

Her time with Gabby, who she had only known for a few days were the most wonderful, scary and exciting days she had ever experienced in her life.

Trem's cheek pressed against Gabby's. "If you'd have me, I'd always say yes." She continued by kissing the pale cheek and letting the warming sensation of the hug flow through her.

"So how was the outside world?" Gabby asked, closing her eyes as she continued to hold Trem.

It was hard to think how she could answer honestly, so she instead replied as plainly and to the point as she could. "It was very big, and so green. But it was fun, with you."

They spent the next half hour going through Gabby's collection of posters, comics and novels, all of the tacky horror variety. In a way, Trem was glad she could indirectly influence Trem's life in this way, it certainly sounded like Gabby had a great deal of pleasure in her passion. It made Trem happy, even if she didn't quite understand it. At ten minutes past the hour, Gabby could hear a car pull into the driveway.

"Oh cool, Dad's back." She got up to her feet and helped Trem up off the bed. "You ready for this?"

The first impressions with Gabby's Mother had been good, with any luck she would be able to not only keep it up, but make a good impression on her Father. "I am."

The two heard a faint murmur of voices. Gabby opened the door for Trem and followed her to the stairs. Once they arrived in the dining room, they saw Craig taking off his jacket and undoing his tie.

"Hi Dad!" Gabby called, waving to him as they entered the room, pausing to share a kiss on the cheek.

"Hi Gabs." He replied. He looked up at the new arrival. "So, this is your new friend." He offered his hand and smiled. "Craig Morgan, pleasure to meet you."

This Human obsession with shaking hands was very bizarre. Still, it would be rude not to. Craig gave her a firm shake, considerably more boisterous than any of the previous ones, causing Trem's body to shuffle slightly. "Pleasure to meet you too."

Mavis slipped on an oven glove and unveiled the individual clay pots of lasagne, steam rising from each of them. She placed them on each mat laid out on the table. Gabby and Trem took their seats with Craig while Mavis put a plate of garlic bread and a bowl of salad in the centre of the table. She placed a cola on Gabby's coaster. "What do you want to drink Trem? We have water, juice, cola, cider?"

That threw the hapless Manzazzu, cola was strange enough. She decided it was better off playing it safe. "Water please." She then drew her attention to the food before her. Blimey, it looked like a lot. While Craig and Mavis discussed his day at work, Trem leant over to Gabby. "So, what is this dish?"

Gabby used her fork to lift the cheese top layer. "It's basically meat and pasta layered up with cheese sauce. Do you know what pasta is?" Trem's blank look saved her having to say anything. "Okay, that's a no. Try a bit, I think you'll really like it."

Given her day spent exploring Human culture, this was going to be another informative experience. Using her fork, she cut a small triangular segment out of the dish, blew on it to cool it down and placed it in her mouth. After swallowing the small piece, she went back for another bite, and another. That was another success.

"I think your lasagna is a hit with another person Mum." Gabby joked, taking a sip of cola.

Mavis passed a slice of garlic bread to Trem who placed some of the meal along with some salad onto the bread and proceeded to consume it all in a few bites. "Blimey, anyone would think you'd never had lasagne before."

"I haven't." Trem replied, having finished her mouth full.

Mavis and Craig glanced at each other before getting stuck into their meals. "So Trem, tell us about yourself." Craig said as he began chewing his way through his mouth full.

Trem began playing with her fork. There was a lot she could say, a lot she shouldn't say too. Gabby had given her a taste of what Humans considered normal, with any luck it should be enough to inform her choice of words.

"Well, I was taught everything I know from my parents for as long as I can remember. I've never left the house until today thanks to Gabby." She stabbed the lasagne with her fork and hung her head. "My parents disappeared when I was young, I've lived by myself for a while before I received some... Help."

Gabby noticed an awkward look from her parents, clearly searching for something to say in response to that. "I'm...So sorry to hear that." Mavis replied, still rather lost for words.

"You have nothing to be sorry for." Trem took another mouthful of food before swallowing and turning to Gabby with a smile on her face. "Besides, Gabby has inspired all new confidence in me. I am very lucky to have her."

Gabby blew her a kiss. "I'm lucky to have you too."

Mavis leaned over and pointed her fork at the both of them. "So, how did you two meet?"

The two exchanged little looks, as if to ask which should go first. When they silently agreed on Gabby, she came up with a rushed response on the fly. "By accident really, but we kind of bonded pretty quickly and before you knew it we became friends."

Mavis reached for her glass of wine. "More than friends, if your sharing your first kisses."

This was news to Craig, who's eyes widened at the revelation. "Really?" He too reached for his glass. "How...How modern."

Gabby couldn't help but laugh to herself. "Oh come on Dad, when have I ever had any real interest in boys? I left enough hints." She teased.

"Oh it's not a problem, I don't have an issue. So long as you're happy Gabby." Craig's tone was sincere, it was clear he really meant that. He just struggled to phrase it correctly.

Mavis posed the next question, after scooping up some of the cheese sauce with the garlic bread. "So, Trem... It's a fascinating name, where is it from?"

Once again, Trem didn't think before she replied, not knowing why the following response left an uncomfortable silence. "Oh, it's Manzazzuan."

Gabby knew her parents were too polite to ask where that was, or what it was, or what it meant. She only knew what it meant a few days previous. "It's eastern. Her family comes from the Middle East so they like to keep the tradition. Hence, you know…" She gestured to Trem's outfit with her fork.

"Well it sounds very interesting. You must tell us about it one day." Mavis continued, taking a spoon full of salad.

Maybe one day, but not today. Nothing would be gained by trying to explain everything now, especially given how strange the thought of Gabby telling her parents she had talked to her Nan's ghost was. In fact going into detail about the fact Manzazzu aren't technically Human, more like ancient Babylonian necromancers, given power by the goddess Ishtar as well as a longer life span, was just not going to happen.

"So you were home taught then? It would explain why we've not seen you in any of the local schools. What are you planning on doing with yourself?" Craig was always one to get to the point, some find it intimidating, but in his line of work, it was expected.

Trem didn't really understand the question. She had to rely on Gabby muttering an explanation before she could answer. "Oh, I'm not sure. It's expected I follow in my parents footsteps."

"Ah, like taking over the family business, that kind of thing?" Gabby's Father was clearly in a probing mood. Still, he wasn't a judgemental person, just a curious one.

Trem drummed her fingers on the table and bit her lip. "Yes, in a way. It kind of involves death."

Just like that, the questions of Trem's occupation and life goals quickly subsided. Trem wondered why that was the case, but seeing how Gabby coped with the passing of her Nan, Humans must be inherently uncomfortable with the idea of death. That was the impression she was getting anyway.

"How's the food?" Gabby asked, breaking the silence with a crunch of garlic bread.

Trem finished pushing some mince into her mouth with her fork. "Amazing." She said through the mouthful. "I won't be able to eat anything for weeks after this, it's so filling."

Mavis chortled, waving her hand in the air. "Oh you're too kind dear!"

Trem looked up from her meal, a neutral expression on her face. "No I mean it."

Thank goodness for her Drama classes, she'd perfected a believable fake laugh that she always planned on using at parties when she needed to look less awkward. "Very good Trem!"

Trem responded with an awkward smile. "Thanks. So, what is your role in the great picture Mr Morgan?"

After seeing off the last dregs of wine in his glass, Craig jokingly straightened out his shirt collar, to the amusement of Gabby and Mavis. Again, Human thing, Trem thought.

"Well I am the store manager of the local Dewsbury's. If you don't know what that is, we're a supermarket catering for all your shopping needs, from locally sourced fresh fruit and vegetables to those handy little essentials..."

The other two in the family caught on immediately to what he was doing, how tacky of him to quote the advert from the TV and mock the voice over as well.

"Dad, you are such a dork!"

They all enjoyed a good laugh, while Trem was wondering why she was tearing up. It was evident very early on that despite the hardship of losing her Nan, Gabby soldiered on, as did her parents. It was clear they had all decided to live and laugh for their departed, which was a noble path to take.

Trem suddenly felt rather angry at herself. Gabby, a Human, someone who her Grandfather would have her believe be an inferior creature... She was thriving, whereas Trem felt like she was festering. She rubbed her eyes with her palm, as stealthily as possible so no one would notice.

"What about you Mrs Morgan?" Trem asked.

"Mavis dear, please call me Mavis I keep telling you. Bless your sweet heart though." She leant back in her seat. "Oh I'm a Mother every hour of every day. Always have been. I used to work in an office, it was the least exciting thing I've ever done in my life and I do not recommend it." She tapped her hand against Craig's back. "Then I met his lordship down the pub one day."

"I remember it well." Craig replied. "August 27th 1988. You were with your friends from the office unwinding after a long day and some drunk idiot tried to put his hand up your skirt."

She began filling her glass and her husband's while continuing the conversation. "Yep, so I smacked his hand away and then this tall dark stranger appeared out of nowhere. What did you to do him dear?"

Making his hand into a fist, he slammed it onto the tabletop, causing all the liquids on the table to shake.

"I robbed him of his two front teeth. That sent him packing." He said with a grin on his face.

Gabby was already a quarter of the way done with her meal, never finding it hard to consume food at a consistent pace. "My Dad, the pacifist. They say chivalry is dead? Nonsense!"

By the time they had finished the food, an hour of relaxed and, for Trem, insightful, conversation had taken place. Whichever Manzazzu said that the Human race was savage and primitive, nothing but bald primates dragging their feet on the Earth's surface, was so very wrong. Trem had never eaten so much in her life, she felt bloated and heavy but would not have taken the experience back, it was wonderful.

The time spent perfecting the meal for her and the others was admirable, the Humans were very good at taking the mundane and the simple and creating a large, impressive event out of it. Consuming food, a necessity for Humans to live, now turned into an enjoyable social event. It was a shame the stance on Humans were what they were, the Manzazzu could really learn something from the Humans, while they were alive.

After a period watching some television, while having her arm around Gabby, Trem's attention was snapped away by a tapping sound. She looked to the window in the kitchen, there was Woody, pecking the glass with his beak.

"Bloody birds." Craig muttered, still focusing on the TV.

Woody took off and flew to the first floor of the house. Trem got up from the sofa and made her way quickly to Gabby's room.

"Trem?" Gabby took off after her, ignoring her parents gaze following them.

She scrambled up the stairs and entered her room, where she saw Trem open her window and hold out her hand. The sun had already set and darkness had already taken hold of the sleepy village. But for Trem and Gabby, their peace was to be shattered.

"What's happened?" Trem asked. Woody began tweeting frantically, even sounding panicked. "Slow down, slow down." The whistles and calls slowed and became clearer. Gabby could tell the news wasn't going to be good.

"...What?!" Trem looked outright horrified with what she was told. She turned to Gabby. "It's Treman..."

Gabby instinctively grabbed her boots and began putting them on as she passed Trem's own pair to her. "Again?" She hopped on one leg, shoving her foot inside as quickly as possible. "Right, tell me on the way. I assume it's bad?"

"Yes. I'm going to send him into the Styx kicking and screaming for what he's done..." She slipped into her robes and footwear, stopping before she got to the door. "Gabby, I really can't ask you to come with me this time. I've put you in too much danger."

Gabby knew where this was coming and quite frankly she didn't want to hear it. "Look we're wasting time, every second we loiter around is time we're wasting." She held out her arm and Woody perched on it, hopping onto her shoulder. She grabbed her phone and joined Trem as they made their way down the stairs. "I'll explain things, you go on ahead and I'll catch you up."

When they reached the bottom of the stairs, Trem bolted straight past Gabby's parents and out the door. Craig and Mavis barely even registered her go past when they turned, reacting to the sound of the door. "Gabby, what's going on?"

294

Gabby didn't even realise Woody was on show for them both to see, as his head twitched and moved about by itself. "I'm sorry but there's an emergency at Trem's house, I don't have time to explain. I've got my phone and I won't repeat the same mistake as before." She gestured to the door and started walking backwards. "I really am sorry but I can't explain now, I'll tell you later but she really needs me and I have to go." She turned and ran out of the door, slamming it shut behind her.

"Gabby wait..!" Mavis called. A few moments after the door closed, she turned to Craig. "Did she have a bird on her shoulder?"

Craig looked rather clueless. "I didn't get a chance to take much notice."

Outside, it wasn't long before Gabby caught up with Trem. "So what happened?" They followed the path back to the house, but now it was dark it became altogether more intimidating. The route through the overgrown brambles was so hard to see, but it didn't slow them down.

"Treman came back into the house and has Jenny and the others sealed away. He's used the same technique we used to make Woody have a physical body. I'll explain it later but it means he's way more dangerous then he was before."

That certainly made Gabby feel a real sense of fear once again. He'd already done a number on her, she'd only just stopped feeling the effects of the attack. "So, what's the plan?"

"...I don't know." Came the rather deflated reply.

They soon arrived at the house. Gabby should have been used to fearing for her life at this stage, but it was an experience she wished she didn't have to keep going through. The thought they both shared was a sobering one. In the fight to come, between Treman and the two of them, one of their stories was coming to an end.

Chapter Seventeen: "Scornful Old Man"

"We still have a duty as Manzazzu, we still have to keep the Styx in order, even in this small and unimportant part of it."
"Unimportant? Any intrusion in the Styx could lead straight to the Capitol."

Gabby followed Trem to the back of the house, where the walled off garden resided. Gabby really hoped it would be the last time she'd have to sneak into the house again, she was getting tired of it in all honesty. Of course, there was no guarantee this way was as safe as just walking through the front door.

"Can you check to see if the coast is clear?" Gabby asked Woody. He gave a confident chirp, Gabby scooped the wooden bird off her shoulder and held him in her hands. She watched Woody fly over the wall and turned to Trem. "He's a good bird."

Trem looked rather impressed by Gabby's resourcefulness. "Smart move." She complimented.

Woody wasted no time returning, perching himself on the top of the wall. Whistling the all clear, Trem gestured to the wall. "I'll give you a lift."

She offered her hands, cupped them together for Gabby's foot as she was hoisted onto the top of the wall. She pulled herself up onto the wall and sat on the side, looking down at the drop. It must have only been a few feet, nothing major. She let her feet dangle off the side and slid off, landing on her feet.

"Trem, will you be able to...?" Before she could continue, Trem landed next to her, perfectly straight on her feet. "...Never mind." Gabby continued. "That's pretty cool."

Trem gestured for Gabby to follow her. They snuck through the garden, being careful to avoid stepping on any of the plants or vegetables growing in the ground. They reached the door which lead into the manor. Of course, that would be too complicated a route to take, with Treman on the prowl. Fortunately, the door was covered by a stone canopy. The window to Treman's room was set on the wall behind the canopy, and had already been smashed in Trem's violent outburst. Climbing in wouldn't be too difficult. Trem jumped onto the canopy, in an acrobatic movement beyond Humans ability.

She lent down and took Gabby by the hand, pulling her up. "You Manzazzu are just better than us in every way aren't you?" She observed.

Trem patted Gabby on the back. "Later, love." She turned to the window, it was large enough for them both to climb through. "Be careful of the broken glass." She instructed, leaning through the empty space where the glass once was as she climbed into the room. She helped Gabby through by taking her hand.

They looked around the bedroom, Treman must have stored his collection of rings somewhere, all Manzazzu had them close by, where they could be easily found. However, Trem had been unsuccessful in finding them.

"What are we looking for?" Gabby asked, remaining still. The room itself had already done a number on her before, she wasn't keen on repeating it.

Trem noticed the fresh hole in the wall, she pointed to it and began slowly walking over the split and broken floorboards. "That, I'm sure of it."

Gabby followed Trem, matching her steps. The house had a new smell to it, it was a mix of fire, smoke and a musky dampness.

With the night well and truly fallen, it gave the house a far more unforgiving feeling. She could just about see what Trem had stashed away. Inside the hole was the rotting box of Treman's, still open and containing the remaining rings. Gabby could hear Trem breathe a sigh of relief. She pulled a sapphire ring from the box, the second and last one in Treman's collection.

"He still had another one. It's not uncommon to have two of the same types after all." Trem explained, slipping it into her robe pocket. "We need four, I have one and Treman had one."

Gabby nodded, following as close as she could. "Right, and you gave me a box of rings too. What about the fourth?"

Trem took the box out as she replied. "My Mother's collection will be in their room. Once we can get them, we can take the fight back to Treman…"

Gabby started to become a little worried when Trem remained silent. "Trem, what is it?" She asked, peering around her, trying to get a look at what she'd seen.

Trem reached into the hole and pulled something out, a porcelain jackal skull, which had lost it's white sheen and was cracked in a few places. Trem stared at it, seemingly unable to take her eyes from it.

"Trem, what's that?" Gabby asked, glancing between the skull and Trem.

She realised the increasing anger Trem was conveying, she held the skull in her hand and squeezed as hard as she could. With one grunt, she shattered the mask, small shards of porcelain falling from her hands and onto the ground. She dropped the remainder and turned to the door. "I'll explain later."

Gabby decided it was best not to ask, answers could come later,

once they dealt with Treman. She kept close to Trem as she peered out of the door. There was no sign of Treman, though the sound of the fire crackling away in the distance was certainly a new thing.
It was a warm night, so the fire was making the house feel rather muggy and humid, though that was the least of their worries.

Trem moved silently down the hallway of doors, barely making a sound. Gabby meanwhile cringed at every squeaking floorboard she happened to stand on, just unlucky she figured. When Trem reached her parent's room she was relieved, the last thing she wanted to do was to draw attention to themselves and blow their cover. The silence was the worst thing about it all though, one could hear a pin drop it was so quiet. The darkness didn't help either.

The door slowly opened and Gabby followed Trem inside. Once they were safely in, they closed the door behind them. There was enough moonlight creeping in through the windows to illuminate the room sufficiently enough to make out the details. It was very similar to Trem's room, with a four poster bed as the biggest difference. Trem made her way to the desk by the window as Gabby looked around.

She noticed a picture on the wall, a portrait of a youthful blonde woman with pale, sky blue eyes. Her blonde hair reached past her shoulders and her head was covered by a military style peaked cap. The headwear also matched her uniform, which was a deep blue with a gold trim, epaulettes and what looked like a black rollneck underneath. Gabby thought she was rather beautiful, and rather sexy, especially considering she was brandishing a blue flaming sword.

"Trem?" She whispered, pointing to the picture. "Who's this?"

Trem glanced up at the picture before returning to her search. "Oh that's the royal highness herself, the Manzazzuan Queen. Third Queen since the birth of our race. She's only been ruling for about two, maybe three hundred years or so."

Trem made hundreds of years seem such a short amount of time. She tore herself away from the picture of the Queen and joined Trem in her search. Together, they went through every drawer in the desk, flicking through cylinders, sculpting tools and other assorted trinkets. Trem dug deep and finally pulled out a dusty box. Blowing the dust off the top, she set it on the desktop. She opened the box and sighed as she saw the important sapphire ring.

"Thank goodness." She put the ring in her pocket and gave a thumbs up to Gabby. "We're good to go. Now, we just need get these on four of the suits of armour in the manor's corridor. You remember where that is?" She asked.

Gabby nodded. "Yeah, but we need to go through the main hall to get to it, don't we? Isn't that where Treman could be?"

"Yes. Leave him to me, I'll distract him while you get those rings onto the armour. That way when we get Jenny and the others out, they can fight alongside us." Gabby would hate to admit it, but there was something in Trem's tone that suggested she wasn't entirely confident with the plan. She hoped it was just her imagination.

While Gabby and Trem made their way out of the bedroom and prepared to make their presence known, Treman stood in the centre of the main hall, watching the fire burn. In the flames, he could see flashes of the past. He could see glimpses of his children at the Academy, the Sisters growing up under his guidance and... The war. He had taken such a minimal role in the war, he worked with a group of Loyalist Manzazzu who collected information on enemy movements and passed them onto the strategists.

He loved the Mutashaeib and everything they stood for, but when the time came to don the jackal masks and take up arms against the Royal Family, he didn't. He was too obsessed with preserving the family name and keeping his sorry self alive as long as possible. He was not a true Mutashaeib, he only followed their beliefs and then only in private. Even he admitted how pathetic that sounded.

Treman was so lost in the disjointed and chaotic flashbacks, he barely heard Trem and Gabby make their way down the stairs and enter the main hall. Gabby sneaked past the fading old man with ease and set about placing the rings that belonged to Trem, her parents and the one she was gifted onto the suits of armour.

Trem stood behind Treman, keeping her distance. "Treman." She called.

The creature that was once her Grandfather slowly turned to face her. The helmet had a crack down the face, the silver armour was now stained with so many blue frost streaks that it would be considered two tone in colour. His posture was much more primal, his dead arm was on the floor and he had hunched himself forward. Several of his ribs hung through the chest plate and with every breath, he sounded like the sheer process of existing brought him pain. He let a low level growl escape the helmet, which sounded like it came from a bear, not an old man.

"I found the mask." Trem said, her voice was as blunt as it was cold.

Treman responded with a growl, a faint hint of his original voice could still be heard. "And?" He managed to force out.

Trem kept her distance, he was still clinging onto whatever small scrap of his original self he could muster. "I always knew you were scum, but this really just defies how awful you were. The Mutashaeib were nothing but arrogant, racist bigots who were so stupid enough as to think they could topple the Royal Family. You didn't even fight in the war, you coward. You just watched, you didn't even do a favour to the world and get yourself killed fighting for your cause. How many of your fellow scumbags died in battle?"

The last vestiges of his uncorrupted form vanished in the low level, guttural scratching noises that came from his helmet.

"You're pathetic Treman. You hypocritical, sad nobody. It's time to die, old man. Your final death, it's been overdue for years now." Trem sounded so cold, so unfeeling. It was a far cry from the lonely Manzazzu Gabby had shown the outside world to.

Treman didn't respond to Trem's words. Instead, he dragged himself over to the doors leading to the Ishtar Gate. He called into the darkness, his voice no longer resemble its former self, it was now a beastly roar. "Now!" He called.

Trem reached for her sword, but before she could draw it, an almighty scream filled the air. Gabby, who had just finished her job, ran back into the hall to see what was going on. Treman stepped aside as a Faragh, as disturbing as the last one they faced emerged. The shredded remnants of a football top hung from his front as the bottom row of large fangs pushed deep into his top lip, coating his teeth with blood. He was on all fours, his spine having burst free from his back and a chunk of flesh hung from the top of his head.

"Treman... What have you done?!" Trem demanded, horrified at the sight before her.

Treman ignited his sword and held it to the Faragh. Spooked by the spitting embers, the corrupted soul charged out of the room and through the door. Treman kept his sword waving in the air as a further four Faragh emerged, charging after the other one with great speed. This was bad, very very bad. The crazy old man had not only corrupted a group of innocent Etemmu, but he was now setting them off into the Human world. Trem ignited her sword, which caught the attention of the last Faragh to emerge. It stopped and stared Trem and Gabby down.

"I think you made it angry..." Gabby shivered, she knew if she made it out of this alive she wouldn't be able to sleep for a week. Rubbish, dated horror movies couldn't really prepare her for this real horrific sight.

The both of them stayed glued to their spot, out of fear or on purpose neither really knew. Before the final Faragh could attack, Treman jabbed it with the side of his sword, causing the beast to turn, get spooked by the flaming sword and follow the others.

Funny, there were supposed to be fifteen. Maybe the Sisters couldn't contain all of them, still, not Treman's problem anymore. Trem was seething with anger now, her knuckles were white as she gripped the sword harder then she'd ever done before. She was about to charge at him when Treman held the Emerald ring up to them.

"Trem...Is that where the others are trapped?" Gabby asked, feeling the sweat on her brow run down her face.

Treman pulled himself into the centre of the room, a maniacal and disturbing laugh filled the air. "It was." Came the fractured voice once again. He held the ring out over the fire and dropped it into the flames.

"Guys!" Trem yelled. She adopted a battle ready stance, holding the sword up, ready to fight him.

Gabby meanwhile jumped into action like a shot. She dived at Treman and ducked between the legs of the armour. Moving quicker then she moved in a long time (coincidently, the time she ran away after she first entered Jenny all those years ago), she forced her hand into the fire. She tried to ignore the seething pain of the heat against her skin. She finally managed to grab the ring. The metal burned her fingers and caused her to yelp, but she kept hold of it as tightly as she could. She scrambled to her feet and lunged back at Trem. "Catch!" She called, throwing the ring at Trem.

She caught it in her hands, cupping both together and keeping a tight grip on the ring.

For both of them, time suddenly seemed to slow right down to a snail's pace. Gabby smiled when she saw Trem grab the ring, but what she didn't see was Treman. He raised the sword high above his head and brought it crashing down onto her. The slash from the sword cut into her back, ripping her t-shirt, staining it with blood. The forward momentum carried Gabby even further towards Trem. She could only watch in horror as Gabby fell to the floor with a hard thump. Trem froze, she refused to believe what she just saw.

As she stood there, her eyes filling with tears and her mouth agape. The green ring began to glow white. The four Etemmu shot out of the ring, so desperate to escape that they barely noticed what had transpired. Jenny and Skye's first reaction was to embrace and Abhay and Hogarth checked their spectral forms to make sure all was in order.

Jenny was the first to see what had happened and let out a scream. "Gabby!"

The scream snapped Trem right out of it. She turned to the four and pointed to the hallway. "You four, into the armour, now!" She ordered.

The four obeyed and disappeared in an instant. Having just escaped one ringed prison, they were now using the same kind of ring to help Trem out. The four flew into the sapphire encrusted rings, reforming inside the armour. When they all gained physical form, they joined Trem's side as she sank to her knees.

She dragged Gabby up onto her lap and looked at her back. The cut was deep but it didn't look like it hit anything. Though given the strength Treman possessed, it was lucky he didn't bust her spine with a blow like that. She dug into her pocket and found the vile of potion she'd used on her arm and Gabby's eyes before. She always made sure she had some to hand, an old thing her parents told her to remember in case of emergencies.

"Gabby, can you hear me?" Trem undid the top of the bottle, her hands shaking.

Gabby struggled to keep her eyes open. The pain in her back was so unbearably bad, it certainly felt like what she imagined being stabbed in the back felt like. She was also feeling increasingly faint, like she was slipping away. She was feeling as desperate as Trem was, she tried to force her eyes to open wide. "Trem..." She strained. Gabby tried to lift her arm, but only managed to move it slightly.

"I'm here..." Trem replied. She was trying her hardest not to start sobbing. "I'm here Gabby." She tried to reassure. "Hang in there, we'll get you patched up, it will be alright..."

Gabby half smiled, feeling her own hand being gently taken by Trem's. "This...Really hurts...." She gasped. Her back felt warm, she knew it was hardly a flesh wound. "Kind of obvious, right?"

"Yeah..." Trem took Gabby's hand in her own, the feeling of her own friend and lovers blood coating her was making it shake. "Come on Gabby, squeeze my hand. We can get through this, you can get through this." She felt Gabby's grip on her hand tighten, it reached the point where it began to hurt, but it didn't matter to Trem. "Think about all the things we've done together. I've only known you for a few days, but you've made my life feel like it was worth living again."

Treman watched on, what little mental presence he had left was half thinking he would throw up at such a cheesy display. "Now who's pathetic?" He jeered.

Trem reached down and kissed Gabby on the lips. "You can do it Gabby, I know you can."

None of the four Etemmu could say anything, they all knew how bad the wound looked. They were so used to seeing how strong and durable Manzazzu were, they had forgotten how frail the Human body could be.

Gabby found herself starting to hyperventilate, each breath becoming weaker. "I'm not... I'm not through just yet..." She gazed up, trying to install a bit of confidence into Trem, though it did rather fail. "We still have to sort that monster out..." She strained, so hard it caused her to cough. Every time she did so, she felt her body sting.

"Yeah, of course we will." Trem replied, placing her clean hand against Gabby's cheek.

A thought entered Gabby's mind, her half smile faded into a sad expression, she had a very sobering realisation. As soon as she began to think about it, her eyes began to close. She fought against it as hard as she could. This was nothing, she could fight it. She had to, she needed to fight it.

"Trem..." Gabby's whole body felt limp and she was welcomed by the embrace of darkness.

"Gabby...?" Trem held Gabby in her arms, staining her robes in her lover's blood. "Gabby!?" She screamed.

Abhay and Jenny knelt down beside Trem, both rested their metal gauntlets on her back. Hogarth reached for the bottle which had been placed upright on the floor. "Trem, we can still save her."

Treman was loving the sight. The look of distraught despair on his Granddaughters face was irresistible, he couldn't help but produce a mocking, hearty laugh at Trem's expense. That certainly snapped some resemblance of collectiveness back into his shattered excuse of a mind. "What a sight! I never thought I could take so much away from you! First your parents and now your pathetic Human lover!" Only after he let out the loud boast that he realised his error.

Trem's eyes shot open. Was he serious, was Treman the one who caused her parent's disappearance all those years ago? All this time, she had wondered who was the one responsible, she had almost given up hope of ever finding out. But he was there, under her nose the whole time... Trem couldn't believe it. She couldn't believe how much of an idiot she was, because it all started to make sense. She had found the jackal mask of the Mutashaeib, he was a sympathiser to their cause. He robbed her of her parents and left her to suffer in the darkness for all these years.

Skye and Abhay put their hands to the hilts of the swords hanging from their armour, they sensed something was going to kick off very soon.

Trem shut her eyes tight, clenching her left hand into a tight fist and gripping the other one against her love. The anger felt like it was building up inside her. The anger towards herself, for her own blindness after years upon years of wondering, of being on her own and having to suffer Treman's toxicity all her adult life. But the anger towards Treman was more akin to blind rage. He had taken away everyone that she had ever cared about. Her Mother, her Father... Now Gabby was unconscious and bleeding out in her arms.

The rage boiled over. She opened her eyes to reveal black voids of rage and despair. She kept them locked on Treman, the sight of them caused the old ghost to feel real fear, which he hadn't felt in decades. "Kill him!" She screamed at the top of her lungs. "Kill him now!"

Skye and Abhay drew their swords and moved their hands up the blades, the sapphire rings providing the spark to ignite the swords. They both adopted combat ready stances and charged towards Treman who wasn't yet ready to ignite his ruby red flaming sword. With one arm out of order, Treman raised his sword and was able to block their joint attacks. Abhay pushed against Treman's blade while Skye forced her gauntlet into Treman's chest plate, causing him to stagger into the wall.

Hogarth took Trem by the hand, his large, cold metal gauntlet pressed against Trem's. "Trem, go help them. I'll look after Gabby, she'll be safe with me."

"But..." Trem began.

"Just go, they need you. I'm never going to be a fighter, I leave that to the others. Gabby will be safe with me. Just go!"

Trem looked to Jenny, who spoke before she could. "I want to get my own back on Treman." She drew her sword.

Trem nodded and ran to the hallway to grab another sword. Jenny meanwhile ignited her sword. Honestly, she wasn't a fighter at all, she didn't actually know one thing about sword combat. But if Skye was going to fight to protect Gabby and Trem, then she made it her duty to do the same.

Skye kicked Treman away, causing him to stagger into the landing. Jenny appeared, swinging her sword around, striking Treman on the side of the helmet. Using the time Jenny bought, Abhay sliced Treman's arm, cutting it badly. Treman swiped wildy at the three fighters, glancing Skye and Jenny with his sword but barely phasing them. They surrounded him, each gaining hits on his body. Treman growled, grunted and roared his way through the pain, struggling to keep his metaphorical head above the water.

Trem removed the sword she had carried all day from her belt and ran past Hogarth, glancing enough to see him begin to use the ointment on Gabby's back. The sight fueled her for a fierce fight, with the spark of hope lighting fires in her will.

"Out of the way!" She called. She hit her two swords together, forming an X shape. She then pulled them apart, resulting in the same shape taking the form of a blue, flaming shockwave that shot past the three Etemmu and into Treman's chest, causing a large cross shaped hole in his armor.

Treman at this point was spewing up blood from his mouth, he was really on his last legs now. He stomped forwards, driving his sword towards Trem. She managed to block his advance by using the same cross formation to hold the blade in place. Skye, Jenny and Abhay jumped into action, Jenny and Skye slashing his legs and Abhay slashing his shoulder. Treman sank to his knees, his arm barely able to hold the weight of the sword.

Skye brought her sword down, but Treman brought his dislocated, hunched shoulder up, allowing the pauldron to take the blow. Abhay drove his sword into a gap in Treman's armour, piercing his side. The blue flames burned the silver plates and caused the fading creature to yell out in agony. Jenny stabbed Treman's foot, pinning him to the ground, allowing Trem to take a long stride, draw her sword back and swipe it at Treman's head, sending the helmet flying off his face.

The skull had dislodged, leaving areas of Treman's face saggy and loose. His mouth was now a mess of shredded skin as his enlarged teeth left nothing around them. His eye sockets were practically on his cheeks they were so low down and his other eye had almost fallen out.

Trem grabbed him by the neck and held him up into the air, his trapped foot coming free from his leg with an almighty crunch of breaking bones. With all her strength, Trem hurled her former Grandfather down the stairs that lead to the Ishtar Gate. With every hard, painful hit on the stairs, the sound of bones snapping and metal crunching filled the air. He hit the floor hard, landing in the pool of water around the gate. Some of his teeth had come loose, his skin continued to droop off his skull, he was barely surviving the attack. His sword landed in the darkness, Treman wouldn't be able to find it now.

He looked up the steps to see Trem staring down at him. With the last resemblance of sanity he retained, he could have sworn he'd seen Trem morph into his daughter, Trem's Mother. The piercing, deathly glare she gave him really installed fear into the old man, which was the last thing he felt before slipping away for the last time.

Trem ran down the stairs as Treman descended into his Faragh state. He let out an almighty roar as Trem hurtled towards him, pushing him into the open Ishtar Gate. They both emerged from the other side, hitting the dirt ground. Trem acted quickly, taking her sword in both hands, bringing it down onto Treman's head, severing his eye. He wailed in agony as he thrashed about, trying to get Trem off him.

Deep in the Styx, lost in the myriad of damp passageways and decaying structures, two figures stirred in the darkness. Alerted by the distant noise, they pushed forward into the darkness, their salvation could be at hand.

Pulling the sword from the old fool's head, Trem turned and made a mad dash for the Ishtar Gate's portal. Treman lunged forward, slashing his gauntlet at her. Trem felt the sharp scratch from this attack as her robe was ripped . She jumped through the gate, landing with a thump on the wooden floor. Treman got on all fours and prepared to follow her, running like the animal he was towards the Gate. He jumped into the air.

Trem desperately held her hands out, drawing the signs in the air to close the gate, which she managed to do in the nick of time. The last glimpse she saw of her Grandfather was his screaming, twisted, beastil face flying towards her. The Gate closed instantly, sealing away Treman on the other side. With his mirror destroyed, there was no other way he could gain access to the manor house.

Trem sank to her knees and panted. It was over. All this time she had spent putting up with him, the Mutashaeib sympathiser, the heartless monster who took her parents from her... It felt good to be able to put the whole thing to rest. Her parents were still out there, there was still some hope. In the end, he failed in his desire. That thought made Trem feel better about the whole thing, that he finally got his punishment. She closed her eyes, she could see her parents once again, smiling at her. They would have been proud if they were there. Trem's smile faded as her eyes slowly opened.

"Gabby..." She muttered to herself. She glanced at the open door at the top of the stairs. "Gabby!" She got to her feet and ran to the stairs.

Gabby had never passed out before, she assumed it was like going to sleep. The severity of pain she sustained from the attack combined with the blood loss caused her to faint, though she couldn't remember much of the vivid details. What was becoming clear though was what she was hallucinating. She slowly opened her eyes, expecting to be back in the manor house, surrounded by Trem and the ghosts like last time, but that wasn't the case. She felt like she was moving, and when her vision began to clear, she noticed she was slowly moving backwards. Infront of her was a figure, wearing blue robes with their back turned to her. They had dark, curly hair just like Gabby.

Around them, it looked like they were in a tunnel, made up of what looked like vines, bushes, and crawling ivy, all of which had turned brown and had started to decay. There was a sound of running water and sure enough, Gabby looked down to see there was indeed a body of water flowing below them. It felt like they were floating, which was odd because it felt like they were suspended above the water.

Gabby drew her attention back to the figure. "Hello?" She called.

The figure turned their head, Gabby could see a brief glimpse of something familiar. The figure then turned their body, and the whole thing became all the more trippy for Gabby. She was staring at a mirror image of herself. The figure's face was identical to her's in every regard except for a scar running down one side of her face, from the forehead, down the eye and onto the cheek. This copy of Gabby also wore blue and gold Manzazzu robes, with a ruby necklace around her neck.

Both Gabby's stared at each other. This was some weird Sci-Fi stuff going on here, like those alternate reality things with timelines where something changed in the timeline. Was this the Manzazzu version of Gabby, or something else?

"You're.... You're me..." Gabby said, blinking as she looked the figure up and down.

The other Gabby tilted her head, looking very confused, she was clearly as lost as the real Gabby was. "I'm you?" She asked.

The two remained silent for a moment, both taking in the sights before them. "Why are you here? What is it you want?" The other Gabby asked.

"I don't want anything, I passed out and suddenly I was here. I got attacked and blacked out, I didn't plan on being here, I don't even know what here is. Why should I anyway? It's not like I've had every little bit of Manzazzu culture explained to me."

The other Gabby began to look concerned. "You mean your not Manzazzu?" She asked, as if it was such a hard concept for herself to understand.

"No, of course I'm not, I'm human." If this reflection was really her, couldn't she tell?

Gabby found herself reaching towards her mirror self, who's hand raised to meet hers. Their palms touched the other. Gabby watched as her twin self and the tunnel around them began fading into the darkness. "Wait...!" She called.

Trem had no idea how Humans worked their technology, why they were so dependant on it was beyond her. Still, she managed to find her way to Gabby's contacts and eventually landed on "Mum." She pressed a button which triggered a series of monotone beeps.

The beeping stopped and a voice came from the device, it was Gabby's Mother. "Gabby? What's going on, are you alright?"

Trem moved the device closer to her mouth. "Umm... Mrs Morgan, this is Trem. Gabby's okay, she's just had a bit of a knock." She turned around, watching as Gabby lay on her side while Hogarth, still in his suit of metal, continued to administer the potion onto the wound on her back. Pale new skin was slowly forming over the cut.

"What happened?" Mavis asked.

"Well...We had a bit of a fight with my Grandfather, he injured Gabby but we're just patching her up now. It's nothing to worry about, we dealt with him."

Of course telling her not to worry would only result in more worrying for Mavis. "Can I speak to Gabby?"

Trem glanced to the bedside. The other Etemmu had shed their armour and were hovering around Gabby. "...She's just having a rest at the moment."

"Okay, I understand. Thank you for telling us. Will you tell Gabby to ring us when she's awake?"

"Of course Mrs Morgan." Trem replied. After a few final thanks, Mavis ended the call.

Trem took her place at Gabby's bedside, next to Hogarth. She looked to her armour clad friend. "Thomas, you can rest now. I'll take over, you can get out of that suit now."

"Are you sure?" He asked, looking down at Gabby's healing wound.

Trem put her hand on his steel pauldron. "I'm sure."

Following her instructions, Hogarth transferred his ethereal body from the suit of armour and back into its previous form, the armour falling to pieces on the floor. Abhay gave him a supportive but firm smack on the back.

Trem leaned over, resting her hand on Gabby's head. It seemed that she was always destined to lead Gabby into danger, she knew Gabby wouldn't want it any other way. Still, with Treman gone, one problem was now dealt with. The issue now was, the escaped Faragh. Once she knew Gabby was okay, she planned to go off into the night and track them down.

It was a good thing that the sixth sense Manzazzu possessed , gave them the ability to detect disturbances in the Styx. This would also help find Faragh, since they certainly counted as a distrubance. Faragh are usually unpredictable, but it was logical to assume since it was fast approaching midnight, there wouldn't be many people on the street to come in harm's way.

Gabby slowly lifted her heavy eyes. She rolled onto her back and looked at Trem and the others staring at her. "....Hello." She groaned, leaning up.

Trem wrapped her arms around Gabby's shoulders. "How are you?" She asked.

"Well, getting far too used to this whole waking up after being saved by you guys malarkey." She joked. She rubbed her eyes and sniffed. "I had a weird dream though."

Chapter Eighteen: "What's TCP?"

"There's more to life than what the Queen and the upper classes dictate. We should do something without lives."
"Such as?"

Trem updated Gabby of the situation, that seven Faragh were now on the prowl in Mortsbury. Still, the good thing was that Treman was now out of the picture once and for all. Gabby sat upright on the bed, the wounds on her back healing nicely.

"I want to help you." Gabby told her, shuffling on the bed.

Jenny leaned forward, keeping her hand in Skye's. "You're still recovering sugar, you should get your rest."

Gabby would usually be concerned about coming off as annoying or arrogant, but this time she ignored all those worries and went straight to the point. "I know you Manzazzu can sense where these things are, but you don't know the village like I do. You won't know where exactly they'll be, sure you know where they are but how would you know if you won't have to break into somewhere? Trem, please, you need me."

The four Etemmu all turned to Trem. She glanced away to have a think. Gabby was hardly wrong, she couldn't deny she would be invaluable. But Gabby was still endangering herself. At this point, it was becoming impossible to argue with her over this, not that she ever wanted to argue with her of course. Gabby had proved in the Styx that she could kill a Faragh, a wounded one.

These were out of Limbo world and were on the prowl. They didn't possess a physical form that would be as deadly as the ones in the Styx, but they could still cause some real damage to a Human with their icy aspects.

Plus, she suspected the reason Treman had created them in the first place was to send a message. It would only be a matter of time till other Manzazzu found out about this and report it to the capital. She looked over to the glass tank on her desk. Woody was perched on the top and Sammy's head was poking out of his hide away.
The Dragon lizard blinked and Woody cooed, almost as if to show support in Gabby's decision.

"...Think you can walk?" Trem asked.

Gabby flexed her shoulder muscles, feeling the wound. It had practically healed, it still felt a little tender though. "Yeah, I think so. That stuff of yours blows TCP right out the water." She joked.

"...What's TCP?" Trem asked.

Well that joke died, oh well. "Doesn't matter." Gabby turned and stood up from the bed. She felt a little shaky, but it was nothing. She felt the rip marks on her shirt though, clearly it was going straight in the bin when they got back to her parents. Speaking of which... "Have my parents called?" She asked, glancing at her phone on the table in the middle of the room.

"Oh yes, I said you'll contact them again when you wake up." Trem replied.

Gabby slowly walked to the table, keeping her head straight. "So, what's the plan?" She asked, picking up the phone.

"There are seven Faragh out there. We're going to track them down and finish this."

Gabby brought up her contacts on her phone. "Okay, I'll just tell Mum I'm okay and we'll head out." She turned and began talking to her Mother, reassuring her as she walked out the room.

The four Etemmu circled around Trem. "Are you sure about this?" Abhay asked.

Trem crossed her arms and sighed. "I don't know. I can't keep asking her to come with me, I just have to keep protecting her as best I can."

Jenny spoke softly as she floated behind Trem. "Maybe she can protect you too."

Gabby did manage to do so in the Styx, though both she and Gabby knew there was a certain element of luck there. Gabby had never picked up a sword in her life, they both knew that. It wasn't as if she magically held a sword and became a master of the blade, far from it. Gabby killed the Faragh in the Styx because it was wounded. After that night, Trem figured she might be able to teach Gabby.

"Maybe..." Trem replied.

She decided to use the time while Gabby spoke to her to top up Sammy's food and water. She stroked her scaly companion and closed the lid when Gabby returned.

"All's fine, I'm telling her I'll sleep here if that's okay? I can crash on the sofa downstairs."

Trem turned and began heading for the door. "We'll discuss this later." She turned to the four Etemmu. "Abhay, you're in charge till I return."

The late soldier scoffed playfully. "Because it went so well the last time!" His jovial attitude gently faded as Trem and Gabby were about to set off. "You can trust us Trem."

"Good. See you all soon." Trem replied as they left the room.

When they reached the main hall, Trem headed straight for the hallway to grab one of the swords for Gabby. While she was absent however, Gabby's attention was drawn to the tapestry above the fireplace. The figures seemed to have moved a few inches, to make room for a new figure. At the end of the depiction, next to Trem's late aunt was a new figure. He had his back turned, only his side profile was visible, his black robes mostly defying his appearance. Treman was now officially dead. Gabby wondered why Treman would show up now when he had died before? Another question for another time.

Trem appeared with a sword and the sapphire ring that she gifted to Gabby. "Okay, are you ready?" She asked. Gabby pointed to the tapestry, and to Treman. "Huh, about time he reappeared." Trem muttered.

Gabby followed her to the door. The night was a mild one, which was fortunate for Gabby given her t-shirt was clawed to bits and covered in blood on the back. Trem would have offered a change of clothes, but her mind was on other things.

"Okay, so where's the first beasty?" Gabby asked, taking the sword Trem held out for her.

Trem took a few paces forward, closing her eyes and reaching out into the night. All she needed to do was feel a cold shiver, which would be easy in the mild evening. It wasn't long before she felt the tell tale shiver. She gestured for Gabby to follow as they charged into the night.

Reaching the main road, Trem pointed up the street, the opposite direction from Gabby's house. "What happens if we keep going up there?"

Gabby, who was several paces behind Trem, caught up and glanced to the direction she was pointing to. "Oh the forest. There's nothing up there, just trees and fields. Is that where one of them is? It'll be hard to get around at night."

Trem unsheathed her blade and bolted into the darkness, Gabby following close behind. While Trem was able to vault over the stone wall that lead to the forest with no difficulty, Gabby was left scrambling ungracefully over the top. The forest was vast, leading to a valley with a running stream, a keen hiking destination. Even in the dead of night, the smell of wild garlic stained the air and the sound of the running water broke the still silence of the night.

Trem battered the branches and brambles away with her sword, fighting her way down the slope to the bottom of the valley, following her senses towards the first Faragh. "What's down here?" She asked Gabby, slashing at a low hanging branch.

"Nothing really, just a path leading to a fishing pond. Then just trees and more trees." Gabby replied, trying to keep her footing in the darkness.

The moon hung in the sky, shining brightly, cutting through the darkness. Gabby glanced up to the sky, there were no stars. A layer of cloud had started to build up. She was glancing at the sky for so long, she didn't see Trem had stopped, so she walked straight into her.

"Oof! Sorry..." She apologised.

Trem held her hand up. "Listen..."

Amongst the sound of flowing water came a familiar clicking, the sound of a Faragh. Trem knelt down among the tall grass, followed closely by Gabby. She squinted and glanced around the area. She pointed to one of the many trees littering the landscape. "There, it's coming from behind there."

Sure enough, Gabby caught sight of a large mass of shadows. It was just standing there by the look of it, never a good sign. Trem began to sneak towards the tree line with Gabby close behind. The river masked the sound of their feet against the grass, while their dark attires went a long way to blend into the twilight.

The two made their way to the water's edge and slowly stepped into the water, the running river barely made it past their boot. They emerged on the other side, the Faragh vast approaching. Trem gestured for Gabby to follow closely as they snuck around the corrupted soul, which was still remaining in place. They waited till they were facing the late Human's back. Sure, attacking from behind was quite the cowards move, but they needed to prioritise speed over ethical sword play.

The Faragh looked as frightening as ever, but Gabby was focused on the slight shimmers of Humanity that remained in the twisted figure. Another from the bus crash full of football fans. She had heard about it from her Dad, so it was surreal to have to face the poor souls in this way, not being able to gain peace in the after life. Did Treman have something to do with turning them? The worrying thing was, she was told fifteen fans perished, by her reckoning only about half that number emerged from the Ishtar Gate. Still, the good thing was it meant there'd be less Faragh to locate. It was going to be a long night either way.

A crack ran through this Faragh's head, with one side of his head having peeled away revealing a punctured skull. A sizable wad of brain was visible, even in the dark. His spine had burst and come loose at the base, resulting in a severely hunched individual. Like the others, he wore his home team colours, which hung loosely from his twisted body. One of his claw like hands was pressed against a tree, which to Gabby seemed very odd.

Trem edged closer, her hand hovering over her sword, readying herself to ignite the sapphire flames once again and do her duty as a Manzazzu. She moved with silence and with the utmost stealth... Till she stepped on a branch. The snap sounded so loud, breaking the silence with an audible echo. Gabby bit her lip and swore under her breath.

The Faragh's neck swung around, dislocating itself in the process. Trem, with much haste and desperation ignited her sword and lunged at the creature. She held her breath and with all her strength, plunged the sword into the Faragh's head. The sound of the impact made Gabby queasy, she figured that kind of sound was reserved for her horror movies.

The Faragh twitched, blood trickling down it's face as the flames spat into the late Human's face. Trem roared as she brought the sword down, slicing the Faragh in half. The segments fell to the ground and slowly faded into small patches of frost, which melted away in the warmth.

Trem panted, fixing her fringe. "One down, six to go."

Gabby was left staring at the spot where the Faragh had been. Trem had been merciless. She was doing what needed to be done, of course, but there was a ferocity in the attack she'd never seen in Trem before. While Trem headed for the river, Gabby approached the tree the Faragh had leant against. She squinted as she tried to make out a faint detail in the bark. Her heart sank when she realised what was there.

Two names had been carved into the tree, many years ago too by the look of it. Dennis and Sylvia, 1987. The writing had faded and moss was starting to grow over, but the words and numbers were just clear enough to make out.

Did Faragh have the ability to retain some the memories of their previous life? That was a kind of horrifying thought, being aware you're trapped in that awful, monstrous form. Trem said the Faragh lose their individuality, but if they could remember even fragments of their past lives... Well, it scarcely bears thinking about. Not only that, but they'd have to end six more Faragh by the time the night is over.

Gabby caught up with Trem as they emerged from the woods, a little emotionally strained but otherwise unscathed. Climbing up over the stone wall, they soon arrived back on the main street.

"Okay, so where do we go now?" Gabby asked, keeping her sword close to her.

Trem reached out in her mind, trying to feel for any Faragh that were close by. "I can't feel any close by..." She began running down the street, her sword jangling around in the sheath as she headed for the bottom of the street.

Gabby was keeping pace well enough, but she knew by the end of the night she'll have had her exercise for the year sorted. "Not found anything yet?"

A slight murmur in the air was enough to get the hairs on Trem's arms to stand on end. A faint tingling sensation rushed through her body. "It's not close, but we can get there quick if we run. You feeling fit, Gabby?"

Feeling her bones aching at the thought of it, Gabby forced a fake chuckle. "Quite fit Trem."

So they continued their journey into the night. The grassy path they traveled ran parallel with the road, which would continue on for a few miles before reaching Mortsbury town. As they ran, the clouds overhead began to grow heavier, with the chance of rain becoming more and more apparent. Still, it was hardly going to stop them.

After half a mile or so, they reached a turning in the road, leading up a small hill. Trem took a deep breath, clearing her mind and feeling out for the Faragh's presence. "Gabby, what's up there?" She asked.

Gabby wiped some sweat off her brow and glanced up the road. "Oh, that leads to some old sheds. Some broken down lorries are dumped there. Makes sense for a Faragh to be up there I guess, the Styx is all kind of abandoned and falling apart anyway." One day she'd ask what the deal with all that was, Gabby thought.

The trek up the hill was steep and tiring, not helped by the mild air causing Gabby to run short of breath much easier than she expected to. When they reached the top, they were greeted with, as Gabby described, several sheds which were in the process of being reclaimed by nature and two lorries , who's paint had long since chipped away, which were being swallowed up by the vegetation as well.

Gabby followed Trem's lead as she unsheathed her sword from the scabbard. There couldn't be that many places for a whopping great corrupted soul to reside. An almighty bellow punctured the silence, resulting in the two women being startled by the noise. They both looked up and ignited their blades. The Faragh was standing on top of one of the sheds. Blood trickled from it's mouth, the lips having been chewed right off with those huge fang like teeth. This one was just as frightful as the last few, with this Faragh's nose having been compressed inwards and a bloody stain where one of the eyes were.

It knelt down and jumped from the shed to the ground, slashing it's arm at Trem. The arm went right through Trem's head, sending her staggering backwards, ice having formed around her face. Gabby drew her attention away to look at Trem for a second and already the Faragh was bearing down on her, it's jaw opening wide. It brought it's jaw down on Gabby. She jammed her flaming sword into the beasts maw, using all her strength to keep it away.

It baffled Gabby how something like this would even exist in real life.

The Human soul must have been such a fragile thing to be so easily corruptible, but to this extent? It felt so wrong. It also felt like the exact reason why Humans were never made aware of the Manzazzu. Not because of confirmation of life after death, but because of the horrors that came with it. Gabby wondered how Manzazzu ever coped, having to deal with these things. Right now though she was more worried about being savaged by the creature.

Gabby's hands shook as she pushed as hard as she could. It felt like such an immense weight behind the Faragh, more than she could handle. She found herself being pushed, her feet sliding backwards ever so slightly. The Faragh's one Human eye stared deep into Gabby's own, the worst thing about it was how sad it looked, as if the last sparks of humanity inside the twisted monster was begging to be put out of its misery. Gabby would have loved to oblige.

Trem staggered to her feet, wiping away the dampness from her face, her skin stinging slightly. When she saw Gabby in peril, she took her sword in both hands, ran up to the Faragh and slashed it's back. Gabby used the opportunity to drive her sword through the Faragh's head. The top of the skull landed on the ground, followed closely by the rest of the body, which soon faded into nothingness.

Gabby sank to her knees, the fire fizzling away from her sword. "Trem, I don't get it..."

"Don't get what?" Trem knelt down, putting her hand on Gabby and whisking the flames away from her sword. "Gabby, what's wrong?"

"Well, in the Styx, these things could hurt us. But here Jenny and the others don't have physical form. So how come I could have one try to eat me and Treman could get into that suit of armour?"

Trem lifted Gabby's head gently with her hand. "Do you want to go back to the house? You don't have to come, I told you before, you've got no obligation to follow me around and endanger your life."

Gabby pulled herself up onto her feet, using her sword to help her. "Look Trem, you can keep telling me that, and I'm going to say the same thing. I'm in it for the long haul. The last thing I'm going to do is let you face this alone. Besides, you've spent way too much time being by yourself."

Trem got to her feet as well and began to head away from the old sheds. "Thank you Gabby, I won't let you get in harm's way though, you've had enough of that already." She returned her sword to it's scabbard and made her way down the hill.

"Oh and to answer your question about the Faragh. Well in regards to the sword, the only reason it could make contact with it is because of the blue flames. From what I can tell, and this may not even be right, but it looks like it's the only thing that can affect them in this world and in the Styx. I don't really know myself but at a guess it might be made up of some substance that can affect Faragh across both planes of existence." She scratched the back of her head. "Well, just a guess at any rate."

That made sense. Just as well because the whole greater Manzazzuan culture and abilities would boggle even the most educated minds, so if an eighteen year old, fresh out of college nobody from England could grasp it, then there would be hope yet.

"I do have one question for you though." Trem asked.

"Hmm?" Came the reply.

Trem stopped in her tracks and smiled. "How are you so good with a sword?"

Gabby couldn't help but burst out laughing. "Good? Are you serious? I wouldn't know good swordplay if it smacked me in the face." She patted the hilt of the blade. "All I can do is just swing it wildly. It was dumb luck I killed that Faragh in the Styx. I chopped it's head off when it was distracted by this big light. I've seen a few fantasy films, so in my mind I try and replicate that. But what they don't show is how heavy the ruddy things can be."

That was rather surprising, she assumed all Humans had a rudimentary understanding of swordplay. Despite that though, Gabby showed potential. "Well, you could have fooled me. What do you say when this is all over, maybe I could teach you some Manzazzuan dueling methods?"

Gabby's face light up. "That would be so cool! Thanks so much, I'll be a good student, I promise."

"I don't doubt it." Trem replied.

When they returned to the road, Trem pointed to the distance. "How far away is the town we visited?"

Gabby stood over what looked like a mole hill but in the darkness she didn't want to assume anything. "Well the actual town only starts two or so miles away. The town centre is further in. You think the other five are there?"

Trem began the long walk to Mortsbury town. "It's a good assumption. They would have had enough time to reach there by now."

Gabby had actually walked to the town before, more than once. When it was a lovely day when she was younger, her parents and her would go hiking to the town, get lunch and walk back in time for tea. It wasn't such a hard thing for her, though she was out of practise. She decided to share that bit of nostalgic information with Trem, who found it rather quaint.

"You are really fortunate to have such a wonderful family." She began to fidget awkwardly. "Honestly, what do they think of me?"

That came as a surprise, Gabby didn't see that coming. "Honestly?" She began, her blushing. "They really like you. Mum thinks your rather cute and Dad thinks your kind of shy but a great friend to me." She shrugged her shoulders. "The only thing they question is your haircut and fashion sense, other then that they've got no issue at all."

Trem tugged at her high collar, she didn't think there was anything wrong with her looks. "Well, these are Manzazzuan robes, we all wear them, it's expected and assumed we all do." She began playing with her fringe.

"Oh yeah, I think your hair's really cool but I've been meaning to ask about that. It's pretty modern, how did you find out about it?"

Trem pointed out a few large rocks on the path which she alerted Gabby's attention to before replying. "I think it was some advertisement shoved through the manor's door. Something that was happening in the town, but I ignored it. The woman on the front though, I liked her hair style so I did this myself."

Gabby wondered what would have been shoved through her door. There was a Taser Laser Action Course that opened in Mortsbury a few years previously, maybe it was that. "Rightly so, you should never listen to the naysayers. I don't know what it's like for Manzazzu, but with us Humans there's a certain way of thinking. I like to think I'm very open minded, try anything and don't hold back. Then there's the opposite, the type of people who won't trust anything they don't know or can't understand. Worse, don't want to understand."

Trem nodded as they continued walking along, glancing back at Gabby. "I can understand that. There was one group of Manzazzu who wanted the Human race wiped off the face of the planet."

Well, that went from zero to one hundred in an instant. "Wow.." Gabby gasped. "Was that what Treman was part of? With that weird skull thing?"

Trem nodded. "Yes, the Mutashaeib. The jackal skull was their symbol. Treman wasn't even a legitimate member, he was a cowardly sympathiser that watched silently from the side lines."

It was all starting to make a bit more sense now. "So what happened to them all?"

Trem ducked under a road sign as she replied. "The Royal Family wiped most of them out, though no one knows what happened to the core leaders. Rumour was they went into hiding. It's all written in a book at the manor, I'll show you it one day. My parents fought in the war, it's in living memory, as of the last generation or so."

It sounded like a certain war the Human race endured. As Gabby and Trem pushed on into the night, Gabby had to wonder just how different these seemingly contrasting race of people were.

Chapter Nineteen "Horseman In The Butchers":

"It's the ideal life for a Human. Settle down in the countryside, raise a child..."
"I'm starting to see the appeal. They aren't the primitive savages your Father would have us believe."

The two would be warriors passed a stone sign, welcoming visitors to Mortsbury town. The new town stretched for several miles, which lead to the old town at the core of the settlement. Gabby's school lay beyond the old town. With any luck, the rogue Faragh would only be around the old town. The journey was a little tiring but hardly a draining one, Trem took it in her stride of course. She seemed to be made of steel or something, whereas Gabby was just keeping herself in check.

She was able to keep up, but was feeling the tiredness get to her a little. It was already 1am, maybe this was what women her age meant when talking about a long night out. Fighting corrupted souls from the afterlife may not have been part of that though.

When they reached the roundabout in the centre of road leading into the town, Trem could feel the sensation of more Faragh surrounding the area. "That's better, it's clear to me now."

Trem looked around, the road separated into three different directions, each leading to another part of the town. One Faragh seemed closer then the other, as if it was on the move. She pointed to the path leading straight on. "What's up there?" She asked.

"Oh the train station. An old steam train does the rounds from here to the other towns." Gabby explained. Many a fun childhood was spent on that train, going on day trips up the coast.

Trem took her sword from its sheath and proceeded up the road, past the line of quaint, picturesque little shops. Gabby glanced round the street far more than Trem, making sure that there was no sign of any innocents being caught in the crossfire. The night was, once again, still and quiet. The population of the new town were all asleep, fortunately, since it was a weekday, it was highly unlikely many would be about.

"Trem, I'm kind of worried about this. Innocent people could get hurt." Gabby said, glancing around continually.

"That's why we have to get the last five dealt with before sunrise." Trem replied.

At the end of the road was the train station. Trem jumped over the wall and onto the platform, leaving Gabby behind. "Trem!" She called in a whisper. "Stay there!" She ran around to the official entrance to the station.

Gabby climbed over the locked gate and bolted onto the platform. "Right, sorry about that. Humans don't jump like they're spring loaded like you lot. So…" Gabby began looking around the platform. "… Where's the awful thing?"

Trem stepped off the platform, onto the train tracks. Gabby bit her hand as she noticed a security camera on the top of the platform. "Trem!" She whispered. She pointed to the camera. "They can see us, we could get in trouble. "

The response was rather quick and without much thought. Trem ignited her sword red with her ruby ring, drew her sword back and slashed the air, the crescent shockwave striking the camera, causing it to short circuit and pop with a fizz.

"Trem! That's criminal damage!" She forced through her closed teeth.

"It is? Is that bad?" Trem asked innocently.

Gabby stepped onto the tracks and removed her sword. "Let's just find this thing and kill it before I have a heart attack." At this rate they'd be arrested for trespassing, damaged property and by the end of the night, who knows how many other offences.

Trem lead the way down the railway line for several yards before the line turned off into a siding, where a line of old coaches were sat. They could see the Faragh inside one of the coaches.

"If these Faragh are supposed to be brainless, then why do they keep coming to these random places?" Gabby had a sinking feeling she knew the answer, but she didn't want to assume.

Trem kept her eyes locked on the Faragh. In close quarter combat, Faragh have the advantage of strength and speed, but their cumbersome size didn't allow them to use those skills very well. It was going to be a close thing. "Well, there's a theory that Faragh can retain slight details of their Humanity, during their time alive anyway. No one's really sure why."

She began to walk towards the carriage, her sword spitting out blue flames. "Stay here." She ordered, forcing the door open.

Gabby watched Trem force her way in and confront the Faragh inside. After a few seconds of deathly silence, the carriage began to rock back and forth. Gabby felt awkward thinking about what any onlooker might have thought of that. Several grunts could be heard, a few unearthly hisses, swiftly silenced with the sound of a brief and sharp woosh.

There were a deathly chill in the air before Trem merged, victorious. She panted as she returned her sword to it's holder. "Done." She strained through the panting.

Gabby walked up to Trem and offered her hand, helping her off the carriage. "You need a rest or something?" She asked.

"Four to go." Came the reply as Trem walked past Gabby and jumped from the rail tracks back onto the road.

Trem seemed to be a woman on a mission, that much was obvious. But it was clear going through the process of killing the Faragh was starting to drain her. Gabby didn't know how she was coping, having to face those horrific things over and over again.

The only reason Gabby felt like she wasn't going to be scared for life over this was because she was getting increasingly numb to the whole affair. The dawning thought of four Faragh left? It was a miracle no one had been hurt as of yet, and hopefully they wouldn't have to deal with that.

Gabby followed Trem, trying to keep pace was proving to be harder than expected. "You can feel one right? It's got to be close by?" She asked.

Trem nodded, the unnerving sensation was indeed growing stronger. They crossed the road and began to climb up a steep, cobbled road, lined with houses. "Is there anything up here of significance?"

Gabby felt like the hike up the street was like climbing a huge hill, with every step she felt her blood stained, ripped shirt cling to her body. Sweat patches were forming and she struggled to talk without panting. "Just some houses..." She began.

Trem stopped and glanced back. "Do you want to stop?"

Gabby's attempts to get her breath back finally proved successful when she stopped, leaning back and taking some deep breaths. "I'll be okay, I just need a minute ." Human beings weren't built for trekking around town at nearly 2am, on a warm, sweaty night. Okay, maybe some could, at a push, but Gabby wasn't used to it. "To answer your question, the road at the top leads to the old town, it's about a mile or two."

"No, it's not that far. There's something on the road to the town, it's closer than I thought. You okay to keep going?"

Gabby replied with a thumbs up, clicked her neck and gestured up the path. "Ready to keep trekking."

When they reached the top of the street, Trem lead Gabby up onto the main road. The houses on either side of the street eventually came to an end, leading onto a stretch of road where only countryside could be seen, prime ground for any Faragh to hide.

"You know, there's something I learned today." Trem began, in a half run down the path running by the road. "There was certainly a lot of beauty here, being shut off all those years meant I never even entertained the idea that there was anything for me here."

Trem really had come a long way in the past few days, and Gabby was really rather proud of her. "Was it because Treman put you off the idea of going outside, or did you think we Humans were inferior?" She hoped she didn't seem too forward with the question, it did seem rather blunt, but it wouldn't have made a difference regardless. She still felt the way she did with Trem, that this bizarre, beautiful and wonderful woman was unlike anyone else Gabby would ever meet again.

"I never thought Humans were inferior like Treman did... Not as advanced, maybe. But it's not like I hold it against you all. Manzazzu are supposed to be Humans blessed by Ishtar centuries ago, so it's kind of unfair to compare the two if that's true." She rested her hand on her sword's hilt. "I've always had a fascination with Humans, granted. But I never expected to..."

Gabby noticed Trem had begun to blush. "Never expected to what?"

Though Trem's head was turned away, her eyes glanced at Gabby's. "...Never expected to grow so close to one."

They both stopped dead in their tracks, Gabby gently putting her hands to Trem's head. She pulled her in gently for a brief kiss on the lips. "I never expected to fall for an advanced ghost summoner, but I'm very glad I did."

Their brief moment of joy was interrupted by the sound of a car's screeching tyres. They both turned their heads to the noise, their smiles fading. There was an almighty crash, followed by a Faragh's unmistakable growl.

"Oh no..." Gabby muttered, the worst case scenario had happened, someone had been caught in the crossfire.

They both removed their swords and ran towards the noise. When they rounded the corner, they witnessed a car which had lost control and struck a street lamp. The driver, fortunately unharmed due to the airbag deploying, was on the ground. He was frozen due to the shock of seeing a Faragh bearing down on him. It's clawed hand closed into a fist.

"Hey!" Trem called, igniting her sword and slashing the air, the blue cresent of fire striking the Faragh, knocking it to the ground. "Gabby, make sure he's alright. I'll deal with this."

Trem chased after the Faragh, ready to take it down as quickly and as mercilessly as she could. In her mind she kept repeating one simple fact. Three left after this one. Gabby meanwhile ran at full speed towards the man, who was still on the ground.

"Are you okay?" She asked, helping him up with her one free hand.

The poor guy was shaking, he looked downright catatonic. "Wh...What is that thing?!"

How was Gabby supposed to explain stuff she spent days trying to get her head round? Simple answer, don't. "Why, do you want to exchange names and addresses? Look, you wouldn't believe me even if I tried to explain, even I don't get it."

They both watched Trem charge at the Faragh, jumping up into the air and landing a blow with her sword through the creature's neck. It staggered back, clutching it's wound.

The man looked back to Gabby. "Who are you people anyway?"

Trem stabbed the Faragh in the leg, throwing it off balance and allowing her to drive her sword through its chest.

"Seriously, long story. You're not hurt are you?" She asked, glancing the man up and down. Now she was up close she couldn't see any visible sign of injuries.

The man glanced back in fear at the creature. "Yeah I'm fine, just filling my pants with fear, nothing to worry about..." He was still panting as he kept his eyes locked on the creature. "Whatever that thing is, it's really messing with me." Well, no surprises there... "Why does it kind of look like Derek...?"

Gabby felt a sinking feeling in the pit of her stomach. "Who's Derek?"

The man ran his hand through his hair. "He used to work the night shift with me... He died in that coach crash coming back from the footy...." He knew the Faragh when he was alive, this Derek was one of the football fans killed in the crash.

Gabby had no idea how awful this must have been. Faragh were terrible enough when they were anonymous. Trem looked ready to end the creature, prompting Gabby to grab the man's hand, causing him to turn and face her. "What's your name?"

"Uhh, Jerry..." He began.

"You'll want to look away for this bit." Gabby advised.

There was an almighty grunt from the Faragh as it faded into nothingness. Another poor soul given the sweet release it deserved.

With the deed done, Gabby let go of Jerry's hand. "Okay, it's over."

The poor guy turned around, seeing only a patch of melting ice on the ground and Trem returning her blade to it's holster. "I'm... I'm not going to even ask. I was just... I was just seeing things, trick of the light." He glanced at his ruined car. "Good thing I have insurance..." He muttered.

Trem joined the two, the exhaustion beginning to show. Even for a Manzazzu, this was becoming hard for her. "Everyone okay?" She asked, focusing predominantly at Gabby but glancing at the tall, bearded stranger.

"Yeah..." Gabby replied, letting her sword slide back into the scabbard around her waist.

Jerry staggered back, his hands fumbling for his phone. "Man I just work at the local radio station, I don't get any of this and I don't want to..." He began typing in the emergency breakdown number. "Thanks for, you know, saving my life and stuff..."

The two women shot worried looks at each other. "Wait, are you sure you're okay?"

The man placed the phone to his ear and staggered backwards, wobbling slightly. "Yeah I just, I just got to sort this mess out..." He then turned his back and walked away to make the phone call.

"Well, I think he took that rather well." Trem retorted, heading along the road to the next port of call, wherever that may be.

Gabby itched her head. "Well, some people just go into full denial, it's one way of keeping yourself sane."

Trem smiled and shook her head. "Humans..." She muttered playfully. She pointed up the street. "What's at the end of this road?"

"The old theatre, a little museum... The supermarket Dad's store manager in, that's off a turning. Aside from that, a little park and a memorial." Gabby listed. "Can you feel anymore of them nearby?"

The lack of Faragh was starting to concern Trem, the longer they waited the more people were at risk. It was a fluke they'd come this far and only had to deal with one person. "Gabby, at a guess, where would you look first?"

If the detail about Faragh retaining some semblance of their humanity was correct, her mind turned to the list of deceased in the crash her Dad listed off from the paper the other day. So far, they had listed the local radio co host and a volunteer on the railway. It was something only mentioned once, so she was trying to focus on recalling the details. "Try the theatre, they had a lot of volunteers and staff." She began walking, patting Trem on the back as she took off. "I'll take point this time, this is my town after all!"

Trem had to admit, this was a much better idea. The last thing they needed was to get lost, she only had instinct and her senses to get them to the next Faragh, it could send them to all manner of places.

Gabby knew this too, she didn't want to explain why she and Trem were chasing monsters through her Dad's store, or the school or anywhere else for that matter. If she could keep the whole thing under wraps, then it would be a success. She was already formulating potential excuses just in case she needed to wiggle out of anything. Always best to be prepared, her philosophy.

The old Victorian theatre was in sight. Gabby had spent some time there, watching and taking part in the odd performance. When they drew closer to the theatre, their fears were soon realised, the doors had two large patches of hard frost burned into the woodwork. On the upside, there was only one more Faragh to track down, and no one would be in the theatre. Downside, there were two beasts left to finish, one was hard, but two...!

"Oh great..." Trem muttered, walking up to the door. She turned to Gabby and reached for her sword. "I'll get us in..."

Gabby quickly grabbed Trem's hand. "No, no, no! No more illegal entering, we're on thin ice as it is." She gestured to the corner of the door, where a key pad was placed. "Maybe a less damaging way of breaking and entering?"

Her hand hovered over the keys, Gabby closed her eyes and tried to recall the code. With any luck, it hadn't changed since the last time she used it. They all memorised a little pattern for the code, but it had been months since she had to use it. Trem watched Gabby silently mouth incomprehensible rhymes. Slowly, she hesitantly and without much confidence, began putting in a four digit code. She waited for the beep to confirm the door was unlocked... But it never happened. Huffing, she tapped her palm on her forehead.

"Seven or six.... Seven or six....?" She muttered and forcefully prodded the six button, which was followed by the long beep, finally.

She grabbed the handle of the door and pulled it open. The lights were motion activated and had already been triggered, which was kind of strange, but now wasn't the time to debate. Gabby led the way from the entrance of the theatre which was lined with posters and the occasional plant. The theatre itself was quite the relic, a piece of old Mortsbury history from the Victorian era. A few mod cons had found their way into the theatre, with a bar recently been added. What never changed was the smell of dust, which never seemed to go away.

A pair of ornate, large oak doors led to the theatre itself, and once again, the frost was melting, dripping off the wood. Gabby gently put her hand against it and pushed the door open a crack, peering inside. She felt herself go stiff and froze. On the stage were two Faragh, snarling and snapping, fighting each other. They sliced at each other with their claws, blood streaming down their faces. Gabby closed the door and slowly turned to Trem, her face pale and drained.

"...Two of them..." She strained, pointing at the door.

Trem's eyes widened. "Oh wonderful.." She whispered.

Gabby looked over Trem's shoulders, there was a flight of red carpeted stairs that led up to the first floor circle of seats. "Trem, hear me out, I got an idea."

She walked past Trem and up to the stairs. "Right, so it's going to be hard to take out two, but can you get the from a distance? You know, with your..." She made a swiping gesture with her hands, making a swoosh noise.

"...That's not a bad idea. But I think I can do one better. Can I have your sword?" She asked.

Gabby didn't hesitate in handing over her blade. "What are you thinking?"

Trem took Gabby's sword in one hand and her trusty weapon in the other. "Can you get me to the highest level? I want to get as good a view I can of the stage."

Gabby began sprinting up the stairs. "Sure, follow me."

Now it was Trem's turn to follow Gabby as they passed the first floor circle, then the second. Gabby led them through a door and into one of the seat boxes. They sank to their knees and peered over the side. The two Faragh were really going at it, pouncing on each other, taking wild swipes at each other's faces.

"So, what's the plan?" Gabby asked.

Trem peered over the box to the Faragh once again, igniting her sword. "Just got to get this timing right..." She muttered.

One of the Faragh battered it's foe onto the ground, and in that brief window of opportunity, Trem striked. She stood from her hiding place and held her blue blazing blade like a javelin. She held her free hand outward, lining up the shot.

She would only get one good shot, so she had to be accurate. She drew in a breath, held it in and took one step forward, throwing the sword. Before the downed Faragh could get to its feet, the sword struck the creature, piercing it through the head, pinning it to the ground. There was an almighty squelch as the creature twitched for a brief moment before fading into a frosty patch.

The other Faragh looked up and let out a rage filled scream, it wasn't very happy to have it's fight interrupted. Trem set the other sword ablaze and quickly lined up another shot, though she wished she had more time to allow for accuracy. She launched the sword at the Faragh and it struck, puncturing the beast's chest, hitting the ground and keeping the creature flailing in agony on the ground, unable to move.

Trem stepped onto the raised barrier around the box and stepped casually off, falling roughly twelve feet before landing upright. She walked through the rows of seats and up onto the stage. She yanked the still flaming sword from the ground and stepped up the helpless Faragh. Trem lined the sword up to its neck, raised the weapon in the air and brought it down onto the monster's head. The twisted and deformed skull rolled away as the corrupted soul faded away.

Trem sighed, only one more to find, then their awful mission was done. Then maybe she and Gabby could actually spend a day without any fear of interruption. She wiped some sweat off her brow and took Gabby's sword from the ground. She then turned on the spot and looked up at the box where Gabby was watching intently. "Why don't you jump down? It'll save the walk."

"...A fall like that would really hurt! I'm Human remember? We're not built like you Manzazzu." She replied.

Trem blinked, staring blankly for a moment. "Oh yeah, I forgot about that. I'll meet you by the entrance."

Gabby began to make her way down the stairs while Trem paused for a moment to look around the theatre. The ornate, highly decorated ceiling was quite the aesthetic marvel, it reminded her of the more reserved Manzazzuan grandeur she'd seen in her books. She had spent a lot of time thinking how similar the two people were. Manzazzu, after all, were born from the Human race when Ishtar apparently "blessed" them with their powers.

If that was the case, the First Queen's Manzazzu must have been quite something. She remembered her ancestor on the tapestry, the dark skinned eastern warrior Manzazzu of old. How brave they must have been, forging a new world. With Trem venturing into a new world of her own, she certainly felt she had a good idea of what they felt.

They both met up by the entrance and returned to the warm, starless night. They could both feel in the air that rain would be on the way soon, but they could also feel something wasn't right. They both felt uneasy, the night was far too quiet. Before, they could hear a slight wind, but now everything was dead silent.

"Trem, any idea where the last one is? I kind of want to get this done so I can get some sleep. If we keep going I think I'm going to pass out." Gabby wasn't joking either, she was hardly the most unfit person but her legs were aching. Her eyes felt heavy and her head felt hazy.

Trem stepped out into the middle of the road, looking around aimlessly. "I don't know... We'll go back the way we came, maybe then there'll be something." She held Gabby's sword out, offering it back to her friend.

"Oh, cheers." She took the sword, fastened the belted scabbard around her waist and let out a big yawn. "Sorry, it's been a long day."

Trem pulled Gabby in for a reassuring hug. "It's nearly over Gabby. Just one more and then we can put this whole ugly mess behind us." Trem looked into Gabby's eyes, the exhaustion was clear on her face. She had never seen her this bad, even when bleeding half to death, she didn't look this drained.

They rounded a corner and walked back down the street, Gabby's feet felt so sore in her boots. When she would eventually sleep that night, it would feel like she'd been awake for days. She wasn't much of a night owl anyway, but walking for miles on end, after a serious injury and nursing blood loss would exhaust anyone. But she kept pressing forward, she had to.

They reached a turning that would lead them back to their starting point when a flash not only startled Gabby, but flushed out any remaining colour in her face. Her arm latched onto Trem's shoulder. Trem reached for her sword but Gabby franticly shook her head. The blue flashes of a police car, which had pulled up on the path behind them.

Gabby realised the blood stained slash marks were still ripped into her shirt, which she wore with no coat to cover. Two women, brandishing swords, one covered in dried blood... Oh this did not look good at all.

"Oh not now... Why did it have to be now?" Gabby muttered, shaking all over.

She could hear the police car door close behind her, the incoherent buzz of chatter on the officer's radio. Her mind raced at what felt like a thousand miles per hour, today was just one test after another. She turned around and wiped as much fear off her face as possible, trying and mostly succeeding to have a neutral expression. She pulled Trem around as well. "What's up officer?" Gabby asked casually.

The tall police officer, in his high visibility jacket put his hands in his pockets. "I could ask you the same question." He pointed to Gabby's shirt. "Is that real blood on that shirt?"

Gabby glanced at her back and pulled at her shirt. "Oh that, it's fake blood. Taught how to whip it up in high school, good for fake wounds." She nodded to Trem. "We were just doing some filming. You know, cosplay stuff. Hence why my friend here's dressed so..." She gestured up and down Trem's body. "...Yeah."

The officer looked down at their belts. "Right, and are those real swords?" He asked.

Trem rather unwisely flashed a segment of the blade out of the sheath for the officer to see. Gabby quickly explained, trying hard not to stutter. "Oh no, prop swords. Trisha here lives in the old town and I live in the new, we just got caught up and didn't notice how late it was so we're walking back to my place."

The officer nodded his head slowly through the story. "Do you need any help getting home?" He asked.

That certainly lifted a lot of the stress off of Gabby's shoulders. They weren't in trouble for breaking into the train station or anything? Great! "Oh thank you, but we're alright thank you." She realised she thanked the guy twice.

"Stay safe okay? Don't hang about, just get to where you're going." The officer instructed, heading towards his car.

Gabby nodded and forced a smile. "Will do sir, thank you for the consideration." She watched the man enter his police car and drive off, waving as he drove off. After a moment stuck in the same position mid wave, Gabby let out an exhausted sigh.

She dragged her hands over her face and through her hair, which was starting to stick to her sweat drenched brow. "Trem, please tell me you've got a handle on where the last Faragh is? At this rate if I keep going, you'll have to drag me out of the ruddy Ishtar Gate yourself."

Trem was really starting to fear for Gabby, her exhaustion was turning her into something Trem hadn't seen before. In fact, there was a brief, dark glimmer of Treman in her angry gaze. Trem found it hit her deep, her face showing her inner worries and fears. "Right…" She muttered. She corrected her fringe and turned to the road before them. "I can feel something, yes. Come on, we've got this. One more trial to face."

She hesitantly walked forward and offered her hand. Gabby glanced down, let out a weary breath and took Trem's hand gently in her own. "Let's just get on with it."

Gabby was able to keep her frustration at bay, long enough for them to arrive back at the start of the village and down the path Trem had pondered on before. The slight incline they found themselves descending began to worry Gabby. "Trem, you sure we're heading to the right place?"

"Yes, why?" Came the reply.

Gabby let go of Trem's hand and looked ahead to the long road lined with shops. "My Dad's supermarket's up here." Trem stopped and shot a worried look at Gabby. "Trem, don't tell me it's at Dad's work, please..."

The young Manzazzu bit her lip, it was almost like she didn't have the heart to tell her. "Gabby, it's a possibility." She had to be truthful in this situation, there was no way to scoot around the facts. "I dare even say, it's a certainty."

Poor Gabby looked like she was going to pass out with exhaustion. "I can't do this Trem, I can't cope with this anymore." She dragged herself over to a wall and slouched on the floor. "All this Manzazzu stuff, ghosts, whatever Treman's skull mask guys are, or were, or whatever... Any wonder why Humans like me don't get involved? We're weak, we're pathetic and stupid." She moped, putting her face in her hands.

Trem rushed over and knelt by Gabby, rubbing her hand on her friend's back. "Gabby... I can't promise things will be easy, we both know they were never going to be. But this is the last one. Come on, we're so close now. I know you can stick with it, because I believe in you. I wouldn't have fallen for you if I didn't know you were perfect for me."

Gabby slowly lifted her head, feeling Trem's slight and tender touch on her hands. Through the trickling tears, Gabby and Trem smiled at each other, a silent reassurance to the other. Gabby got back onto her feet, her head spinning slightly. "Let's get this over with so I can sleep."

"Sounds like a plan."

When they arrived at the local branch of Dewsbury's, their concerns were confirmed. The Faragh was on top of the shop, plain and clear for all to see. Trem watched it act like a sentinel atop the food shop. "Gabby, you don't mind sitting this one out, do you?"

Considering the roof of the shop was pretty darn tall, Gabby felt no guilt in her reply. "I don't mind at all. Give it hell."

Trem readied her weapon for the last time on this long and rather painful day. "With pleasure." She grinned.

She charged at the building and jumped as high as she could onto the roof. She landed softly, eyeing up the creature. Finally, the last Faragh. Treman will have failed in his plot to send a message to the Royal Family that the Mutashaeib would never return. The safety of Gabby and who knows who else, was in her hands, and she wasn't going to stand down or give the Faragh any mercy. She drew her sword straight, turned her hand and dragged it up the blade, setting the weapon on fire once again.

Immediately, the Faragh charged at her, letting out a bellowing roar as it prepared to close it's maw into Trem. Before it was on top of her, Trem drew her sword back and scored a well timed blow to the creature's belly, causing it to recoil in anguish. It's bloodstained face contorted with a mix of extreme anger and pain.

It tried to raise it's hand but Trem was fast, she caught the hand with her sword, cutting it with the blue flames. The once strong and stable attack turned into a helpless flail of wounded wrist. Trem was starting to feel cocky, but it would be in vain however as the Faragh's other hand struck her on the head.

Trem staggered back, ice having formed over her lower face. Gabby tried to get a look to see what was happening, but her view from the ground was frustratingly limited. Trem used her fingers to grab hold of the ice on her face and rip it away, leaving a painful looking red mark across her face. Trem smiled a malicious and evil little smirk. "Oh you're in for it now." She took her sword in one hand and raised it up to her head. Her other hand was stretched outward, beckoning the Faragh to attack her. "Come on, good thing." She teased.

The Faragh rose to its feet, limp arms left hanging in front of it's hunched body. It began to run at great speed towards Trem, who remained locked in her position.

From the ground, Gabby could hear a sound that made her feel sick, a wet, meaty squelch like before. When she managed to get a good look at what had happened, she saw Trem standing upright and victorious with her sword having run the Faragh straight through the head. The crumpled form hit the roof of the store and like a passing breeze, melted into nothingness.

Gabby didn't know why she had begun to cry again, but the relief she was feeling was the best she'd ever felt in her life. They had beaten Treman's plot, they had won and come out unscathed. As shattered as she felt, Gabby still kept beaming from ear to ear as Trem made her way back onto the ground. When Trem was close enough, Gabby pulled her in for a hug. Chuckling, Trem dropped her sword and let the warm, slightly sticky embrace of her friend warm her to the core. "It's over now." Trem whispered.

The two heroes, riding an exhausted but triumphant high from their victory were on their way back to Trem's house, having left the scene of the fight behind them. They spent the journey back holding each others hand. Trem certainly felt unstoppable, with a real thriving power going through her body. The last few days had been unbelievable for her, and it was all because of Gabby. She knew she'd have plenty of days in the future to show her appreciation in all sorts of ways.

Gabby meanwhile was looking at Trem's eyes, admiring their strange jet blackness. To many people, it would be a sign of distrust or something evil or malicious. But for Trem, there was a sense of fragility about them that Gabby could never feel anything but empathy for. As for Trem, Gabby's seemed to be full of bright, energetic optimism, something she had been lacking. What felt like years could likely be decades for her.

Their tender moment was interrupted when they both began to feel specks of rain on their faces. Soon enough, the heavens opened and began a downpour. How lovely. Gabby looked around the surroundings, they were at the patch of greenery between old and new Mortsbury, which was just a stone's throw away from the new destination she began dragging Trem to. There was a small bridge on the off road, which lead to a small outcrop of houses and a farm. Gabby led Trem down a small dip in the land and they both scrambled under one of the arches, sheltered from the rain.

"Ahh, that's better. We can wait it out here if we need to." Gabby said, finding a level patch of earth to sit on.

Trem took her sword and ignited it with the red flames. She gently pushed the blade into the soft soil, using it as a makeshift campfire. "That's even better, some warmth." She looked down and noticed Gabby had begun shivering. Sitting on the dirt ground, Trem took off her robe and placed it around Gabby, wrapping it around her. "There you go, that should help you warm up."

Gabby let out a little moan as she could feel herself warming up every second. "But won't you be cold?"

Trem shrugged her shoulders, wrapping a bare arm around Gabby. "Cold never bothers me." She gently kissed Gabby on the forehead.

"I'm the blanket burrito now." She joked.

Trem wasn't quite sure what that meant but she chuckled all the same. "That you are."

Gabby watched the flames crackle and dance around the metal blade, in a way they were rather soothing to watch. She rested her head on Trem. "Can I ask you something?"

"Of course."

"What were your parents like?" Gabby asked, at the halfway point between being awake and asleep.

Trem gently ran her fingers through Gabby's thick, curly hair. She didn't need to think long or hard about it. "They're wonderful, the best parents I could have ever asked for. Dad was always such an optimist, always the showman, always doing his best to make me happy. As for my Mum? Well, she's always so calming. Just with her voice she could stop me crying as a baby. She just always made me feel like everything would be alright. Even now when I see them looking down at me from that painting in the house, I still feel... Well, safe."

She felt Gabby reach up and take her hand, pulling it closer to her chest. "That sounds lovely." Gabby's voice started to trail off into a murmur. "How did they meet...?"

The ruby ring on Trem's finger began to glow a bloody shade of red as she reached into the flames, pulling out a small ball of fire. She flexed her fingers as the ball split in two. The spheres then spiraled upwards until they transformed into the shape of a man and woman, both in long Manzazzuan robes judging by their vague outline.

"There was a big event at the Manzazzuan capital, all the big houses were there. Mum was meant to mingle with the famous and important men so she could marry into wealth and power to keep Treman happy. But she didn't do that, she fell for Dad instead. This nobody, out of his depth Manzazzu in such an elite society would become her husband and my Father. This is how they met, at a dance."

She began to hum, moving her fingers to manipulate the figures. They bowed to each other, took each others hands and began to slow dance. Gabby watched with misty eyes as Trem began to sing, more specifically, the song that they danced to the other day in the manor house. In fact, the dancing was almost identical to their romantic moment. Gabby continued to watch the figures dance around the sword, flaming robes spinning around blazing bodies.

Gabby could feel herself falling into the warm embrace of sleep at last and while Trem continued to sing, Gabby finally fell asleep. Trem chuckled as she snuffed out the figures, she deserved her rest.

Chapter Twenty: "What Now?"

"I'll fight to protect my family, if I have to."

The Boatswain's Mate was one of the most well regarded and expensive restaurant in Mortsbury, complete with a sea view and everything. The only way Gabby had a chance of ever taking someone there is if she won the lottery, or if she was dreaming... Which in fact she was. She was sat in front of Trem, both laughing and enjoying themselves. Even though Gabby was aware she was dreaming, she didn't really care.

The moments she spent with Trem felt so good and worth treasuring, even fake ones still gave her a sense of wonder. Her laughter subsided however when she caught a glimpse of something in the glass. She expected to see her reflection, but the mirror image was wrong. She leaned in for a closer look, to see her dark, curly hair now long and gray, with a deep scar running down her eye. The closer she looked, the more the cheeks and eyes began to change, till she was looking at another person. They wore the same blue and gold Manzazzu robes as the mirror Gabby in her hallucination. Just as she was about to speak, she was yanked suddenly out of the vision and found her eyes had opened almost by themselves.

A quick glance of the surrounding area confirmed Gabby's suspicion, she was back in Trem's house. She sat up and rubbed her eyes, she felt like she had the best night sleep in a very long time. She glanced down at her chest, her ripped up, bloody shirt had now been replaced by the same black and white high collared, sleeveless tunic Trem wears. Gabby began to blush when she considered that Trem would have to had seen her topeless. She checked to make sure she was still wearing her bra, breathing a sigh of relief.

The door to the bedroom was gently opened by Trem, who had a cup of steaming liquid in her hand. "Oh good, you're awake. I was going to wake you up if you were still out of it." She closed the door behind her and walked up to the bed, sitting on it's side and offering the drink. Another cup of the rose water tasting tea like liquid. "This should help get your energy back up."

"Thanks." Gabby said as she took the drink, blowing off the steam. "What time is it?"

Trem dug into her robe and pulled out Gabby's phone, which was upside down. Flipping it the right way up, Trem squinted at the read out. "8.38am." Trem handed Gabby the phone. "Your parents rang again, I think I have the hang of that device, I told them you were resting. They know Treman attacked you. As far as your parents know, my Grandfather was suffering from something called senility and he lashed out at us both before dying of a heart attack."

Gabby sipped the drink and listened intently, nodding as she went along. "Makes sense, it's not exactly a lie."

Trem drew her attention to the sound of a little wooden chirp. She smiled and held her hand out as Woody landed on her. "I think he wants to make sure your alright." She joked, lowering her hand onto the bed, allowing Woody to hop off.

The little bird hopped up to Gabby and jumped into her hand. She drew Woody closer to her face, allowing him to gently nudge her nose with his beak. Gabby chuckled and stroked the back of his head. "You're adorable you are." She glanced up to Trem. "Like mother, like son."

Trem blushed slightly. "I'm not adorable..."

Gabby was about to open her mouth when she heard a familiar voice. "Trem, is she awake?" Whispered Jenny.

"Why don't you ask her yourself Miss Abernathy?" Gabby jokingly replied.

After a brief pause, the four Etemmu emerged through the door, leaving patches of frost on the wall as they entered. "How are you feeling?" Abhay asked.

"Twas quite the epic saga you endured yesterday." Hogarth continued, in his usual theatrical way.

Skye pulled the two away from the bedside. "Come on you two, give her some space."

"Guys, seriously, I'm fine. I feel pretty great actually, I think I needed a good rest and I got one." She paused while Woody jumped up her arm, hopped onto her shoulder and flapped his wings a few times till he perched himself on top of Gabby's head.

"That is just plain adorable..." Jenny grinned.

Gabby rubbed the sleep from her eyes. "The last few days have been, well, mad." She explained, blinking away the last of her eye crust. Yawning, she continued. "I think I need to see my parents, we've got some stuff to take care of."

The four Etemmu knew all too well what she meant. "Of course." Abhay replied, speaking for the group.

Gabby looked up at the four lowered heads and smiled. "Hey, you guys have been so good to me. I've only known you all a few days and you really treated me well." Her face morphed into a cheeky, devious little smirk. "Except you Skye."

"Hey!" She called.

Gabby chuckled to herself. "Just joking, you're great too."

Trem stood up from the bed and addressed the group. "Okay, so Treman is gone. His little plan to release the Faragh into the world of the living failed. I've locked him in the Styx and we destroyed his only way to get back. We managed to get through that relatively unscathed." Her voice wavered slightly as she clenched her fists. "...I found out who took my parents from me. I got to pay Treman back for that and all the years I had to put up with him." She rested her hand on the bed frame. "I was the one who summoned him, it was my fault you were all put in danger. I can't say I'm sorry enough."

Gabby gently got up out of the bed, being careful of Woody. "Trem, I know I've said this a lot, but it strikes me when you summoned these four they came over because they wanted to." She turned to the Etemmu. "That right guys?"

"Of course." They all agreed.

Woody hopped onto Gabby's shoulder as she continued. "So we all know you don't mean it in any kind of malicious way. You couldn't know, so try not to worry about it okay?" She drew Trem into a hug. While embracing her friend, Gabby felt her phone vibrate. She pulled out of Trem's grasp and checked the device.

"Is it your parents?" Trem asked.

Gabby read the text message slowly, keeping her eyes fixed on the screen as she spoke. "Yeah, Mum's just checking up on me." She began typing her response, glancing back at Trem. "Trem, do you want to come with me?"

Trem wasted no time replying, answering as soon as Gabby asked the question. "Yes please."

At first the suddenness threw Gabby, but she smiled widely

nonetheless. "Cool."

Trem turned to the quartet of spirits. "Will you all be okay if I leave for a few hours?"

The last time she asked that, they were all sealed into a Manzazzuan soul ring and nearly incinerated, so the silence that stayed in the air for a fleeting moment was understandable.

"...Well if there's any issue we can send Woody again." Skye reassured.

Hogarth pulled awkwardly at his ruff. "If thou fool us once, thou must know us as the fool. Twice? The fool doth become a wiser man.... Or ghost."

Gabby really tried hard not to laugh. "That statement kind of went away from you there, didn't it?"

"...Yes." Hogarth was always the one to lighten the mood, ever the comic. He had come to terms with the fact that this was the role he played in life, both on and off the stage, and it was one he aimed to continue in this after life as well.

The group shared a good chuckle before they started to go about their day, eventually leaving Gabby and Trem alone. Before they left the room to head to the Morgan family house, Trem paused to feed Sammy. As she placed the food gently in the tank, the small wooden box in which Tremadore's letters arrived in activated. A small flash of light leaked out of the gap in the box, indicating a new message arrived. This didn't go unnoticed to Gabby, who gently placed Woody on the bed.

"What's that?" Gabby asked, pointing to the box.

Trem lifted the lid and took out the rolled up paper inside. "Oh it's another Manzazzu I'm in contact with."

That little detail really stumped Gabby, she knew another Manzazzu all this time and never said? More to the point, why weren't they ever present? Trem was only able to write to the only other member of her race? That was odd.

Trem scanned the paper and put it in her pocket. "I'll get back to this later."

After the now familiar and much traveled journey to the house, Trem and Gabby arrived at the doorstep. Trem stayed behind a few paces, giving Gabby enough space as she opened the door. The moment when Gabby saw her Mother, she charged at her and threw herself into her arms. Trem watched her tearful reunion with her Mother, which honestly made the young Manzazzu feel misty eyed. Mavis looked Gabby up and down.

"I'm so glad you're alright..." She pulled at Gabby's tunic. "...You've changed." She noted.

Trem put a hand up and leaned her head around to glance at Mavis, her posture indicating she was rather nervous and angsty. "I gave her one of my tops. Her last one had blood on it."

Gabby bit into her lips and tightly shut her eyes, this was going to take some explaining.

"Blood?!" Came the reply.

Gabby tried to make the response sound as innocent and casual as she could. "Yeah but don't worry, it was only Trem's Grandfather." She failed to make it sound innocent at all.

Trem stepped into the room and intercepted the conversation before it escalated. "Let me explain Mrs Morgan."

Trem spent the next half hour explaining the elaborate lie about Treman, that he had gone mad in his senile state and attacked Gabby before having a heart attack and dying. Gabby helped flesh it out, including an ambulance that pronounced him dead at the scene and how she had spent the night getting some much deserved rest.

Soon though, it was time for them to go into Mortsbury town , to the funeral directors to sort out Eliza Morgan's service. Gabby felt awful because due to the drama of the last day or so, she had forgotten all about that. She asked her Mum if Trem could join them, which she allowed without a second thought.

Craig was still at work, still trying to decipher the strange security camera footage. There was no evidence of a break in, just something odd going on late at night. Trem and Gabby should have got away undetected, turned out the Faragh had shorted out the one camera that picked up the car park when it was on it's rampage. But Mavis understood, it was a family matter on her side and he didn't want to intrude on her personal wishes.

There seemed to be no reports of the Faragh attacks, they had succeeded in being undetected and the Faragh were never picked up on any security camera either. Even the radio presenter, Jerry James kept silent about it on the wireless that morning.

An hour later, Trem waited outside the simple brick building that rested at the bottom of a dead end turn off in the middle of Old Mortsbury. Inside, Gabby and Mavis sat on rather comfortable wooden seats as they spoke to the director of the business, Miss Aduba. She was a kindly woman, in her mid forties by the look of her. She had a soft, delicate Nigerian accent and turquoise eyes that peered from the fringe of her brown bob cut.

She wore a simple white shirt and jacket with red trim and a pair of black trousers. On the desk she had her back to was a bust, with a three point metal headdress placed atop it and around the cream coloured office was an assortment of unique items, including some strange sculptures and a metal mask hanging above a small fireplace for the winter. A very homely arrangement.

Miss Aduba was writing down the list of requests in a little leather bound notebook. "Okay Mrs Morgan, just to recap. You have asked for a simple ceremony at the crematorium, non religious. A eulogy to be read by one of our celebrants followed by Elizabeth's favourite piece of music."

Mavis was holding onto Gabby's hand the entire time they were there. Gabby found the time to slip into her old outfit, the Trem inspired garb didn't seem appropriate given the circumstances.

"That's right. She never wanted a fuss, like her husband, they wanted to let people have their time to come to terms with it and move on." Mavis spoke, in a respecting and hushed tone.

Miss Aduba nodded her head slowly and smiled. "Of course. The venue is all booked, we'll make sure the flowers arrive on time as per your instructions and ensure you don't have to worry about a thing."

Gabby kept her Mum's hands close as she lowered her head. "Thank you." Mavis replied. "Can I ask where your loos are? I just need to use your facilities."

Miss Aduba got to her feet and opened the door leading further into the building. "It's your first door on the right. Take as long as you need."

Mavis thanked her before disappearing into the other room,

leaving Gabby alone with the funeral director as she took her seat. "Miss Aduba, can I ask a question?"

"Of course you can." She replied, sinking into her armchair.

Gabby glanced around the room, taking in the sights of the strange oddities. "You've collected a right menagerie of cool looking things."

Miss Aduba chuckled to herself. "I'm a hoarder really. I guess you could call these... Relics of a past life." She said, turning in her chair and running her fingers over the lion engravings on the head piece. She looked up from the desk and out of the window. She caught a glimpse of Trem standing outside, causing her smile to fade. She caught enough of a glimpse to register her black Manzazzuan robes.

Putting the smile back on her face, she turned around, back to Gabby. "Have you ever been abroad Gabby?"

Gabby was away with the fairies, staring at the mask mounted on the wall. "Umm, no I haven't. The furthest we went was the Drama overnight trip to Braisingstoke. We've been around the UK a lot but I've yet to go out of the country. Dad says he's saving up for a big splash next year."

Mavis returned almost on cue and sat back down on the comfy chair. "Sorry about that."

"Not at all Mrs Morgan. I'll just get some papers for you to sign and we'll all be set."

When she went through the open door, into the other room, Gabby had to do a double take. She caught a glimpse of something hanging on the wall before the door closed.

They looked like the same high collared tunic and robe that Trem and Treman wore, the standard Manzazzuan garb. This time, the robes were white with a red trim. Before she could get a good look at them, the door closed.

She turned to her Mum quickly. "I'm just going to check on Trem, back in a sec." She got to her feet and sprinted out the room. She swung the door open and patted Trem on the back. She then pointed to Trem's robes. "Only Manzazzu have those robes right?"

Trem stared back at Gabby, slightly befuddled by the question and the sense of urgency surrounding it. "Umm, yes why?"

Gabby pointed into the office. "The woman who runs this has got the same type you have, except they're white and red. When she comes out the office can you see what you think?"

"Yeah, of course."

Gabby gave Trem a wink as a thank you and slid back into the building, sitting back down on the chair. Aduba entered the room soon after with the papers.

"Here you go, just on the dotted line." She instructed, handing Mavis the papers and a pen.

While Mavis was doing so, Gabby watched Trem peer in through the window. She scanned the room with her eyes, taking note of every nook and cranny of the room. When Aduba turned around in her chair to use the desk, Trem ducked out of sight. Once she was done, she left the papers on the desk.

"Okay, I think we're all set. You have my number if you require everything." She turned round and glanced at both Gabby and

Mavis. "Is there anything else you'd like to discuss?"

Gabby and Mavis looked at each other. Everything had been considered, the venue, the menu, the seating, there wasn't much left. "I don't think so." Mavis replied.

With that, they bid Miss Aduba farewell. When they left the building, Gabby pulled at her Mum's shirt. "Hey I'll be with you in a minute if that's okay? I just want to talk to Trem before we drop her off."

"Of course love. I'll get the car started." Mavis replied.

Trem glanced into the room once again, her head remaining locked in position. "I think she is a Manzazzu you know."

Gabby peered in as well, getting as good a look as she could before being noticed. Aduba drew her eyes away from the paperwork and blinked, her turquoise eyes changing to pupil-less rings of gold. Gabby ducked out of view, it was starting to get a little crazy for her. "Trem...?" She looked up, Trem was still looking through the window.

The Manzazzu known as Aduba was working on some paperwork when she peered out the window. Her golden, featureless eyes widened as she slowly raised her head and she locked eyes with Trem's own. The two stared for what felt like hours, both taken aback at the other's presence. Aduba eventually broke the staring contest with a smile and a wave. Before Trem could wave back, she was dragged down by Gabby.

"What was that?!" Gaby whispered.

Trem felt like she was almost hypnotised by those eyes. "Uhh, well... Manzazzu clans, big families, we all have genetic traits." She pointed to her jet black eyes. "Mine are pretty obvious. But those are really impressive. I think Dad may have mentioned her once... I'll need to go through some stuff when I get back."

They tore themselves away from the funeral home and the newly discovered Manzazzu inside and back to Mavis' car. They dropped Trem off at her house and Gabby and her Mum returned home for lunch. Once she was pleasantly filled up on sandwiches and crisps, Gabby made her way back to the manor house. After a brief meet up with the quartet of ghosts, she arrived at Trem's room. Trem was in the middle of writing a response to the letter which had arrived. She paused and watched Gabby enter the room.

"Hello Gabby." She called.

"Hiya." Came the reply as she sat down on the bedside. "You still writing?"

Trem finished the last few words before rolling the paper up and putting it in the box, watching the muted light flash and vanish within a second. She turned around in her seat and smiled. "No, all done. So, how have you been?"

Gabby crossed her legs and got comfortable. "Yeah, good. Still can't get used to the idea Manzazzu live among us simple humans."

Trem rubbed her forehead and sighed. "I feel the same way honestly. If I'd have known there were Manzazzu in the local area, I'd thought I would have seen them."

All the time spent alone, shut off in the manor and not only did the Human world hold no real danger for her, but she had fellow members of her race nearby. Her seclusion, hearing the bile from Treman about the outside world had cut her off from being with the only people she needed. It must have been part of Treman's big plan, to intimidate her and make the world of the Human race seem so hostile.

Of course, summoning the Etemmu proved that at least in history, the Human race wasn't so awful, but Abhay came from a time of war and Skye came from an era of conflict. Jenny was killed by her fellow man, accident or otherwise. None of these facts urged her to venture forth into the outside world.

Gabby had started to put the facts together too, Treman would have been the big reason she wouldn't have ventured outside. Her head perked up however as she glanced to the box on Trem's desk. "Hey, that reminds me, who have you been writing to?"

Trem had been scowling all the time she had been thinking of Treman. He was now a brainless Faragh locked in the Styx for another Manzazzu to off and he was still making her furious. But when Gabby asked her question, her scowl faded fast.

"Oh Tremadore? He's a friend of Dad's. We began writing to each other when he sent a letter a few years ago. He didn't know what happened to my parents, so I told him all about it. We've been writing to each other since then. Why do you ask?"

Gabby rested her chin on closed fists. "Well, if he's living anywhere near here, we could go see him. Do you know where he is?"

Treman would never have allowed Tremadore anywhere near the house, and with him convincing Trem not to go outside, she'd never actively searched him out. "He said if I ever needed him, he was at the Ye Olde Abode. Is that anywhere near here?"

Gabby's heart skipped a beat, she felt her soul begin to lift as a massive grin crept over her face. "Yes I do! It's on the Morstbury pier, it's just a short trip on the bus, not far at all!"

Trem got up from her seat. "Really? Excellent...!" She began, but was seemingly distracted by something.

Gabby detected this change of mood too. "Trem, what's up?"

Before she could get an answer, Trem was already out of the door, dashing down the stairs and over to the two globes that sat in the living room. Gabby ran after her, shocked at the speed Trem could muster. She peered over her friends shoulder, trying to get a look at what was going on.

Trem traced her finger over the globe till it laid to rest on one region. She spun the other globe with her free hand and her finger landed on the UK, slowly moving up England till it landed almost on top of them.

"That's us, is there another Faragh in the Styx?" Gabby asked.

Trem peered up at the wall where the tapestry and the portrait of her parents hung. "No, better." She said, with tears forming in her eyes. "So much better... We need to see Tremadore."

So, plans were set in motion. Gabby raced home, collected her wallet and explained the situation to Mavis, by which she meant lie, telling her they were going into town again to meet Manisha and Bobbi. But still, it would be too long to explain everything. She promised herself that one day, her Mum and Dad would learn the truth.

It would be hard, very hard, and maybe not the right move at all. But keeping things hidden was going to get increasingly harder the longer she had to keep it up.

The bus ride was one of impatience, Gabby could tell Trem just wanted to get there as quickly as possible, though the schools and workplaces were closing up and the home run had begun, slowing the bus' progress. Trem had begun to bite at her nails, unable to sit still. Gabby put her hand on Trem's, trying to calm her down as much as possible.

Finally, the bus pulled up to the stop, along a stretch of road that overlooked the rolling beach of Mortsbury. The pier itself stretched for about five hundred feet, with two shops on opposite sides of the pier as one enters through the ornate entrance, which doubled as a tourist information centre. At the end of the great stretch was Ye Olde Abode, a wooden structure which contained a circus ring style theatre.

Trem ran towards it, Gabby struggling to keep pace. "Trem wait, I think it's closed..." She began. That didn't stop Trem from knocking on the door.

"Hello?" She called at the closed door. "It's Trem, from the letters?"

Trem was like a little child at a sweet shop, she was so desperate to get inside, to see the Manzazzu she had spent years talking to, via letters. Even Manzazzu for all their advances still had pen pals.

The door slowly opened, creaking as it did, like in horror movies. Gabby knew this song and dance well, entering into a mysterious place full of the unknown. It was becoming second nature to her quite frankly.

From out of the dimly lit entrance peered the unmistakable form of an Etemmu. His receding hairline emphasised the severity of his sculpted face and piercing eyes. His apparel and all round demeanor meant one thing, he was a butler in his former life.

"Miss Trem, the master is expecting you." His voice just oozed with Victorian class and sensibility. As for the look he gave poor Gabby, he nearly turned his nose up at her. "...Who is this, pray tell?"

Trem took Gabby by the hand and pulled her gently forward, given that she was a few paces behind her. "Gabby Morgan. If Tremadore is expecting me, he'll be expecting her too."

The butler's expression remained the same, though he gestured into the darkness all the same. "This way then, ma'am."

Trem slowly walked into the darkness. Before she followed, Gabby looked up at the floating ghost. "Don't I get a ma'am?" She snapped.

"No." Came the reply.

Gabby sneered as she entered the darkness. When she emerged, they were in a large room that was lined with fake, painted shop fronts. There were some stalls set up behind the painted facades that sold refreshments and snacks. Tables and chairs lined the lead up to the ring that sat at the back of the room.

"If you would care to take your seats, the master will see you after the rehearsal." The butler jeered as he floated past Gabby, deliberately making her shiver.

"Knock it off!" She yelled. "What's your name anyway?" She demanded.

The butler straightened his waistcoat. "Stride." He replied.

Trem had already taken her seat, so Gabby walked over to her, pointing back at Stride. "Yeah well, you'd better watch yourself." What an empty threat, and they both knew it.

The whole arrangement looked like a typical circus tent. The ring's floor was covered with hay, with individual bails spaced around the circular stage. There was apparatus set for high wire and acrobatics and a mock circus entrance for the performers to appear from.

The lights dimmed, Trem and Gabby held hands, watching the

stage intently. Two bright spotlights lit up the stage while music filled the air. The mock entrance to the stage opened up, revealing a tall figure in a suit of grey armour, decorated with ornate golden decals.

The figure's face was hidden by a great helmet that matched the armour. With every step leaving a loud metallic clunk, the figure stood on one side of the stage, brandishing a zweihander sword. Gabby couldn't help but notice the Manzazzuan rings on the fighter's hands.

Suddenly, there was a flash of light which startled both Gabby and Trem. A mini tornado of fire erupted out of thin air, spinning in a tiny circle, rising up and up into the sky. Emerging from the burning maelstrom was the figure of a man. When the flames burned themselves out, the figure became clearer. He was a man in his early forties, with thick black hair that reached to his shoulders.

He looked to be from the Middle East or India, in the lighting and from such a distance, Gabby couldn't quite tell. He wore a burgundy velvet tailcoat with black embossed patterns trailing throughout. His black Manzazzuan tunic was underneath and a sash was tied around his waist, where his sword hung.

The two duelists held their swords up, emerald flames igniting around the blades. The two combatants adopted ready stances and waited for the chorus of the music. Once it begun, the duel commenced.

The armored figure drew the sword back and fired off a bolt of green flames at the other dueler. The man dodged the attack by running towards it then dropping to his knees, allowing the momentum to carry him another few feet as he swung his blade towards the knight. The figure jumped back to avoid the swipe, unable to block in time.

Once the knight landed, they fired off another fiery bolt. The man mirrored the knight's attack, sending out one more bolt in return. Both jets of green fire met in the middle of the stage, struck and cancelled each other out.

The man got to his knees and brought his sword down onto the knight's zweihander, causing them to plant a steel boot into the ground to stay in place. The man showed off his toothy grin and pushed harder onto the blade.

The knight responded by pushing against the sword and lurching forward with all their might. The man somersaulted back landing on his hands and then back onto his feet.

The knight charged at him, slashing at him with the large blade. Each strike was skillfully blocked and mirrored, constantly keeping his foe on their toes while making sure there were no gaps in his defence. He ducked to the ground to avoid a slash and brought his sword upwards, causing the knight to stagger back.

Gabby watched, white knuckled and on the edge of her seat. This was real dueling, this is what she had always wanted to learn. The fact she had gone this far on luck and just wildly swinging her blade was rather sobering. She needed to learn how to defend herself properly, maybe this guy would be the one to teach her, as well as Trem of course. She glanced over to Trem, she was sucked into the action as well, unable to look away.

In the ultimate act of mockery, the man jumped to avoid a low strike from the sword, then he jumped onto the blade itself, chuckling and giving the knight a pat on the head. He jumped off and attacked, spinning his sword to gain as much momentum as possible.

They entered into a fast paced dance of sword play, each taking offensive and defensive strikes in quick succession, the knight landing hard, precise blows while the man danced around with speed and agility. Each strike was made with strategic precision.

The combative stalemate lasted over a minute, both foes seemed evenly matched despite having opposing combat styles. What swung the tide though was actually a genius move by the man. He seemingly weakened his attacks, as if to suggest he was suffering from fatigue. Trem and Gabby seemed to think it was real and luckily for him, so did his opponent.

The knight knocked the man to the ground with a strike from the gauntlet, his sword landing several feet away. The armored opponent raised their sword high to strike him, then he grinned. He reached out for his sword which flew at breakneck speed into his hand and with one quick slash, he struck the knight's sword from his hand.

As the music they had been fighting to came to an end, the man got to his feet and pointed his sword at the knight, who slowly sank to their knees. "Guess I won." The man smiled.

Trem and Gabby both shot to their feet and began cheering. The knight's head spun round and they got up from their knees, they began marching aggressively towards them. The knight pulled the helmet off their head and dropped it on the floor. The tall, muscular knight was revealed to be female, with short scraggly blonde hair. Her face was semi translucent like the Etemmu at Trem's manor.

"Just who are you and who let you in here?" The new Etemmu demanded, a thick Slavic accent booming from her lungs.

Gabby immediately began to back away, the new figure was intimidating the living daylights out of her.

"Iskra!" The man called. He walked up to her and gently smacked her armour with the back of his hand, producing a metallic clunk. "Stop being so overprotective. These two are friends, calm your Slavic passions." He joked.

The man stepped over one of the bales of hay and up to the two women. "So you must be Trem!" He put his feet together and bowed. "It is an honour to meet you in person..." Before he could continue, Trem had already thrown her arms around him.

"It's so good to finally see you, Tremadore." She said, keeping her arms tight around him.

Gabby put her hands together and placed them to her mouth, it felt so good to see Trem with one of her own people.

"You too my lady." He replied. "You really are your parents daughter, you truly have their best traits, if I may say so."

Oooh, he was quite the gentleman... Gentle Manzazzu, Gabby thought. If she wasn't already spoken for or cared for such things, Tremadore would have been rather attractive.

Tremadore straightened himself out and gestured to his comrade. "Allow me to introduce Iskra Kuragina. You must forgive her, she's rather a protective soul, but loyal."

Gabby could tell that made the Slavic muscle machine feel awkward. "Sir..." She strained through her teeth, clearly embarrassed.

The butler Etemmu emerged from behind Gabby and Trem, having flown through the stage seats. Tremadore gestured to him as he floated to his master's side. "This bundle of joy is Landon Stride. He stops me from having too much fun." He teased.

"Very drole sir." Stride replied.

Well, these two were winning no points for charm but to be fair, Skye didn't when they first met too. Gabby thought she was just getting used to the idea of Etemmu too. With these two, the Manzazzuan world would always be full of surprises.

Tremadore noticed Gabby's presence and stood to attention. "Ahh, you must be Miss Morgan."

Gabby was quick to offer her hand. "Yep, and you can call me Gabby."

Her hand was drawn into a gentle shake. "A pleasure, my dear." He smiled. "So, what can we do for you?"

Trem clutched at her robe and squeezed tightly. She had yet to tell Gabby of her discovery, but if they could do this, then Trem may be able to answer all the questions that had plagued her for years and finally accomplish what had been her goal since she was a lost, scared little child. She looked to Gabby for reassurance, and when the two locked hands, she felt the strength she had needed all this time. "Tremadore, I'd like to ask for your help." She proclaimed boldly.

"Of course, anything for Tremarda and Tremera's daughter."

With a smile on her face, finally brimming with confidence , Trem held her head up high and replied. "I want you to help me bring my parents back!"

Epilogue: "What Next?"

Treman's Faragh clawed and scratched at the wall, trying desperately to get through to the other side. He had totally turned, the armour that once held his form was now a mess of metal on the dirty ground. A few impatient growls left the wall of thick teeth that grew over his non existent top lip. As he filed away at the wall, there was a slight murmur in the air, which caused Treman to pause. A second passed and suddenly, a spear, wrapped in blue flames appeared, striking him through the head, pinning his corrupted soul to the wall. After a few lifeless twitches, the twisted form of Treman vanished into nothingness. Nothing was left behind but the spear. Once the fires sizzled away, Tremalor appeared, pulling the spear from the wall.

The three Sisters removed their masks and watched the cold smear left behind melt away. Treman's last instructions were their final trial, to cut all ties with anything that would hold them back. Treman was their instructor, mentor, he was like a Father to them, and his death would teach them to let go and move on. The life of a Mutashaeib was a dangerous one, where forming close attachments could lead to a lack of focus, maybe even death. That was something Treman had taught the Sisters from the very beginning, that his role in their lives, no matter how important, was always temporary. The trio of young Manzazzu sank to one knee and bowed their heads, paying a moment of respect for their fallen mentor.

When they all got to their feet, Tremalee rubbed her fuchsia eyes. "What are we going to do now?" The reality was struggling to sink in for her, they always knew the day would come and they had been preparing for it
for years. But now it had happened... It was all so strange for her.

Tremalor however was less remorseful, keeping any trace of her emotions hidden beneath the veneer of apathy. "We go ahead with the plan."

Tremalee turned to Tremalan, who moved her eyeless head to the younger sister and bowed her head, reassuring the child like assassin. On Tremalor's orders, they all pulled their masks over their faces and jumped across the Styx river onto the other side of the rotting bay. They soon arrived in the complex, into the maze of rusting metal girders, corrugated sheets and thin walkways. In the darkness, the three moved stealthily, the endless maze of corridors and walkways stretched upwards, seemingly to infinity. It would take centuries to traverse if you got lost inside. Fortunately for the Sisters, they knew the route well.

Making their way up several dimly lit stairs, they eventually reached a structure built onto the walkways. A small box made of wood and corrugated metal plates, the Sister's home since Treman took them in. Tremalor approached what was seemingly a solid wall of wood, but when she placed her hand on the surface, a door morphed into existence. The three Sisters entered the simple accomodation, the door sealing behind them. The room was featureless, just three beds and a chest in the side of the room. In the corners of the room were frosted glass orbs which, when Tremalor clicked her fingers, lit up, bathing the room in a warm glow.

Tremalor and Tremalee removed the weapons from their backs and put them under their beds, with Tremalee's large axe leaving a dull thud as it hit the ground. She looked like a slight, petite girl with no visible muscle. But the way she swung her axe around, her outward appearance betrayed the real strength, which was far greater than her other Sisters.

Tremalee pulled her mask off and threw it on her bed, resting on it's side. Tremalan lowered her hood and gently pulled her mask away from her face. The blank patches of flesh where her eyes would have been, haunting to anyone else, but to her Sisters, Tremalan's lack of eyes made her special. Not just because they granted her the ability of clairvoyance, but because she was the glue that held the group together. Her visions of the potential futures gave them hope in their darkest time.

As Tremalor began to speak, she was interrupted by a metallic clunk. The Sisters looked to the chest, the large lock on the front had come off and dropped like a stone onto the wooden floor. The Sisters suddenly became anxious, inside were the final instructions from Treman, which were only to be read on the event of his final death. Since Tremalor was the one to terminate Treman, the duty fell to her. She slowly approached the chest, pushing the lid open.

The air was still as she peered in. "What is it?" Tremalee asked, leaning forward from her bed.

Slowly, Tremalor's hand dug deep into the chest and pulled out a jackal skull, the same type the Mutashaeib wore. Much like Treman's, this was a mock porcelain skull and thus wasn't authentic and certainly didn't give them legitimate Mutashaeib status. Unfortunately Treman never told them that.

Tremalee dropped off the bed, onto her knees and crawled towards the chest. "Oh my... Sister, is that real? Is it happening?"

Tremalan walked over and knelt next to Tremalee, putting her hand on her young Sister. Even without her eyes, she was still facing the skull. She could see it clear as day in her mind's eye.

Tremalor nodded, staring at the skull. "It's official." She looked into the chest and pulled out two more, which she handed to her Sisters. She also found a scroll of paper deep in the bottom of the darkness. She took it out, placing her skull on the floor and unrolled it.

She pulled herself onto her feet and began to read. "My warriors, as you are reading this, I will have completed my time in this world for the last time. If my faith in you has been true, then you will have done the deed for me. I assume you succeeded with efficient results."

All three Sisters took a moment of silence. The procedure hadn't been perfect, and they knew it. Not all Faragh they set free went through into the world of the living, some escaped to who knows where.

Tremalor continued. "The first stage of the plan is complete, the Faragh will have wreaked havoc in the Human world and sent a message to the Royal Family. Below is the plan we discussed in finer detail. Do me proud, be the Mutashaeib you were raised to be." Though the plan for the overthrow was listed below, Tremalor didn't read it.

She folded the paper and turned to Tremalan. "Well, did we succeed?"

Tremalee glanced to Tremalan, the latter using her inherent abilities to peer into the future, to see all the potential outcomes of this situation. Her heart sank as she replied with a short and blunt... "No."

"You're kidding?" Tremalee looked so disheartened, this was to be their first major glory.

Tremalor meanwhile looked like she was seething with anger, her gloved hands forming tightly clenched fists. "I thought Treman had dealt with his Granddaughter, just like he did with her parents?"

The clairvoyant shook her head, strands of dirty blonde hair brushing the blank top half of her face. "She had help. A Human called Gabby Morgan."

Now all three of the Sisters were on their feet. Tremalor looked like she was ready to murder someone, which wasn't too far from the truth.

"We will still go ahead with the plan, but as the eldest here I move for a slight alteration to the plan. If this Human thinks she can interfere with our plans then she has another thing coming."

Tremalan continued looking through the potential streams of future events, one causing her to swallow hard. She chose to ignore the majority of the unlikely outcomes, worrying about potential futures had kept her up that night. "She and Treman's Granddaughter are planning another excursion into the Styx."

Tremalee stared off into the distance with widening eyes. "Wait, is that who I saw the other day?"

"What do you mean?" Asked Tremalor.

The youngest Sister pointed to the blank wall where the door once was. "I was out there having a walk and I saw some girl in the Complex, near the light at the end." She could tell Tremalor was about to ask her something, so she intercepted the question. "Yes, I had my mask on, don't worry."

"Good." The eldest Sister rubbed her forehead and sighed. "You two get some rest. Tomorrow we work on amending the plan. Nothing would make Treman more proud than seeing us end those two pests once and for all."

Tremalor and Tremalan went to their beds, placed the skulls on the pillows and began changing out of their leather suits when Tremalee approached the chest. She peered inside and caught a glimpse of something white. She pulled it out of the chest and examined it. It was another roll of parchment. She began to scan through the writing.

"Oh no way..." She exclaimed. "Hey Lor? Treman found out about your parents! You're never going to guess who they are!" Tremalee was ecstatic, energy bouncing off her.

"Sister, you're not supposed to read that..." She couldn't deny her curiosity though, as much as her family, whoever they were, took the lowest priority for her, but maybe that would change. "Who are they?"

Tremalee was getting so excited she looked like she would burst at any moment, even after all this time, she was still brimming with childlike joy. "Only the leaders of the Mutashaeib! They're still alive!"

For the first time in years, Tremalor actually smiled. She took the paper from Tremalee's hands, just to make sure. Her younger Sister was right, she was born of the blood of the founders of the Mutashaeib. The leader, Cyrus and his wife.

"What about Lanny?" Tremalee asked, nodding to Tremalan.

Tremalor scanned down the page, her eyebrows raising. "You come from the bloodline of the Queen's personal oracle. The finest and most sought after clairvoyants in Euphretia."

Of course Tremalan had no idea how to take this information. On the one hand, she was happy to know her origins, finally. But on the other hand, she was brought into the world by the same elitist snobs they were trying to overthrow. She chose to respond with a quiet nod.

"What about me?" Tremalee asked excitedly.

Her upbeat smile slowly started to fade when she watched her older Sister reach the bottom of the page. "...I'm sorry Tremalee, Treman couldn't find anything out about your clan. He thinks they may have been killed in the war."

Tremalee's heart sank, her head sinking along with it. "Oh..."

Tremalor was never very good at being sisterly, but she certainly tried her best to comfort her little sister. She put her bare hand on her sisters. The other two removed their gloves, locking hands together. "When we take Euphretia, we'll do all we can to find your family, okay?"

Tremalor held up her skull mask and stared into the eyeholes.

"We aren't Mutashaeib yet, we have this task to perform before we can call ourselves true members. But when we do, we will be welcomed with open arms... Welcomed by my parents..." The reality of that still hadn't quite sunken in.

She patted her sisters on the back and lead them to the beds. "Come on, you two need your rest before tomorrow. We've a lot to prepare for and I need you two to be dependable."

As the Styx Sisters rested, something restless was on the move in the Styx. Treman being sealed caused a faint ripple throughout the Styx, the River itself becoming ever so slightly choppy. In the maze of dull, grey gangplanks that stretched onwards and upwards, into infinity, something unexpected was on the trail of the disturbance. A wolf like Northern Inuit sniffed the stale air. It glanced around the structure, looking down at the layers of walkways still to go. Though this time, for the first time in over two decades, there was that glimmer of hope. The noble animal barked, alerting it's owners.

Two figures dashed towards the dog, peeking over the side of the walkway. Below them lay a faint light, it must have only been a dozen levels down. Feelings of hope and happiness flooded the couple who grabbed hold of each other in a tight embrace. They both wore Manzazzuan robes, the colours fading under years of dirt and ash. The woman's snowy white hair had lost it's short, stylish cut and her fringe was long and full of knots. Her jet black eyes were beginning to well up at the thought of seeing her daughter again. As for the man, his soft brown hair still retained it's metallic sheen, as did his eyes, but his tunic had seen better days. Both of their black robes were full of holes, with scratch and burn marks. The husband and wife duo were Tremarda and Tremera, Trem's parents. The dog was Tremera's, much like how Sammy belonged to Trem.

"Good boy Neti." Tremera complimented, kneeling down to pet her companion.

Her husband leant against the guardrail and looked to the dim light leading to the exit of the Complex. "We still have a way to go my love. We need to wait until our house's Ishtar Gate opens."

He noticed his wife was still on her knees, looking into the ether, lost in thoughts. He knelt down next to her and gave Neti a stroke or two. "We'll see her very soon. I bet you she'll be doing great."

Trem was so young when they disappeared, in Human terms, no older than twelve. Every day they both worried about her, but what kept them going was the thought of seeing her again. She'd have grown a lot in that time too.

Tremarda wiped a tear from his wife's face with his thumb. "I don't know how long we've spent here, and I'm so damn tired. Every day I think how I swore an oath to protect you and how I screwed it all up. I don't think I'll ever make it up fully to you, but.." He stopped himself and tried to hold back the oncoming tears. "Nope, I've set myself off now."

Tremera gazed up at her husband, her black eyes gazing into his metallic irises. She shuffled closer and put her arms around her lover's head. "Hey, don't say things like that. It wasn't your fault,

Treman was the one who attacked us. You helped keep me and Neti alive all these years. I wouldn't be able to keep going if it wasn't for you." She held her husband gently by the head. "We're so near the end."

He sniffed and wiped his eye with his palm. "Doesn't feel real does it? When was the last time we ever felt like that?"

Tremera smiled rather cheekily as Neti lifted his head curiously. "The night of the dance at Euphretia, maybe?"

The two enjoyed a good laugh together, remembering back to that great night at the Venusian Eclipse Ball all those years ago. One of the best nights of their lives. The socialite and the showman, it was like something out of a fairytale.

"Before we get lost in misty eyed nostalgia, let's push on. I can't wait to find out what sunlight feels like once again." Tremera joked, helping Tremarda to his feet and gesturing for Neti to follow.

The duo were full of not only a newly kindled sense of hope, but also fond memories of that fateful night in the Manzazzuan home land.

Euphretia was not only the seat of the Royal Family, but the capital city of the race. The high society of the race reside in the immaculate grandeur of the upper city. Euphretia itself, an island in the Indian Ocean resided close to Africa and Australia, but due to issues resulting from the war with the Mutashaeib, it was only accessible by sea. The centre of the enormous island was the Royal Fortress, a grand and decadent castle complete with turrets and towers galore.

Below the fortress was the high city, rings of buildings built into the rock face. Structures such as the Manzazzuan Lyceum went under the surface of the rocks. There Manzazzu from all walks of life are mentored in the history of the race and hone their

individual clan powers. Trem's Mother and aunt had both attended, their ability to animate objects thrived during their time there.
At the city's heart was the Bazaar, the trading hub of the land. Thriving with indoor and outdoor markets, with everything from spices to hookah bars. Below that lies the Under City, a cramped but livable area where those not blessed with the financial riches of the elite reside. There was rarely any talk of a class divided as those in the lower city still had access to the Lyceum and Bazaar.

For Treman and his daughters, Euphretia wasn't a home. They had a cozy estate in Switzerland, with servants and isolated comfort. Tremera and her sister were bored senseless by the whole thing, they both yearned something more. They wanted to be like other Manzazzu, cavorting with attractive men, drinking and having a good time on the twisting streets of Euphretia. All this pomp and circumstance was numbing to the two of them.

The family approached the golden doors that lead to the main ballroom in the Queen's fortress. The corridors were lined with polished white pillars and tiled floors. An entire wall was a window to the world below and the vast expanse of ocean below them. The lights from the city bathed the view in an orange light, cutting through the night time sky.

"As the eldest, the responsibility lies on you." Treman began. "It's the family you're representing, Tremera. Remember to make a good first impression. You're here to secure our legacy."

"Yes father." Tremera replied, bowing her head.

Two guards stood by the door. They both wore the distinctive silver armour with gold trim, mesh sleeves protruding from the gaps in the steel plates and helmets with sculpted face engraved on their fronts. They stood to attention as the trio passed, opening the doors for them.

The ballroom revealed itself to the nervous family. The enormous structure amazed Tremera, not only was the scale quite literally awe inspiring, but there must have been hundreds of Manzazzu there. Many of them would come from noble houses, brushing shoulders with the Queen herself. Never before had the two young Manzazzu felt so out of their depth.

Treman turned to Tremera's sister and waved her away with his hand. "Now you, make yourself scarce, I have to secure your sister's future before I worry about you." With that he took Tremera by the arm and pulled her into the crowd.

The soon to be aunty to Trem was left standing in the middle of the room. Eventually, several men came to her side. What she always managed to do better than her sister was socialise and flirt, it opened many doors for her in the past and would continue to do so again. Treman had left her by the wayside and she was evolving into something far greater than any other of his pawns. Her Mother died in childbirth, Treman refused to say anything about her to either of them, of course. At first, one would think it was due to the immense sadness of losing a loved one. But this was Treman, that would be giving him far too much credit.

Tremera was lead to a tall Manzazzu, with a middle eastern complexion and thick black hair. "Tremera, allow me to introduce Lord Tremadore, heir to the title of the Asud Manzazuu."

She gave a courteous bow to the Manzazzu. "Hello. It is a pleasure to meet you, my lord." She glanced up as she heard him chuckling to himself.

"Tremadore please my dear, formalities are such a waste of time." Tremadore smiled, taking a glass of wine from one of the passing maids, offering it to Tremera. He waited for Treman to disappear before handing it to her.

She took the glass gently, possessing all the physicality of a frightened mouse. Tremadore smiled and leaned in closer, whispering. "Hey, don't worry. I know this isn't your sort of thing either." He thanked a passing maid as he intercepted a glass for himself.

"Really?" Tremera was both surprised and relieved someone thought the same as she did. She couldn't imagine she was the only Manzazzu who didn't want to be there.

"Besides..." Tremadore continued. "...I can guarantee I won't be your type. You don't want someone like me cavorting about your life, making the place look untidy. Besides, I'm sure you're a wonderful woman who will make someone very happy, but I don't think it could ever be me. I don't, you know, beat to the sound of that drum."

Tremera knew what he meant. "Of course. Well, thank you for your honesty. It is rather refreshing to see."

She was gestured to move closer to Tremadore. "I can recommend a far more suitable Manzazzu, someone far more sensitive and more relaxed."

"Oh?" She asked.

He pointed one finger away from his glass, to a certain awkwardly standing Manzazzu with a metallic shimmer to his hair. "What about Tremarda? He's been staring at you all evening."

She met eyes with this Manzazzu, who, when staring back at her, began to fidget. "Well... Father wouldn't approve." She muttered.

"Father's not here is he?" Tremadore replied, raising his eyebrows and carrying a certain condescending tone when he said the word "Father." He pretended to meet the gaze of another Manzazzu and left Tremera on her own.

The couple who would be destined to marry both slowly approached each other, side stepping a few passing Manzazzu on the way. Both struggled to hide their nerves. Tremera knew she was viewed as a social elite by association with her Father but Tremarda knew he was a nobody in the eyes of high society. It wasn't long before they were standing in front of each other, Tremarda towering above Tremera by a good foot and a half.

"Lord Tremarda I presume?" Tremera asked, bowing her head in respect.

Tremarda however didn't bow, instead his eyes darted around the place. "Not exactly..." He whispered.

Tremera's head lifted, tilting to the left ever so slightly. "You're not a nobleman?" She asked.

"Well..." He began, unsure on how to explain. "I like to think of myself as a noble man, but I'm far from being a nobleman."

That triggered a little laugh from Tremera, which was the perfect ice breaker. "That's very witty."

Tremarda chuckled too, the light relief felt like such a weight off his chest. "I just thought of it. Rather proud of it myself."

With her smile still present, which Tremarda was finding adorable with every second, she continued the introductions. "I'm Tremera. It's a pleasure to meet you."

"Likewise. So your Treman's daughter eh?"

Her smile slowly turned into a worried expression. "Yes, is that a bad thing?"

Tremarda shrugged his shoulders. "He's known by reputation. But from what I've seen, his daughters are nothing like him. In fact I dare say, if the rumours are true... If you don't mind me saying, I believe his daughters will have more charm, beauty and grace than he will ever have."

The young Manzazzu nobel's eyes widened. "Well, those are very strong words I must say." Her smile slowly returned however. "They're also very refreshing. Not many have the strength or courage to speak their mind."

Glancing at his glass and taking the last sip of wine that remained at the bottom, Tremarda continued. "Well, it's one of the advantages about not being a high born. We speak our minds in the lower regions. If we don't like someone, they know it." He looked around the Manzazzu that surrounded him. "Having said that, I'm also not stupid enough to tell these snobs where to stick it, not in the Royal Fortress anyway."

One of the maids passed with an empty tray. Like all the others, her black and white uniform was complete with a ruffled frill on the chest, high collar and jewelled brooch in the centre, along with a skirt made of black feathers. Tremarda passed the empty glass, the maid's black gloved hand took it and placed it on the tray. "The dance will begin soon, sir."

"Oh good, thank you." He responded as both he and Tremera both returned her bow.

Tremera began playing with her hands, which she hid behind her back. She was trying to pluck up the courage to ask the question. "Umm..."

Before she could ask, Tremarda intercepted and quickly and rather ungracefully blurted. "May I have this dance?"

It was almost unheard of for the man to ask for a dance, Treman taught her it was the duty of the lady to ask. But Tremarda was proving himself to be the strangest yet most liberating person she'd ever spoken to. She was dreading this day for weeks, worrying about her legacy and how the elite would view her, but at that one moment, she didn't care. All she wanted to do was hear more about the world where Tremarda came from. Treman would have her believe that the lower areas of Euphretia was a hive of scum and villainy, but she struggled to believe that.

"Y...Yes! Yes you can!" She replied, a wide smile on her face.

The hundreds of assembled Manzazzu all stood by their chosen partners. Tremera glanced besides her to see her sister standing with a Manzazzuan lord, one that would offer her social security and more importantly, since Tremera knew her partner from the Lyceum, she knew they would be a good match. If her sister chose to be with that Manzazzuan lord, then at least Treman would get his wish of continual legacy. But that didn't seem to matter to Tremera. All she wanted to do was spend more time with this strange but brilliant man.

All the Manzazzu assembled stood a few feet in front of their partners and awaited the cue to begin. The Manzazzuan Queen, clad in her blue and gold uniform, her long blonde hair kept under her peaked cap, stood up from her throne and took a few paces forward. "My Manzazzu, we are assembled once again on this important date to honour Venus passing the sun. Now that day has passed and we are gathered to close off this important day with the traditional Midnight Ball."

The Queen gestured for a Manzazzu to stand upon the stage. This Manzazzu wore a hood over her eyes and bowed. While the Queen took her seat, the woman turned to the crowd. Music began to sweep into the room as she began to sing. The male dancers stepped towards their partners and took a hand, placing the other on the back of the female dancers.

Tremarda was as gentle as possible, and his efforts to be as light and delicate, was felt by Tremera. The white haired beauty now felt so close to the strange new man, but she was immediately taken by his gaze. The metallic eyes were striking at first, but oddly beautiful at the same time.

Along with the crowd, the couple began to move slowly, side step following side step. With their hands still locked, they held their arms to the sky and Tremarda span Tremera on the spot, the Manzazzu around them following the same steps. The music began to grow and swell and with it, the dancing became faster and more passionate. It was a complex fusion of ballroom and tango dances, with short, swift kicks following long spins and twirls. Both parties led the dance in perfect synchronization, moving in circles around the dance floor. Above them, the full moon cast it's light on everyone.

With the ballad in full swing, Tremera was lifted from the ground and held up by Tremera who, along with his fellow Manzazzu, span their partners while pirouetting on the spot. Lowering his flustered but otherwise ecstatic partner, Tremarda fixed a lock of snowy white hair that had come loose from Tremera's braid around her head.

The dance continued till the Moon's light no longer lined up perfectly with the stained glass roof of the ballroom. When the dance came to an end, Tremarda dipped Tremera theatrically, following the example set by the other Manzazzu around them. He helped her back on her feet, panting.

"Well, that was a work out.." He wheezed.

Tremera wiped a thin layer of sweat off her forehead, she had to agree there. "That was... That was wonderful."

Before Tremarda could reply, he caught the sight of Treman pushing through the Manzazzu, smacking a maid's tray out of the way. He grabbed Tremera by the arm and dragged her out of the circle. This action did not go unnoticed by the Queen. One of her advisors was about to rise from his seat to alert the guards. She held her hand up and left her throne.

"Father..!" Tremera yelled, being dragged to the side of the circle and pinned to the wall.

Treman pointed back at the crowd, barking out his words, almost spitting them out. "I forbid you from fraternizing with the likes of him!"

Tremera pushed against her Father, sending him staggering back. "You're in no position to order me around, I'm the one who will inherit the titles after you." Tremarda must have installed some new found confidence in the previously introverted Manzazzu.

"I will not have this family's name dragged through the mud!" He raised his hand to strike Tremera, but his hand was grabbed mid air by another.

Tremera's sister held tightly onto her Father's hand. "I think you'd better leave, Father."

Treman forced his hand out of his daughter's grasp. "We'll have words later." With that, he stormed off into the crowd of Manzazzu.

Tremera watched her Father disappear from view. "By the end

of tonight, I may have ruined Father's expectations..."

"Good." Her sister replied.

"Yes. Because I'll have gained something far more important." Tremera walked back into the crowd.

The crowds parted as she froze, feeling as if the blood inside her had frozen. The Queen was approaching her. She towered over the noblewoman and put her hands gently on Tremera's arms.

"Are you alright? Did he hurt you at all?" She asked, a motherly tone coming from her that Tremera found relaxing.

"N...Not at all, your majesty. Thank you..." She stuttered.

The Queen spoke in a hushed tone, though all the eyes in the room were directed at them, it felt like they were the only two in the room. "Your welcome. If he causes problems again, don't hesitate to report him to my guards. They'll remove him." She took Tremera's hand in her own gloved hand. "This is a new day, don't let people like him have dominion over you."

All the poor young Manzazzu could do was blush. "I won't, thank you so much ma'am." She bowed.

"Now, go back to your partner, he looks like he's going to pass out any minute." She joked. As she turned to her throne, Tremera caught a glimpse of Tremarda and walked up to him as the staring crowd dispersed.

"Where are you staying tonight?" She asked.

Tremarda was rather surprised by the suddenness of the question. "In the Under City, in one of the complexes. Why?"

Tremera glanced around at the crowd. "Let the families squabble amongst themselves. By the time they notice, we'll be long gone."

"You make it sound so romantic." Tremarda chuckled.

"How else am I going to keep you for myself?" She flirted, causing Tremarda to blush.

The duo slipped away from the party and made their way out of the Fortress. The Euphretian night was warm, with a slight breeze coming off the ocean. The waves could be heard even from the height of the Queen's abode. They progressed down the spiraling path from the Fortress and into the Upper City. It wasn't long before they found themselves a Paternoster elevator which took them into the Lower City.

This would be the first time Tremera would have visited the Lower City. When they left the elevator, she was taken aback how windy it was, it blew her robes and hair around. She marvelled at the sheer scale of the place. They had arrived down a spire which formed the centre of the Lower City and had stopped on the top floor. There was a deep, golden light which shone up from the seemingly endless base of the city. The lights of all the buildings was responsible for this, with hundreds of them either built into the rock face or were suspended off the hundreds of circling walkways surrounding the spire. Everywhere in the Lower City was a short walk away.

Tremarda took her hand and guided her down one of the walkways, the city below them growing larger as they descended. Soon, they arrived at a large building, built on huge stilts. Once they entered, Tremera found herself in a maze of corridors. Tremarda checked the numbers of the doors till he found his own.

"Here, my lady, is my temporary home away from home. We're renting it for the celebrations." He explained, pressing his hand against the door.

"We?" She asked.

He opened the door to reveal a small wooden room, with three bunk beds and a window looking onto the Lower City. Inside were five Manzazzu, including Tremadore from earlier. He was sat atop one of the beds. Also there was the Manzazzu who would be known to Trem and Gabby as Miss Aduba. Two Manzazzu of African descent sat on the other bed. They were twins, one wore a brown Manzazzuan sleeveless tunic, the other wore a purple one. One of the twins had thick dreadlocks with a hair chain while the other had short hair, red gem earrings and a wing tiara. They all looked towards the door as Tremarda opened it.

"Hey everyone. I've brought a visitor." He teased as Tremera entered the small room.

The five Manzazzu all looked to the new arrival with great interest. Tremadore began chuckling to himself. "My match making skills prove to be infallible." He joked.

The twins jumped from their bed and approached Tremera, sniffing her gently.

"Oh, umm... Hello..." Tremera said, shuffling awkwardly.

The twins turned to the others. "She's good."

Tremarda gently nudged the twins away. "Make way." He scooted to his lower bunk, presenting it to Tremera who sat down.

"So, introductions. Tremadore you already know." He gestured to the waving Manzazzu. "Here we have the Lycan Twins of Kenya."

Tremera stared at Tremarda then back to the twins. "...Lycan? As in..."

Before she could continue, the Twins flexed their bodies, thick golden fur rising from their skin, their ears growing and their mouths extending to form wolf like snouts.Once they were fully transformed, the fur protruding out of their sleeveless tunics, they both smiled toothy grins that showed off their sharp fangs. "Woof woof." They both teased in unison.

"Impressive aren't they?" The Aduba Manzazzu complimented, scratching behind the Twins ears, causing them to purr contently. She introduced herself and her status as team medic.

Tremera was so taken aback at this strange yet wonderful world. "They are.... Who are you all?"

Tremarda took a wooden stick from the corner, coating it in steel in his hands. "This is our show. Well, not everyone could make the journey." He explained. "We go to Manzazzuan settlements all over the place and put on a bit of a spectacle. Occasionally we open the doors to some Humans."

Now that really surprised Tremera. "I thought we weren't supposed to reveal ourselves to Humans?"

"Call it exploiting a loophole." Tremadore explained.

The Twins both morphed back into their humanoid forms. "They don't even suspect we're not who we say we are." The dreadlocked twin explained.

"Yeah, they just think we're just some clever effect or something, it's kind of humbling really." The other joked.

Tremera couldn't resist the temptation anymore. "Where are you going after this?" She asked.

"The Manzazzuan colony of New Naresh and then across the ocean to wow the Human crowds of Britain." Tremarda described in a theatrical fashion.

Tremera walked up to Tremarda. "Can I join you? Just for a few days?"

"Are you sure?" He asked. "Won't your family be worried?"

She shook her head. "No...Let's do it Tremarda, just you and me."

The showman bowed his head and sank to his knee. "Tremera, it'd be my honor."

Tremera spent the night in the Lower City, dancing, playing and joking with the strange group of wonderful Manzazzu. She'd never felt so alive, so free. With this group, she felt no social expectations, no stress of following etiquette and protocol. She had let her white hair out of it's braid and taken off her white robe during the festivities, without them, she looked far less reserved than before.

The next day, she returned to the world of pomp and circumstance, in order to get her bags packed for the long boat ride. However, the destination would not be the family's owned land in Switzerland, but with the five strong group of Manzazzu bound for New Naresh.

She arrived in the lavish complex which Treman had rented for them and stealthily made her way to her bedroom, without being seen. She'd already begun packing her bags, making sure her box of rings was kept safe and secure, along with her collection of books and other personal items. She was so lost in her thoughts of a new, exciting life of romance and wonder that she didn't notice her sister at the door.

"Sister, what are you doing?" She asked.

Tremera wasn't interested in what she was going to say. She loved her sister dearly, but she knew all she'd do is try and convince her to stay, to try and play with her guilt to make her realise her mistakes. She wasn't going to have it, last night taught her that she needed to be decisive."You can deal with Father, I'm removing myself from the family." She tried to walk into the other room, to avoid her sister's gaze.

"Tremera, don't walk away from me!" She ordered. Her tone sank as she almost spoke in whispers. "Please think about what you're doing. Don't leave us... You wouldn't leave me would you?"

If it was just Treman, she'd have no issue in leaving. But she still loved her sister. "You could come with us?"

Her sister shook her head slowly."I can't..." Her voice quivered ever so slightly. "Father's health has taken a turn for the worst. The stress of last night put too great a strain on him."

Tremera kept her gaze away from her sister. She didn't want to leave her sister in this position, but if she was going to go with the others, she didn't have any choice. She was conflicted, that much was obvious. But her sister was a strong Manzazzu, she could look after herself.

"If Father isn't long for this world, someone's got to look after him. One of us has to be the loyal daughter." Her sister continued.

Tremera finally turned to face her sister, their gazes meeting each other's with unsure and anxious eyes connecting."Are you trying to make me feel guilty?" She asked.

"No, I'm sorry..." She said, wiping her eyes. "It's just... He'll find out at any moment..."

With her new found confidence, Tremera proclaimed clearly and sternly... "He can't stop me." She closed the bags containing her belongings and crossed over the room, giving her sister a hug. "I'll keep in touch. I'll write to you every day, okay?"

Her tearful sister nodded. Even she was starting to realise this was for the best. Every bird must fly the nest, and one day she would have to do so as well. With any animosity between them settled, Tremera began her journey to the doors of the complex.

She stopped as she saw Treman, his face gaunt and his eyes heavy, propped against the wall. He really did look awful. He knew exactly what was happening, but had no energy to stop it. "You foolish girl..." He strained.

"I am my own Manzazzu, Father. You can't stop me. " She replied, which would prove to be the last words she'd say to her Father for years.

Tremera opened the doors, the early morning sunlight pouring in, revealing Tremarda waiting for her.

"I think it's time we were going. " Tremera said.

"Yes..." Tremarda took one of her bags as they made the journey down the spiraling walkways, down to the docks where his group were waiting.

As they walked, Tremera spoke up, silencing some feelings and doubts in her head."I wouldn't worry about Father. Even Manzazzu aren't the exception to the rule. Everyone dies eventually."

As they reached the bustling bay, Manzazzu from both cities boarded their respective ships to their home continents, Tremera took one last look at Euphretia. "This world of Manzazzu and Etemmu isn't the be all and end all. There's a whole other world out there."

Tremarda put his hand on her shoulder and smiled. "Yes, a Human world."

That got Tremera thinking. "After we go to New Naresh, where did you say we were going?"

"Britain, an island off the coast of Europe. I think that's right anyway. Why'd you ask?"

"I know a place, out of the way, miles away from prying eyes." She explained.

"Go on." Tremarda said, fascinated with where this was going.

The show's run in New Naresh was incredibly successful, with Tremera herself taking on a spot in the group using her inherited clan powers to bring inanimate objects to life. Once a month had passed, it was time to take the show to Britain. There was a small manor house that once belonged to Treman's wife's family. It was out of the way, perfect for the show's group to settle in once they had finished the show for the day.

"To have an Ishtar Gate in a place like this, will it be dangerous?" Tremarda asked.

"To a Human, this will all be meaningless." Came the reply, with a smile. "We still have a duty as Manzazzu, to keep the Styx in order, even in this small and unimportant part of it."

"Unimportant? Any intrusion in the Styx could lead straight to the Capital."

He had a point. As much as they wanted to separate their lives from the other Manzazzu, they couldn't ignore the greater roles they had to perform.

"There's more to life than what the Queen and the upper classes dictate. We should do something with our lives." Tremera continued.

"Such as?"

She stood in front of Tremarda and put her hand on his chest. "Tremarda, would you accept my hand in marriage?"

There wasn't even a second of silence separating the question and response, Tremarda let out a fast and passionate... "Yes!"

Tremera practically jumped into Tremarda's arms as he spun her around. They both felt like they could take off and reach the moon. They shared a kiss and were both even brought to tears at the thought of spending their life together.

"It's the ideal life for a Human. Settle down in the countryside, raise a child..." She knew a child was something Tremarda was certainly all for, and it was truthfully something she always wanted.

Tremarda agreed with her, especially the idea of starting their own family. "I'm starting to see the appeal. Humans aren't the primitive savages your Father would have us believe."

"No, maybe they're not. But I know one thing. We're going to start something beautiful here. I know something else as well, I'll fight to protect my family, if I have to."

With that, they shared another kiss on the steps to the manor house.

Over the next few months, the show would continue on the Mortsbury pier, attracting Humans and Manzazzu alike. The performers all would go on to find other accomodations in the village. As for Tremera's family, her sister would eventually move out of the family home, leaving their beautiful Northern Inuit Neti with Tremera. She went off to live a life of security and luxury with her husband and would remain happily married till she passed away decades later.

Tremarda would eventually become more preoccupied with his new life and find himself floating away from the show, which still survived without him. Eventually, Tremadore was left to keep the flame alive, the others finding the thought of settling down all the more appealing.

Then, on one rainy night, Tremera gave birth to a beautiful baby girl, Trem. The couple spent a decade looking after their daughter, playing with her, teaching her the Manzazzuan ways, according to their own take on the world, and gifting her with her pet Dragon Lizard Samiel. For all three of them, it was the happiest years of their lives.

Eventually, Treman was unable to keep his luxurious accomodations in Switzerland. Feeling guilty over the way things ended between them, Tremera allowed Treman to stay in the house, to live out his final weeks. Unfortunately, in his withered state, what neither Manzazzu could have guessed was how bitter Treman had become. In the dead of night, Treman was able to set up his final act. He managed to draw his daughter, husband and their dog into the Ishtar Gate, under the pretence that he detected something in the Styx. Using his inherent powers, he brought one of the suits of armour in the manor to life and with it's great strength, it rendered Tremera and Tremarda unconscious and threw them and their dog into the Styx River. His mission completed, Treman soon succumbed to his illness.

Years later, the trio from this lost family were making their way back to their daughter, but the journey there would be paved with peril. They would face opposition, fight against the Styx Sisters and once more brave the River Styx in order to reunite with Trem, for the first time in decades.

Printed in Great Britain
by Amazon